The Trials of the Honorable F. Darcy

A modern *Pride & Prejudice*

Sara Angelini

Sourcebooks Landmark™
An Imprint of Sourcebooks, Inc.®
Naperville, Illinois

Published by Sourcebooks Landmark, an imprint of Sourcebooks, Inc.
P.O. Box 4410, Naperville, Illinois 60567–4410
(630) 961–3900
FAX: (630) 961–2168
www.sourcebooks.com

Library of Congress Cataloging-in-Publication Data

Angelini, Sara.
The trials of the Honorable F. Darcy / Sara Angelini.
p. cm.
1. Darcy, Fitzwilliam (Fictitious character)—Fiction. 2. Bennet, Elizabeth (Fictitious character)—Fiction. 3. San Francisco (Calif.)—Fiction. 4. Legal stories. I. Title.
PS3601.A54T75 2009
813'.6—dc22

2009018720

Printed and bound in the United States of America
VP 10 9 8 7 6 5 4 3 2 1

Dedicated to Dominic
and all the readers at Austen Underground,
Hyacinth Gardens, and A Happier Alternative

Chapter 1

CHARLES BINGLEY LOOKED UNDER the hood of the Lamborghini Murcielago and crossed his arms over his chest.

"How much horsepower?" he asked.

"It's a 580," replied his friend, Fitzwilliam Darcy.

Bingley stroked his chin and nodded, his eyes still caressing the engine. "And zero to sixty in…?"

"Zero to sixty-two in 3.8 seconds, top speed 205."

"Have you driven one?"

"Yes. I wasn't impressed—traction control," Darcy said, a hint of disdain in his clipped British accent. Bingley looked up at him.

"Isn't that a good thing? I don't want to plunge over the Pacific Highway, no matter how good I look in it."

"For God's sake, Bingley, it's an Italian super car! If you're afraid to drive it, buy a Honda."

Bingley chewed on his thumbnail absently. "I bet it costs a fortune to insure."

Darcy laughed. "Insurance? Don't buy it if you can't afford to wreck it."

"It looks scrumptious," cooed Bingley's sister, Caroline. "I'd look divine in it." She bent over to peer in the window and surreptitiously looked behind her to ensure Darcy had a good view of her rear.

"What do you think, Darcy?" Bingley asked.

"If flash is what you want, this is the car to buy," Darcy replied with a noncommittal shrug.

Caroline wiggled out of the window and turned to Darcy.

"Whatever happened to that funny little car you had—the one with the driver's seat in the middle?" she asked.

"I sold the McLaren to Ralph Lauren a few years back. He refuses to sell it back to me," he said ruefully.

"You know Ralph Lauren? Ugh, tell him I hate his latest line." Caroline wrinkled her nose and checked the polish on a fingernail. Darcy allowed one side of his mouth to curl into a smile as he envisioned himself flipping open his cell phone and saying, "Ralph. Darcy. Hate the line. Want my car back."

"I'm getting it!" Bingley declared. "Let's go." He walked resolutely toward the dealership's office. Darcy looked at his watch.

"Bingley, I have to get back to court. Don't you want to think about it overnight?" he called after him. Bingley continued toward the dealership door, shaking his head.

"I'll have it in yellow!" he announced, giving Darcy a dismissing wave in farewell. Darcy sighed and climbed into his non-flashy Audi.

"Fucking Ralph Lauren," he muttered to himself.

Darcy pulled into the parking lot of the Meryton Courthouse behind a blue MINI Cooper whose driver was bobbing her head and clearly singing at the top of her lungs. From the adjacent parking slot, he watched in fascination as she slammed out a drumbeat on the steering wheel. He wondered when she would pull out the air guitar. Laughing silently to himself, he grabbed his briefcase from the passenger seat and climbed out. The driver of the MINI Cooper was apparently doing an encore, as she did not exit.

One of my favorites, he thought, recognizing the song as he passed the car. He hummed the tune to himself, fingers twitching at his side as if working over the frets of a guitar. His long legs took him quickly across the lot and up the five flights to his office.

"Good afternoon, Your Honor," an attorney greeted him in the hallway. Darcy nodded in greeting and passed through the judges' entrance, slipping his dark-rimmed glasses on as he did. A state budget crisis left the building with slipshod security at best, and in an effort to slightly alter his appearance, as well as to appear older, during court, Darcy wore glasses and gelled down his hair the way his father had done. It was amazing how little attention to detail most people paid. He was rarely recognized on the street by attorneys with whom he regularly worked, let alone a one-time defendant with a grudge. Still, better safe than sorry, so Darcy lived in a secure high-rise building in downtown San Francisco and made the daily commute to Meryton.

Just as he was passing her, his secretary said, "Judge Clayton went home sick. You'll have to take her afternoon calendar."

Instantly annoyed, Darcy swung back to his secretary.

"Sick? What's wrong with her?"

She shrugged and handed him his phone messages, studiously avoiding his frown. A moment later, Presiding Judge

Wendell Boyd knocked briefly on Darcy's door before letting himself in.

"Sorry, Will," he said, shaking his head and handing Judge Clayton's docket to Darcy.

Darcy removed his glasses and pinched the bridge of his nose. Judge Clayton's "illnesses" had become a near-ritual occurrence, and the fallout always landed on Darcy's shoulders.

"Any word on appointing a new judge?" he asked, tossing the docket on his desk. Boyd held his hands up defensively.

"My hands are tied until either California miraculously finds a couple hundred million dollars lying around or until the hiring freeze is lifted. Even when the money starts flowing again, you know that Meryton is the bastard stepchild of San Francisco. The city gets priority for filling their vacancies. I was lucky *you* were appointed; there were two other vacancies I *didn't* get to fill. So don't hold your breath."

Darcy shook his head in disgust, and Boyd turned to exit. He paused by the door and said, "If you leave at the end of your term, I'll really be in a bind. Have you considered running for re-election?"

"I've considered it and decided not to."

"Come on, Will. Dockets are backed up two full months, and you're the best damned judge in the county. You'll be doing everyone a disservice if you quit when we need you the most. If it's the money, I'm sure I can figure something out."

"It's not the money. It's that fighting the good fight has lost its charm."

Boyd nodded in understanding and opened the door. "Just think about it," he urged, then left.

"Don't hold your breath," Darcy muttered.

Sighing, Darcy sat at his desk and rubbed his tired eyes. Money was the least of his concerns. Like his barrister father before him, Darcy had inherited a large fortune and estate in England. And like his bohemian Californian mother, Darcy felt that money was rarely the remedy for one's ills. She was as influential as his father on Darcy's decision to become a barrister specializing in family and criminal law. His fondness for all things American presaged Darcy's path to become an expert in United States jurisprudence. Shortly after obtaining his barrister's license, Darcy's firm quickly tapped him to spearhead their foray into international law by opening an office in California. His dual citizenship allowed him to move freely between countries, and his natural ability—he had always been a quick study—allowed him to easily pass the California bar exam. Despite his young age, within two years, Darcy had gained a solid reputation for his skill in complex international litigation. The judges appreciated his decorum, his colleagues appreciated his intelligence, and the community as a whole appreciated his integrity.

When the then-presiding judge keeled over in his mistress's bed, Wendell Boyd was appointed to fill the vacancy and charged with the task of finding a scandal-free replacement to fill his own vacancy. Will Darcy immediately came to mind. He encouraged Darcy to submit an application, and with barely ten years of practice under his belt, Darcy became the youngest judge appointed in the county.

But four and a half years into a six-year term, Darcy was disillusioned, overworked, and bored. The inter-office politics, from the lowest clerk all the way up to the governor, disgusted him. Although the workload was staggering, it was also monotonous.

The same tired issues, the same weak arguments, and the same gray, shouting faces. It was enough to drive Darcy insane.

Well, no use dodging it, he thought resignedly. He looked at Judge Clayton's docket.

Six trials.

"Fucking Judge Clayton," he muttered under his breath.

Still irked by the sudden transfer of Judge Clayton's calendar, the Honorable F. Darcy entered the courtroom with an annoyed swirl of black robes. Sometimes he imagined himself as Professor Snape when he wore them. Considering how frequently he wished he could zap some people out of existence, it was fitting. This afternoon would be one of those days. He hated cleaning up other people's messes, and yet, it somehow always fell to him. He was "responsible" and "reliable" and "respectable" and "rich"—all qualifications that made everyone think he enjoyed taking care of their problems.

He thought they could all go fuck themselves. *Christ, I need a vacation,* he mused, surprised at the vehemence of his own resentment. He was practically counting the days until he could return to England and assume the life of a country gentleman. Or maybe he'd loaf on a beach for a year, or travel, or visit relatives in France, or… he pulled himself out of his reverie and turned his attention to a new face in the courtroom.

Well, if it isn't little drummer girl, he thought, amused. *Probably here to contest her speeding ticket.*

She was talking to Charlotte Lucas, a defense attorney from Gardiner & Associates. She was lucky; he was a softie for speeding tickets. If the policeman didn't show up, he routinely dismissed them. As he didn't see a California highway patrolman anywhere in the courtroom, he figured she'd be free to play air guitar within the hour.

"Anybody ready?" Darcy asked, handling his docket on a first-come, first-served basis.

He was surprised to see Ms. Drummer Girl lead a pudgy, slightly sweaty man to the defense table while Mr. Johnson, the prosecutor, took his side.

"Elizabeth Bennet for the defense, Your Honor," she announced. Darcy gave her a critical eye over his glasses and returned his gaze to the file before him. *New attorney*, he thought, disappointed. *Tedious*.

Tedious as it was to break in new attorneys, Ms. Bennet at least gave a concerted effort to defend against the charge of solicitation of prostitution. Her client, Bill Collins, was a habitual offender who Darcy had sentenced on several occasions. He wondered how long before Mr. Collins contracted a flaming case of herpes.

While he was not impressed by Ms. Bennet's hypertechnical arguments—and made sure she knew it—he let enough of them stand to force the prosecutor to reduce the charges. He sentenced Mr. Collins to thirty days probation and called the next case.

The prosecutor then brought the prostitute before Judge Darcy for trial. She was represented by a barracuda defense attorney from DeBourgh & Associates, slumming on a pro-bono case. Darcy groaned inwardly. He hated that firm—they *never* took a plea bargain. He would have to try the case.

"What am *I* in trouble for?" the prostitute whined, outraged.

"*Fucking* Bill Collins," Darcy thought irately.

***

"Fucking Judge Darcy," Elizabeth Bennet swore as she punched the elevator button to the ninth floor where Gardiner & Associates was located. Even though she knew they were weak, she had been humiliated by his pointed dismissal of her defenses. It was an inauspicious way to start her legal career.

"I think you've just been *Darcied,*" Charlotte teased. "He's actually a pretty good judge. He's never been overturned on appeal, you know," Charlotte said, winking at Elizabeth.

"I think Buddy Holly needs to work on his interpersonal skills," Elizabeth replied. They dumped their briefcases in their offices and met again at the door as they left for the evening.

"Want to go for a drink?" Charlotte proposed.

"I'm meeting a friend. Mind if he comes along?"

Charlotte shrugged, and soon they were walking toward the local legal watering hole, the Assembly Room. Elizabeth found her friend sitting at a table by himself.

"Hi, Lou. This is Charlotte Lucas. Make nice."

Louis Hurst, Elizabeth's best friend since junior high, was a slender man with deep blue eyes, dark hair, and who worshipped Rupert Everett. With little direction in life, he had never been driven like Elizabeth. He drifted from job to job, somehow always managing to land on his feet. Right now, he was a massage therapist at a day spa. Their opposite attitudes were largely what glued their friendship together—that and their fashion sense.

Charlotte and Lou gave each other friendly greetings and Lou handed Elizabeth the cocktail he had pre-ordered for her. They were just arguing over what to order from the menu when something caught Lou's attention.

"Who is *that?*" Lou gaped with raised eyebrows. Both Elizabeth and Charlotte turned toward the door.

"Ugh, it's Judge Darcy! Let's get out of here!" Elizabeth exclaimed, grabbing her purse.

"Too late," Charlotte groaned. Darcy was standing a few feet behind Elizabeth talking to another attorney and inconveniently blocking their path to the door.

"Come on, Darcy, join us. It'll be fun," Elizabeth overheard Darcy's companion say.

Darcy shook his head. "No, I'm busy tonight."

"But she's *crazy* about you. You could get laid tonight!" the attorney pressed.

"Thanks, Jim, but no," Darcy declined politely.

"Hey, did you see Gardiner's new attorney? Eleanor... Elaine, what the hell is her name? Elizabeth, that's it! She's hot. You should ask her out."

Elizabeth's face flushed as Lou's eyes widened in disbelief and Charlotte laughed outright.

"She's all right, I suppose," Darcy said dismissively. Elizabeth's jaw dropped in indignation, and Lou clapped his hand over his mouth in mortified mirth while Charlotte snorted seltzer out her nose.

"C'mon, she looks like she's got a great body," Jim cajoled, oblivious that Elizabeth was sitting directly behind him.

When she thought it couldn't get any worse, Elizabeth heard Darcy say firmly, "Look, she's not pretty enough to tempt me. Do you have any idea what kind of headache even the *appearance* of impropriety would cause? I could get kicked off the bench for shagging an attorney who practices before me."

Elizabeth was the first to burst out laughing at the absurdity of their conversation, joined by the howls of her friends.

Annoyed by the explosion of laughter behind them, Darcy and Jim moved away from their table, never registering the identity of its occupants. Elizabeth, having heard enough, gathered her keys and purse. The trio lapsed into another fit of giggles as they brushed past Darcy on their way out.

"*She's all right, I suppose*," Charlotte mimicked, then laughed again.

"But not pretty enough to tempt *me*," Lou finished with a spot-on impression. "Maybe *I'm* pretty enough to tempt him," he suggested hopefully. "Ooh, the shagging we would do!"

"Oh, Lou, the only shag about you is your hairdo," Elizabeth snorted.

Despite the humor she found in the situation, Elizabeth could not ignore that she had just been rather soundly insulted by Judge Darcy. She continued to laugh and joke with Lou and Charlotte as they went to dinner, but a slow burn of resentment began to glow inside of her.

Darcy really was busy that night. He had plans for dinner with Caroline. Dinner, of course, meaning sex. He wasn't quite sure when he had decided it was acceptable to have sex with his best friend's sister, but it had been occurring on an occasional basis for the last two years. He drove to her apartment and absently ate dinner. They pretended to watch a movie until she straddled him on the couch, then the action moved to the bedroom. Although he was physically aroused, Darcy felt empty, detached. Caroline writhed and moaned beneath him, and he performed those acts which brought her pleasure. His breathing was hardly quickened by the effort; she was easy to please. He allowed her to orgasm and then reached his own quickly, in an almost businesslike manner. Afterwards, he leaned against the headboard and drew his knees up, draping his elbows over them.

"What are you thinking?" she asked him sleepily.

He was thinking that he was ashamed of himself for taking advantage of her when he knew that she wanted more.

"I was thinking about work," he lied. She rolled over and nestled closer to him while he gazed into the darkened bedroom.

"You think about work too much. You need to relax," she murmured.

He did not respond. He was not happy with this "relationship." It went against everything he believed in—sincerity, honesty, integrity. He resolved at that moment that he would not sleep with another woman until he felt some genuine affection for her. It didn't have to be love—he wasn't a romantic—but it *did* have to be more than a need to scratch a physiological itch. He mentally prepared himself for a long period of celibacy. Then he made an excuse, dressed, and went home.

It wasn't just his insult that made Elizabeth dislike Darcy, although that played a significant role. It was his superior demeanor. She always had the feeling he was looking down his nose at her, peering over those ridiculous horn-rimmed glasses as if he could actually see better without them. He made her feel like he could see right through any clever arguments she made and that if he'd been her opponent, he'd have ripped her to shreds.

In court he was not an easy man. He was impatient. He liked to bark orders and was known to banish unprepared attorneys from his courtroom, telling them to come back when they wouldn't waste his time. If paperwork had staples or was not hole-punched, it was rejected. If a brief had no citations, it was rejected. If an argument began to sound the least bit desperate, it was rejected. Elizabeth quickly learned to avoid the imperious glare that signified impending rejection.

She honed her legal skills by memorizing codes and statutes until she could quote them with confidence. She always had case law at the ready while her opponents floundered and shuffled their notes. In time, she forgot how intimidated she felt by that first appearance.

But his insult was not as easily forgotten. Having experienced the mortification of being found not tempting, Elizabeth found it very hard to take Judge Darcy seriously. On the contrary, she thought of him as a sort of joke. She showed her indifference to him by refusing to take the bait when he said something offensive—as he did on a daily basis. While professionally she was without fault, she danced on the edge of disrespect with pert glances and cryptic *Yes, Judge Darcy*s. She dubbed him Clark Kent—without the sparkling personality—and made fun of him at every opportunity. The ember of resentment had taken root and burst into a full-fledged flame of defiance.

Oblivious to her true feelings, Darcy quickly concluded that she was one of the most capable and intelligent attorneys he had the privilege to work with, crafting creative settlements and persuasive briefs. He was always impressed by her dedication when he ran into her at the elevator after hours or on weekends. She met each of his challenges with spirit and never backed down when he ruled against her; he enjoyed sparring with her. If he found himself looking forward to her cases, it was in a purely intellectual sort of way. It had nothing at all to do with her velvety brown eyes.

While Judge Darcy avoided meditating on the very great pleasure a pair of fine eyes in the face of a pretty woman can bestow, he could not help but notice that Elizabeth had a streak of determination that some might call "fiery." He could always count on her to liven up the courtroom by pressing her opposing counsel's patience to its limits. Sometimes, her own patience was tested and those brown eyes snapped and sparkled as her razor tongue lashed into the other attorney. On one particular occasion, she had been provoked by the plaintiff attorney's absence—a stalling tactic no doubt intended to bring about a more lucrative settlement from Elizabeth's client—who then had the nerve to suggest to Darcy that Elizabeth was stonewalling the settlement discussions.

"Miss Bennet, are you refusing to negotiate?" Judge Darcy inquired over his glasses.

"Well, Your Honor, I would have been happy to continue negotiations, had Mr. Franklin not disappeared for the last two hours," she replied with sarcastic sweetness. "As it is, I've made several proposals, all of which he has refused. I will not be bullied into an unfair settlement, and with the case law in my favor, further negotiations are against my client's interests," she answered, tossing an annoyed look at Mr. Franklin.

"I see. Mr. Franklin, I'm sure you've done your best," Darcy cocked one eyebrow and glanced at Elizabeth, "but Ms. Bennet is a hard negotiator. I'm afraid you'll have to set it for trial."

Elizabeth thanked him and left the courtroom. Darcy thought he detected a hint of triumph in her confident stride and hid a smile. She must have known how much he hated it when parties tried to play the system, especially a system as overburdened as theirs. Had he been in the same position, he would have done the same thing as she; at least taking a calculated risk was intellectually honest.

He hoped nobody had noticed that he had complimented her negotiating skills in open court. He would have to be mindful of that in the future. But *bollocks*, when her eyes shone like that, how could he not admire her? She was more than just a pair of warm eyes in a pretty face: he was beginning to *like* her.

A week later, Darcy was struggling over an egregiously bad brief—it warranted dismissal of the case purely on its grammatical errors, let alone its total lack of legal basis—when he noticed Elizabeth wander into his courtroom. Apparently she had not seen him, as she went directly to the bulletin board at the back of the room and began reading the latest appellate court ruling. She rocked back and forth on one of her high heels, her well-shaped legs showing beneath the pleated fringe of her modest skirt. With his view uninterrupted, Darcy allowed himself a leisurely admiration of her rear, the silver-blue silk of her skirt hugging it just short of indecently. He found himself slightly jealous of that nubby material. He was, after all, not made of stone.

Realizing that his thoughts were wandering into unacceptable territory, he cleared his throat and said, "That case will be of benefit to you, I think, in some of your toxic mold cases."

She turned, startled, when she heard his voice.

"Yes, it looks like insurance companies can now avoid paying out on mold resulting from catastrophic water damage," she said.

"One more thing for victims of hurricanes to worry about," he said.

"If you're the victim of a hurricane, I think you have more

than mold to worry about. But I'm sure you'll find a way to apply the law fairly." She gave him a little smile and turned her attention back to the case.

"You like insurance defense, then?" he asked trying to make small talk. She turned back to face him.

"Insurance defense allows me to indulge my inner evil overlord." She raised her eyebrow and steepled her fingers under her chin in a posture of evil contemplation. "All defense attorneys are bad people at heart, you know."

"You're very good at it," he commented, a smirk playing at the corners of his lips. She laughed as Charlotte came into the room.

"Hey, there you are. Hello, Judge Darcy."

"Ms. Lucas."

"Judge Darcy was just telling me how great I am at victimizing the already victimized." Elizabeth cocked her head to the side as she tossed a mischievous glance at him. Of course she was deliberately misunderstanding his compliment in order to tease him. She was the only attorney who *ever* teased him; he wondered if he should be flattered or worried. He suppressed the urge to tease her back and instead smiled cryptically.

"You should see how she treats the staff," Charlotte grinned. "You ready?" she asked Elizabeth. Elizabeth nodded and walked toward the door.

"Have a good day, Judge," she called over her shoulder as she left. She didn't wait for him to reply.

Over the next few days, Darcy noted with some concern that his eyes were drawn to Ms. Bennet with increasing frequency. There was no denying that he was beginning to find her attractive. Of course, as a judge any personal connection with one of his attorneys would be highly questionable and would probably lead to an investigation, and that would undoubtedly be a major headache. But he could still look, and look he did. *Plenty*.

Her face was beautiful—not exotic or glamorous, but intelligent and classic with good cheekbones and a small chin. Her peaches-and-cream complexion contrasted against mahogany hair, which was always pulled back into a professional chignon. That a curl usually found its way free, only to be tucked behind an ear, struck him as somewhat charming, as if somewhere inside a wild child was begging to be let out.

He often found himself smiling inwardly when those warm, chocolaty eyes rolled in contempt at her opponent's argument. One could easily predict her thoughts by observing how high her eyebrows arched. Hitching the left one conveyed sarcastic disbelief, while a double raise meant *outright* disbelief. Usually, he was in complete agreement. It was as if they shared some coded communication, a secret banter beneath the mundane small talk they traded every day.

But on a more basic level, Darcy finally acknowledged that Jim was right. Elizabeth Bennet had a damn fine body. She was not particularly tall, perhaps five-foot-four, and her curves were shown to their advantage by well-cut suits in light blues and greens, which Darcy thought suited her better than black. Those colors flattered her eyes and made them sparkle. And if there was anything Darcy had to admit to himself, it was that he was definitely beginning to notice her *sparkle*.

Chapter 2

WHILE ELIZABETH BENNET WAS busy impressing Judge Darcy with her impertinence and legal acumen, her sister, Jane, was impressing another gentleman in an entirely different way.

Jane Bennet had begun her residency at Meryton Hospital in late June. In the four months that had passed since that time, she had secretly lusted after the unsuspecting pediatric surgeon. Dr. Charles Bingley was cheerful, talented, good with children, and *oh-so-hot*. She had a notion that he might be gay, but if he wasn't, she was determined to bed him. It was with great delight that she found him sitting alone in the cafeteria.

"Hello, Dr. Bingley," she said as slid into the chair next to him.

"Jane! How nice to see you again. How is it coming over in urology?"

"I wanted to thank you for lending me this text," she said, placing it on the table next to him. "I've learned a great deal about the male anatomy from studying this book."

"I'm glad you enjoyed it. I thought it might be a little hard for you," he replied.

"Not at all. I think I understand it pretty well. In fact, I've taken the liberty of putting my phone number on the post-it note in chapter sixteen if you wanted to call with any questions about the text." Jane licked her forefinger and paged over to the chapter entitled "The Male Sexual Response" and pointed to the post-it note with her cell phone number on it.

"Please feel free to call me, Doctor," she said.

"Call me Charley," he said a little breathlessly.

She smiled. *Not gay*.

"Oh, come on, Darcy, it will be an absolute bore without you," Caroline said as she sipped her coffee.

"It will not!" Bingley cried indignantly. Caroline gave him a disbelieving snort and turned back to Darcy.

"It will be full of scrubs and nurses," she pouted.

"I *do* know people outside the hospital, you know!" Bingley said hotly. Darcy watched the interaction between older sister and younger brother with amusement. He could almost envision Caroline holding Charles out at arm's length, her hand on his forehead while he swung fruitless punches at her.

"Aren't you inviting any of your friends, Caroline?" Darcy asked, sipping his tea.

"I'm inviting *you*, aren't I?" she replied, leaning over the table and poking her finger into his chest.

He looked down at her red lacquered nail. There was something about Caroline, a strange mix of socialite and slut that never ceased to fascinate him. It must work on some level, because she'd made a bloody fortune in real estate, but it never quite fired on all cylinders for Darcy. He supposed that was one of the reasons he had never really been serious about her.

"Halloween is a tedious holiday. Everybody thinks it's their one time in the year to get *outrageous* by dressing up in costume," Darcy said derisively.

"It is!" Bingley grinned. "I'm not sure what I'm going to be yet—"

"No doubt it will be *outrageous*," Darcy drawled. "Maybe you could be a surgeon. You could wear one of those little paper hats!" he said with mock excitement. Then he shook his head and leaned back in his chair. "It's a time for everyone to get drunk, act stupid, and hide behind a disguise while doing it." He took a sip of tea to emphasize his teetotaling point.

Bingley sat back with his arms crossed. "Honestly, Darcy, sometimes I think the wart on Caroline's ass is more fun than you."

Darcy choked on his tea, and Caroline swatted Bingley on the head before turning her attention back to Darcy. "Will, really, I'll be desolate if you don't come," she purred. "Bring Georgie; she'll have fun."

Darcy rolled his eyes and put down his teacup. Caroline was under the impression that his twenty-five-year-old sister, Georgiana, was perpetually fifteen.

"I'll make it worth your while," she sang, tracing a little circle on his hand with her fingertip.

Darcy pointedly ignored her and looked at Bingley. "What time should I come?" he asked with resignation.

Bingley grinned. "The party starts at eight." His smile disappeared. "And you'd better not come dressed as a judge!"

***

"Come on, Lizzy, you have to come with me. I won't know anybody there!" Jane pleaded.

"Jane, you're perfectly capable of making friends. Besides, you'll know *him*," Elizabeth pointed out.

"Pleeeeeeeeeeeeeeeeeeeaaaase!" Jane said, clasping her hands together. "I really like Charley, and I'd like you to meet him."

"And what better time to have an intimate one-on-one than when he's hosting a party in a mask?" Elizabeth snorted.

"If you don't come with me, I'll... I'll... I'll think of something," Jane finished weakly.

"You are so lame," Elizabeth laughed. "Fine, I'll go, but I won't dance, and I'm leaving at eleven o'clock. I have an early massage tomorrow. You'll have to find your own way home."

Jane squealed with pleasure and planted a juicy kiss on Elizabeth's cheek.

"How do you like it?" Caroline asked as she twirled in a circle before Darcy.

"What is it?" he replied, tilting his head. She was wearing a bright orange jumpsuit that ended in short-shorts and fishnet hose. The suit was unzipped halfway down her ample chest, and she was wearing handcuffs.

"It's a prisoner costume," she pouted, turning around again.

"*Property of the penile system,*" he read on her back, laughing.

"Maybe you should put me in jail, Judge Darcy," she cooed as she sashayed toward him. He laughed again as she put her hands on his hips and did a little grind against them.

"Caroline, what are you wearing?" Bingley's dismayed cry interrupted Caroline's seductive routine as he swept into the room wearing a Darth Vader costume. "You were *supposed* to be Princess Leia!"

"Don't you find it a little, um, *incestuous* for us to have coordinating costumes?"

Bingley put the helmet on his head and raised his fist in the air. "You have failed me for the last time!" came the electronic voice from within the helmet. Darth Bingley then turned to Darcy and raised an accusing finger at him. "What the hell are you?" he demanded with a dramatic shake of his fist, clearly enjoying the power of the Force within him.

Darcy, dressed in a black, flame-retardant auto-racing suit, put on his helmet and lowered the tinted visor.

"Are you Evel Knievel?" Darth Bingley asked. Darcy shrugged and gave a thumbs-up. Bingley was lucky Darcy had followed through on his promise to attend the party in the first place. Unfortunately for Caroline, Darcy's change of costume had foiled her plan to appear as his prisoner.

She stuck out her lower lip and groused, "I thought for sure you'd be a judge again."

"Where the hell is this place?" Elizabeth frowned as she held a flashlight to the map. They were in the middle of nowhere, having taken a winding road off of the Pacific Highway. It had been a good ten minutes since they last saw any signs of civilization.

"Did we take a wrong turn?" Jane asked nervously, gripping the steering wheel and flicking on the high beams. She slowed as the road twisted around a bend.

Up ahead was a row of parked cars, and around the bend an enormous mansion came into view. Jane and Elizabeth looked at each other in disbelief. Just in front of them, a woman in a ballerina costume climbed out of her car. Jane giggled nervously. "Do you think this is the right party?"

"No, most bazillionaires normally keep ballerinas on their grounds just for fun," Elizabeth quipped.

Jane rolled down her window and tapped the horn lightly.

"Is that Charles Bingley's place?" she called to the ballerina

"Yes," the tutu-clad woman replied.

"Oh my God, Jane, your boyfriend is Bill Gates' *rich* brother," Elizabeth breathed, awed by the grandeur of Bingley's house.

"I don't think I need to tell you there's probably security here, so don't stuff any silverware into your bra."

"Me? You were the thief when we were kids!" Elizabeth laughed. Together they began the trek up the driveway toward the brightly lit entrance. At the bottom of the steps, a crowd of costumed guests hovered near a yellow Lamborghini. Darth Vader sat behind the wheel. His head turned to them as they approached.

"Jane!" came his electronic voice. Jane looked at him startled, until he took off his helmet. "Jane, it's me!" Bingley laughed. He climbed out of the car and walked over to her, giving her a light kiss on the cheek. "I'm so glad you came. You look great! What are you?"

Jane was wearing thigh-high vinyl boots and fishnets, short biker hot pants, and a black leather vest. Her blond hair was curled into a sedate bun at the nape of her neck, a black cap perched jauntily on her head. She turned her back to Bingley, who read the lettering across her vest.

"She's a Hell's Angel!" Bingley laughed with delight. After Elizabeth was introduced to Bingley, he led them inside, where the party was already in full swing.

***

Darcy was perusing the drink selection and wondered how he was going to drink with his helmet on when a particular costume caught his attention. The woman was wearing a white tank top and low-slung leather pants with a studded belt and motorcycle boots, but what drew his gaze were the large black feathered wings strapped to her back. The dark kohl smudged around her eyes could not disguise them; he would know those eyes anywhere.

What the hell is Elizabeth Bennet doing here? he wondered. He slipped the dark visor of his helmet down so that she would not recognize him and watched her as she looked nervously around the room. She smiled when a blonde biker chick came to her side and squeezed her hand.

So, she's a lesbian, Darcy thought, slightly disappointed and slightly turned on.

He stepped aside as they approached the drinks table, heads close together. Elizabeth looked up at him and smiled.

"Nice costume!" she grinned. "Is that your Mach 5 out there, Speed Racer?" Darcy shrugged and gave as bashful an expression one could while wearing a helmet with a tinted visor. Never mind that he wouldn't be caught dead in such a blatantly ostentatious pimp-mobile.

"Do you know which one is Caroline?" Jane asked Darcy. He pointed to Caroline's orange back. Just then, Bingley raised a gloved hand and beckoned Jane to him. "I feel an irresistible urge to obey his command," she droned.

"Okay, Speed and I will be here when you get back—if you survive," Elizabeth finished ominously. Jane walked toward Bingley who was already pulling Caroline over to meet her.

"I'm Azrael," Elizabeth said to Darcy, offering her hand. *The Angel of Death,* he thought, impressed, as he shook her hand with his gloved one. "Nice to meet you, Speed." He nodded and picked up a bottle of wine, gesturing toward her. "Why, thank you." She smiled as she held her glass to the bottle. He filled her glass and was about to pour one for himself when he realized he couldn't drink it without removing his helmet.

"Do you know many people here?" she asked him. He shrugged. She looked at him and tried unsuccessfully to repress a smirk. "Talkative, aren't you?" He shrugged again and waved his hands in the air. She laughed.

Christ, she's good looking, he thought. He had never before seen her with her hair down, and he found it unnervingly attractive. She hadn't come to the party all tarted up like a lot of the women here, nor had she chosen an immature, cutesy costume like, say, a bunny. He had no doubt she knew that in addition to the Angel of Death, Azrael was also the Angel of Law.

"I have a confession," she said. He crossed his arms over his chest in an expression of interest. "I don't know anybody here. My sister there works with Charley at the hospital. He invited her, and she dragged me along. I'm a party crasher. It's always nice to have Death drop in, don't you think?" she chewed on a swizzle stick and looked at him through her lashes.

Inside his helmet, Darcy grinned.

"Can you believe this place?" Elizabeth mused, taking in her surroundings. "I had no idea that people actually lived in places like this." Darcy looked around him. It was a bit opulent for his taste, and it was larger than his estate in England, but then Bingley was always one for form over substance. He had no idea why he liked the guy so much.

Darcy turned his attention back to Elizabeth, who was talking to a man in a pirate costume.

"*AAAAAAARRRRRRRRR* you having fun?" she asked. The pirate laughed and waved his rubber hook at her.

"*Shiver me timbers*, I need me some rum!" the pirate growled.

Darcy moved aside and watched in amusement as the pirate fumbled with his hook, a wineglass, and a bottle of wine. Elizabeth raised an eyebrow at Darcy and then rescued the pirate by pouring the wine for him.

After the pirate had gone, she turned to Darcy and said, "Talkative *and* helpful." He put his hand over his heart and bowed slightly in apology. She laughed. "It's really quite sad that I am completely entertained by a mime."

He laughed again inside his helmet. They stood in comfortable silence as the party became more raucous. As the crowd became thicker, Elizabeth was jostled and spilled red wine down her white tank top.

"*Goddamit!*" she exclaimed. "This was my last white tank top!" Darcy grabbed a bottle of seltzer water while she dabbed at her top with a paper napkin. He wetted a towel and began to press it to her chest, unwittingly groping her. When her gaze rose sharply, he snatched his hands back and gave her the towel and seltzer water, then watched as she drenched her shirt with it. The stain came out, but now he could see the lacy pattern of her bra underneath. An unexpected surge of excitement thrilled in his core—with that covert bit of lace, her sex appeal had just skyrocketed.

With the sweltering crush of the party around them, Elizabeth's wings began to wilt, as did Darcy's social fortitude. Ignoring her questioning look, he gently pulled her arm, and they squeezed through the crowd toward the front door. There he rifled through the drawer of an antique card table where Bingley had predictably left his garage door opener.

Darcy grabbed her hand and led her down the steps of the house and toward the garage.

"What are you doing?" she asked warily.

He held his hand up to her in a reassuring gesture.

"You're not going to axe murder me, are you?"

He stopped and assumed a pensive expression, helmeted chin resting on palm, finger tapping against the helmet. After visually debating with himself, he shook his head. Then he threw his hands up in the air and tugged her by the hand again.

Although Elizabeth had slight misgivings, no mental alarms were ringing, so she let the mysterious stranger lead her to the garage. With the garage door opener pilfered from Bingley's foyer, he opened the garage and turned on the light. Elizabeth gasped. Bingley had a car collection! While she gaped, Speed rifled through a key cabinet until he found the set he was looking for. Jingling the keys in his hand, he walked confidently to a Ferrari Enzo. When she hung back, he turned to her and beckoned her to follow him. She did, and after helping remove her wings, he assisted her while she climbed into the low-bodied car. Then he jogged over to the driver's side and expertly slid in. Clearly, this was a man with experience in getting in and out of outrageously expensive cars.

The engine started with a throaty growl, and he carefully maneuvered out of the garage and onto the driveway. The serpentine back road lured the purring motor of the car, and Darcy felt the call in his soul. It hadn't been that long ago that he tore recklessly across these very roads; he knew their twists and dips like he knew the lines of his own face.

"Are you stealing this car?" she asked. He laughed and shook his head. Pausing at the end of the driveway, he leaned over and adjusted the racing safety harness that crossed over her chest. Then he revved the engine and looked at her—she looked apprehensive.

"Do you know what you're doing?" she asked, her hand gripping the door.

He nodded. He pointed at his helmet, his gloves, his jumpsuit, and his racing shoes.

"Authentic?" she asked. He nodded. "Authentic eBay?" she clarified.

He shook his head and jabbed his thumb into his chest. Then he gave her thigh a comforting squeeze. Then, with a thumbs-up, he revved the engine. He stepped on the gas and the sleek machine glided forward.

Elizabeth felt her heart lurch as they surged forward. Images of being arrested—or worse, crashing—flitted through her mind as Darcy increased their speed. They took a curve, the car hugging the asphalt like a reunited lover, and suddenly, she was *exhilarated*. He gave the car more gas, the force pushing her back into the seat as they took another twist.

While the restraining harness brought Elizabeth some comfort, it was the skill of Speed that allowed her to enjoy the roller-coaster thrill of the ride. Each curve swung her toward the door or toward Speed, and she screamed with laughter when he caught air cresting a low hill.

Next to her, Darcy was grinning like an idiot in a joke store. The car belonged to him, stored in Bingley's hermetically sealed automotive museum. Some motor enthusiasts were afraid to drive their sports cars, fearing to scratch the paint or get dirt on the leather seats. But not Darcy. He felt true joy when pushing the performance of a car that was more like a wild animal than a machine.

With Elizabeth in the car, he was barely going over the speed limit, but in an Enzo it was still an exhilarating ride. He didn't know what impulse had made him decide to take her for a ride, for there was no telling how she would react, but deep inside, he had somehow known she would enjoy it.

Finally, when her hair was wind whipped and her eyes were bright with breathless excitement, Darcy steered the car back to the garage. As they pulled under the florescent lights, he glanced at her. With a child-like grin, she gave him a double thumbs-up.

Elizabeth extricated herself from the car, her wobbly knees forcing Darcy to offer her a steadying hand. As he helped strap her back into her wings, his gloved finger brushed her bare shoulder, raising tiny bumps on her skin. She turned to face him and peered into the dark reflective visor.

"Who *are* you?" she breathed.

Caught up in anonymous flirting, Darcy nearly lifted his visor before remembering himself. He was sure the half-smile on her face would fade when she knew she'd just been taken for a spin by Judge Darcy. So instead of revealing his identity, he shrugged and looked away, then walked her back to the house with his hands clasped behind his back.

He spent the rest of the evening by her side, a silent sentinel warding off any potential flirts with his blank gaze. He stood near when she stepped outside for air, followed her to the buffet, and held her drink when her hands became full. He diminished the destruction wrought by her wings, gently pulling her away from sneezing guests or catching goblets as she brushed by the wine station.

When Jane squeezed out of the crowded dance floor and grabbed Elizabeth's hand, laughing, "Come and dance!" Elizabeth looked questioningly at Speed. Although he regretted it, he could not possibly dance while wearing the helmet—and he certainly couldn't take it off now. Instead, he stroked a finger over one bent and broken feather on her wing.

"You're right, I've done enough damage." Elizabeth nodded. "Thanks, but no," she said to Jane.

Jane was just about to beg when Bingley grabbed her hand and pulled her back into the crowd with a yelp.

"You think he'll slip her the light saber later tonight?" Elizabeth smirked. Darcy did his best to interpret her glance as anything but inviting and looked out to the dance floor where Caroline was showcasing in tangerine glory. She waved at him, and Darcy raised a hand in acknowledgment.

"Is that your girlfriend?" Elizabeth asked.

Darcy looked down at Elizabeth and shook his head unhurriedly. Elizabeth's lips curled into a coy smile, and she looked at him from beneath her thick lashes. Hooking her thumbs into her belt loops, she swung her hips to the music. She did a slow turn, giving him a generous view of her shapely behind as she continued her dance, throwing a warm look over her shoulder.

Darcy leaned lazily back against the wall, arms crossed. *Is she doing a little dance for me?* he mused, smirking. Her sex appeal was undeniable, and Darcy was definitely feeling its pull. It wasn't just the room temperature that was fogging up his visor.

He watched as she faced him, singing a line to him. It was amazing how sensual her lips were, caressing the words. He fell completely under their spell, his pulse quickening and his groin stirring to semi-erection. Almost too late he realized that she was undoing the strap of his helmet, that luscious lower lip tucked mischievously between her teeth.

He stood up straight and firmly caught her wrists, wagging a reproving finger at her.

"Okay, Speed," she laughed, "your secret identity won't be revealed tonight."

He gave an inward sigh of relief as he released her arms. That had been dangerously close to disaster. At least the scare had killed his emerging erection.

Her attempted seduction unsuccessful, Elizabeth looked ruefully at the clock and sighed. "I should be going."

There was no doubt in Darcy's mind this time—her look was definitely an invitation. He sorely regretted that he could not take her up on her offer and could have kicked himself when he saw her brows scrunch in disappointment.

"Well, anyway, it was nice meeting you," she said as she offered him her hand. He shook it, holding it just a fraction too long. Then she was gone, and he had not said a single word.

Darcy pushed his way outside and tore off his helmet, shaking his soaking head and gulping in fresh, cool air. A moment later, Caroline emerged from behind, giving him a playful swat on the butt.

"Miss me?" she asked playfully. He didn't answer but looked out into the night. "We still have time to use these." She waved her handcuffs at him.

He laughed shortly and shook his head. "No thanks," he answered, his mind still distracted by the unexpected—unexpectedly pleasant—company of Elizabeth.

"I told you I'd make it worth your while, and I never break a promise," she sang as she slipped her arms around his waist. She pressed against him and looked at him invitingly.

"No need, I enjoyed myself. I won't hold you to it," he said.

"But will you hold it"—she pressed against his groin—"*against* me?"

"No thanks, Carrie. Not in the mood." He pushed her gently away, and she looked at him in slight confusion and amusement.

"Okay," she said and took a step back. "Are you all right?" she asked.

He nodded. "I'm fine. Just a little overheated. I think I'll head home."

"Is it possible to be completely sexually turned on by someone whose face you haven't seen and who didn't say a word for the whole evening?" Elizabeth asked Lou as he kneaded her back the next day.

"It depends. Did he weigh 300 pounds?"

"No. I wish I knew what his face looked like."

"Have Jane ask what's-his-name who it was, then see if you can get his number," Lou suggested.

"Christ, he was sexy!" she sighed. "I thought I felt some chemistry, you know?"

"With someone who wore a helmet all night?" Lou repeated skeptically. "He didn't even lift the visor to say good night?"

Elizabeth laughed. "No. I'm being stupid, aren't I? If he didn't even bother to say anything to me, he couldn't be interested, could he?" She turned on her side to face Lou as he massaged her arm. "It's just that, well, it was like he was playing a game. I mean, he didn't say anything, but he didn't ignore me. He followed me wherever I went, he didn't dance with anyone, and he didn't talk to anyone else. I think everyone thought he was my date, and I kinda think he wanted to give that impression. What does that mean?"

"Mmm," was Lou's response. Elizabeth rolled back onto her stomach and sighed again.

Chapter 3

BY THE NEXT WEEK, Jane and Bingley were dating. All those characteristics that had made her doubt his sexuality now convinced her of the opposite. His great fashion sense was easily explained: he was heavily influenced by Caroline. What Jane initially mistook for disinterest in her turned out to be a disarming lack of conceit; he simply hadn't thought that someone as lovely as Jane would be interested in him. However, the night of the Halloween party had been a revelation to both of them. After introducing her to everyone, Bingley had stayed glued to her side all night. After the party, a two-AM make-out session in his professional-grade kitchen led to a three-AM sleepover, and a ten-AM hangover the likes of which neither had ever known.

They complemented each other perfectly. Bingley had a child-like quality about him that took to Jane's maternal persona. She brought him a measure of comfort and stability that he'd lost when his own parents died. On the other hand, he made her laugh and explore her inner goofball without shame.

In the end, all that mattered was that they adored each other and were inseparable.

"Since when are you a karaoke maestro?" Elizabeth asked Jane as she peered into her closet.

"Charley loves it," Jane answered as she pulled out a pair of black pants. "Wear these."

"Do I have to?"

"Yes, you have to go to karaoke, and yes, you have to wear these pants. Think of it this way: a blind date can't get any *worse* than karaoke, so there's only room for improvement."

Elizabeth sighed. Ever since she'd started dating Bingley, Jane had become decidedly pushy. Even Elizabeth was not able to withstand her wheedling, and had finally agreed to a date—sight unseen—with one of Bingley's friends, Richard Fitzwilliam.

"What's this Richard guy like?" Elizabeth groused as she pulled on the pants. She had mixed feelings about blind dates; they were an uncomfortable confirmation of romantic desperation.

"He's very cute, very funny, and likes karaoke. That's all you need to know."

Elizabeth rolled her eyes and undid one of her blouse buttons. She might feel like an old maid, but damned if she'd look like one. The addition of an amber beaded necklace ensured Jane's sanction.

"Very sexy." Jane nodded approvingly. Her silver mandarin-style dress that stopped six inches above the knee was, naturally, stunning. Strappy silver heels set off mile-long honey-kissed legs. With an almost careless gesture, Jane swept her long blonde hair into a sleek twist. Elizabeth brushed an uncooperative wave of hair behind her ear and once again envied Jane's sophisticated beauty.

The doorbell rang and Elizabeth gave Jane a moment to greet Bingley before following her downstairs. She need not have worried. If Richard Fitzwilliam was what desperate old maids got "left" with on a blind date, she'd sign up for the next one in a heartbeat. He was tall, built, well-dressed, and had laughing blue eyes set off by fashionably shaggy brown hair. She had to give Jane credit—Richard was a hottie.

"Ready?" Bingley asked, and they all piled into his SUV. Across town they found a club where, instead of pulsing dance music, the out-of-tune strains of karaoke devotees floated out the door. Elizabeth shook her head in disbelief.

"I can't believe I'm actually going to a karaoke bar," she muttered before flashing Richard an impish grin.

Jane immediately found a table near the stage and ordered a round of drinks. The audience, already four drinks ahead of them, cheered as singers boldly took the stage to belt out their favorite songs. After two drinks, Bingley found the courage to leap onstage for a rousing rendition of Journey's "Don't Stop Believin.'" He strutted on the stage, pointing at ladies in the crowd and rounding up with a finale of jumping up and down on the stage.

While Jane performed the latest pop ballad, Elizabeth downed another drink. She was determined that serene Jane wouldn't show her up. After all, Elizabeth had always been the *fun* sister.

Under the orders of Captain Morgan, she made her way up to the stage. The bright lights blinded her as she looked out into the audience. Her inability to see beyond the first row of tables brought her an irrational sense of comfort. If she couldn't see them, surely they couldn't see her.

With the microphone in her hand, Elizabeth waited for her selection—Donna Summer's "Hot Stuff"—to begin. She tapped her heel to the disco beat and let herself be carried away by the music. She strutted and sashayed her hips, kneeling to sing to the front row and jumping up again to run her hands through her hair. Feeling the moment, she flashed Richard a grin. He responded by shouting, "Spank it!"

Never one to refuse a challenge, Elizabeth turned her back to the audience and gave herself a single slap on the behind, while tossing a saucy grin over her shoulder. The catcalls and whistles that followed gave her a case of the giggles, and she finished off the song with another swing of her hips and a charmingly girlish curtsey before jumping off the stage and rejoining her party. She was rewarded for her efforts by a kiss from Richard that said much more than, "Nice job."

At the rear of the club, Darcy stood motionless, agape at the spectacle before him. He had been invited by Bingley, and without his little sister insisting he go along, Darcy had declined. But Georgiana was out of town, Darcy was bored, and Bingley was always good for a laugh, so Darcy found himself standing just inside the doorway.

He was just searching for Bingley's blond head when he saw the most amazing thing he had ever seen in his life. Elizabeth Bennet was on the stage singing and… undulating… in a very unprofessional manner! At first he couldn't believe it was her, but he recognized that saucy grin that she flashed partway through her routine. Darcy was stunned.

Her shirt was open halfway down her chest with a glittering necklace that served only to draw his eyes to her breasts, jiggling under her shirt with every move. Her hair was a wild halo of dark curls around her face—*holy Christ*, did she just *slap her ass?* Darcy swallowed with a parched mouth. It couldn't possibly be her. It just couldn't. That wasn't fair. She had no right to be hiding all of—*that*—under a suit everyday, and then parading it around in front of him where he had absolutely no chance of ever seeing it!

She finished her number and everyone started to clap. She grinned and curtseyed like a kid, laughing at herself. He remembered that Bingley was dating Elizabeth's sister and that Elizabeth had no idea that he was Speed Racer. She could have no reason to expect him to show up. Meeting her now would only embarrass them both. Darcy decided not to join Bingley after all. He turned quickly on his heel and left.

Elizabeth's performance did nothing to push thoughts of her from Darcy's head; she'd already been on his mind too much for comfort since Halloween. For the next few days, visions of her smacking her rear would intrude on him at the most inopportune times—while making toast, on his morning commute, in the shower. Seeing her in her business-smart suits, hair groomed, and blouse buttoned to her throat was a maddening tease.

He had the urge to tell Elizabeth that he knew her little secret. He imagined she would get a great laugh out of it, if she didn't first peg him as a pervert. Instead, Darcy contented himself with his private knowledge of her performance skills. But when he saw her in the cafeteria the following Monday, Darcy couldn't help himself.

With an inward smirk, he passed her in line and said, "Watch out for the chili. It's hot stuff."

In his chambers later, Darcy sighed. It was absolutely impossible to ignore his attraction to her, especially after that display in the karaoke bar, but it was equally impossible to act on it. To act on his impulse would only cause professional trouble for each of them. He didn't need to have a rule against office romances—the State of California did it for him.

Judicial ethics prevent even the appearance of bias, let alone the real thing. How would it look if he were to date her *and* rule over her cases? Even if he could remain impartial—and he believed he could—it was not likely that anyone else would believe he was. She would be forced to take all of her cases to Judge Clayton, which was a problem in itself. Reassigning all of her cases to Judge Clayton would skew the caseloads and deprive Elizabeth's clients of a basic right: to bump a judge they didn't want.

No, asking Elizabeth out—having a relationship with her of any sort—wasn't a viable option.

He sighed. So why was it that even in his thoughts, they were already on a first-name basis?

His random musings on the various attractive parts of Elizabeth's body—she had very cute, pert ears—were disturbed by the buzzing of his cell phone. Glancing at the screen, he saw that it was his sister, Georgiana.

"Georgie, how's London?" he answered with a grin.

"Bloody freezing," she laughed. "I'm spoiled by San Francisco's weather."

"Yes, cold and rainy, such a step up from the UK. Have you been to the house?"

"Yes, Mrs. R. says hello and something about getting your bloody arse back over to see her for Christmas."

"I know, I know…" Darcy groaned at the oft-repeated plea from his long-term housekeeper-cum-maternal-figure to visit.

"She also wants to know when she can expect her first grandchild."

Darcy laughed. "Not that again."

"You should have married Sylvia Matlock when you had the chance. I heard she just got engaged."

"Good for her," Darcy replied diplomatically. His old flame Sylvia had not taken their breakup well, and he counted himself lucky on his narrow escape.

"I could give her a call and tell her you're still available," she teased.

"Uh, no." Darcy shivered a little at the thought. For a woman so beautiful, intelligent, and accomplished, Sylvia had been quite certifiably insane. The scathing messages she left on his phone after their breakup had made him glad he didn't own a small pet that she could have left dismembered on his doorstep.

"Was she that bad?" Georgiana laughed.

"No, of course not." Yes, she had been that bad. But he wouldn't impugn her character, both out of a sense of honor and for fear of retribution.

"I've been instructed to ask you if you're dating anyone."

"That's none of your business."

"I'll take that as a no. Will, you really need a girlfriend."

"I do not."

"Yes, you do. You're commitment phobic, do you know that?"

"I am not!"

"Then why haven't you had a serious girlfriend in the last ten years?"

"I don't know—I'm busy, I'm lazy, I don't want the hassle, there's nobody I'm really interested in making the effort with."

"So you sell yourself short to Caroline Bingley because she's convenient?" she challenged.

"There's nothing going on with Caroline," he stated. He heard her snort.

"Why do I find her underwear in your laundry?"

"Why are you looking in my laundry? And you haven't found it there since last July, I'm quite certain."

"Caroline Bingley is not what you deserve, Will. I can't believe you dip your stick in that."

"The mouth on you!" Darcy laughed. "I've done a poor job raising you." He could hear her smile.

"No, you've done a great job. I'm not a crack whore, right?"

"Who knows what you do in your spare time," he replied dryly.

"Seriously, Will, I don't want you to be an old bachelor. You're too good to waste on that. You'll be a great dad. I should know."

"Raising you did me in—I'm not having any kids," Darcy joked. He glanced at the framed photo on his desk—a skinny sixteen-year-old boy and a four-year-old girl with white-blond hair and freckles. Twelve years her senior, Darcy had always been protective of Georgiana. Losing their mother when he was sixteen and their father a mere six years later had made the two nearly inseparable. Except for his first summer in California, they had never been separated by more than an hour's drive. That she wanted him to settle down was more than just sisterly affection. It was a wish that he would have the full and fulfilling domestic life that had been taken from them long ago.

"Do you really not want kids?" she asked, sounding hurt. Darcy ran a hand over his face. To be perfectly honest, he did want kids. He just didn't want them to become teenagers. Georgiana had had a few rough years when Darcy was sure he'd lost her. He didn't think he could take that from his own offspring.

"Of course I do."

"So what's the holdup?"

"Look, I'm just lazy. Finding a woman takes a lot of effort. There's the whole problem of where to meet them, weeding out the uglies, getting rid of the sots, avoiding the golddiggers—there's really not much left in the pool once you're done. At least there are no illusions with Caroline. She only wants what's in my pants. She's made her own money, she doesn't want to be tied down, she's not bad looking, and she's tolerable company."

Georgiana made a sound of disgust. "Are you listening to yourself? Are you really that jaded? Don't you want something more?"

He sighed. "Of course I do, Georgie. It just hasn't happened yet."

"Get off your ass, and make it happen," she replied.

They rang off and Darcy brooded. During Georgiana's "rough patch," complete with promiscuity and drug use, Darcy had dropped nearly everything to straighten her out. For five years he devoted himself to Georgiana and work and nothing else. He didn't have any girlfriends. He didn't have a social life. He wanted to set a good example for her, and he wasn't sure he could, so the example he set was one of celibacy.

He had his discreet flings, of course, but things never advanced further than that. He always seemed to back away from anyone who showed any serious interest. At first he told himself that he needed to be there for Georgiana. Then, once she had moved out to live on her own, he convinced himself that it was how freewheeling bachelors lived. But eventually, it became monotonous and lonely. He had a hard time relating to people his own age because they did not have the experience of crushing responsibility as he had. He was too serious for most, and too young for others.

Even when Bingley's sister, Caroline, hinted at something more serious than a one-night-stand, he'd initially backed away. But eventually, loneliness gave way to familiarity and comfort. It hadn't been a perfect relationship, but it had been satisfactory for a time. This recent realization that it wasn't enough was a completely new development, made worse by his sudden infatuation with Elizabeth Bennet.

November in San Francisco was cold and rainy and it put Elizabeth in a foul mood. It put her in an even worse mood when she had to go out into the drizzle the weekend after Thanksgiving to put the finishing touches on yet another appeal of one of Judge Clayton's misguided rulings. She would much rather spend the day splayed on her couch in sweat pants and a tank top eating pumpkin pie cheesecake. Instead, she was trapped in front of her computer, her eyes burning and her stomach growling.

With a sigh, Elizabeth stood and stretched, then looked out the window. Nine stories below, a man ran a circuit of the park across the street. The distraction of watching his long, lean form loping along the path was a welcome one. Although she couldn't make out his features, something about the runner's movements reminded her of Speed Racer. Both were tall and lean, and she smiled as she pictured a helmet on the running man. Yes, they were nearly identical. She watched him make another quick circuit before he stopped and bent over, panting. As if sensing her, the man looked up toward her window. She instinctively darted aside to avoid discovery.

***

Darcy completed another circuit around the park, trying to beat his last time. He had been dismayed to find his racing suit so snug over Halloween. Even though the years had not been unkind to his body, his sedentary job made it all too easy to become "soft." Besides, running helped him clear his mind and focus on what was important to him. Right now, he was thinking about a trial decision he'd been working on an hour ago. When he became too confused at his own musings, he'd decided to go for a run in the park across from the office building.

Bent over his knees, panting, he suddenly knew how he had to rule. As always, the run had brought him clarity. He glanced up at the office building, wishing that he could simply dictate the decision while he ran instead of typing it himself. A brief flash at a window caught his attention, but the cloudy sky cast strange reflections, so he could not be sure of what he saw.

One more slow lap allowed his muscles to cool before he doubled back to the building's entrance. He swiped his security tag and let himself into the foyer where out of the corner of his eye he saw her: Elizabeth Bennet. For an instant he considered asking her what she was doing there, but he was sweaty and he was wearing nylon running shorts and a T-shirt. He might even smell bad. Thinking quickly, he ducked his head over the water fountain, hiding his face, and drank until she was out the door. Then he jogged up the five flights to his office and soon immersed himself back into his trial decision.

With her brief mostly done, and thoughts of leftover turkey and stuffing distracting her from finishing, Elizabeth stuffed her legal research into her messenger bag and grabbed her keys. When the elevator doors opened in the foyer, she noticed that the jogger was inside. He must have a security pass to enter, so he must work there, but she could not simply stare at him. Besides, she was in no mood to socialize even if it did turn out to be someone she knew. So instead, she dropped her eyes to the floor and let herself look at his legs as he stopped at the water fountain. Then she dashed out the door to her car before the rain began again.

"Another Christmas at home..." Jane sighed.

"Another year of '*Why aren't you married?*'" Elizabeth finished in her mother's shrill tone.

Her prediction came true as Mrs. Bennet took another disappointed poll of her daughters.

"Lizzy, you're not getting any younger! Believe me, before you know it, your eggs will be rotten, and you'll have to adopt from some Third World country. Then where will you be?"

"Mom, I'm only twenty-seven, give me a break!"

"I had Jane when I was only twenty, and I tell you it's better to have them when you're young. With my nerves, I don't think I could have handled children if I had waited until your age, Lizzy."

Elizabeth smirked. Her mother's nerves, indeed! She looked over at her father, who gave her a secret smile.

"Why don't you pick on Jane? She's not engaged either!" Elizabeth protested.

"Oh, but she'll have no trouble. She'll always be beautiful. But you, Lizzy, you must work to be married before your looks go! Besides, Jane has her surgeon!" their mother said with glee.

Jane looked at Elizabeth, and they rolled their eyes. It didn't matter that Jane was also a surgeon. Jane had practically begged

Elizabeth not to mention Bingley's wealth—the attack of nerves would be intolerable.

Their mother claimed to be of a delicate constitution, always complaining of flutterings and nerves, but she could often be seen in a fuchsia nylon running suit, working out on the elliptical machine in the garage while she watched the *Dr. Phil* show.

Their father preferred to spend his evenings in the solitude of his study with one of his scientific journals or puttering on some invention in the garage. He had been extremely proud of Jane and Elizabeth when they went on to professional careers. Their other sisters each had less illustrious career paths. Mary wanted to be a novelist, Kitty wanted to be an actress, and God knows what Lydia wanted to be—perhaps a stripper.

"Well, Lizzy, do you have any prospects at all?" her mother asked, refusing to let the subject die.

Sadly, she did not. Richard had not called her back, and she had never had the nerve to ask Jane to discover the identity of Speed Racer. She supposed he was long gone. When she shook her head, her mother wailed.

"I'll be in the garage," said her father.

That evening, Jane and Elizabeth spooned in their old beds, which had been pushed together into a king sized bed by Lydia.

"Lizzy," Jane said sleepily.

"Mmm?"

"I really like Charley."

"Good for you."

"I wish he weren't so rich."

Elizabeth opened her eyes. "Why?"

"Because people will always think I only want his money, and I don't. I wouldn't care if he were a shoe salesman, except

I don't think I'd like the constant smell of feet. But really, I wouldn't care."

"Then you really deserve him. How did he make his money, anyway?"

"His father was a computer billionaire, and his mother was an actress. They died in a plane crash a couple of years ago."

"Oh, how sad!"

"Yes. His sister is his only family now. She's in real estate. She's rich in her own right."

"They have a very impressive home."

"He wants to sell it. He thinks it's too much. It came with the helicopter, and he's never used it. I told him he should just buy something a bit smaller, maybe with a little more land and raise a few horses. He liked the idea."

Elizabeth smiled and hugged Jane. "He seems like a really sweet guy." She drifted to sleep wondering if she would ever find her own sweet guy.

"This is when I miss England most," Darcy said thoughtfully as he and Georgiana put the last Christmas ornaments on the tree. "I miss the snow and Mrs. R and seeing the house decorated. You know, I'm thinking about moving back in a couple of years."

"Really? I think I'm content to stay in California forever," Georgiana said. She turned off the overhead lights, and they sat close together on the floor, the tree glowing before them. "It's warm here, and I have friends," she continued. "England is just dead parents and an empty house to me."

He looked at her in surprise. "Dead parents and an empty house? How depressing," he said. "It's got a lot of good memories for me. It will be good to live there again. Maybe get married, pop out a few kids, liven the place up a bit."

"When you do, invite me over." They sat in silence for a few minutes. "This is for you," she said, handing him a little box.

"Christmas isn't until next week," he protested.

"Open it anyway." He slipped the ribbon off and removed the lid. Inside was a little black book. He looked at her sardonically.

"Start filling it," she said with a smile.

Chapter 4

LOU HURST LOOKED CRITICALLY at himself in the mirror and adjusted the hat on his head.

"You look fine," Elizabeth grumbled as she pulled on her gloves. "Come on, we can still get a few runs in."

"Do you think that snowboard instructor is gay?" he asked her, still studying the angle of his knit cap.

"Yes, I do."

He smiled. "Want to take some lessons?"

"Lou, I already know how to snowboard."

Lou released an exasperated breath. "So do I. Honestly, Lizzy, you have no imagination!"

"You go ahead. I'd just cramp your style anyway. How about I meet you back at the lodge for dinner at six?" Lou nodded.

They headed out together and separated at the base of the slope. Their annual ski trip usually ended like this—with Lou hitting on every metrosexual in sight and Elizabeth snowboarding until dusk, only to meet up again for dinner, drinks, and a facial. It was one of the things she loved about Lou. He wasn't clingy. When they were on vacation together, they didn't have to *be* together.

She slid down the hard-packed snow, the brisk wind brightening her cheeks to a rosy sheen, before ducking into the ski café for a hot chocolate. She was just licking whipped cream from her lip and looking for a place to sit when she received the shock of her life.

Towering before her, his face an open expression of surprise, stood Judge Darcy.

"Ms. Bennet!" he stammered.

Her own surprise was so great that all she could manage in response was a weak, "Judge Darcy! Wha... what a surprise!"

"Yes, indeed." He seemed at a loss for words.

Just the sight of him outside of court worked a knot on her stomach. She didn't like him, and she didn't want him ruining her ski trip. She wracked her brain for a polite comment that would allow her to escape from the café gracefully.

"Do you ski often?" she blurted, then groaned inwardly. *Don't invite him into a conversation!* she chided herself.

"Yes, well, when I can. A few times a year. And yourself?"

"No, usually only once a year." There was an awkward silence, and Darcy looked around as if searching for their next topic of conversation.

"I see you snowboard?" he said almost triumphantly, gesturing toward her board. *Poor guy*, she thought. *He really doesn't have any social skills*.

"Yes, I took to it more easily than skiing," she replied. *God, how long is this going to go on? I can't talk to this old fart forever, I've got a manicure at three!*

"I learned both at the same time in high school," he replied.

In high school? They had snowboarding back when you were in high school? she thought. Just how old *was* he?

While she pondered Darcy's age, they were joined by a willowy blonde in a pink cap. The blonde looked up expectantly at Darcy, but he was looking at Elizabeth with a strange expression on his face.

"Yes, they did," he frowned.

Good lord, had she said that *out loud?*!

The blonde, evidently giving up hope that Darcy would introduce her, offered her hand to Elizabeth.

"I'm Georgiana."

Darcy shook himself back into the conversation and said, "Georgie, this is Elizabeth Bennet. She's an attorney in my courtroom."

Out of nowhere, Lou appeared at Elizabeth's side.

"Going to introduce me?" he asked pleasantly, rubbing his hands together. He took Elizabeth's drink from her, sipped it, and handed it back.

"Judge Darcy, this is my good friend Lou Hurst. Lou, this is Judge Darcy and Georgiana, his… daughter?" she finished quizzically.

Georgiana threw her head back in a hooting laugh, and Elizabeth saw Judge Darcy's eyebrows slam down across his nose. *Yikes!*

"Georgiana is my sister," he said dryly, his ire showing in the flare of his nostrils.

"No, come on, Dad, stop teasing her," Georgiana laughed. "You're what, fifty?"

Darcy looked at his sister in dismay. "Excuse me," he said shortly. He strode over to a bench and sat down.

"I think you struck a nerve," Georgiana mused, watching

her brother sit on a bench and begin fussing with his boot bindings. "I'd better go sooth his ego. For the record, he's thirty-seven. It's the judge thing. People always think he's older than he is."

"Sorry," Elizabeth mumbled, blushing bright red from chest to hairline. She watched Georgiana join him and pull off his cap and muss his hair. Elizabeth realized that without his glasses and with his hair boyishly ruffled, Judge Darcy didn't look anywhere near as old as she thought he was. As she watched them, Georgiana said something to Darcy, who nodded curtly in response. Then he rose from the bench, tall and lean in his dark blue ski suit, which put her in mind of another man entirely. *Oh, Speed Racer, who are you?* she wondered wistfully as she watched Darcy's surprisingly shapely backside stride away.

Later that evening, Darcy and Georgiana were enjoying a quiet dinner at the lodge restaurant when a waiter brought them a nearly-empty bottle of wine and a slip of paper.

"From the young lady by the fireplace," the waiter explained, nodding toward the other side of the room. Darcy followed his glance and spied Elizabeth, the glow of the fire shining softly off her hair and bathing her in warm color. Even from across the room he could see the shadow her long lashes cast on her cheek. She was completely oblivious to her own beauty—completely unaware that she was stirring feelings inside of him that he'd long ago buried. It took him a moment to register that she was sitting with her friend, who was eyeing him with curiosity.

"Why would she send you an almost empty bottle of wine?" Georgiana asked.

"Rules. You can't give a judge anything worth more than five dollars," he explained, tearing his now obvious stare away from Elizabeth to look at the note. *Sorry about the daughter thing.*

He looked back at her, and she raised her wine glass to him in an apologetic salute, a half-smile playing on her lips. He was seized with the sudden urge to march over and kiss her. Instead, he nodded once and then quickly looked away.

He passed the rest of dinner in silence, casting furtive glances at her when he thought she wouldn't notice.

"You're looking at her an awful lot," Georgiana remarked.

Darcy forced his attention back to his sister with a careless shrug. "She's pretty. Why can't I look?"

"Why can't you ask her out?"

"A: She's with someone. B: It's against the rules of the profession. C: She thinks I'm your father," he ticked off on his fingers.

"I just have to say that it's very sad that you bought a Valentine's Day ski package and took your sister." She sighed, shaking her head. "Almost as sad as her taking her gay friend."

"What do you think precipitated the makeover?" Charlotte Lucas whispered on Monday.

"Maybe Clark Kent called and asked for his glasses back," Elizabeth joked.

"And Superman is emerging. Look at those eyes!" Charlotte continued. Darcy had stopped gelling his hair down and wearing his glasses, which revealed his eyes to be an almost startling shade of green.

"Maybe his girlfriend decided she didn't like getting her fingers stuck in all that gel," Elizabeth suggested. "I heard the lead partner at DeBourgh & Associates was trying to hook him up with her daughter."

"Anne? And Judge Darcy? I doubt it," Charlotte replied. "I met her several times when I worked at DeBourgh. She's an *Artist*, with a capital *A*. No watercolors, if you know what I mean. I think she sculpts with hamburger." Elizabeth clapped a hand over her mouth to stifle her laugh.

Their humor was short-lived. Darcy criticized Elizabeth's case harshly in front of everyone, making her angry. Then he did it again to the next attorney. And the next. Soon it became apparent that the judge was in a foul mood. For days. On end. February was a very bad month to appear before Judge Darcy.

Darcy had exactly one entry in his little black book: Anne DeBourgh. Unfortunately, he found her slightly repugnant. She always seemed to smell like meat, and her art was absolutely frightening. But it was a start, and she was a good conversationalist, especially if it could be done in fresh air. Which was why he invited her to the Springtime Symphony in the Park.

"Thank you so much for inviting me," she said as they found a spot to spread out their blanket. Anne was a short, thin woman with her black hair cut in a severe bob slashing past her chin. Her blue eyes were too big for her face, her cheeks had a pinched look about them, and her skin was dreadfully pale. Her lurid purple sundress hung like a tent on her tiny frame.

"It was my pleasure," Darcy replied. He laid out the blanket and sat down, elbows slung on his knees. "Your mother thought you would enjoy it." Anne looked down and smiled.

"I'm sorry for that," she said. "She is very determined. Just so you know, I do not share my mother's motives." She looked at him and gave him a friendly smile that said, "Hands off." Darcy inwardly sighed. He would have to scratch that lone entry from his black book.

"Yes, well…" He cleared his throat and smoothed a hand over his jean-clad thigh, then examined his tennis shoe.

"My mother tells me you have some connection with the symphony?" Anne tried to fill the awkward silence.

"Well, I was on the board a few years ago, but I'm not really that involved anymore," he answered. "And my sister is a violinist in the symphony."

"Really! I had no idea!"

Pleased to have found a comfortable topic—his sister's talent—Darcy leaned back on his elbows and stretched his legs out. Immediately, someone tripped over them.

"Oh, I'm so sorry!" he exclaimed, jumping up to help the poor woman he had just tripped. He was astonished to find that the hand he held in his own belonged to Elizabeth Bennet. "… Ms. Bennet," he finished somewhat weakly. She looked up at him with her big brown eyes, as surprised—but perhaps not as pleased—as he was. He pulled her to her feet, all the while feeling an electrical zinging where his skin touched hers.

"Watch your step, Lizzy!" came a shrill voice from behind her. *Lizzy?* Darcy thought. *Not Beth, or Liz, or Eliza?* He thought it suited her, and wondered how it would feel to call her Lizzy, to whisper it in her hair, to breathe it against her warm skin while… *Stop it!* He was giving himself the shivers.

Elizabeth gave him a tight smile. Then she turned toward the voice. "I'm fine, Mom." She turned back to Judge Darcy. "I'm sorry, are you okay?" she asked him.

He nodded; his mouth was too dry to say anything.

Elizabeth's mother joined them with a little huff. "Why, this looks like the perfect spot!" Her blonde hair frizzed about her face as the breeze ruffled it, and her cheeks were pink with exertion.

"No, Mom, let's go on over there," Elizabeth said, pointing in a general direction away from Darcy.

"Nonsense! This is perfect!" With that, Mrs. Bennet flicked out her lawn chair and sat resolutely in it.

"Mom, this spot is already taken by *these* people. Have a little consideration!" Elizabeth exclaimed, flushing deeply to Darcy's amusement.

"Consideration! They should have some consideration for my nerves! I can't walk another step in this heat. I'll faint. You don't mind if I sit here, do you?" Mrs. Bennet concluded, turning to Darcy.

Elizabeth looked away in embarrassment. Her father and Lou caught up with her and began to spread out a blanket for them, putting an end to her efforts to find another spot.

Darcy shook his head, looked to Elizabeth, and said, "Not at all, Ms. Bennet, I'm happy to share the space."

Mrs. Bennet looked at Elizabeth. "Do you know each other?" she said sharply. Elizabeth sighed and hung her head. Then she looked up with a grim smile.

"Mom, this is Judge Darcy. Judge Darcy, this is my mother, Fanny Bennet, my father, Tom Bennet, and you've already met Lou Hurst." Darcy began to shake hands.

"A judge, Tom! A judge!" Mrs. Bennet waved her hands excitedly at her husband, then looked over her sunglasses at Darcy. "And so young too!"

"*Mom*, this is Judge *Darcy*, before whom I appear nearly *every day*," Elizabeth emphasized, her embarrassment growing by the minute.

"Have you met Anne DeBourgh?" Darcy intervened, introducing Elizabeth to Anne. "Anne is my date." *Not my daughter and not my sister*, he thought irately. Anne looked at him with one brow arched in amusement.

Elizabeth shook hands with Anne and looked for a place to sit. Darcy moved over to give them more space, and Elizabeth and Lou sat on the ground next to them.

"You are Catherine DeBourgh's daughter?" Elizabeth inquired politely. Anne nodded. They had a brief, friendly conversation and then each ran out of things to say. Darcy did nothing to assist them. Elizabeth turned her attention back to her family and tried to forget his presence.

"I've been looking forward to this concert quite a bit, Lizzy," Mr. Bennet said to her from his lawn chair.

"What is it again?" Mrs. Bennet asked, looking at the program.

"It's the San Francisco Symphony playing Led Zeppelin," Lou supplied.

"Remember seeing them in concert before we were married?" Mr. Bennet said to his wife.

"No, I don't," she said, creasing her brow.

"I shouldn't be surprised, my dear, we were very, very high."

"I am *so* able to see you guys spaced out on LSD, getting the Led out," Elizabeth laughed.

"Don't you look down your nose at me, little Miss Lizzy! And it *was not* acid; it was just a little pot. Besides, I seem to recall you loved to twirl around in your little tutu to Elton John." Mrs. Bennet turned her attention to Lou. "She wanted to be a ballerina, you know. Got too heavy."

"Thanks, Mom." Elizabeth blushed and glanced out of the corner of her eye at Darcy, who was studying the program and appeared not to hear their conversation.

"But oh, how she wanted to star in the *Nutcracker!*" Mrs. Bennet continued.

"Nutcracker, ball breaker, it's all the same," Lou muttered to Elizabeth.

"Tom, remember how she split her chin open when she decided to hula-dance on the freshly waxed floor?" Mrs. Bennet reminded him. "Lord, what a fright! I looked up and there was blood everywhere!" she said to Lou. Then she laughed. "She was only four, and she had taken her shirt off and was in just a little skirt, because that's how the women did it on *Hawaii Five-O!* We had to take her to the emergency room like that!"

Now Elizabeth was sure she could see a little twitch at the corner of Darcy's mouth, but she was determined to ignore it.

"That was when we decided she'd better have dance lessons, or she'd be a danger to herself and others," Mr. Bennet added.

"You haven't seen her at a nightclub, then. She's still a danger," Lou snorted.

Elizabeth cringed but couldn't help laughing with them. Besides, what did she care what Judge Darcy thought of her? At least she wasn't dating a member of the Addams Family. With that thought in her head, she put him out of her mind completely and enjoyed an evening at the symphony with her family.

Darcy was a terrible date, so he was fortunate that Anne had no interest in him at all. He made little conversation with her because he was focused on eavesdropping on the Bennet family. He listened and tried not to laugh when he heard her parents talk about Elizabeth—*Lizzy*—dancing. He could very easily envision her as a little girl scampering about in a pink tutu. Lou's comments on her club dancing, however, took him back to the karaoke bar, and his thoughts took on a less innocent but infinitely more enjoyable bent.

His eyes crept over to her. She lay on the ground, knees bent up, and kicked off her sandals, digging her toes into the grass. Her green sarong skirt fell open revealing a good portion of her leg and thigh that Darcy's fingers itched to touch. He surreptitiously admired the curve of her breasts under her fitted T-shirt. The stab of jealousy he felt when he watched her talk easily to Lou, joking with him, and watched Lou touch her arms and legs in a familiar way surprised him. The emotion was not dulled when Lou put his arms around her and tapped melodies out on her arms. She closed her eyes and moved her hands to the music, and still Darcy watched her.

It hadn't escaped Lou's attention that Darcy seemed unable to take his eyes off of Elizabeth.

"He's got the hots for you," he commented as they drove home.

"Who?" she asked, mystified.

"The judge."

"What? Are you deluded?" she laughed. "I'm just 'all right,' remember? Anyway, he's no Speed Racer."

Lou shook his head. He recognized the signs of a man's attraction—the judge had it written all over him.

"Maybe he's having second thoughts about how 'tempting' you are," Lou suggested. "If you try really hard, maybe you could get him kicked off the bench for improperly shagging you."

"I'm not sure if he could give a proper shag if he tried," she dismissed with a smirk.

"He's a good looking man, Lizzy. You should consider it," Lou said pensively.

"A: EEK! B: Are you insane? C: EEK!" she said, ticking off her fingers. "Besides, even if I were interested, it's unethical for an attorney to date a judge who decides her cases. And I'm not interested."

"Okay, okay, methinks the lady doth protest too much!" Lou ducked Elizabeth's playful swat. "If you find out he's gay, give him my number, would you?"

Chapter 5

THE IRONY OF DARCY'S life was that his best friend was dating Elizabeth's sister. In an effort to resist the temptation to learn more about Elizabeth from Jane, Darcy had avoided her. He hadn't even bothered to tell Bingley that he worked with Jane's sister. Bingley would undoubtedly try to play matchmaker. So rather than become embroiled in an awkward mix of professional and social encounters, Darcy kept mum on the whole thing. The less he knew of Elizabeth, the better. Ignorance, as they say, was bliss.

"She's perfect," Bingley sighed over lunch. Darcy cocked an eyebrow and turned the page of his newspaper. "Do you know, I haven't made a single impulse buy since I've been dating Jane!" Bingley grinned proudly. Darcy laughed.

"I'm thinking of asking her to move in with me," he confided to Darcy.

Darcy stopped laughing and looked up in concern. "Really? Don't you think it's a bit early?"

"Early! We've been dating for six months!" Bingley exclaimed. "She thinks I should sell the house."

"No doubt to buy a bigger monstrosity," Darcy said absently but with a hint of derision.

Bingley's face reddened with anger. "Darcy, you're a dick! She actually suggested I buy something smaller and with more land and a couple of horses. I think it's a great idea. But maybe that's too *nouveau riche* for you!"

Darcy looked at Bingley in surprise. He could count on one hand the number of times Bingley had been angry with him, and this was one of them.

"*Nouveau riche?* What are you talking about?"

"Old money doesn't buy and sell estates. It's not *aristocratic* enough. Only new money *spends* money." Bingley stirred his coffee angrily.

"Don't be absurd, Bingley. You can do whatever you want with your money. I don't give a damn. What's this all about?"

"You think you're too good for her!"

"Even if that were true, why the hell would it matter? She's *your* girlfriend," Darcy retorted.

"You think she only wants my money!"

"I said no such thing."

"You said she wanted me to sell my house to buy something bigger!"

Darcy quelled his angry retort and bit his tongue.

"Why don't you like her?" Bingley asked, his anger giving way to agitation.

"I *do* like her. I just think you should be careful. I always think that, no matter who you are dating. It's a consideration for any wealthy man." Darcy paused. "But obviously you know her better than I do. I apologize. I didn't mean to insult her or you."

Bingley seemed somewhat placated but was not completely satisfied. "She's very important to me, Will. I'd like you to get to know her better." Bingley looked at Darcy with an almost pleading expression; he was so eager to have the approval of his closest friend and ally.

Darcy felt ashamed and, despite his own misgivings, said, "Look, Charley, I'm going to England in June for two weeks to attend a legal conference and take a little vacation time. Why don't you come along and bring Jane. It will give you a chance to spend some time with her and see if you really want to live with her, and it will give me a chance to get to know her a little better."

"Really? You'd do that for me?" Bingley said, surprised.

"Bingley, you're like a brother to me. I only want you to be happy."

Bingley grinned with delight and agreed. Darcy pushed down the little well of anxiety in his stomach. Whether it was excitement or dread, he couldn't say.

"So, what are you doing during the first two weeks of June?" Jane asked. Elizabeth switched the phone cradle to her other ear and spread the *California Bar Journal* on the desk before her.

"Um, same thing as usual. Bill ten hours and work fourteen. Go home, eat Lean Cuisine over the sink, and go to bed convinced that I'm never going to meet Mr. Right. I blame Mom. Oh, and I'll probably have Lou give me a massage."

"I think you should go on vacation."

"Who would take care of my twenty cats?"

"I'm serious, Lizzy! Charley and I are going to England for two weeks, and we both want you to come along."

"Oh, please, Jane! There's nothing I'd love more than being a third wheel on your pre-honeymoon."

"Actually, you'll be the fourth wheel; we already have a third."

"Great."

"See, Charley's friend has this vacation home outside of London, and he's invited us to use it. But he's also going to be there."

"You've *got* to be kidding. You want me to go along to keep your host company while you canoodle with Captain Conundrum?"

"Well, yes, actually. It's not like you wouldn't have any fun. We'll go sightseeing and shopping, see a few shows..."

Elizabeth half-listened while Jane ran off a list of tourist traps she wanted to visit. Three half-hearted "uh-huhs" in, she spotted an ad in the journal—a legal conference in London during the first week of June.

She'd never been to England, and she needed a vacation. If she went to the conference, at least she would be fulfilling part of her educational requirement. She was sure Charley's friend wouldn't want to pair off with her, so she was practically assured free time to explore on her own. Suddenly, it sounded quite tempting.

"Has Charley's friend actually extended the invitation?" she asked, now devoting her full attention to Jane.

"Of course!"

"Have I met him? What's his name?"

"To be honest, I've only met him once. I think maybe his name was Greg. He looked like a Greg, anyway. Oh, I don't remember! But Charley says you met him at the Halloween party, he saw you talking to him."

"Was it Speed Racer?" Elizabeth gasped, bolting upright in her chair.

"I don't know. Charley can't remember what costume he wore. Actually, I'm surprised Charley can remember anything about that night, he got so trashed. Did I tell you—"

"Wait! I have to know, is it him?"

"Honey, I don't know. But even if it is, he's off-limits. This guy dates Charley's sister Caroline."

Elizabeth flashed back to the Halloween party and Speed Racer slowly shaking his head when she asked if Caroline was his girlfriend.

"Must be the pirate, then," she sighed, crestfallen. "He wasn't that bad. Okay, I'll do it if I can get my boss to let me go."

Jane's squeal, accompanied by girlish clapping, made Elizabeth smile. After being assured that Charley would make all the arrangements—"All you have to do is pack and show up at the airport, I *promise*"—Elizabeth hung up. Then, glancing at the clock, she groaned. She was scheduled for a hearing with Judge Darcy, who had been in rare cranky form lately.

"I'm going to need this vacation," she grumbled.

The last week of May was some kind of cruel endurance test for Darcy. Somehow, his thirty-eighth birthday had snuck up on him, and he'd spent it alone in the dark, not answering his phone. That he was still single, without even a potential girlfriend, was suddenly galling. The only person he was interested in was Elizabeth.

She floated in and out of his courtroom every day, those sparkling eyes teasing him. He could almost imagine that she was flirting with him. Maybe she *was*. Maybe she was in the same boat, interested but unable to act.

Understandably—or so he thought—he was frustrated. It bled into every other aspect of his life. Caroline had stopped calling, and even Georgiana said he needed a vacation.

"You're obviously sexually frustrated," she announced over a salad. "Why don't you try to get laid while you're in London?"

"Piss off," Darcy replied tiredly—but did not deny her assessment.

"You need a hobby. Are you still playing guitar?"

"Yes, of course. I don't need a hobby. I'm already too busy."

"Well, you should channel some of that energy somewhere. Can't you write some legal treatise or something?"

"Georgiana—" Darcy cut off his annoyed retort, a lightbulb going off in his head. Of course! He could invite Elizabeth to collaborate with him on a law journal article! She was smart, nobody would question his choice. And it obviously would be an honor for her, a real boost to her legal career. It was an offer she couldn't possibly refuse. Then, once they were working closely together over the next few weeks, he could get to know her, see if she was interested in him. By the time his term was up, he'd be free to ask her out. It was a brilliant plan. He couldn't believe it had taken him so long to come up with it.

"I have to get back to work," he exclaimed.

"But your lunch just arrived!" Georgiana protested.

"Not hungry." He tossed some cash onto the table and flung his arms into his suit jacket.

Two hours later, Darcy paced angrily in his chambers. The moment he'd returned from lunch, he'd called Elizabeth's office and summoned her to his chambers to offer her the position. It hadn't gone well.

He supposed he should have noticed her displeased expression, but he wrote it off as having interrupted an office day, and didn't give it another thought. He took her evident discomfort as nervousness and was all confidence when he said, "Ms. Bennet, how would you like to write a law review article with me?"

He was so sure that she would accept that he brushed it off when she answered, "Thank you, but no, I'm not interested."

"I've been very impressed by your work," he continued, passing a glass paperweight from one hand to the other to mask his excitement. "I think this would be a good move for your career."

"Thank you, Judge Darcy, but no."

It was her firm, insistent tone that caught his attention.

"Did you say no?" He frowned, resting the paperweight on his desk.

"I'm afraid so."

"I chose you personally. This is a once in a lifetime opportunity," he said, a tiny drip of dread beginning to spread in his stomach. Could he have read her wrong?

"I understand that, and I appreciate it, but I'm really not interested."

He looked at her as if he did not quite understand which planet she was from. "May I know why not?" he asked.

"It's for personal reasons. But I do appreciate your thinking of me."

"Personal reasons?" His frown deepened. "Boyfriend?" he asked. Oh God, what was he saying?

"Judge Darcy, you know very well that is a completely inappropriate question!" she exclaimed, standing up. Of course it was, and of course he knew it, but some sick force compelled him to pursue it.

"But that's the reason?"

Two bright pink spots appeared on her cheeks, and he recognized her expression as anger.

"Of all the *arrogant*—do you honestly think I would let a boyfriend—or *anyone*, for that matter—dictate my career? You want the truth? Fine. I can't stand you. You're rude, condescending, and you think your opinion is better than everyone else's. I can't think of anyone I'd *less* want to spend my free time with. So thanks, but no."

Even through his own shock, Darcy could see that Elizabeth was as surprised as he at her outburst, although for entirely different reasons. He had merely been wrong; she had just committed career suicide.

"I see," was all he could manage to choke out. There was a heavy, awkward silence, then he said, "You've said quite enough. I understand. I'm sorry that I interrupted your day." He turned his back to her and opened his door, eyes cast to the ground as she hurried out the door.

Well, at least she doesn't have a boyfriend, he thought ironically.

"Are you kidding me? You said *that* to him?" Lou exclaimed over coffee.

Elizabeth nodded. "I'm afraid I did."

"You are so screwed," he laughed. "You just lost every trial you'll ever have with him for the next twenty years!"

"I'm going to try to avoid him for the next week, then I'm gone for two weeks. Hopefully, he'll have forgotten all about it by then," she said, grimacing.

"Not likely! Really, Lizzy, you need to learn to watch what you say!"

"This from the man who told my father he'd *like* to sleep with me, if only he weren't gay?"

Lou scowled. "I was feeling pressure from your mom," he grumbled.

"You know, in her eyes, being gay is no excuse for not marrying me."

Chapter 6

THE DEPARTURE DATE FOR their vacation fell on Saturday, the first day of June. After the last week she'd just endured at work, it couldn't come soon enough for Elizabeth. She boarded the plane with relieved excitement. Boredom quickly followed. While Jane and Bingley played footsie, Elizabeth worked a puzzle book, read—then discarded—a trashy romance novel, and tried to sleep.

"How do you know this guy?" Elizabeth voiced six hours into their transatlantic flight.

"College roommate." Bingley's response was muffled by the magazine tented over his face.

"Was he the pirate at your Halloween party?" she asked.

"I can't imagine Will dressed as a pirate," Bingley laughed, pulling the magazine from his face. "But honestly, that whole night is such a blur. Jane swears we made out, but I can't remember a thing."

Elizabeth sighed in frustration. Bingley was a sweet guy, but he had the most annoying habit of ignoring the most basic details. He seemed philosophically opposed to organization, schedules, or planning. He liked to just let things work themselves out. He was maddeningly vague about where they were staying, when their host was arriving, and even whether Elizabeth was expected to share expenses. He simply couldn't be bothered with the details.

"Lizzy, just relax. We're going to have fun, and you really need to wind down. Look how tense you are!" Bingley said, kneading her forearm with his fingers. Try as she might, she couldn't stay mad at him. Being an airhead seemed to be part of his charm. Elizabeth shook her head, picked up her book, and soon was pulled into the sweeping story of "forbidden and savage love."

When they finally got off the plane, a car was waiting for them at the airport. Bingley greeted the driver cheerily, their luggage was loaded, and soon they were on their way.

"You guys are going to love this place," he said as they sat cozily in the car. "I used to spend holidays there when I was in Cambridge. The house is spectacular, one of those country estates that goes back hundreds of years. I always feel like I should wear a tuxedo to dinner," he said with a grin.

They drove for some time out into the country. The late afternoon sun cast a golden glow on everything. As the road curved around a lake, a huge sandstone mansion crept from behind the trees.

"Behold Pemberley," Bingley said with quiet drama.

Elizabeth was speechless. The driver stopped by the lake to allow them to get out and take a look.

"I thought you said it was a summer home!" Jane cried. Bingley laughed.

The mansion, lined with rows of symmetrical windows, was a majestic edifice. Elizabeth could easily imagine seventeenth century aristocrats converging here for a month-long hunting party. Elegant ladies would take tea in their glittering gowns while the gentleman in frock coats smoked and stroked their hunting hounds by the fire. Or so she presumed.

An old forest framed the rectangular, golden building with lush, deep greens while the rolling lawn was accented by a water lily-filled pond. There was a comfortable grandness about it—stately but not stodgy, formal yet still inviting. It had none of the intimidating ostentation of Bingley's house, yet somehow seemed more sophisticated—more *genuine*—for it.

They continued on to the main house where a tall, slender woman with graying hair and blue jeans was waiting at the door.

"At last!" she laughed, wrapping Bingley in a hug and kissing him soundly on the cheek.

"You keep getting younger, Mrs. Reynolds!" Bingley said, returning her hug. Her introduction to Jane and Elizabeth, although less enthusiastic, was no less warm.

"Will's flight is delayed. I don't think we'll see him until tomorrow," she said over her shoulder as she led them inside.

Elizabeth was as impressed by the interior of the home as she was by its exterior. Rooms were tastefully furnished in dark woods and rich carpets. While the house had a masculine feel, lighter touches of flower-filled vases and fringed throw pillows belied a woman's presence.

Mrs. Reynolds led them to the family dining room, where a light dinner of sandwiches and salad awaited them. The trip had taken its toll on Elizabeth. The flight itself was exhausting, and the time change left her feeling ready for bed before the sun had barely touched the horizon. She soon found herself yawning between bites, unable to concentrate on the conversation. She actually jerked awake when she felt a hand on her shoulder.

"I'll take you straight up to bed, if you like," Mrs. Reynolds said gently.

"I'm so sorry. I didn't expect to be so tired," Elizabeth apologized.

"It's no trouble. Come along, I've got to take clean towels up anyway. You can have a soak before bed."

Mrs. Reynolds' maternal presence was the best feature of the estate, Elizabeth decided as she wearily climbed the stairs to the second floor. She was definitely a different sort of mother than she was used to. After showing her how to work the antique showerhead, Mrs. Reynolds left Elizabeth to prepare for bed. Elizabeth didn't bother to shower; she was far too exhausted. Instead, she changed into her pajamas and climbed between the sheets. Her last thought before falling asleep was that she hoped Will Reynolds was as nice as his mum.

Darcy's flight was some kind of nightmare designed to torture the homesick traveler. First they were delayed in San Francisco by fog for two hours. Then the flight was cancelled altogether and he had to transfer to a flight that had a stopover in New York. Once in New York, a mechanical problem delayed the flight for another three hours. By the time he was finally over the Atlantic, Darcy no longer cared whether he plunged to his death, as long as it ended the misery of smelling his neighbor's body odor—something even first class could not cure—for the next seven hours.

Attempts to sleep were largely unsuccessful, but he was glad to be going back to England. It always restored his spirit to go home. Mrs. Reynolds was indeed the closest thing he had to a mother, and though he hated to admit it, he often missed her. At home he didn't have to worry about work or politics. He could ride horses and motorbikes like he had all his youth. He had no intention of spending much time with Bingley; he did not want to intrude, and besides, Bingley and Jane were likely to spend a good deal of time in London anyway.

Even more than just recharging, Darcy needed this vacation to do a little soul-searching. Elizabeth Bennet had given him a set-down like none he'd ever experienced. He supposed he had let his manners lapse and had allowed his frustration to show too often. But it had gone beyond that; she'd said she couldn't *stand* him. It had hurt him. He should have known that her teases weren't flirting; they were well-aimed barbs. He was as dense as Bingley.

He steered his car from the airport toward his family estate—Pemberley. The sun was just beginning to creep over the horizon when he finally swung past the lake. As he always did, he stopped to admire the mists rising from the water, the water fowl stirring, and the warm glow of the house behind the lake. This was home, where he could be himself again.

He pulled his bags from the boot of the car and quietly made his way upstairs to his bedroom. It was the same as it had been for generations: huge four-poster bed with oversized mattress, heavy antique dresser and nightstands, fluffy down comforter and pillows. He had eschewed such trappings when he was younger, but after his father died, he had moved into this room. He felt as if the master of the house should be in this room. He found it surprisingly comfortable: masculine and old-fashioned. Aside from lengthening the bed, he hadn't changed anything.

It suited him perfectly. *Home at last,* he thought. Time to get Elizabeth Bennet out of his system for good.

Elizabeth woke the next morning to light filtering in between the cracks of the heavy drapes on her window. It had been too dark to see the view from her window last night, and she sprang from her bed and pulled the drapes aside. The view was lovely. There was a green sweep of grass curving over a gentle slope that framed the edge of the pond, a swan gliding around the lily pads.

Hiking her pajama pants up and her tank top down over her belly, she found her slippers and washed her face. She brushed her teeth but not her hair, and, after a couple of false starts, found her way downstairs. On the terrace she found Jane and Bingley, sitting in their pajamas, sipping coffee, and munching croissants. Two weeks of meeting Bingley in their own kitchen every morning had erased any shyness she had about meeting him in her jammies.

"Good morning!" she sang as she stepped out onto the terrace. Too late, she realized that their host had arrived. He leaned on his elbows against the balustrade, looking over the edge. At the sound of her voice he turned to her.

Recognition set in.

Long seconds of silence drew out. Finally, he managed to choke out, "Ms. Bennet!"

"Judge Darcy!"

After an agonizing moment that seemed to stretch into eternity, Elizabeth turned and bolted back to her room. She was pacing, wringing her hands, and saying "ohmygod-ohmygod-ohmygod," when Jane found her moments later.

"Lizzy, what just happened?"

"Oh my God, I can't believe this is happening. You said his name was Will Reynolds!"

"No, I never knew his last name. I've only met him once before. And the *housekeeper's* name is Reynolds." She paused for a moment, watching Elizabeth stride back and forth across the floor. "So this is the Judge Darcy you've been complaining about?"

"Jane, I have to get out of here. I can't spend two weeks with him. We'll kill each other." Elizabeth was already tossing toiletries into her half-unpacked suitcase.

"Where are you going?"

"To a hotel."

"Don't be ridiculous. Lizzy, *stop*." Jane grabbed Elizabeth by the shoulders and spun her around to face her. "You've never run away from anything in your life. Whatever problem you have with Will, I'm sure it's all a misunderstanding."

"Huh!" Elizabeth huffed humorlessly. "You're such an optimist."

"A misunderstanding," Jane continued, "that you can resolve here. Away from the pressures of work. No matter what, Lizzy, you have to go back and work with him. Which do you think is the better course: run away and let it fester, or try to work it out and not get an ulcer every time you go to court?"

Elizabeth rolled her eyes and crossed her arms over her chest.

"I'm not going to let you ruin our vacation—this is *your* vacation too, Lizzy. So get dressed, come downstairs, and let's see what he says. If he's a tool and asks you to leave, we'll go with you, I promise." Although Elizabeth was not anywhere near convinced, she nodded once. Jane gave her a squeeze and left her to get dressed.

She looked down at her appearance—rumpled pajama bottoms with skulls and crossbones, a tank top with no bra, and her hair was a spectacular mess. The glass eyes of her pink bunny slippers seemed to laugh at her, their bent whiskers twitching as she paced.

Could it possibly get any worse?

Darcy stood, rooted to his spot, not quite able to process the image of Elizabeth dashing away from him. To say that her appearance was unexpected might be the understatement of the century. All of the resolutions he'd made—stop thinking about her, find someone else—flitted out of his mind with the realization that she was here. It was too cruel to be coincidence, so either it was fate, or Bingley.

"Bingley!" he shouted, wheeling to confront his friend.

"What!?" Bingley looked genuinely surprised at his reaction, and it took Darcy a moment to recall that Bingley didn't know that Darcy and Elizabeth were co-workers. He took a deep, calming breath and ran a hand through his hair.

"You didn't tell me you were bringing anyone else," Darcy said in a tight, controlled voice.

"Yes, I did! Two weeks ago! I left you a message. I told you Jane was bringing her sister."

Darcy swore. He never listened to Bingley's messages—they always rambled on and never got to the point. It was easier just to wait for Bingley to call back and then steer the conversation in a coherent direction. But two weeks ago he hadn't been answering his phone much, wallowing in birthday pity as he had been.

"Didn't Mrs. R tell you? I emailed her to let her know. I thought for sure you knew!"

Darcy shook his head. Mrs. Reynolds was a capable housekeeper; she didn't need Darcy's input about anything. She probably assumed that he already knew.

Darcy sat at the terrace table and buried his face in his hands. Their last encounter—where he was soundly shaken from his delusional belief that she might be interested in him—had left him angry and hurt. But it had done nothing to erase the persistent longing he felt. He liked her. He wanted her. And he was helpless to do anything about it.

Well, at least this would give him an opportunity to show her that he wasn't some sort of ogre. He was a generous, kind, easygoing man who just happened to be at the end of his rope. And now, the woman he couldn't get out of his mind had been tossed into his lap at a secluded country estate over which he was lord and master. *Surely*, he could make it work to his advantage.

"Is this going to be a problem?" Bingley asked, sitting across from Darcy. Concern creased his forehead. "We can go to a hotel."

Darcy leaned back in his chair, his hands still covering his face. Then with a groan and a short laugh, he looked at Bingley.

"No, of course not. I want you to stay. But I think you should know that Jane's sister and I work together, and she doesn't like me. So if you were planning on some kind of matchmaking, just forget it."

How Elizabeth had made it all the way to England without knowing that he was their host was a mystery. But knowing Bingley, he just hadn't told her.

"I'm going to go… somewhere," Darcy said, standing. Hide was what he wanted to do.

"Will, I'm sorry," Bingley said softly.

"I know. You're an idiot, Charley. You can't help it. It's part of your charm."

Careful to avoid any of the common areas where Elizabeth might unexpectedly pop up—much like a carnival game, except Darcy was the one dodging the shots—he made his way to his private study near the rear of the house. He sat down in a well-worn, leather easy chair and heaved a deep sigh.

It wasn't just her being there that so unnerved him. It was that she looked so winsomely sexy with her rumpled clothes, tousled hair, and the intimate informality of a simple tank top with no bra. *This is what she looks like first thing in the morning,* he thought, which led him to wonder what she looked like sleeping, or naked, or fucking.

"*Stop!*" he groaned to himself, a shiver coursing down his spine. He was at the end of his rope, yes, but there was no need to wind it around his own neck.

He made himself wait for a half hour before emerging from his study and approaching the terrace. There she was, standing in the same spot where he'd stood before, looking over the view of the lawn and pond. She was dressed now in khakis, a turtleneck, and a long-sleeved button-down shirt over it. He swallowed and worked up his nerve. No time like the present to start making amends.

"Ms. Bennet, I want to apologize," he said quietly as he stood beside her.

She turned to look at him, her face was an unreadable mask. "There is no need to apologize, Your Honor. It appears there was a gross lack of communication between myself and my sister. I would be happy to go to a hotel," she offered.

"Don't be silly. It's an awkward situation, but we are adults, and I'm sure we can get beyond it and enjoy the next two weeks." He was disheartened that she appeared surprised by his conciliatory tone. It made him more determined to shatter her impression of him.

"Of course," she replied stiffly before she resumed her intense viewing of the landscape. Sensing her discomfort, Darcy tried to ease the tension.

"Well, the house is plenty big enough, and if my ego is too large to fit in the same room as yours, I could open a wing for you." A small smile tipped the corners of her lips.

"I'm sorry, you're right. About being adults, not about the egos," she added quickly. "I'll do my best to act like a grown-up, Your Honor."

He laughed. "Ms. Bennet, we are *five thousand miles* away from work." He assumed a stage whisper. "Nobody will know if you call me Will and I call you Elizabeth."

A smile crept to her lips. "What does the 'F' stand for?" she asked.

He blinked a moment in confusion, and then recalled the nameplate on his desk: Hon. F. Darcy.

"What do you think it stands for?" he countered.

"Do you really have any doubt what *I* think it stands for?" she said, smirking.

"Contrary to popular belief, my mother did *not* name me Fucker. It's Fitzwilliam." They both burst out laughing, and for at least that brief moment, Darcy felt as if things were looking up.

***

Well, that wasn't so bad, Elizabeth thought as she let out an unsteady breath. She had had a little while to think about what Jane said—that no matter what happened, she would still have to work with Darcy. She had also come to the conclusion that she had been way out of line with her outburst. He could be Attila the Hun, but she still had to respect him as a judge. And really, he was a fair and even-handed judge; she had always thought his decisions were sound. It was just his demeanor that had put her off. He always seemed to be in a bad mood. She also had to admit that after his initial rejection of her at the Assembly Room, she hadn't really given him much of a chance.

It couldn't be easy to be in his shoes. He was a relatively young man in a position of power that had to be handled responsibly and fairly. It wasn't until recently that she'd even realized that hardly any attorneys held trials with Judge Clayton; everyone preferred Darcy. So while both judges might have the same number of cases, his were inherently more labor-intensive. Perhaps she had judged him unfairly. He was supposed to be an impartial officer of the court, not her friend.

It was this conclusion that convinced her to follow Jane's advice and try to iron out her issues with Darcy. Hopefully, they would learn to understand each other and make both of their lives easier in the future. Besides, with her sister dating his best friend, chances were good their paths were going to start crossing a lot more.

Now, as he stood next to her on the terrace, she appreciated the obvious effort he was making. She *would* make the most of this opportunity.

"I assume you are attending the London conference?" he asked. She nodded. They discussed the topics and after some offers and refusals, agreed to attend together.

"Would you like a tour?" he asked.

"That would be nice, thanks." They strolled through the house, stopping whenever he remembered some historically significant item or anecdote.

"I'm afraid Mrs. Reynolds does a much better job than I do," he said as they reached the portrait gallery. "She leads tours on a regular basis. These portions of the house are open to the public," he explained.

As if on cue, Mrs. Reynolds led a small party of elderly women into the gallery. Elizabeth watched as Mrs. Reynolds recited a complete history of the estate, using the portraits of prior occupants as illustrations. As she examined the paintings, Elizabeth was struck by Darcy's resemblance to another Fitzwilliam Darcy, dressed in Regency period clothes.

"You look very much like him," she said quietly so as not to disturb Mrs. Reynolds.

"That is my great-great-great-great-great grandfather Fitzwilliam Darcy," he said, counting the "greats" on his fingers. "The name Fitzwilliam is somewhat common in our family. It started when *that* Fitzwilliam's father married a young lady with that surname. After that, there's always been a Fitzwilliam Darcy floating around, and there is also a line of cousins with the last name Fitzwilliam. Family gatherings can be a little confusing."

Elizabeth was still staring at the portrait when Mrs. Reynolds moved the group down to the more recent portraits.

"Now you will see the portrait of the current Master of Pemberley, Fitzwilliam Darcy," Mrs. Reynolds called to the group.

Elizabeth turned to Darcy and mouthed, "*Master?*" with an amused smirk. He shrugged and gave a slanted smile. She followed slightly behind the group to see the portrait, half-expecting to see him dressed in costume, but it was a very tasteful informal painting. He was sitting on a sofa with a young woman and a large gray wolfhound.

"This portrait was done about eight years ago. That is my sister, Georgiana. You met her at Tahoe," he said close to her ear. "She's a musician. In fact, she was playing at the concert we attended in April."

She wondered if he knew how stately he looked standing there. Although he was casually dressed in a blue check button-down shirt and gray slacks, she thought his carriage left no doubt that he was completely comfortable in the formal surroundings. He stood almost posed in graceful relaxation, hands behind his back, one leg turned slightly.

A few of the older ladies looked at Darcy with recognition and nodded politely. He returned the nods graciously. As the group prepared to exit the gallery, one of the ladies turned and said, "Thank you very much, Mr. Darcy, for sharing your lovely home with us."

"You are most welcome. I am very pleased that you are enjoying it," he replied warmly. Mrs. Reynolds nodded approvingly and herded them out for the remainder of the tour.

Darcy motioned Elizabeth into the hallway and quickly concluded the tour of the house. Next, they explored the grounds and gardens. He was surprisingly knowledgeable about the gardens and the landscaping, telling her about the major landscaping renovations in the late 1700s that produced the current delightful aspects.

"It is honestly the most beautiful home I have ever seen," she said appreciatively as they strolled back to the main house. Elizabeth turned to take another look at the grounds. She could not imagine growing up in such luxury. Even harder for her to imagine was abandoning it.

"It must have been difficult to leave," she ventured.

He shrugged. "Pemberley has always been here and will always be here. It didn't seem to make much difference whether I stayed or left. So I left to see what else there was in the world."

"Do you miss it?"

"Very much. I shall not be seeking a second term," he replied.

"Then you mean to come back here?"

He shrugged again. "Eventually. It's my home."

He steered her toward the house where they met again with Bingley and Jane and sat on the terrace to have tea.

That evening in her bedroom, Elizabeth ruminated over the day's events as she brushed her hair before the antique vanity. Darcy had been more than polite and considerate. He had been… well… *pleasant*.

It was funny, just a week ago Elizabeth would never have looked at Darcy twice, so prejudiced was she against him. But today he had shown himself to be something more than what she'd known. When he talked to her, he held her gaze with those striking green eyes until she had to look away from their intensity. He ran his fingers absently through his hair when he was thinking, erasing the austere image she'd always had of him. Before today, she never would have noticed him. Before today, she would never have called him handsome.

But today was today, not yesterday, and there was always something new to learn today. And today, to her surprise, she had learned that perhaps Lou's idea that Darcy had the hots for her wasn't such a bad idea after all.

***

At the other end of the hallway, Darcy was getting ready for bed. He was exhausted, having avoided sleep until now in order to stave off jet lag. He felt grimy and stepped into the shower, allowing hot water to sting his face. The shock of seeing Elizabeth had not quite worn off, but all things considered, he was pleased. They'd had a good day, he'd made her laugh, and he managed not to think about how much he wanted to change her mind about him and instead set out to just be a normal man around her. He supposed she was thinking the same thing he was: with Bingley and Jane dating, they were probably going to be seeing more of each other outside of work, and they'd better learn to play nice.

He'd had a will of iron all day, pushing aside every thought regarding how attractive she was, but now he was just too tired, and he gave in. She was undeniably beautiful, and he found her sexy in unusual ways. Something about the way her hair curled about the nape of her neck when she wore it up drove him to distraction. He imagined it would be wonderfully intimate to kiss her there, to ruffle those curls with his breath, to taste her skin on his tongue...

He turned the shower temperature over to cold and thought to himself, *It's going to be a very long two weeks.*

On Monday morning, Darcy offered to show Elizabeth some sights in London after they had attended the day's seminar. She thanked him, and after breakfast, they climbed into his car and he steered toward London. She took a deep breath and forced herself to make the apology she knew he deserved.

"I wanted to say how very sorry I am for my behavior when you offered me the law journal article," she said as she looked out her window at the countryside. "I was terribly rude, and there was no excuse for it."

His face flushed as he glanced at her. "Really, there's no need to apologize. I've thought about what you said, and you were right. I guess I'd let my manners slip, and that's not acceptable. Everyone deserves respect in the courtroom. You said nothing that I didn't deserve."

They fell into an awkward silence, and he cleared his throat, grappling for a new topic.

"How do you like your MINI Cooper?" he asked, finally.

"How do you know I drive a MINI Cooper?" She frowned.

"I've seen you in the parking lot."

"Oh. It's a lot of fun to drive. I've been thinking of taking one of those racing courses."

"Really? How interesting. I used to race cars, you know."

She turned in her seat to face him. "You used to race cars?"

He nodded. "I did in college, a brief stint of about three years of semi-professional racing. My father hated it—it caused a minor scandal in my family," he related. "I eventually quit after a particularly bad crash."

She was not listening to his story.

"*You* are Speed Racer?"

Her question took him by surprise, and he didn't answer right away, but his cheeks reddened.

Her face flushed, and she sat back in her seat, looking forward.

"Oh my God," she said in wonder.

"I'm sorry, I should have said something at the party," he said and glanced at her. "I didn't want to embarrass either of us."

"Wow," she said quietly. "I would never have guessed. Never in a million years."

"Yes, I know. You made it quite clear in Tahoe that you thought I should be eating strained peas in a retirement home," he teased her.

She cringed. "You know, you did it to yourself. You wore those ridiculous glasses and plastered your hair down; you looked like a fully vested member of AARP," she grumbled.

"Yes. Would it surprise you to learn that was the point? I was only thirty-three when I became a judge, and young judges don't get much respect."

They rode on in silence until he pulled into the Ritz where the conference was being held.

"Should I have worn something nicer?" Elizabeth asked, glancing down at her black floral jersey wrap dress and beaded sandals.

"You look fine. Why do you ask?"

"You're in a suit," she pointed out. "I'm not."

"I have a reputation to maintain," he said to her with a half-smile.

"Nobody here knows you're a judge."

"Everybody here knows I'm a Darcy," he replied simply.

Entering the foyer, the concierge greeted them immediately.

"Welcome back, Mr. Darcy. Will you be staying the week?" he asked politely.

"No, I am here for the conference, thank you," Darcy said almost absently. The concierge bowed slightly in deference.

"If there is anything you need, please let me know."

Elizabeth sat through the seminar distracted by the man beside her. He was so different than the image she had always held of him. He had an easy elegance and comfortable manner that she'd never seen—or perhaps never noticed—before. She stole a glance as he stood across the room, pouring coffee for both of them.

How could she *not* have known that he was Speed Racer? His height alone should have given it away; he towered over everyone and stood at least six-foot-four. His movements and gestures were familiar now that she looked. Even seeing him in his ski suit in Tahoe hadn't made the connection for her. How incredibly unobservant *was* she? But now there was no doubt. When he looked at her, she felt that same little flutter of excitement in her stomach she got whenever she thought about Speed.

He got the same deferential treatment wherever they went. When they went to a museum after the session, they were greeted by the curator, who offered to personally show them the best exhibits. For dinner, they got the best table without waiting, despite the long line out the door. Tickets to the sold out play? No problem, Mr. Darcy, front and center.

On the way back to Pemberley, Darcy had the misfortune of being pulled over by a traffic cop. But once again, the family name saved him. The officer greeted Mr. Darcy pleasantly and asked him to take care and watch his speed, not everyone was as skilled a driver as he, then sent Darcy on his way with a friendly wave.

As they pulled back onto the motorway, Elizabeth blurted out, "Are you royalty?"

Darcy threw his head back and laughed. "No, I am *not* royalty. The Darcy Policeman's Pension Fund gets me out of tickets *all* the time." He laughed again and shook his head.

By now, each was comfortable sitting silently together, so Darcy turned on the radio. He was about to change the channel when he recognized the disco beats and heard "Hot stuff, baby, tonight." Instantly he recalled her karaoke performance, and he pulled his hand away from the dial. He still wasn't prepared to admit that he'd seen her performance, but in the dark of the car, he allowed himself a little smile as he relived her routine, every hip thrust burned into his brain by the lust he'd felt for her.

Some time later, they pulled onto the gravel at Pemberley and climbed out of the car. Darcy busied himself pulling his jacket from the backseat and brushing it off while secretly watching her walk toward the house, her dress swinging alluringly off her hips. He wondered if she knew how sexy she was. At that moment, Elizabeth looked over her shoulder at him and smiled. He swallowed and looked down, then he locked the car and jogged to catch up with her.

"Thank you for a wonderful day, Will. You are a great host," she said as they walked up the stone steps together.

"The pleasure was mine." *Entirely. Completely. Absolutely.* He was doomed.

It was nearing midnight as they walked upstairs together. They stopped at her bedroom door, just down the hall from his own.

"Well, good night," she said softly, her hand on the doorknob.

He looked down the hall to his own room and sighed. He looked back at her.

"Good night." He turned and walked to his own bedroom, closing the door firmly behind him.

Once inside her bedroom, Elizabeth admitted it to herself—she was attracted to him, and she thought he might be attracted to her. She lay on the bed and thought about what it might be like to kiss him. She wished Lou were here to dare her into it.

Ten minutes later, after some hesitation, Elizabeth rapped lightly on Darcy's bedroom door. He must have presumed it was Bingley because he opened it without bothering to re-button his shirt.

"Sorry, is there an Internet connection?" she asked hesitantly, her laptop held tightly to her chest. He blinked at her. She studiously avoided looking at his chest.

"Of course," he replied. He hastily buttoned his shirt and led her downstairs to his study. Within moments, she was set up.

"Thanks," she said, smiling at him.

"No problem, feel free to use it anytime. Good night again," he said.

"G'night."

As soon as he was gone, Elizabeth logged on to her Instant Messenger account. As expected, Lou was logged on. She ping-ed him.

<Hiya!> she wrote.

<Whassssup?> Lou replied.

<"Will" = Speed Racer = Judge Darcy = HOTHOTHOT>

<LOL. I told you so. In his bed yet?>

<Can't do it—rules.>

<Rules are meant to be broken, sweetie. I break God's rules of nature every day!>

<Enough about your wardrobe. What should I do?>

<You should go for it. Rules don't apply when you're not in the country.>

<Jurisdictional issue. I like it. What about when we get back?>

<Think about that in 2 wks. Gotta go. Ciao.>

<Ciao, bella>

***

Once back in his room, Darcy lay awake in bed, his hands folded behind his head as he stared at the ceiling. He had tried not to notice that she was again in pajama bottoms and a tank top, but it was no use. At least this time she was wearing a bra. But the way her hair fell on the smooth sweep of her shoulder and her beguilingly rumpled appearance did not let her escape easily from his mind. He wondered what it would be like to see what was beneath those pajamas. Then he ground his teeth and mentally berated himself. *Get a grip, man!*

Chapter 7

ELIZABETH SLEPT SOUNDLY, DREAMING of green eyes and running her fingers through dark wavy hair. She woke up flushed, the vividness of the dream leaving her heart pounding. She rubbed her face and groaned—this was terrible! She couldn't be attracted to Judge Darcy; that was just all shades of wrong! No, the best thing to release this pent-up energy was vigorous exercise. After slipping on her track pants and halter, she knotted her hair at the back of her head, and flitted lightly down the steps and out the door, iPod blasting in her ears. She ran along the main road until she found a path leading to the fields, and splashed through a puddle with childish pleasure.

She had run hard for about two miles when she stopped, leaning over, and gasping for breath. Panting, she put her hands on her knees to rest, when she felt something nuzzle her rear. She turned and jumped back with a violent start and a yelp as she came face-to-face with a large horse. It took her a moment to see Darcy sitting on the horse looking amused. She jerked her headphones from her ears.

"That was not nice!" she exclaimed, putting her hand on her chest. "You nearly gave me a heart attack!"

"I'm sorry, he's a very rude horse," Darcy laughed. "You should sue him for sexual harassment."

Elizabeth laughed a little, over the worst of her shock, but her heart still pounded. Darcy looked… *magnificent* was the only word she could think of… astride his horse. He had on riding breeches and boots, clinging to the sensual curve of his strong legs. She was fairly sure her heart wasn't pounding from just shock anymore.

The horse pranced a little as Darcy looked down at her. "Listening to 'Hot Stuff?'" He smirked.

She narrowed her eyes at him. "How do you know about that?" She looked up at him accusingly, hands on her hips. "*How?* Did Bingley tell you?"

He laughed and swung down from the horse. "No, I was there. It was quite a performance. Especially the part where you spanked yourself." Her face turned bright red. "Now Ms. Bennet," he teased in a superior tone, "don't be bashful. You are very skilled at… er… what was that? A strip show?"

"And just what were you doing there, *Judge* Darcy?" she replied archly, amusement winning out over mortification.

"I had been invited by my very good friend, Bingley. I got there late, saw your performance, and decided that there was no way I could compete with that. I left."

Elizabeth turned her head away from him in embarrassment and laughed. She looked back at him. "Well, I guess you know my dirty little secret." She took a step closer to him, hands on hips, pert challenge written all over her body, and arched her brows at him. "What's yours?"

He took as step closer to her, closing the space between them to inches. He looked down at her upturned face. "That I enjoyed it."

There was no denying the electricity that was flowing between them—she had goose bumps on her arms. Elizabeth swallowed hard but did not back away from him, her eyes fixed on his pulse, visible at the hollow of his throat.

Overcome by the scents of her sweat, her shampoo, and her natural scent of pears, he raised a hand and touched a strand of her hair with his forefinger.

She raised her eyes to his. "It doesn't get much more inappropriate than this," she murmured, not at all appearing offended.

"Oh, yes it does," he assured her. He dipped his head and kissed her. She returned his kiss without hesitation, her heart pounding in her chest. "I've wanted to do that since Halloween," he murmured.

"Coincidentally, I've wanted that since Halloween," she answered huskily. "I just didn't know Judge Darcy could give it to me." She raised her face to his and kissed him again, this time taking the initiative.

"That does present a problem, doesn't it?" He broke off the kiss a moment later.

"Yes, but I believe we have a compelling argument that we are outside the jurisdiction of the American Bar Association," she replied against his lips. He kissed her again.

"We have the same rules in England," he reminded her. She dismissed his point with another kiss.

"You're not a judge here in England, are you? And I don't have a license here. As far as I'm concerned, for the next two weeks, I'm just a tourist, and you're just a barrister."

"I have always admired your legal reasoning, Ms. Bennet." He smiled. She arched a brow in acknowledgment, and yielded when his lips descended hungrily on hers again. With one hand caressing the side of her neck, he snaked his other arm around her waist, pulling her close. She deepened their kiss by opening her mouth under his. Standing on tiptoe, she wrapped her arms around his neck, curling her fingers into that dark, wavy hair. His arousal was evident, pressed into her belly, and she felt her own tingling excitement between her legs.

Only when she felt his thumb slip under the strap of her halter did she bring herself back to reality. She stepped away from him, laughing shakily, and crossed her arms over her chest. Much more of this and she'd be stripping naked and doing him right there. At least his breathing was as heavy as hers.

"We're in the middle of a field," she observed, as if he had no other senses to discern it himself. He ran a shaky hand through his hair and looked around him, as if he had indeed forgotten where they were.

He took a deep, steadying breath, and said, "We'll miss the seminar. I'll give you a ride back." He held his hand out to her, and she hesitated nervously before remembering that this was Speed Racer; she trusted him with her life. Then she smiled, took Darcy's hand, and stepped toward the horse. He helped her into the saddle then swung easily on behind her. With his strong arms wrapped around her to grip the reins, she could feel his heartbeat against her back.

She could also feel his erection against her back.

As the horse began to trot, Darcy let a pained grunt slip out.

"Are you okay back there?" Elizabeth asked innocently.

She snuggled her bottom against his groin, a mischievous smile hovering on her lips.

"This is wrong on so many levels," he said in an aggrieved voice.

Elizabeth scrubbed her skin in the shower, excitement still coursing through her veins. At last she'd found that chemistry she'd been searching for since Halloween! Finally, she'd found Speed Racer, and he hadn't turned out to be some dud. He'd turned out to be an amazing, funny, sexy man.

Who just happened to be off-limits.

Elizabeth paused midway through her exfoliation and frowned. Now why did her conscience have to go and kick in gear? Hadn't she been a good girl all her life? Hell, even Jane had shoplifted when she was eight, but not Elizabeth. Elizabeth had always played by the rules.

She squeezed her eyes shut and shook her head. No. She was on *vacation*. That *had* to count for something. It wasn't like she was going to tell anyone—*ever*—and if there was one thing she could be sure of, it was that Darcy would be discreet. They would have a fling, then go back to work, two sexually sated adults perfectly capable of carrying on a professional relationship. This wasn't high school; they could pull this off. And she was determined to make the most of it. She poured her ethical concerns down the drain with her rinsed shampoo.

Darcy looked in the mirror, shaving cream smudged on his chin, as he shaved. He couldn't help grinning—hell, he felt like *giggling*. He couldn't believe that he'd just kissed Elizabeth, that she'd kissed him back, and that they had some tacit agreement that it was going to continue. How long had he wanted this? Why hadn't he done this before?

You know why, his reflection seemed to say. The grin slipped from his face. *You are asking for trouble*.

Darcy put the razor on the sink and sulked. The problem was right in front of him: he was a judge, she was an attorney, and never the twain shall fuck.

"Oh, come on!" he said angrily to his reflection. Hadn't he spent his entire adult life helping others? Hadn't he been a bedrock of reliability and respectability? For God's sake, he was thirty-eight, and he couldn't remember when he last felt like this. Didn't he deserve to have some fun? Couldn't he have a guilt-free fling for once in his life? Who cared if they worked together—he knew with every fiber of his being that it wouldn't affect his judgment, and he knew that Elizabeth would never try to use their relationship to sway his opinions on the bench.

"It's a stupid rule," he grumbled. "And she's right. The ABA has no jurisdiction in England. Or in my bed!"

With firm determination, he tucked the nagging feeling of guilt into the same brain compartment where he stored recipes and unsolicited phone numbers—never to be retrieved again.

"I can't make heads nor tails of this flowchart," Darcy muttered quietly, trying not to disturb the other attendees of the seminar. He rotated the page in front of him. Elizabeth leaned over and rotated the page in the other direction.

"This way," she said, her voice low next to his ear. Something about the timbre of her voice made him glance over at her. She had one corner of her plump bottom lip tucked coyly between her teeth.

"Thanks," he murmured, his eyes drawn away from her lip to her hand, which now touched his thigh lightly.

"Glad to help."

A little smile spread across his lips as he realized that she was flirting with him. She returned the smile with one of her own, acknowledging that he had called her on her game, but not conceding defeat by any means.

Seconds later, her pen fell to the floor. She bent over to retrieve it, glancing up at him as she did.

"Excuse me," she whispered, her hand on his thigh for balance. As she rose back up, he had a generous view down her blouse, creamy cleavage accented by delicate lace. He smirked and tried to pay attention to the presentation to no avail. Every few seconds he glanced at her from the corner of his eye to find her toying with a tendril of hair that had fallen from her bun, or doodling aimlessly on her writing tablet. When she caught him watching her, he saw her little satisfied smile return.

Then she stood, her gray pencil skirt pulling snugly over her hips as she squeezed out of her space. She returned a few moments later, presumably from the restroom, and tried to squeeze back into her seat space.

"Tight seating," she laughed apologetically as her rear brushed against his arm.

"Indeed," he agreed with a twisted smirk.

She fidgeted for a moment, then yawned, the buttons of her crisp white blouse straining against her breasts as she stretched her arms and arched her back. He now dropped any pretense of attending to the presenter and gave her his undivided attention while trying desperately to hide his own grin.

She tapped her pen thoughtfully against her teeth, admiring the doodle that she'd just drawn. Then, apparently completely by accident, the pen fell down her blouse. Darcy pressed his fist to his mouth, stifling his laugh.

"Oops!" she whispered, making his shoulders shake harder. She fished the pen from her cleavage, tongue poking from the corner of her mouth as she did. The pen rolled slightly as she placed it on the table between them.

Darcy picked up the pen and nonchalantly tapped it on his upper lip, as if composing his notes into a legal opus. A subtle sniff pulled the scent of pears from the pen to his nose.

He opened his writing tablet and wrote the word "TEASE," then passed the tablet to her. Elizabeth studied the word, nodding gravely. Then she jotted a response and returned the tablet to him. He read it. *Hot Stuff*.

His legs crossed under the table, Darcy nudged her foot with the toe of his shoe. Without taking her eyes from the slide show, she uncrossed and re-crossed her legs, drawing one black stiletto pump along his calf. Acknowledging that she was much better at this game than he, Darcy rested his chin in his palm and watched her through lowered lids.

Once the presentation had ended and attendees were shuffling their papers and filing out, he leaned toward her and murmured, "I hope you enjoyed yourself."

She glanced down at her hands then raised her lashes to look at him.

"It wasn't for *my* enjoyment."

Blood surged to Darcy's cheeks, roared in his ears, and

flooded his groin with that simple, sultry statement. It was a full minute before he could speak, and by then, Elizabeth was putting her arms into her trench coat and slinging her purse over her shoulder.

"We should go. We'll be late for dinner with Charley and Jane," she said, acting as if she had not just teased him into a frenzy. Darcy had never wanted to skip a meal so badly in his life.

Dinner was a struggle, to say the least. The soft light of the restaurant reflected warm peach tones onto Elizabeth's skin, inviting him to caress her cheek. While Bingley and Jane told story after story of their mundane adventures, Darcy watched the clock tick. The only piece of information he gathered was that they were going to a play after dinner, which meant that he and Elizabeth would be alone for hours.

He couldn't taste his dinner—the only taste he craved was Elizabeth's lips. She was listening intently to Jane, and then she closed her eyes and let out a long, easy laugh. It was a wonderful laugh—not too loud, not too high, not too husky. The perfect laugh. Everything about her entranced him: her face, her voice, her scent, even the way her eyebrows arched and scrunched, knit together and sprung apart, as she talked. Her playful flirtation at the seminar had undone him; he wanted her so badly that his teeth ached.

She joked and smiled, and tried to draw him into the conversation, but he was tongue-tied. When she gave his thigh a gentle squeeze and tossed him a questioning look, he shook his head slightly. Nothing was wrong. In fact, everything was perfect.

He didn't recall paying the bill or standing to leave. While he held Elizabeth's coat for her, he subtly grazed his forefinger against the side of her neck.

"I surrender," he murmured to her. She glanced at him over her shoulder as he ran one hand over her arm. "I am yours completely." She nodded and looked away, a small smile on her lips.

The drive home was a blur of white dashes and nearly-missed exits as Elizabeth kissed his jawline for much of the way.

"Please stop, you'll make me wreck," he laughed hoarsely as she tugged his earlobe with her teeth.

"Not so grouchy anymore, are you, Judge Darcy?" she hummed seductively in his ear.

"You have no idea," he swallowed.

"I think I do." She took his hand and pressed it to her chest. He felt her heart hammering against the skin of his palm. "I want it as much as you do."

Somehow he managed to resist pulling into a deserted car park and fucking her in the car. He clung to the knowledge that he was going to have her in his bed for hours on end, and he was not going to ruin it by a quick rutting.

They pulled to the front entrance of Pemberley, and Elizabeth dashed out of the car before he had even cut the engine. She was halfway up the stairs when he overtook her, grabbing her hand as he did. Without hesitation he led her to his bedroom. Only then did he stop, giving her one last chance to change her mind. She reached across him and pushed the door open.

They tumbled into the room, the door thudding closed behind them as they grappled in a hungry kiss. Elizabeth pushed Darcy's jacket off his shoulders and began working on his shirt buttons while he tugged her blouse from the waistband of her skirt. As he began to unbutton her blouse, she worked at his cuffs, all the while kissing in shorts bursts and long draws, tasting and savoring the flavor of finally admitted desire.

Shoes were toed off, skirt and pants pooled to the floor,

until he stood in only his boxers and socks, and she stood in lacy panties and bra. Her eyes swept over his broad, smooth shoulders. She brushed the sprinkle of dark chest hair with her fingertips, stroking the lean and toned muscle beneath. Darcy traced his fingers over the lace edge of her bra, then deftly unhooked the front clasp, freeing her soft, firm breasts. Her rose-colored nipple peaked under the gentle stroke of his palm.

He pulled her close and kissed her again, running his hands down her back to cup her bottom. She tipped her head back, breaths coming short now, and gave a quiet moan as he kissed her throat. Then she clasped her hands over his and together they pushed her panties from her hips to the floor.

With little grace, Darcy scooped her up, strode across the room, and dropped her on the bed. She hit the mattress with a giggle. He was already ripping open a condom package when she hooked her toes into the waistband of his boxers and tugged them down. After making quick work of the condom, Darcy crawled onto the bed beside her. Elizabeth immediately drew close to him, pulling her leg over his hip and trailing her hand along his arm. Darcy traced the dip of her waist to the rise of her hip, her smooth skin warm beneath his palm.

They twined their fingers together while his lips left hers to taste the skin of her chest. She arched beneath him when he pulled one nipple into his mouth, tongue rasping lightly over the puckered skin.

She drew him from her breast for another kiss, and he freed her hair from its clasp. Her dark, chestnut waves tumbled onto her pale shoulders, framing her face. It nearly took his breath away. He knotted his fingers in her hair and buried his face in it; she smelled like sunshine and pears.

"Elizabeth," he breathed.

"Will," she whispered, a hint of pleading in her voice. Darcy settled his hips between her legs, closing his eyes as she opened for him.

"Say you want me, Elizabeth," he whispered.

"I want you, Will."

"Say you surrender."

She closed her eyes and said huskily, "I surrender."

They both let out gasps of pleasure as he pushed deep inside of her. She was lithe and limber beneath him; he was supple and hard on her. Each of his thrusts was met by her own, breath for ragged breath. With a hand under her hip, he pulled her closer to him, feeling her undulate in synchronized rhythm. Her pace quickened, and she pushed her hips to meet his with insistence. She buried her face in his neck and panted as she built toward her climax. Then she rolled her head back, thrust her hips up, and uttered a long, gentle moan from the bottom of her throat as she reached ecstasy.

Each pulse within her pushed him to the brink of his own release, but he pulled back. As she descended from her peak, he rolled to his back, pulling her astride him. He stroked her nipples with his thumbs and watched her face, still flush with pleasure. She squeezed him from within as she rode him in long, slow strokes and dipped her head to slide her tongue over his nipple. His hands on her hips pulled her closer with each thrust. She raised her lips from his chest and trailed a line of hot kisses from his throat to his mouth.

"Yes, yes," he pleaded against her lips, her hair falling around them in a thick curtain. He wrapped his arms around her waist and pulled her tight, falling into a crashing orgasm with a guttural groan.

Slowly, slowly she eased her rhythm, allowing him time to

enjoy and recover from his climax. He let out a helpless moan and tousled her hair with limp fingers. She laughed softly, tickling his cheek with her breath and making him smile.

"That was..." he whispered, unable to complete his thought, let alone the sentence.

"The best ethical violation of my life," she finished. He laughed softly and nodded in agreement.

Gently sliding off his hips, Elizabeth pulled the covers over them and curled into his side, her head resting in the hollow of his shoulder. They lay together in the darkening room, the sound of their breathing returning to normal.

She thought he had fallen asleep when he said, "Maybe we should talk about the elephant in the courtroom."

"Yes," she sighed reluctantly.

"I presume that what happens in England stays in England?"

"Absolutely," she quickly replied. Then, to soften the curtness of her response, she propped up on one elbow and fingered his chin. "Do you think I want anyone to know that I slept with Buddy Holly?" she teased. He smiled and caught her finger in a kiss.

"Then we should make the most of it. Let's not have any silly arguments or fights. If I do something to hurt your feelings, please tell me. I'll do the same. I don't want to have any regrets."

"No games, no lies." She nodded in agreement.

"I'll never lie to you, Elizabeth. Never."

"I know," she answered, and soothed away his earnest expression with another kiss. He pressed his forehead against hers and stroked her upper arm with his thumb, before opening his eyes. She gave him a reassuring smile, then turned to snuggle against him. He rolled to his side and she nestled her bottom in his hips. His arm draped across her waist and his knees tucked behind hers in an intimate, protective spoon. She closed her eyes and felt his fingers sweep the hair from the nape of her neck.

"I have wanted to kiss this spot for weeks," he admitted drowsily, pressing his lips to her neck just where her hair curled. "For weeks," he repeated with another kiss.

Elizabeth smiled lazily. She was dropping off to sleep with the sexiest man alive wrapped around her and kissing her. Dreams didn't get much better than that.

Chapter 8

DARCY WOKE WEDNESDAY MORNING just as the sun was illuminating Elizabeth sleeping beside him. She was on her belly, one arm dangling over the edge of the bed, the other tucked under her chest. Her hair was swirled around her head, over her shoulders, and across her back. Its scent pulled him down for a quiet sniff, and he placed a soft kiss on her shoulder, careful not to wake her. Cautiously scooting closer to her to feel her skin touch his, he put his head on the pillow and watched her, waiting for her to wake.

A little while later, she stirred and turned her face toward him, giving him a drowsy grin. She twisted to her side and placed one hand on his chest. He covered it with his own, then pulled her fingers to his lips for a kiss. She snuggled closer, drawing one leg over his waist, while he slipped his arm under her for a hug.

"Good morning," she mumbled into his neck.

"Good morning," he answered, laughing as her breath tickled his skin. "Are you all right?" He ran his hand tenderly over her arm.

"Mm-hmm," she replied contentedly, kissing his chest.

"Anything I can do to make you... better?" he asked hopefully, kissing the top of her head. Elizabeth snickered then raised her face to his for a kiss. She was fresh-faced, with a dusting of freckles over her nose and cheeks. What he'd always thought were dark brown eyes, he could now see were shot with reddish hues, like rich cherry wood. Her thick lashes framed her eyes with a dark fringe, without benefit of mascara. She had a simple, natural beauty that he far preferred over made-up perfection.

"I might be better if you kissed me here," she suggested, tapping her cheek. With a smile, Darcy complied and landed a gentle, lingering kiss on her cheek.

"Better?" he asked, shifting to kiss the other cheek.

"Mm-hmm. How about here?" She pointed to her shoulder, and Darcy obliged her with pleasure. They played this game for a while longer, until they were entwined. In hushed whispers, he gently encouraged instruction from her, and gave her whatever she asked without hesitation, telling her that she was beautiful in every way. It was the most intimate, sincere sex Darcy had ever had; it almost startled him to realize he was making love to her. Climax was long and slow and gentle.

They basked, content in the morning sun for a while longer, then Elizabeth reluctantly pulled herself from his arms.

"Where are you going?" he asked.

"I'm sneaking back to my room." She smiled as she pulled her things together.

He snuggled down deeper into the pillows and pulled the blankets up to his nose.

"It's much more fun in here," he coaxed.

She leaned across the bed and pushed the blanket away from his nose, kissing his lips warmly. "It's *too* fun in there. We'll starve."

He watched as she slipped out and ran down the hall to her own room, the faint click of her door following shortly behind. With a sigh, he tossed the blankets off. It bothered him a little to operate in secrecy. For one, it meant lying to Jane and Bingley, and he abhorred lies. But more importantly, it meant not holding hands or kissing when anyone else was around. Secrecy meant car rides, stolen nights, long walks in the woods. Not sharing dinners, not putting his arm around her at a play, not holding her hand at the museum. It meant restrictions. He didn't like restrictions. But something was better than nothing, as he could now definitely attest. And so he would follow her lead until she indicated otherwise.

Even though Elizabeth behaved herself at that afternoon's seminar, Darcy couldn't concentrate. He was distracted by her scent, her closeness. All he could think about was touching her, holding her, being with her with no outside distractions. *We're wasting time*, he thought impatiently.

She saw his unhappy expression and jotted a note to him: *What's wrong?*

He read it and replied *I don't want to be here.*

Where do you want to be?

I think you know.

Is that all you can think about?

Yes.

This is a very important seminar!

Want to skiv off?

Yes!

Darcy could not believe he was acting like a schoolboy, skiving off classes, chasing a pretty girl. They gathered their things as unobtrusively as possible and left the room. Once outside, Darcy broke into a wide grin, grabbing her hand. They walked, hand-in-hand, through London's crowded streets. He waited patiently while she window-shopped, and when she ducked into a store to try on a pair of shoes, he surprised her upon her return with a bouquet of flowers. That she actually blushed charmed him beyond words.

"Everyone has to have this picture. You'll thank me when you're eighty," he said, posing her before the granite lions of Trafalgar Square. He snapped a picture with her cell phone and nodded with satisfaction at his handiwork.

"What about you?"

"I grew up here, I don't need it," he dismissed.

"Yes, you do. Come here," she insisted, pulling him to her side and holding the phone out. As she snapped the picture, he kissed her cheek.

"You've ruined it!" she giggled.

"That's not ruined!" he exclaimed, feigning hurt feelings.

"Stand still and be good!" This time he cozied his head close to hers and smiled contentedly as she snapped a picture. When she was satisfied, she tucked the phone into her purse. He wrapped his arms around her waist, whirled her around, and kissed her laughing mouth. Then they walked away, fingers linked.

"Can we ditch tomorrow too?" she sighed as they walked back toward the hotel.

"You're reading my mind."

"What would you like to do?"

"Need you ask?"

"I mean besides *me*," she laughed.

"Maybe we should go to a karaoke club," he suggested with his best attempt at a lecherous smile.

"You are far too fixated on that."

"It did make an impression."

She sniffed her flowers and gave him a sly look.

"I'll have to show you something else then."

"I'd like that. Let's make it a date. Tonight." His voice held a hint of challenge.

"I'll consider it. Right now we need to meet Jane and Bingley."

He groaned. Elizabeth snatched her hand from his and took a step away, then waved at Jane and Bingley halfway down the block.

As they waited for them to catch up, Elizabeth coyly asked, "What would I get in return?"

"Besides the night of your life?"

She laughed again, tossing her head back.

"What *would* you like?" he asked, perplexed.

"That riding getup was pretty sexy," she suggested. He laughed, but was prevented from replying by the arrival of Jane and Bingley.

Darcy was far more relaxed at dinner, joking and participating more in the conversation than he had on the previous night. Knowing that he would be spending another night with Elizabeth had improved his mood immeasurably. While he was eager, he was no longer impatient. He could savor the anticipation.

When Jane mentioned that she and Bingley were attending the ballet after dinner, Elizabeth saw the subtle shift in Darcy's expression, a slight brightening in his eyes. She knew he was hoping for another long night together when she felt his foot brush against hers.

As the two couples waited outside for their cars, Darcy casually suggested, "Why don't you take my suite at the Ritz tonight. The performance will be three hours, and you shouldn't drive back so late." Bingley smiled with pleasure at the invitation, but Jane demurred.

"Thank you, Will, but we don't want to be any trouble."

"It's no trouble. I own the suite."

"Well, I don't have an overnight bag. I'd have to wear this tomorrow!" Jane protested, indicating her dress, heels, and shawl.

"Oh, Georgie has clothes there. I'm sure you'd fit into them. She's about your size. She wouldn't mind, even if she knew!" Darcy assured her.

Jane looked hesitant, and Elizabeth could see Darcy beginning to be dismayed. He wanted to have Elizabeth to himself all night long.

Elizabeth took Jane aside and said in a low voice, "Jane, can't you see Will wants to give Charley a night to romance you? He's very happy for him. Let him give this to Charley. Besides, when will you ever get the chance to stay at the London Ritz again?"

Horrified at the thought of coming between some kind of manly bonding, Jane immediately nodded.

"Thank you, Will, you're very sweet. I can pick up some things if I need them."

Darcy whipped out his cell phone to arrange the hotel. Jane and Bingley waved as they climbed into their car and drove away.

"Clever girl," Darcy murmured in Elizabeth's ear, patting her bottom.

"You don't know Jane. All you have to do is suggest somebody's feelings might be hurt, and she'll do whatever you want."

"Lucky for me, I got the saucy one." He nuzzled her ear.

"Really? You don't think Bingley's getting blowjobs like there's no tomorrow?" she murmured. Darcy's jaw hung slightly open at the notion.

"Anyway, why aren't you taking *me* to your suite at the Ritz?" she asked petulantly.

"Much too tawdry for you, my dear," he replied, pulling her into a kiss. "Besides, everyone there knows me," he added more seriously. Elizabeth understood: he didn't want any rumors circulating about him and his penchant for a little afternoon delight.

The ride home was rife with teasing comments and sexual innuendo, and they raced up the steps laughing.

"Meet you in the billiards room," he said as she stopped at her room.

"Why there?"

"That's where the music is." He grinned, walking backwards toward his room.

A frantic search of her suitcase provided only marginally sexy articles: a skimpy bra, a lace thong, and a pair of leather pants that she couldn't even recall packing. Paired with a white tank top—and nothing else—the pants, if not exactly sexy, were at least sexpot-ish. She fluffed out her hair and dotted some gloss on her lips before tiptoeing barefoot downstairs to the billiards room.

Peeking her head around the billiards room door, she spied Darcy sitting in the chair, feet propped on the ottoman. He'd worn his riding breeches and boots, as she requested, and was toying with something that she could not quite make out. She smirked and surreptitiously snapped a picture with her cell phone before playfully skipping over to him. She sat on his lap and traced his collarbone with her finger.

"Very dashing," she purred.

He put a hand on her leather clad thigh and squeezed. "Very sexy," he replied, nuzzling her neck. "I thought you might need this," Darcy said, producing the riding crop he'd been toying with before she came in. He ran it over her leg and gave her a light flick.

"Hey, slow down. I'm not that kinky!" she laughed. "Yet."

"I'm waiting for my show," he teased, nudging her in the ribs.

Elizabeth grinned and stood up. He flicked her rear with the crop, making her yelp out a laugh and dart across the room.

She plugged her iPod into the dock and played "Hot Stuff," prancing around the room in a humorous reproduction of her karaoke performance. By the end, both were giggling breathlessly as she curled on his lap again.

"I think your number needs more spanking," Darcy suggested, giving her rear a light slap.

"That was just my warm-up number, to limber up the joints," she said as she climbed off his lap.

"No, it's okay," he protested as she pulled away, but she shook her head and gave him a seductive smile as if to say the *best is yet to come*.

This time, her dance was to a sultry, jazzy song. She skimmed her hands over her body, letting her fingers catch the bottom of her top, exposing a sliver of her belly to him. Her eyes never broke contact with Darcy's; there could be no doubt that the lyrics she sang about being *turned on* were directed at him. At the end of the song, she turned her back to him and walked away, hips undulating in a sensual rhythm to the music, pulling her shirt up to show him her bare back.

Before the song had even faded from the air, Darcy was behind her pressing her to the door, turning her toward him, crushing her lips with kisses. He lifted her to his hips and braced her against the door, kissing her neck. Elizabeth wrapped her legs around him and twined her arms around his neck as his hips ground against hers. His hands were on her breasts, feeling them through her shirt, pushing it up to touch her flesh. He ran his hands over her bottom, feeling the slick leather under his palms. Finally, he put his arms around her waist, swung her away from the door and carried her to the pool table. He sat her on the edge of the table and kissed her while he tugged at the zipper of her pants.

"You"—*kiss*—"are"—*kiss*—"so"—*kiss*—"phenomenally"—*kiss*—"fuckable," he breathed as he struggled to pull the tight leather over her hips. Elizabeth laughed in surprise as she leaned back to help him, and her pants finally fell to the floor. Darcy didn't bother to take his off. He unzipped, fumbled into a condom, and thrust himself into her against the pool table. The act was quick; he had been aroused to an absurd degree by her performance. He came quickly and buried his face in her neck.

"Oh, God, I'm sorry," he groaned into her throat.

"It's okay," she reassured him, tucking a curl of his hair behind his ear.

He looked up at her, his eyes soft and pleading. "Lizzy, what have you done to me?" She laughed softly in his ear, and he hugged her tighter and kissed her lips. "Give me a minute, let me make it up to you," he murmured, closing his eyes. After a moment, he pressed his forehead to hers and said, "Can I take you to bed?"

"Yes, please," she smiled. He picked her up and carried her to his bedroom, where he placed her in the bed and made love to her until she cried out his name.

Chapter 9

ON THURSDAY MORNING, DARCY woke up bleary-eyed from a night of sex, alternating between lusty to tender. He had been out of control in the billiards room the night before. What was supposed to be a fun romp had turned into an electrifying seduction. He felt that Elizabeth would never have made such a display unless she felt something more than mere attraction for him. The realization sparked more than physical desire in him; it lit a sort of feral, possessive need to take her, to mark her as *his*. He was not embarrassed, except that she had no opportunity to take her own pleasure in that episode. He made up for it twice more during the night, once with tenderness and once with mutual hunger. He had never been so sexed up in his life.

Elizabeth was lying next to him, sleeping peacefully on her back, arm draped over her stomach in the dim light of the bedroom. She had kicked the blankets off and lay naked, breasts rising with each breath. He felt as though he could watch her for hours. His eyes took in every inch of her body, from her red toenails to her pale thighs, her soft tummy, her firm breasts, her long slender fingers, her strong arms, the slope of her shoulders, the neck that he loved to taste, her beautiful face framed by her dark hair and arching brows. How in the world had he lucked out and turned her from hating him to sleeping with him?

Stealthily, he crept to the foot of the bed to examine her toes. They were freshly painted a deep, glossy red. He brushed his lips over her toes, and her foot wiggled in protest. Darcy smiled and rested his nose on the top of her foot and kissed it softly. Then he moved down on his elbows to kiss the inside of her ankle and trailed kisses up the inside of her calf, stopping at her knee. When he glanced up, he found Elizabeth watching him with a subtle smile on her face. He winked and kissed her kneecap. Blazing a trail up her thigh, he kissed the patch of hair between her legs, her fingers stroking his ear before he moved on to her belly.

Deep, moist kisses to her tummy made her giggle. He made his way up her ribs to her breasts, his tongue exploring their peaked softness from all angles. Eventually, he landed at the base of her throat, dipping his tongue into the depression there, and feeling her pulse. A brief stopover at her lips ended when he moved on to kiss her eyelids.

He gave the same tenacious attention to her back, kissing her shoulder blades, and sucking on the skin at the small of her back. He continued his sensual itinerary with a long exploration of her bottom and thighs, only to nudge her onto her back again. At last, he reached his destination, the fragrant delta between her legs. He ruffled the soft hair there with his breath, spreading her sex gently with his thumbs and kissing the space between. He had his first taste of her when he dipped his tongue in. Tangy, warm, and wet.

"Will," she murmured, tugging gently on his hair with a smile. "Come up here." He shook his head.

"This one is all for you."

Elizabeth lay back on the pillows, spreading her legs for him. His thumbs pressed expert swirls on her pubic bone, and he slid his tongue along her folds slowly, delicately, as if savoring a gourmet delight. A quiet sigh escaped from her lips.

Encouraged by this soft whisper, Darcy continued. Her moans became longer, closer together, and more urgent. She curled her fingers in his hair and arched her hips toward him. To her unending surprise, and his unending satisfaction, he brought her to orgasm with his tongue and fingers alone.

Once her pulsations subsided, she opened her eyes and pulled his face to hers for a deep kiss. She reached for a condom from the nightstand, but he stopped her.

"I said it was all for you." With a tender smile, he gave her another kiss and rolled out of bed. She cocked her head as she watched his firm, bare bottom stride away from her to the bathroom. While he adjusted the shower, she forced herself from that warm cocoon of lazy satisfaction and out of bed. At her feet in a rumpled heap was Darcy's shirt from the night before. She picked it up and pressed it to her face. It smelled like him: mossy, masculine, and clean. She slipped her arms into the sleeves and wrapped the too-large shirt across her chest.

"You could join me," he called from the bathroom. Elizabeth turned to see his wet head poking from behind the white shower curtain. Barefoot, she padded to him for a kiss.

"I'm going to get my own shower," she replied. His wet hand came out and cupped her chin.

"Everything okay?" he asked, his green eyes searching her face.

"Yes." She nodded. He pulled her close for a deeper kiss, nibbling her lower lip.

"You'll tell me if anything's wrong, won't you?" he murmured.

"Well, the truth is... I'm a bit sore," she laughed. They'd been fucking like bunnies for two days, and she just wasn't used to using those muscles so vigorously.

"Oh, sorry," he laughed.

"Don't be, I'm just going to relax in my room for a bit. I'll be down in an hour or so."

She hadn't lied, exactly—her calves were killing her, and she was sure she was waddling like, well, like a duck that had been fucked—but she also needed to spend a few minutes away from him. Never in her life had she been so closely entwined with anyone. Lou had always given her independence, and her family well knew her need for space. She wasn't yet feeling smothered, but she thought she should head it off at the pass before she did something to anger or hurt Darcy.

Showered and dressed in jeans and a black tank top, Elizabeth flopped onto her bed, novel in hand. She had been devouring the book on the flight, and couldn't wait to get back into it. But despite her best efforts, the words on the page blurred and merged before her eyes. The hero's name kept inexplicably popping into her mind as "Will," and although it was a medieval fantasy novel, Darcy's face peeked from under the warrior's helmet. When she'd read the same paragraph three times without retaining any of it, she gave the book up as a lost cause and tossed it aside.

She lay on the bed and toyed with the sleeve of his shirt, then draped it across her face. The scent of his deodorant wafted to her nostrils, calming her unacknowledged agitation.

It struck her a moment later—she didn't want her space from him. She missed him already, even though he was only a hundred feet away.

The realization that she wanted to spend every last millisecond of this vacation with him almost frightened her. Was she losing her independence? Was she becoming clingy? That thought alone forced her to lie on the bed another ten minutes before giving in and heading downstairs in search of him.

"Feeling better?" Darcy asked over the edge of his newspaper as she came into the kitchen. Without thinking, she nipped a piece of toast from his plate and nodded while she crunched it. Unfazed by her brazen theft, Darcy merely sipped his tea and allowed her to read the newspaper over his shoulder.

"What are you planning today?" she asked.

"The weather looks nice, I thought I'd take a ride on my motorbike." A question hung in the air—he unsure whether to invite her, she unsure whether he wanted her to come along. As a sort of compromise and in an effort on both sides to allow the other a chance to voice their preference, she walked him to the door.

"Can I—" she began.

"Do you—" he said. They both laughed, and Elizabeth leaned against the console table in the foyer.

He made her feel almost shy, and it took an effort for her to say, "If you want some breathing space, just let me know."

"I don't," he answered, pressing close to her.

"It's going to be difficult to keep this from Jane and Charley," she faltered, breathless from the sheer seductiveness of his nearness.

"Is it a secret?" He drew a deep, slow kiss from her, pulling on her lower lip and touching his tongue to hers. Her hands gripped his strong shoulders, and the weakness in her knees forced her to lean against the table. She was completely insensible to the sound of the front door opening.

"I guess that answers that question," he murmured against her lips, breaking the kiss. It took a second for Elizabeth to register that Jane and Charley were standing, agape, in the open doorway.

With a guilty squeak, Elizabeth clamored out from under Darcy's arms, tugging down the tank top that had somehow made its way halfway up her torso.

Darcy took a step back, his own cheeks flaring red.

"Walk! Yes, I was just going for a walk!" Elizabeth stammered, frantically smoothing her hair back into a ponytail.

"I'll come along," Jane said sternly, her expression one of mixed shock and disapproval.

"That's not necessary," Elizabeth laughed hastily, glancing pleadingly at Darcy, who was having his own problem fielding Bingley's beaming grin.

"Oh, I think I need a walk," Jane firmly assured her and swung back outside and down the steps, heedless that she was wearing a black cocktail dress and stiletto heels.

Feeling like a chastened twelve-year-old, Elizabeth trudged out the door. Jane fell in step beside her, stonily silent. Elizabeth picked up the pace, hoping to lose Jane, but Jane's long legs compensated for the uneven terrain and unstable shoes.

"Here I've been worried sick that I left you with someone you can't stand!" Jane began in a shrill tone.

"Oh, please, you sound like Mom. Take it down a notch, okay?" Elizabeth retorted. Jane paused long enough to take off her shoes, then ran to catch up with Elizabeth.

"Stop!" she pleaded. Elizabeth swung to face her, arms defiantly crossed over her chest.

"You're right. I'm sorry," Jane panted. "I shouldn't have come on like that. I was just surprised."

"Join the club," Elizabeth mumbled, dropping her arms to her sides.

"I thought you hated him."

"He's Speed Racer," Elizabeth revealed, as if that explained everything. And, really, it did.

"But you *work* together!" Jane exclaimed.

"Not technically. He's employed by the state, I work for a private law firm." It sounded weak even to Elizabeth's ears.

Jane threw her arms in the air, a sarcastic gesture of "Oh, *now* it's okay."

"You and Charley work together!" Elizabeth countered defensively.

"That's different, Lizzy! Charley's not my boss. He has no say over anything I do. Even *I* know an attorney can't date a judge!"

Elizabeth brightened falsely. "We're not dating—we're just sleeping together."

Jane gave an exasperated shake of her head then laughed. She hooked her arm through Elizabeth's, and they began to walk slowly.

"Lizzy, be *careful*. I told you, he dates Charley's sister." Elizabeth had forgotten all about that, and it sent a near-physical pain into her stomach.

"It'll be okay," Elizabeth tried to reassure both of them, biting her thumbnail. "It's just a fling. We both know it will end when we leave here."

"Yes, but will you *want* it to end?"

"It doesn't really matter what I want, does it? It's not allowed, and that's all there is to it."

Jane put her head on Elizabeth's shoulder and squeezed her arm. It was all she needed to do—they both knew Jane would be there to help Elizabeth pick up the pieces.

Back at the house, Bingley was air-punching Darcy on the shoulder.

"You old dog!" he laughed. "You never said a word!"

"Stop it," Darcy said, trying to look over Bingley's shoulder to see how Elizabeth was handling Jane.

"Been going at it all week long!" Bingley continued.

"Stop it!" Darcy barked, turning his attention to Bingley. He lowered his voice. "It's not like that."

Alerted by Darcy's lack of humor, Bingley's grin faded.

"What *is* it like, then?" he asked. Darcy shoved his hands into his jeans pockets and looked away without answering.

"Don't screw around with Jane's sister," Bingley warned.

"I'm not screwing around with her. We both know what we're doing."

"What *are* you doing?"

"Look, it's none of your damned—" Darcy began, but stopped himself, knowing he sounded defensive and petulant. "We're having a two-week affair, that's all," he admitted.

"And then...?" Bingley prompted.

"And then it's over. I can't date one of my attorneys, you know that."

"But fucking her is okay as long as it's out of the country?" Bingley retorted sarcastically. Darcy laughed.

"That's the theory we're working on, yes."

"Don't be an idiot, Darcy. I know you. This isn't like you."

"I know." Darcy ran a hand through his hair and looked at Bingley with an open, honest face. "I don't know what's going to happen. All I know is that I'm happy right now, for the first time in years."

Over Bingley's shoulder, Darcy saw the ladies heading back toward the house. He went outside and down the steps to meet them, desperate to reassure himself that Jane hadn't talked Elizabeth out of anything. Jane slipped her arm out of Elizabeth's with a farewell squeeze and gave Darcy a shrug and a half-smile that he didn't even see. All he could see was Elizabeth smiling at him, sunshine glinting off the cherry wood highlights in her hair and illuminating the cinnamon freckles on her nose. He felt his heart melt just a little as he put his arms around her waist.

"Want to go for that ride?" he asked softly, nuzzling his nose along hers. She nodded and closed her eyes.

For the rest of the afternoon, they sped over the countryside, warm air whipping their hair, her body pressed tight against his back. Darcy felt a freedom he had never experienced before with her behind him. He didn't think about any of the responsibilities of being a judge, an older brother, or the Master of Pemberley. All he thought about was being her lover.

That evening, Elizabeth moved into Darcy's room. After the last of her things had been transferred, she leapt into his arms, wrapping her legs around his waist.

"You, Judge Darcy, are too sexy for your own good. Now that I have no excuse to run away, I think you will be imprisoned in this room for the next week," she said as she wiggled her groin against him.

"Ms. Bennet, I believe you are a nymphomaniac," he laughed.

He carried her to the bed, dropped her on it, then stripped off his shirt. She sighed as she caught sight of his finely muscled torso. She pulled off her own shirt as he crawled onto the bed beside her, and he leaned over, kissing her softly.

"I'm glad we were caught," he murmured against her lips. "Now I can kiss you anytime I like." Her heart fluttered at this, and she nodded in agreement. He ran his hand over her collarbone, over her bra, down her waist.

Was I even alive a week ago? Darcy wondered. He had never been so consistently inflamed by anyone. He was in a constant state of awareness of where she was, what she was wearing, who she was talking to, what she was doing. For the last week, his entire being had been focused on her, like a satellite in orbit. He felt as though it was his sole purpose to make her laugh, cry, moan, whatever. If *he* didn't give it to her, it wasn't real.

He slipped easily into her. They were, after all, made for each other. He sighed in her hair and kissed her ear. This was where he belonged. The fantasy was the reality, everything else was illusion. He met her eyes and held them while he made love to her. It was as if Elizabeth could read his mind, hear his thoughts. She responded to his body, touched every spot where he ached to be touched, was rough or tender at the right times. They took a long time before they allowed themselves to apex. She whispered encouragement and endearments in his ear that made him shiver. He didn't know who he was or where he was anymore. He was only a part of her.

Chapter 10

"THIS IS GETTING RIDICULOUS," Darcy gasped, rolling off Elizabeth for what seemed like the hundredth time since the beginning of the week. Late morning sunshine glanced off his bare, damp shoulders.

"I think I'm getting judge burn," she agreed, rubbing her inner thigh. "Ease up on the little gavel, would you?"

"I categorically oppose your characterization of my gavel as 'little,'" he replied.

"Do you prefer Junior Justice?"

"It's your pro bone-o work."

They giggled, snuggling together in the tangle of sheets. Pillows were strewn across the bed, and the comforter had fallen to the floor.

"Georgiana says I'm always in a bad mood because I'm sexually frustrated. I think I've solved the problem," he said. Elizabeth considered for a moment, then laughed.

"You *have* been in a much better mood."

"You try doing my job," he said, propping his head on his hand. "There's no staff, everyone bumps Clayton for trial, then

I have fifty hearings a day with attorneys who can't be bothered to hole-punch their documents. I can't do *everything*."

"You don't have to yell at me. I always hole-punch my stuff," she chided gently.

"Yes, you always were one of the best," he said, stroking a tendril of her hair away from her face before lying back down.

Elizabeth nestled her head into the hollow of his shoulder and trailed her foot along the inside of his ankle.

"Can I ask you something?"

"Mm-hmm," he answered drowsily.

"Do you have a girlfriend?"

His hand traced lazy circles on her shoulder. "No."

She remained silent for a moment, then said, "Jane said you were dating Charley's sister."

His hand stilled. "Jane is misinformed. Caroline and I dated on and off for a couple of years, but I haven't been with her for almost a year." He began tracing the lazy circles again. "Would it have mattered?" he asked after a short silence.

"Probably not, but I hate to think of myself as the other woman."

"You're the only one," he laughed quietly, giving her a squeeze. It gave her a warm satisfaction to hear that. "And you? Am I breaking up your marriage to your high-school sweetheart?"

"No, there's no one."

"Not even Mr. Hurst?" he teased.

"You're more his type than I am."

They lay together for a while longer, and had a playful bout of lovemaking during which he stroked her with his riding crop and called her the Wicked Mistress of Pemberley, before admitting that they really should get out of bed. Because they had been outed by Jane and Bingley the day before, they saw no reason to continue to act as if nothing was happening. Besides, Darcy was a fool if he thought Mrs. Reynolds didn't suspect something. So without hesitation, he held Elizabeth's hand as they entered the kitchen for breakfast.

"About time, lazybones," Mrs. Reynolds chided as they sat at the kitchen table.

"Don't blame me, the missus here doesn't like to get out of bed," Darcy protested, his eyes sparkling with mischief. Elizabeth blushed. Not only had he called her his "missus," but he had indeed been *up* hours before. The man was a sex fiend.

"You're not fooling me. I've known you since you were in your nappies, and you're no early riser," Mrs. Reynolds replied, rolling her eyes and sliding a plate of toast before them.

"Mrs. Reynolds, please. It won't do for you to ruin my carefully-crafted image."

Mrs. Reynolds chortled softly and ruffled Darcy's hair. If Elizabeth had not known better, she would have sworn they were mother and son.

"What can I get you, dear?" Mrs. Reynolds asked as she placed a hand on Elizabeth's shoulder.

"Oh, nothing. I'm fine, thank you," Elizabeth assured her. But even so, moments later she found herself staring at a fluffy omelet, sliced tomatoes, and freshly squeezed orange juice.

"This is quite a step up from my usual breakfast of cold coffee and toaster pastries," Elizabeth sighed before slicing into the mouthwatering omelet. "Oh my God…" she moaned upon tasting the melted cheese and sautéed onions.

Mrs. Reynolds joined them for breakfast, and it became apparent to Elizabeth that Darcy held her in close regard and affection. She teased him and joked with him as much as Elizabeth did. Firmly setting aside Mrs. Reynolds' protests, Elizabeth helped clear the table and wash the dishes.

"Mrs. Reynolds, my mother taught me that a good houseguest always takes care of herself and doesn't cause any extra work for her hostess. Knowing her, it's probably the only way she ever got a return invitation," Elizabeth laughed as she wiped the kitchen table. "And now, I'd really like to wash some clothes, so can you please tell me where the laundry is?"

Once Elizabeth was gone, Mrs. Reynolds wrapped one arm around Darcy's waist as he stood at the sink rinsing his mug.

"I like her," she said, giving him a squeeze.

"So do I," he said with a smile.

"Don't you let her get away." She *tut-tut*-ed him with another squeeze. Darcy looked fondly down at the woman who had been his surrogate mother for as long as he could remember. How disappointed she would be if she knew the truth of his relationship with Elizabeth.

"I'll see what I can do about that," he answered and gave Mrs. Reynolds a brief hug.

"It's so good to have you back," she sighed before dabbing her eye and pulling away from him. "Now, let's see if I can find any embarrassing baby pictures to show your girlfriend."

"Mrs. Reynolds, you wouldn't!"

"Why not? You were an adorable baby."

"Mrs. R… Gretchen… *Mum*," he pleaded, resorting to the title that he always used in desperate times. She laughed him off, shaking her head.

"I don't know why you care. She's already seen your bum, and you're still a baby."

***

For Elizabeth, the question of Darcy dating Caroline had nagged her since Jane's reminder the day before. She had almost been afraid to ask, for if he was involved with someone else, her opinion of him would undoubtedly have plummeted. But the more she thought about it, the idea of him cheating on anybody was preposterous. He had far too much integrity to do that to anyone.

Even if he had been involved with someone else, Elizabeth wasn't so sure that she would have been able to break off their affair. For try as she might, she could not deny that she was beginning to feel more than a sexual pull. He was charismatic—funny, considerate, attentive, handsome—all the things she looked for in a man. But more than that, there was an intangible element, a mysterious magnetism that made her eyes follow him wherever he was, like a fish following a shiny object. She knew she'd spent far too much time watching him when she realized that she knew exactly how he liked his tea.

There was a connection between them, an understanding that allowed them to communicate without words. Granted, those communications often ran along the lines of "Want to go do it?" but sometimes it was as innocent as "Please pass the sugar," or as complex as "Can you believe what an idiot Bingley is? Doesn't he know that Jane is vegetarian by *now?*"

Now, in the nightfall after late dinner, they sat in the living room. Darcy strummed guitar while Jane, Bingley, and Mrs. Reynolds drank coffee and talked. Elizabeth observed them in quiet contemplation. Just moments ago, Darcy had rescued Mrs. Reynolds from a large basket of laundry, taking it from her with a chastising look and reminding her that she should not be lifting so much. That he had such an obvious soft spot for the woman, far beyond that of a mere housekeeper, warmed

Elizabeth through and through. He wasn't just a great guy; he was a good man.

Everything about Darcy, from the way he treated Mrs. Reynolds, to the way he ran his courtroom, to the way he took care of Bingley, pointed to his strength of character. And the way he treated her… well, he was a man without fault in that regard. Elizabeth loved the way he smelled and the way his skin felt against hers. She loved the way he let out little muffled grunts when they made love. She loved the intensity of his eyes and the way his smile softened his face. She loved… him.

The realization was so unexpected that it jarred her, like a broken string on a guitar. It jolted her from her private, tender musings and thrust her into the present. He was there, just across the room, completely oblivious that his two-week tart had fallen madly in love with him.

Oh, what a cruel trick, she thought. To know beforehand that a relationship was impossible, and yet to stumble blindly into the trap, was a tragic irony. Did he suspect her feelings? If he did, surely he'd want to end the relationship now… possibly even send her away for the remainder of his vacation. It was possible that he could tell from looking at her; he was a good judge because he could read people despite what they said.

Suddenly, the room's lights were much too bright. Elizabeth felt as if she had the word IDIOT tattooed across her forehead.

"You feeling all right?" Jane asked, noticing Elizabeth's deer-caught-in-the-headlights expression.

"I'm fine," Elizabeth squeaked, sinking deeper into her chair, hoping to be swallowed by the cushions.

"You do look pale," Mrs. Reynolds agreed, touching Elizabeth's damp forehead. "And clammy, too."

"I'm fine, really," Elizabeth replied, darting her eyes away from Darcy's scrutinizing gaze. "Maybe I had a little too much coffee. It makes me jittery. I think I'll just call it a night." Before anyone could question her weak excuse, Elizabeth sprung from her chair and dashed up the stairs. Once she reached Darcy's bedroom, she locked herself in the bathroom and sat on the toilet, pressing her palms against her eyes and willing herself not to dissolve into hopeless sobs.

I'm such an idiot, she thought. *I should never have started this stupid affair. What was I thinking?* She rocked on the seat and hugged herself, crying quietly and feeling sick. She hoped that Darcy would not want to have sex tonight. Making love to him while trying to hide her feelings was a losing proposition. And it was imperative that he not find out.

Downstairs, Darcy wondered whether going to bed was the wisest remedy for over-caffeination and suspected that something else was the root of Elizabeth's sudden departure. She looked worried or panicked, and his first thought was *Oh my God, she's pregnant.* It was an irrational thought because they had been diligent about birth control, so he dismissed the idea immediately. It surprised him that the dismissal was accompanied by a sense of disappointment.

He followed her upstairs a moment later, first because he wanted to be sure she was all right, and second because it simply felt strange not to be in the same room with her. It wasn't so much that he wanted to have sex—God knew they'd been having a nearly non-stop fuck fest for days, and he could use a break—as it was that he felt an empty space beside him when she wasn't there. He entered the bedroom and saw that the bathroom door was closed.

"Elizabeth?" he called softly.

"Yes, I'm just getting ready for bed. Be out in a second. Could you kill the lamp? I've got a raging headache."

Her voice sounded normal, though perhaps a little tired, so Darcy dismissed his suspicions as paranoia. Perhaps she really had a headache. Anyway, it gave him the perfect excuse not to initiate sex—because honestly, he thought he might injure himself if he kept up this pace.

He turned off the light and undressed before slipping between the sheets on his side of the bed. *God, she's taken over one side of my bed,* he thought with a grin. How preposterously domestic that during this torrid affair, they'd staked out which side of the bed to sleep on.

A moment later, he heard Elizabeth emerge from the bathroom. He felt the mattress sink under her weight and waited for the comfort of her warm body against his. It did not come.

His eyes snapped open.

"What's wrong?" he asked, immediately awake.

"I told you, I have a headache," she replied wearily. His suspicion returned, and he rolled over, only to find her back to him. He gently pulled her shoulder until she lay on her back. Even in the dim moonlight, it was plain she had been crying, and it both alarmed and softened him.

"A headache so bad that it made you cry?" he asked, stroking one finger tenderly over her cheek. She closed her eyes as if fighting off more tears. "Tell me," he prompted.

"It's stupid."

"Then tell me, and we'll have a laugh over it tomorrow."

She hitched out a little laugh and wiped the back of her hand across her eyes.

"Okay. But I'm warning you, it's so incredibly stupid that you might not believe me." She paused for dramatic effect, and Darcy waited patiently. "It was the guitar."

Darcy frowned. "Was it that bad?"

"No," she laughed. "It was good. Ridiculously good. I've always been responsive to music, and there you were playing these beautiful Irish folk songs and… well… you made me cry. Now I'm embarrassed *and* have a headache from crying."

She looked up at him, biting her lower lip. When he didn't respond right away, she said, "See, I told you. Incredibly, unbelievably stupid."

"I'm speechless," he said. "I mean, to think that I've got these astounding powers of seduction right in my fingertips and never took advantage of them before." He winked at her.

Elizabeth swatted him playfully then turned her back to him, settling in for the night. Darcy nestled in close, tucking his knees behind hers, and laid one hand on her breast.

"Don't even think about it," she muttered sleepily.

"Preaching to the choir, Lizzy," he answered tiredly. He nuzzled his nose in her hair and kissed that spot at the nape of her neck that so entranced him. There was just something so fundamentally *right* about being with her. *I don't need to prove my manliness by shagging her every night*, he drowsily reassured himself. *It's enough to put my arms around her and let her know I love her*.

His eyes snapped open again.

Chapter 11

"WE SHOULD GO INTO town tonight," Bingley suggested Saturday morning over marmalade and toast. Darcy met Elizabeth's glance over the table, reading her pleading expression: days upon days of hot, mind-blowing shagging were all well and good, but this was her first time in England. He couldn't hold her prisoner as his own personal sex slave, much as he would like to.

"I hear there's a new jazz club," Bingley continued, opening his traveler's guide to London.

"A jazz club?" Darcy asked warily. He didn't particularly like jazz, or clubs, or Saturday night crowds, which made Bingley's suggestion sound like a perfect storm for a stultifying evening. An evening that could be more productively spent. Or if not productively, then at least enjoyably.

His misgivings, however, were wiped away by the enthusiastic light in Elizabeth's eyes.

"Oh, that sounds like fun," she said, grinning eagerly.

Well, if she wanted to do it, Darcy would do it, no matter how painful. Although he'd pushed last night's random thought of love from his mind as exhausted musings, he did have to admit that he *cared* about Elizabeth and wanted to make this vacation memorable for more than a case of "judge burn."

"Oh, but I don't have anything to wear," Elizabeth recalled, her expression falling.

"Why don't you and Jane go to town and shop, then Bingley and I will meet you at the Ritz. We'll stay the night there," Darcy suggested, hoping to avoid a detestable day of shopping.

"Oh, no, I want Charley to come along," Jane pouted prettily, and all hope Darcy had of just meeting them for dinner was dashed. He sighed, then felt Elizabeth's foot touch his ankle. Her expression again melted his formerly stony heart, and he smiled, defeated. Perhaps he would benefit from a lingerie show of some sort.

A few hours later, the two couples were walking through the shops of London. Darcy quickly learned to find a comfortable chair while waiting for Elizabeth, Jane, and Bingley to try on clothes.

"You look miserable." Elizabeth hugged him from behind as he flipped through a magazine at another trendy boutique. He glanced over his shoulder and received a kiss on the cheek for his patience.

"I hope to be rewarded later." He smiled, rubbing his hand affectionately over her forearm.

"Yes, sir. I'll pay for these shoes the only way I know how—by kicking them up to the ceiling." She planted a tickling kiss on his neck as Darcy craned for a look at the aforementioned shoes. They were red python stilettos with a long, skinny, pointed toe. He had never paid much attention to women's shoes before, but if these were the norm, he imagined that millions of women were walking around hobbled by crippling—but sexy—shoes.

"Don't those hurt?" he asked.

"Only when I dig them into your kidney," she retorted with a wink.

Eventually everybody was satisfied, and they headed to the hotel for dinner and drinks before going to the club. Darcy was surprised to see that after hours of shopping, Elizabeth chose to wear a simple black suit. It was not staid by any means, hugging her curves and plunging to reveal a generous expanse of cleavage, and accented by the red shoes. The sophisticated vampishness of her outfit was tempered by the soft waves of hair that tumbled around her face.

"You look beautiful," he murmured in Elizabeth's ear as he ushered her out the door and into a cab. She tossed a glance at him beneath lowered lashes and flashed a secret smile that set his pulse pounding.

The club was already crowded and smoky when they found their reserved seats. They sat in a two-by-two arrangement, facing the stage: Darcy behind Elizabeth and Bingley behind Jane, the couples separated by a drinks table. The room was dim, cigarette smoke was burning his eyes, and a poorly placed stage light was glaring straight at Darcy. He closed his eyes and sent a silent prayer that the night would be neither long nor tedious.

When he opened his eyes, Elizabeth's bare back faced him. Startled, he realized she was wearing a low-back, black silk bustier. A tiny ribbon of red edged the top of the bustier and laced through the back closure. Elizabeth had done him the favor of sweeping her hair over one shoulder so that his view of her bare flesh was unimpeded.

He swallowed and doubted that the evening would be tedious.

That smooth expanse of skin held Darcy's attention all night. At intermission, when Elizabeth turned to talk to him, he could see a seductive swell of flesh pushed against the edge of the bustier.

"I misspoke earlier," he said, leaning forward so that only she could hear. "You don't look beautiful. You look sensational." It never failed to charm him that she blushed whenever he complimented her, as she did now.

Empty glasses began to fill their table, and Darcy began to feel light-headed. He vaguely remembered the singer inviting the audience to dance and seeing happy couples of all sizes and colors swaying in rhythmic flow to the jazz. What he couldn't quite recall was Elizabeth pulling him to the floor. He must have protested, because they were in a dark corner away from the thickest part of the crowd.

Her arms were around his neck, and she was smiling up at him, mischief sparkling behind her sooty lashes. Darcy realized that his hands were on her bottom, one thumb stroking over her curves as he held her close to him.

"Am I dancing?" He grinned, definitely feeling the effects of too much alcohol.

"If that's what you call it," she teased, seemingly unaffected by her own consumption.

Darcy slid one hand up from her rear to caress her bare back, and dipped his head down to smell her hair.

"God, Lizzy, you're so fucking sexy," he breathed in her ear. "You make me crazy. All I want to do is shag you, then shag you some more."

"Then why don't you take me back to your suite at the Ritz," she suggested, drawing his face to hers for a kiss, and whispered against his lips, "and you can shag me all night long."

It didn't take a second invitation for Darcy to pull Elizabeth from the club and hail a cab. They made out in the backseat, sliding across the vinyl bench as the driver swerved in and out of busy nighttime traffic. Only when they were unlocking the suite door did Darcy remember Jane and Bingley.

"Where are Jane and Charley?" he asked.

"No idea. They left the club before we did."

Darcy closed the door behind him and watched as Elizabeth removed her jacket before running her hands over his torso, pulling his shirt from his trousers, and kissing his skin. Her tongue rasped over his taut nipple, causing him to expel a gasp. Then she stepped away, walking toward the dining area. Tossing a saucy smirk over her shoulder, she undid her trousers and dropped them to the floor, revealing black lace panties, garters, and seamed silk stockings. She turned to face him, leaning against the edge of the dining room table, and crossed one red stiletto-clad ankle over the other.

"Still sensational?"

A sly smile curled Darcy's lips as he tugged his tie from his neck. He met her at the table and pulled her to him, drawing a deep kiss from her lips. His hands drifted over her hips while his lips trailed along her throat. Caressing her thigh, he pulled her knee to his hip and stroked one palm over her calf. Elizabeth was a beautiful, intelligent, witty woman… who happened to be wearing deliciously trashy shoes. The red of those shoes inflamed Darcy's passion.

Elizabeth had already worked his shirt to the floor when he said, "Charley and Jane could come back any minute."

"Exciting, isn't it?" Her hands made their way to his belt, and she slowly unfastened the buckle. "I mean, we could get caught.

Someone might see us," she whispered, her fingers tracing teasing lines over his stiff erection. "Maybe we better hurry." Her tone implied, however, that she was in no hurry at all.

Darcy kissed the line from her ear to her shoulder, then turned her to face the table. As he began to unlace the bustier, she leaned forward. He braced himself on the table and kissed her neck. His hands ran over the smooth skin of her rear, running a finger along the edge of her panties. When he slid a finger inside, brushing along her moist sex, she let out a soft groan.

"You like it dirty?" she asked.

"You want it dirty?"

"I think I do."

With one hand, Darcy pushed aside her panties, while with the other he dipped a finger into her. She arched against his hand and squeezed his finger. He pressed his hips against her, leaving her in no doubt of his arousal. Still stroking his finger inside of her, he finished unlacing the bustier with his free hand. It fell open and lay flat on the table, her bare back now in full view.

He pulled his finger from her and put it in his mouth, savoring her tangy flavor as he released himself from his boxers and quickly unrolled a condom. Pulling down her panties, he slid into her wet, supple core. Both let out soft cries.

Darcy leaned over her, his teeth scraping over her shoulder on his way to kiss her neck. His hands folded over hers, and together they braced against the table as he thrust into her. The silverware clinked and glasses rattled under them.

Her body was so familiar to him now, he could read every cue. Her skin began to flush, and her lips parted as she breathed against the wood, climbing toward orgasm. Before she could crest, Darcy turned her over.

"I like to see you come," he rasped as he thrust back into her. His fingers gripped her thighs, pulling one of her knees high and wide. The other hand kneaded her breast, pinching and rolling her nipple.

Suddenly, she arched against him, hips thrust up and head tossed back. With a sharp intake of breath she let out a cry, almost a sob of relief, of "Oh, yes!" Her fingers grabbed at his hair and her legs pulled his hips closer, a rhythmic pulsing taking over her body.

Her uninhibited release pushed Darcy to his own climax. An uncontrolled groan escaped his throat as he sent a final thrust home, rattling dishes and toppling stemware. The tight coil of desire unwound, the tension ebbed as pleasure pulsed.

Now well and truly light-headed from alcohol and sex, Darcy clutched Elizabeth's hips for balance. As the ecstatic flush began to recede, he let out a little laugh. The settings on the table had been destroyed; crystal lay shattered on the floor. The tablecloth was askew, gathered under Elizabeth's hips. The centerpiece had tipped over, cracking two dishes.

"That's going to cost a lot," Elizabeth said, observing a broken candlestick beside her head.

"Well worth it," Darcy panted. He grinned down at her, his hazy mind trying desperately to recall some important bit of information.

"Bingley!" he gasped, eyes wide.

"Shh," she laughed. "They went bar hopping. They won't be back for hours."

"You mean… there was never any chance they would walk in on us?"

She shook her head. "Fun, wasn't it?"

Darcy buried his face in her hair, laughing softly. "Oh God, I love you, Lizzy," he chuckled. Elizabeth put her arms around his neck and tightened her legs around his waist as he lifted her from the table.

"Take me to bed, lover," she cooed. He carried her to the bedroom, intent on making love to her for the rest of the night. But his head was swimming. He fell on the bed beside her and passed out.

Despite waking to what felt like old gym socks in his mouth that even two brushings could not quite dispel, Darcy's hangover was not nearly as vicious as he anticipated. His headache was eased by a hot shower, and he shuffled in boxers and socks to the living room to watch the news. He heard Elizabeth stir and get in the shower, and a few moments later she emerged in fresh white panties and bra, her hair hanging in damp ringlets on her shoulders.

"How are you feeling?" she whispered.

"Not nearly as bad as I should."

"You were pretty smashed."

"I remember all the good bits."

"That's all that's important," she agreed, curling on the floor next to his feet. He slid off the couch and onto the floor next to her. She smelled like soap and pears.

"How do you feel?" he asked.

"I didn't have much to drink. Makes you fat," she said, patting her tummy. "How do you stay in such good shape?" She ran a finger over his lean stomach.

"Lots of push-ups," he said. He rolled to his stomach to demonstrate and did a quick set of five push-ups. Elizabeth slipped onto his back.

"Now try," she said. He pushed up quickly, making her giggle and hold tightly to him. He laughed and pushed again, trying to shake her from him, but she wrapped her legs around his.

Just then, the guest bedroom door swung open and out stumbled Bingley, clad only in boxers.

"Christ, my head!" he moaned. Then, as his bleary eyes focused on the table, "What the hell happened here?"

"I tripped," Darcy said simply.

"And fell," Elizabeth supplied helpfully.

"Onto my girlfriend."

Elizabeth, still clinging to Darcy's back, grinned and gave him a squeaky kiss on the cheek. Bingley shook his head, scratched himself through his boxers, and ordered room service.

The party drove back to Pemberley mostly in silence. Bingley and Jane were nursing hangovers, and Elizabeth was content to watch the scenery pass by as Darcy steered them home. The rest of the day was spent lounging on the terrace with Mrs. Reynolds, sipping iced tea and laughing while Darcy picked out tunes on his guitar.

"You remind me of your mother, sitting there strumming," Mrs. Reynolds mused. "She and your father used to sit out here with their friends, just like this, before you were born."

"I remember her playing." Darcy nodded, studying his fretwork.

"Your mum was a bit of a hippie. She used to play folk music—Peter, Paul and Mary, John Denver, Bob Dylan. You used to run around naked right over there." She pointed to a shady patch of lawn.

"That's quite enough, Mrs. Reynolds," Darcy said in mock sternness. Mrs. Reynolds hid her laugh behind a sip of iced tea.

"Why can't you reminisce about what a great race car driver I was?" he grumbled.

"I can do that." She turned to face Elizabeth. "His father hated it—"

"Isn't it time for dinner?" Darcy interrupted with a withering glance. Mrs. Reynolds laughed again and patted Elizabeth's thigh.

"If you help me, I'll tell you all of his secrets."

"Sounds juicy." Elizabeth followed Mrs. Reynolds to the kitchen, and along the way, Mrs. Reynolds pointed out family photographs: Darcy as a baby, naked on a rug; two proud parents in seventies leisure suits next to a toddler Darcy on horseback; a grinning Georgiana in pigtails and missing her two front teeth; a teenaged Darcy clad in a racing suit, cocky grin on his face as he leaned against his race car, helmet tucked under his arm. These glimpses of his life, rarely seen outside the Darcy family, gave Elizabeth a better understanding of the man she'd come to love.

As the sun sank below the horizon, Elizabeth and Darcy crept up the stairs hand-in-hand. They undressed and curled into bed, content for the moment to be together without more.

"I can't believe how much I've enjoyed this vacation," Elizabeth sighed, nestling her head into his shoulder.

"You hated me two weeks ago."

"Now why do you have to bring that up?" She sat up on her elbow and touched a finger to his lips. "Besides, my feelings now are quite the opposite."

Darcy's eyes searched her face, and he pulled her down for a kiss. "Lizzy," he whispered, his thumb stroking her cheek. She was solemn and gave him a soulful look. Their eyes connected, and he understood: they were going to *Make Love* and it was going to *Mean Something*.

Darcy let himself go, let himself feel those emotions that clamored in his chest. He gasped in pleasure when she touched him, felt cold when she pulled away. He told her she was the loveliest woman he'd ever known, that she felt right in his arms. He told her that she'd shown him how to make love, and he wanted nothing more than to make her happy. He meant every word.

Chapter 12

ELIZABETH WOKE UP MONDAY morning in Darcy's arms again, his chin resting on top of her head, his arm draped over her waist, one leg pushed between hers. She tried to extricate herself from his grasp, but as she moved, his arms tightened about her. He made a sound of protest as she tried again. She laughed quietly into his chest.

"It's too early to get up," he mumbled.

"You have become idle aristocracy, you know," she teased him.

"Yes, but you won't let me enjoy it."

"I need to be outside in the fresh air and sunshine. I'm beginning to feel cooped up!"

Only after he was rewarded with a kiss for every effort—sitting up, standing, getting dressed—did she get Darcy down to breakfast. They declined Jane and Bingley's invitation to lounge with them on the terrace, instead opting to go for a walk. When they reached a sloping meadow of wild flowers, Darcy flattened down a patch of grass and spread his jacket for Elizabeth to sit on.

"I love wildflowers," Elizabeth said, picking one and holding it to her nose.

"Then you shall have them," Darcy declared valiantly, and set out to gather a bouquet for her, calling out the occasional, "Do you like this one?" or "This won't give me a rash, will it?"

Soon he returned with a large bunch of flowers: buttercups, daisies, violets, clover, pimpernels, and even blackberry brambles.

"Wounded," he grimaced, showing her the thorn in his thumb. Elizabeth pulled it out and kissed away the prick of blood. Pulling the flowers to her chest, she lay her head in Darcy's lap and closed her eyes under the pleasant caress of sun and breeze.

"Not quite ripe yet," she said with a sour pucker when Darcy fed her one of the berries he had picked.

They sat there for a while, Darcy stroking away a wayward tendril of hair from her forehead as it was ruffled by the breeze. He broke short the flower stems and arranged blossoms in her hair while she chewed on a blade of grass. She pulled a few dandelions from the bunch and broke the stems, letting the milk drop onto her tongue. Then she placed the yellow crowns in his curly hair.

"Very fetching," she declared with a satisfied nod.

He trailed a finger across the bridge of her nose and over her cheeks. "You are freckling," he said affectionately.

"It's a curse," she sighed.

"They're like a dusting of cinnamon on cream."

They fell silent again, enjoying the weather, the solitude, and the quiet company, until Darcy's stomach grumbled, reminding them that it was lunchtime. Elizabeth laughed softly and sat up, brushing spent stems off her peasant blouse, which had slipped off one shoulder. With her hair full of color and swept by the wind into its natural spirals, she had a timeless, fantastical quality, like a fairy princess who belonged dancing in a forest circle. She was beyond beautiful, and though he felt his eyes couldn't bear it, Darcy continued to gaze at her.

He felt a thunderclap in his chest, as sure as if he had been struck by lightning. He knew, without hesitation, that he was in love with Elizabeth.

Those niggling thoughts from the previous evenings, hinting at his true feelings, did not prepare him for the magnitude of what he felt now. He thought his chest might burst with it. He wanted to tell her that he loved her, that he wanted to marry her, father her children, and stay here until they were old and gray. But the possibility of rejection, the possibility of ruining this perfect bliss, prevented him.

Instead, he said, "I think this has been the most perfect day of my life."

She smiled and nestled back into his lap, and said, "Then we won't end it just yet."

Darcy struggled with whether or not to tell Elizabeth his true feelings. They had agreed to keep no secrets and tell no lies, but this was something different. This had real potential for disaster. She hadn't responded to his drunken declaration a few nights ago, which was just as well. For although he'd meant it at the time, the intensity of what he felt now so outweighed what he felt then that it made the entire incident laughable. Before now, he'd had no idea what it meant to be in love.

His feelings forced him to keep quiet. He didn't want to tell her until he had some inkling what her feelings were. While she was affectionate, did she *love* him? Would he simply scare her away if he admitted what was in his heart?

"You're awfully quiet," Elizabeth commented Tuesday as they headed toward the stable. They were going on a picnic, but she wanted to see the horses first.

"Just thinking." He shrugged, stuffing his hands in his pockets. They reached the horses, and Darcy watched Elizabeth feed them bits of carrots.

"Would you like to ride?" he asked her.

"Oh, no, I'm too chicken to ride by myself," she laughed.

"We can ride on the same horse. Starfire here can carry both of us." When she seemed hesitant, Darcy took her hand. "Come on, it'll be fun." She nodded her assent, and he grinned. Riding always helped clear his mind, and perhaps he would come to a decision about whether to tell Elizabeth that he loved her.

He made small talk, telling her about the horses and riding in general, the differences in English and Western styles, and how to best approach a horse. Then he helped her into the saddle and easily swung on behind her.

"You really are too dashing, Mr. Darcy," she murmured over her shoulder as they set out from the stable at an easy pace.

"It's all for your benefit, Ms. Bennet," he replied, wrapping his arms around her to grasp the reins. They rode for a while, Darcy pointing out places he remembered from childhood as they passed them. When they found a spot under a willow tree, they dismounted and spread out their picnic blanket. After a light snack, they lay back, dozing under the dappled sunlight.

Darcy turned the dilemma over in his mind and resolved to adhere to their bargain and tell her the truth.

"Elizabeth," he began. But he stopped. She'd never given him any reason to believe she wanted anything more than a two-week fling. His admission might not only be unreciprocated; it might be unwelcome. Until he knew her feelings, he wasn't ready to reveal his own.

She looked at him expectantly, and he shook his head.

"Nothing," he said, and propping his head on his hand, stroked a wayward strand of hair from her cheek. She closed her eyes and smiled under his touch. It made his chest ache.

He dipped his head and kissed her. Her arms crept around his neck, and soon they were tangled in a passionate embrace. A sudden gust of wind rustled the leaves above them, reminding Darcy where they were. He broke the kiss and pulled away from her.

"No, don't stop," she murmured, pulling him back to her.

"We are in the middle of a field," he protested gently.

"Then we are full circle," she answered, reminding him of their first kiss. It struck him as ironic that she would say that, because he had gone far beyond full circle. He had traveled a very great emotional distance since that first kiss.

He lowered himself to her for another kiss, and soon they were making love under the willow tree, the sun warming their skin. He breathed in her scent of sunshine and pears, and ran his hands over her body. She was a natural beauty, and he loved her flaws as proof of her authenticity. Their journey to bliss was slow and relaxed, and the afternoon sun was beginning to wane as they lay together.

Elizabeth lay with her head in the crook of his shoulder while he stroked her hair. With her fingertip, she traced a circle on his chest.

"I will miss this," she said quietly. He kissed the top of her head and ran his hand over her arm in a gesture of warmth and tenderness.

After a moment, he said quietly, "You smell like pears—always, no matter what perfume you are wearing or whether you are sweating or just stepping from the shower, I always smell pears. For the rest of my life, Lizzy, I shall never be able to eat a pear without thinking of you."

The thought made them both solemn. They lay still for a while longer and then both felt there was nothing more to say. They rose by mutual agreement and dressed quietly. Darcy plucked blades of grass from her hair with a smile and kissed her again.

He went to fetch the horse and then helped Elizabeth mount it.

Before he swung onto the horse himself, she said, "Your fence is broken. You ought to get it fixed before some animal gets hurt."

She pointed to a gap in the barbed wire fence, and without thinking, Darcy dropped the reins and went to examine it. Before he had gone five steps, he heard her shriek and turned just in time to see the horse rear her onto the ground. He saw her head bounce off the ground with a sickening thud. He immediately ran to her.

"*Elizabeth!* My God!"

He fell to the ground beside her where she lay with eyes opened to the sky. She was obviously dazed but was conscious. Reassured, he hurried to secure the horse so that it would not desert them and then rushed back to her.

"Elizabeth! Lizzy! Are you okay? Can you hear me?" he said as he held her hand.

"Yes, I'm all right. I'm just stunned and had the breath knocked out of me," she replied, pushing herself up on shaky arms.

He touched the back of her head and paled when he saw bright red blood on his fingers. He knew from experience that it was probably not serious, but nonetheless, it was a disturbing sight.

"Lizzy, lie still, you are hurt," he said quietly.

"I am?" she said, sounding a little dazed.

"Yes, you have a cut on your head. Lie still," he said gently. He took a handkerchief from his pocket and held it against the back of her head and was dismayed to see red blossom through a few moments later. He pulled open his cell phone and dialed with a shaking hand.

"Bingley? Elizabeth fell off the horse. Her head is bleeding." He was listening to Bingley's instructions when he saw Elizabeth struggling to sit up again.

"Lizzy! Lie still!" he commanded, pocketing his phone. She promptly lay down again. Darcy removed the handkerchief and folded it over, pressing a clean section to the back of her head.

"I didn't think anyone carried handkerchiefs anymore," she commented. Darcy smiled.

"I also wear clean underwear everywhere. My mother taught me well."

"It better not have any boogers on it," she grumbled and he laughed.

"I see you haven't damaged the humor lobe of your brain."

"Lucky for us we have two resident surgeons," she said.

"Yes, let's get you back to them and see if we can patch you up."

He pulled her gently to her feet, holding her in case she became dizzy. She took a moment to steady herself, leaning against him. When at last she was ready to face the horse again, he led her gingerly to its side.

"Now, be careful," he said as he lifted her up to the saddle. He immediately swung up after her, and with one arm around her waist holding her securely to him, he cantered back to the house. The pace of the horse jarred her, and she let out an "OW!"

"Sorry. Can you still feel your toes?" he asked.

"Yes."

"Then you're fine," Darcy concluded, making Elizabeth laugh through her pain. As they approached the house, Darcy tightened his hold on Elizabeth.

"I'm so sorry, Lizzy. It was incredibly stupid of me to leave you on the horse. I wasn't thinking at all. I won't forgive myself until I know you are okay," he said.

"Neither will I," she groused. He didn't laugh. "I'm just kidding. It was just an accident. I probably did something to make him rear up like that," she said, soothing his arm.

"No, he's a high-spirited horse. I was careless."

"You like a high-spirited horse, do you?" she teased.

"As, I've discovered, I like my women," he said into her ear. "You, Elizabeth Bennet, are very high-spirited."

"Well, it's a good thing you brained me, or I might be positively wild."

Darcy laughed and hugged her tight before helping her off the horse. Then, although she could walk under her own power, he helped her into the house and up the stairs where he laid her gently on the bed. Bingley, Jane, and Mrs. Reynolds sprang into action around him, gathering the first aid kit and disinfectant. Darcy kept the handkerchief pressed to her head, which was still bleeding, while Jane performed a quick examination by checking her pupils, her ability to name everyone in the room, her ability to count her fingers, and her reflexes.

"Will you be checking my head at some point?" Elizabeth asked crossly.

"Just making sure there's no neurological damage. Now, let's take a look at that cut," Jane said, her medical training taking over. "Lots of dirt and leaves here. What were you doing, rolling around on the ground? Let's clean that up," she said and asked Mrs. Reynolds for a bowl of warm water and a washcloth. Elizabeth looked at Darcy with an arched eyebrow, and he looked away, the corners of his mouth twitching.

Bingley and Jane gathered over Elizabeth's head, and between the two of them, made quick and relatively painless work of a few stitches.

"She looks a little pale and shaky," Darcy said. "Should we take her to the hospital?"

Both Jane and Bingley shook their heads. "She's fine, although I suspect she's in for a headache for the rest of the night and probably some sore muscles," Bingley said. "She should probably have a little something to eat and a hot bath, then go to sleep."

"Yes, I'd like to wash the blood out of my hair."

"Would you like me to stay?" Jane asked, stroking Elizabeth's forehead, caring sister taking the place of the business-like surgeon. She looked at Jane and smiled, then looked at Darcy.

"No, I am in good hands already."

"I'll start a bath for you now," Darcy said, his expression one of undisguised love.

The others left and Darcy ran the tap before helping Elizabeth undress. He offered her a steadying hand as she stepped into the tub and swept a lathered wash cloth over her legs in long strokes, massaging the muscles as he did. Lacing his fingers through hers, he stretched out her arm and ran the cloth along it, then made soothing circles over her shoulders. He tilted her head back, tenderly rinsing away the dirt and blood from her hair. Working shampoo between his hands, he lathered her hair gently before rinsing it out.

He wrapped his own terry robe around her as she stepped from the bath with his help. Then he carried her to the bed, shushing her when she laughed a protest. When Mrs. Reynolds knocked with dinner, he was lovingly combing out her wet hair.

"Here you go, sweetie," Mrs. Reynolds said as she set the tray on the bed. "I thought you might not want anything too heavy, and Jane suggested soup and grilled cheese. I hope that's okay."

"That's perfect. It's what my mom always made for me when I was sick. Thank you."

"Will, just give a shout if you need anything else. There should be enough there for both of you," she said as she left the room.

Darcy sat on a footstool by the bed, head resting on his folded arms on the mattress.

"How do you feel?" he asked after she had eaten some of her grilled cheese.

"I have a headache, but otherwise, I feel fine."

"I feel terrible. I feel responsible."

"Sweetheart, please, it was just an accident. Don't get all worked up," she said gently. Both were aware it was the first time either of them had used such an endearment. He caught her hand and kissed her palm.

"It could have been much worse."

"It wasn't."

"You're very lucky."

She stroked her thumb across his cheek. "Yes, I am."

Chapter 13

THE NEXT MORNING, ELIZABETH was understandably sore and stiff. She lay in bed, listening to the deep, steady rhythm of Darcy's breathing as he slept beside her. He had taken good care of her the night before, massaging sore muscles and bringing her plenty of aspirin. She did not have the heart to wake him and instead lay quietly, waiting for him to wake on his own.

Bored, she picked up his cell phone from the nightstand and examined it, curious to see whose numbers he had programmed in. She opened it and noticed that he had not personalized the screen with any screen saver. On impulse, she snuggled down next to him, held the phone out, smiled, and took a photo of them. She dared not set it as his screensaver, but hoped he would look at it and laugh before he erased it.

She replaced the phone on the nightstand and picked up his watch. It was heavy, made of brushed nickel perhaps, a masculine, sophisticated watch. Its main face was currently set on California time, and a smaller face set on UK time. A third dial seemed to be a stopwatch but she couldn't figure out how to work it. She put the watch on her arm and fastened the clasp; even fastened, it slipped off her hand easily. Turning it over, she read, "Happy Birthday, From Georgie" engraved on the back.

The watch was returned to the nightstand and his wallet was the next item to be examined. It was brown leather, well-worn, and European in style, meaning it folded in half rather than in thirds. The outside was examined for any initials or signs of it being a gift. She opened it and looked at his driver's license. *Lord, even the DMV couldn't ruin this guy's good looks*, she thought.

"What are you doing?" he asked sleepily next to her.

"I'm stealing your money and credit cards," she replied, continuing to look through his wallet. There was a condom neatly tucked into the pocket. She pulled out his business card, examined it, and replaced it. He watched her, amused, while she rifled through his other business cards: one from Bingley, one from some attorney, one from a dry cleaners.

"You don't keep any photos in your wallet," she commented.

"No, I guess I don't."

She closed his wallet and put it back on the nightstand.

"How are you feeling?" he asked, reluctant to move from his current, very comfortable, position.

"A bit stiff and sore, but nothing that will last more than a day or so."

"I have to say, the fall looked really awful. If I were you, I'd insist on staying in bed all day today."

She grinned. "That sounds like a fine idea. Do you think Mrs. R would bring breakfast up to us? I'm thinking two eggs, over medium, with some toast and bacon. Yes, lots of bacon, please."

He smiled at her and sighed. He would have to resign his very comfortable position after all. He put on a pair of shorts and a T-shirt and went downstairs, returning about a half hour later with a breakfast for both of them.

After a quick check-up from Dr. Bingley, Elizabeth was pronounced as not dying and advised to take it easy. Intending to do just that, Darcy and Elizabeth spent the day in bed, talking about trivial things that somehow seemed important to know. He learned that as a child she wanted to be a ballerina; he wanted to be a fireman. She showed him the scar on her chin from stitches after her hula accident gone bad at age four; he had broken the same arm twice in grade school, both times a result of falling out of the same tree.

When he asked about her mother, she replied, "My mother is insane. If she knew we were involved, she'd have us registered at Macy's before you could count to three. She's got a very determined idea that all her daughters should marry well and retire to have children, which should then also be married well. You should hear her go on about Bingley. 'Oh Jane, a *surgeon!* You'll have such a big house!' Never mind that Jane is also a surgeon."

"My mother was a wonderful person, very warm and funny. I think you remind me of her sometimes. She was a musician, and she and I used to play together a lot before she got sick. It all happened very quickly, you know. She was diagnosed in June with breast cancer and was gone by August. I became very serious for a while until I went off to college and met Bingley. I found him funny, easy to be with, and he drew me out of my shell a good deal. He's my closest friend—like a brother to me."

Between conversations, they made love. As dusk began to settle in, she nestled in his arms at last, each completely physically exhausted.

After a long silence, she looked up at him and laughed softly. "You're very quiet," she said. "I—"

"Shhh," he said softly. "Just be." He closed his eyes and tightened his arms around her, satisfied to have nothing more for the moment than the warm comfort of her in his arms.

Darcy could clearly see now that he had been badly mistaken in his hope that a two-week fling with Elizabeth could quench his desire for her. He fully realized that he was in love with her, as impossible as it seemed. How could he feel so strongly about her in such a short amount of time? Granted, he had been attracted to her for months, but this was insane! How could he, after only two weeks, be ready to spend the rest of his life with her? He tried to analyze the situation, to see if he was in the throes of infatuation.

She was smart, kind, and funny. She was warm to her friends and family and had a tendency to flirt with just about everyone. She was open-minded to new things, new ideas, different viewpoints. While she had her own opinions, she didn't dismiss those of others. What she didn't know about a topic, she was eager to learn. It was her intelligence and wit that drew him to her in the first place, but her openness and humor held his attention.

And her damnably warm, sultry, laughing eyes. Yes, she had a lovely body, soft and warm when it pressed against his. Yes, she had a wild mane of uncontrolled curls that usually wound up in his mouth at some point. Yes, she was a generous and eager lover. But it was her eyes, always her eyes, that held him.

God help me, I don't want it to end, he thought.

He watched her as she slept beside him. It was four a.m., and he was having trouble sleeping. She knew him as well as anyone in his family, as well as Bingley knew him. He felt comfortable with her—safe. He felt like he could tell her anything—except how he felt about her. Except that he wanted her to quit her job and stay here with him forever. He had no illusions—this was no fairy tale, this was *real*.

But perhaps for her it was different—the holiday syndrome where outrageous behavior was excused. Perhaps she could tune him out when they stepped off the plane. The thought gave him a bitter taste in his mouth.

He rose from the bed and went to the window seat overlooking the lake. It was still dark out, and the moon was not in sight. He sat on the cushioned bench and drew his knees up to his chest. He sat at the window for some time, contemplating his situation. Not only would he have to end his relationship with her, but he'd have to keep its existence secret from everyone. And he'd have to see her every day at work—in the building, in the parking lot, in the cafeteria. Not to mention that Jane and Bingley were definitely *on*, and they would undoubtedly continue to cross paths through them. This was going to be very, very difficult.

How had he gotten into this mess?

He heard a rustle and looked toward the bed. Elizabeth sat up and looked around, disoriented.

"I'm here," he said softly. She turned her head toward him. After a moment, she got out of bed and went to him, drawing a blanket behind her. He smiled slightly as she draped it over his shoulders wordlessly and then settled onto the seat between his legs, pressing her warm back against his chest. He drew the ends of the blanket around them and held her close.

They sat together in silence as fingers of sunshine began to creep over the horizon. He put his face into the crook of her neck and let his breath warm her shoulder, and she nestled her head against his. He kissed her neck briefly then put his lips to her ear.

"I don't want this to end," he whispered. He was asking her, making a tentative proposal that it didn't have to end.

"I don't want to talk about it," she replied miserably.

He chickened out. He was a persistent man, yes, but he would not ruin the remaining two days of their vacation trying to convince her to continue to see him when they got back. He would wait.

He put his chin on the top of her head and closed his eyes. He would think of something.

The option of continuing a relationship with Darcy had already been considered and dismissed as impossible by Elizabeth. Even if, by some miracle, they were able to avoid the ethical conflict—a moot point considering how deeply they were already in unacceptable territory—she had no idea whether Darcy would even *want* to.

Of course, he didn't "want it to end." It was a fantastic fling they were having. But that didn't mean that he wanted to take it to the next step: an open, honest, committed relationship. The thought that his feelings might match her own, that he might love her, was inconceivable to her. She could hardly believe her own feelings, which made her doubt herself and whether she'd bought too deeply into this game. Maybe, once she was back in the real world, her common sense would return. But until then, she remained painfully in love with him.

She spent the day drinking in every last sensation that she could. She studied Darcy carefully so that she could remember every intimate detail of his body, of his laugh, the taste of his lips, the smell of his skin. Every thought, every smell, every sound somehow wound itself back to him, until she was saturated, and still it was not enough. The day passed far too quickly, and they retired to their room early to be alone and drown in each other once again.

The last day of their vacation arrived without welcome. Elizabeth was coiled with nervous tension, and Darcy was called away for much of the day to meet with his staff on closing the house and approving business in his absence until his next return.

Bingley drove in to London for reasons unknown, leaving Jane and Elizabeth alone for the day. Jane noted Elizabeth to be unusually quiet and pensive. She did not respond to Jane's teases or questions. She seemed preoccupied. Jane correctly assumed that Elizabeth was having serious doubts about her relationship with Darcy, but whether it was regret, or desire to continue, or how to disentangle herself, Jane could not tell. For the first time ever, she felt unable to read her sister. And for the first time ever, she felt it better not to try.

Darcy joined them briefly for lunch, and they chatted amiably enough, though there was a strain in the air. Jane watched them closely and saw Elizabeth stop him in the hallway as he was about to return to his business in the study. Darcy gently caressed her sister's face and kissed her with a warmth that could only mean that he loved her, Elizabeth returned the kiss with equal tenderness. Then he pulled back and held Elizabeth's hand and he told her that he was sorry, that he would see her in a few hours. She watched as Elizabeth nodded and looked down with either shyness or sadness.

Bingley returned in time for dinner with Darcy, Jane, and Elizabeth. He was taken aside by Jane, who quietly told him that Elizabeth and Darcy seemed to be in some sort of trouble. He nodded, and they agreed to provide what comfort they could.

The couple watched as Darcy and Elizabeth pretended to eat their dinner. Jane saw them give each other miserable glances but exchange no words. She watched Darcy rub the back of his neck in discomfort, saw Elizabeth look away and blink back her tears. Later, Jane overheard their soft exchange.

"Are you angry with me?" Darcy asked her.

Elizabeth looked at him with surprise. "Of course not, how could I be?"

She touched his hand on the table. He squeezed her hand tightly for a brief moment, then drew his hand away. They resumed their miserable silence until the dinner plates were cleared. Then they retired to their room to pack.

Elizabeth seemed not to pay attention to what was going into her suitcase. It was obvious that she was having a hard time keeping her composure, and did not speak for fear of crying.

Darcy packed robotically. He wanted to reach out to her, to hold her one last time, but she seemed detached. Would they spend this last night together in cold silence? Would she even stay with him?

"Elizabeth," he said behind her. She turned at the sound of his voice. He thought she looked fragile, her eyes wide and shiny. "Come here," he said softly, holding his hand out to her. She went to him, and he folded her in his arms. She wrapped her arms around his waist, and he kissed the top of her head.

"Let's not be distant on our last night," he said into her hair. She looked up at him and finally, a tear slipped over her lashes.

She did not sob or cry—she didn't seem aware of the tear until Darcy wiped it away with his thumb. She closed her eyes and two more tears slipped out. She turned her face into his hand and kissed it.

Darcy cupped her face in his hands and kissed her cheeks. He felt his own throat tightening but absolutely forbade any prickling tears to come. He would not break down in front of her.

Somehow, their clothes were removed and they were entwined in bed but neither took much pleasure in their lovemaking. It was bittersweet, a desperate avoidance of the truth that this was the last time they would ever be together. Finally, Darcy entered her with something like a sob in his throat. He buried his face in her hair, gripping her body tightly with his fingers. She wrapped her arms around him like a drowning woman clinging to a lifeboat. He pushed deep into her, swallowed hard. His breath caught uncontrollably as he spilled into her.

Then he whispered, "I love you, Elizabeth. I love you."

Chapter 15

EARLY THE NEXT MORNING, the two couples drove in silence to the airport. Darcy waited with Elizabeth at the gate, unable to stop touching her. He draped his arm around her waist, threaded her fingers through his, or brushed his thumb across the nape of her neck. Elizabeth leaned her head against his chest and closed her eyes, savoring their last hours together for as long as possible. Their separation was hastened when they finally boarded the plane, because Darcy had purchased a first-class seat, while Bingley had purchased coach for the other three. Elizabeth's heart sank when his fingers slipped from hers and she filed back to her seat. A moment later, he reappeared in the aisle and spoke to the man sitting next to her.

"Sir, I wonder if you would exchange seats with me so that I can sit next to my friend."

"Where are you sitting?" the man asked warily, not wanting to give up his aisle seat for a middle.

"In first class," Darcy replied. He showed his ticket to the man, who eagerly gave his seat to Darcy and practically ran to the front of the plane.

"You didn't have to do that," Elizabeth said as he tucked his bag into the overhead bin.

"Yes I did," he replied, settling in next to her. "The person next to me in first class wouldn't take my bribe to give up his seat." He grinned.

"Your legs are too long," she laughed as he struggled to fold his feet under the seat in front of him.

"It'll be a hellish flight." He nodded then met her gaze. "But well worth it if it gives me a few more hours with you." He pressed her fingers to his lips, then leaned over to kiss her cheek. She turned her head and brushed her lips against his. When she broke off the kiss, he said, "It's an eleven-hour flight."

"Yes, but we need to start breaking up in five hours." She smiled sadly.

"But until then, I'm still your lover." To make his point, he kissed her again, heedless that he was in the middle of a packed international flight. He broke off only when he felt his groin begin to stir. If he hadn't been so depressed, he would have loved to join the mile-high club in the bathroom with her. But he was sure she wouldn't be up to her usual playful lovemaking. She was clearly miserable, maybe almost as miserable as he was.

Stowing the armrest, Elizabeth leaned her back into him while he wrapped his arms around her. For the majority of the flight, they talked quietly, rehashing the last two weeks with soft laughter. Then, true to her word, after five hours, Elizabeth began to withdraw. She put down the armrest, creating a physical barrier between them, and her responses to his queries became shorter, putting an emotional distance between them.

By the time they approached San Francisco, both had sunk into depressed silence.

The plane plunged to the landing strip followed closely, apparently, by Elizabeth's heart and stomach. It was a rough landing, and Darcy had held her hand tightly, but now he released it.

That's it, it's over, thought Darcy. Elizabeth had barely spoken for the last thirty-six hours and seemed unlikely to start now. Both filed out of the plane as if going to their death sentences.

Jane and Bingley watched them anxiously as they awaited their luggage at baggage claim. There was an unspoken agreement between them that they would swoop in for the rescue if needed. Darcy blindly watched the carousel spin, vaguely recognized Elizabeth's bag, and pulled it off for her.

"Let me drive you home," he pleaded as she took the bag from him.

She shook her head. "No, it's better this way." She couldn't meet his eyes with her own.

"Can I kiss you good-bye?" he asked.

She shook her head. He reached to touch a lock of her hair but she pulled away, avoiding the contact. She swallowed the lump in her throat, and she shook her head again. He pulled his hand back, hurt. This was really, *really* the end.

"Lizzy—" he began, his voice strangled.

She cut him off with a shaky voice. "Thank you for a wonderful time and for being such a wonderful host, Your Honor."

She could not have stunned him more had she slapped him. They were back in reality, and she had just crashed him unceremoniously through the gate. His face hardened, and he nodded curtly. He bit back his hurt and anger. His mind began to go numb against the realization that it was definitely over. How was this happening? It would be easier to live without his vital organs than to go on without her; the heart was already gone in any event.

Bingley looked at Jane. "I'm driving Darcy home," he said to her. He gave her his keys. "Take my car. I'll call you tomorrow." He kissed her briefly and steered Darcy toward the exit without protest.

Elizabeth followed Jane meekly to the shuttle, to Bingley's car, and then home. She didn't have the stamina or fortitude to assure Jane that she was perfectly fine. She had no energy to lie convincingly.

Jane drove Elizabeth back to the house and led her to her room. She hesitated briefly, unsure whether Elizabeth would prefer company or to be alone. Jane decided to leave her alone but to keep an eye on her. When Jane returned to Elizabeth's room with her suitcase, Elizabeth was sitting motionless on her bed, staring into space.

"Can I get you anything, Elizabeth?" she asked.

Elizabeth showed no sign that she heard Jane. Instead, she opened her suitcase and began to unpack. She would try to distract herself until that awful time when she had to get into her cold, empty bed. Jane watched for a few moments, completely at a loss. She had never seen Elizabeth in such a state. She didn't know what to do, how to help her. She backed out of the room, leaving Elizabeth to find her own comfort. A moment later, she passed the room and found Elizabeth sitting on the bed sobbing into a shirt.

Elizabeth did not see or hear Jane until she sat next to her on the bed and put an arm around her shoulders. Elizabeth wiped her eyes and nose on the shirt, then waved it at Jane.

"It's his," she laughed mirthlessly. "Somehow it got in my bag."

Jane squeezed her, and Elizabeth stiffened slightly. "Lizzy, it's okay. I'm here for you. Go ahead and cry."

With that, Elizabeth relaxed and leaned against Jane and had the longest, most desolate cry of her life. Jane left over an hour later when Elizabeth had cried herself into exhaustion with the shirt clutched tightly to her chest.

Darcy wordlessly gave Bingley the keys to his car as they walked to the parking lot of the airport. His mind was completely blank. He didn't remember anything between the carousel and getting into his car. Bingley drove them to Darcy's condo in the middle of downtown, attempting small talk, but Darcy did not respond—he did not hear. The doorman recognized them both and let them in without question, seeing the dazed look on Darcy's face. Bingley took Darcy up to his door and pulled his bag in for him.

Darcy allowed his friend to herd him into his living room and switch on a lamp. He nodded wordlessly when Bingley called himself a cab, and sat quietly in an armchair while Charley poured him a drink.

"I'm sorry," Bingley said softly. Darcy nodded, still staring off into space. "Is there anything I can do for you? Anything I can get for you?" he asked.

Darcy did not respond. He had already stopped listening again and ignored the drink Bingley offered. The door intercom rang and the cab driver announced his arrival. Bingley told Darcy to call him if he needed anything, but again, Darcy did not respond.

After Bingley was gone, Darcy turned off the lamp and

sat in sullen darkness. He was already berating himself for his impulsive behavior during the past two weeks. What had he been thinking? He mechanically went through the routine of getting ready for bed and climbed into the cold sheets in darkness. He lay awake for hours stifling the wellspring of emotions in his chest, stamping them down with grim determination. He would get her out of his system. There was no other option.

"Lou, you need to come over," Jane said quietly into the phone on Sunday morning. "It's Lizzy. I've never seen her like this. I don't know what to do."

"What happened? I haven't heard from her for over a week," came Lou's concerned voice.

"They broke up. Now she has to work with him, and I don't know if she can handle it. Please come over."

"I'm on my way," Lou said and hung up. Elizabeth had always confided in him, and he in her. She had been his staunchest supporter when he came out to his parents. He would never, ever abandon her.

Elizabeth was still in her pajamas and had not showered for two days. Lou knocked on her door and entered when there was no answer.

"What are you doing, honey?" Lou asked softly.

Elizabeth did not answer. Lou sat on the bed next to her. She had apparently been up at some point, as she was now lying on top of the blankets instead of under them, but otherwise appeared not to have moved for quite some time.

"I brought you a bagel. Are you hungry?" he coaxed, pulling out a toasted bagel.

"Not really," Elizabeth replied. She looked awful—her eyes were puffy and swollen, her hair was a mess, and she had dark circles under her eyes.

"You really should eat something." Lou rubbed Elizabeth's leg. "And maybe get up and move around." He wrinkled his nose. "And maybe shower. You're kinda smelly." He meant it as a lighthearted tease, to see if he could get Elizabeth to smile even a little. To his dismay, Elizabeth's eyes welled with tears again.

"I can smell him all over my skin," she whispered. "He's got this earthy smell, it reminds me of moss on a tree. He told me I smell like pears. He said he would never be able to eat a pear without thinking of me." She dissolved into tears again, as she had so many times over the past twelve hours. She had not slept at all.

"Oh god, honey, come here," Lou said, and he lay down to spoon her from behind, letting her cry, stroking her hair. When she had stopped crying, he put his chin in the crook of her neck. "Tell me what happened."

"I spent almost every minute of the whole two weeks with him," she said. "It was surreal. I've never met anyone like him. I don't know why it clicked, but it just did. We were all over each other—we couldn't keep our hands off each other. It was like being in a different world. Every morning I wondered if I was going to wake up from it, but it never ended."

"And obviously you don't want it to end?"

She shook her head. "No, I'm crazy about him."

"Did *he* want it to end?"

"No."

"Then why did you end it?"

"Because we work together, and it would be an ethical violation for an attorney to be involved with the judge on any of their cases. And really, Lou, it was so perfect, I can't believe that it was real, that it would have lasted."

"Why not?"

"It was so intense and so wonderful and so… so…" She swallowed hard. "He told me that he loved me," she finished.

"Do you think he meant it?"

"I think he meant it then, but I don't know if he would mean it now."

"Do you love him?" he asked.

She struggled for a minute, then nodded once.

Lou sighed heavily. "Look, I know there has to be a way to get around the judge-attorney rule somehow. You can get your cases reassigned and take someone else's cases. You could get a special dispensation or something, right?" he said.

Elizabeth laughed shortly. "In theory, yes, but in practice, no. We'd have to reveal that we're involved and that would put all of our old cases into question and everything would be a big mess. Plus, there's only one other judge who handles any of our cases, and it would be a big pain to have everything before her. She never decides anything right, anyway. I can't make that kind of investment and risk finding out that our relationship doesn't translate to the real world."

They lay together for a while longer and then Lou said, "Let's get you up and washed, and then we'll figure out what to do." He gently pulled Elizabeth up into a sitting position, then pulled her to her feet. He pulled the crumpled shirt from her arms and began to toss it in the hamper.

"No!" she cried, grabbing the shirt from him. He looked at her in surprise. She blushed and balled the shirt under her pillow. "It's his," she mumbled.

Lou nodded in understanding and led her shuffling over to her bathroom before pulling the tank top over her head and pushing her toward the shower. Five or six hickeys dotted her low back. He touched one as she pulled off her pants.

"They're his too," she said quietly.

He sat on the toilet while she showered. When he felt she had been in long enough, he flushed the toilet.

"HEY!" she yelled.

He smiled.

Darcy had not slept at all. Thoughts of Elizabeth had plagued him all night long. He had not yet progressed to logic, to see if there was any way to get around their situation. He was indulging in self-pity at the moment. He finally rose from bed as the sun came up and sat at his kitchen table looking out over the city. Once the sun had risen, he opened his suitcase and absently set about pulling out clothes. His phone rang, but he ignored it. He heard Bingley's voice over the machine, checking in on him. He ignored it—didn't even listen to the message.

He followed his usual routine: pull out the dirty clothes from his suitcase and put them in the hamper for the housekeeper to wash on Wednesday. Something slippery brushed across his fingers, and he pulled out a pair of Elizabeth's white silk panties. She had not washed them, and he put them to his face and smelled pears mingled with her tangy scent. He crumpled them in his fist and threw them in the bathroom garbage can.

Moments later, he retrieved them and lay down with them on his pillow, finally able to sleep.

Chapter 15

ELIZABETH MANAGED TO PULL herself together enough to report to work early Monday morning. In fact, she got in so early that nobody was yet in the front offices, allowing her to avoid any painful questions about her vacation. She closed her office door and looked at her calendar. Although she had no court appearances today, she had a full calendar for the rest of the week, many of which were set before Darcy. It was bound to be an incredibly trying and exhausting week. She put her head in her hands and wondered how the hell she was supposed to cope.

Charlotte noticed immediately that Elizabeth did not look as refreshed after a two-week vacation as she should. When Elizabeth used the excuse of getting caught up on her messages to decline her invitation to lunch, Charlotte let it go. But later in the afternoon, concern for her friend made Charlotte try again. She picked up Elizabeth's favorite coffee and knocked on her office door. With evident reluctance, Elizabeth let her in. "So, want to tell me about your vacation?" she asked as she sat in a chair across from Elizabeth's desk.

"There's not much to tell. I didn't go BASE jumping or anything. I just caught up on my sleep."

"Then why don't you look relaxed?" Charlotte said directly.

Elizabeth shrugged. "Maybe I got too much sleep. Thanks for the coffee, Char, it was just what I needed to get through the rest of the afternoon. But I've really got to prep for my case tomorrow. Can we catch up later this week?"

Taking Elizabeth's hint with grace, Charlotte stood up. "Sure." As she turned to leave, she glanced at Elizabeth's appearance calendar.

"Ugh, you have Judge Darcy tomorrow? He was in an absolutely foul mood today. I guess he didn't enjoy his vacation, either. That dude seriously needs to get laid," Charlotte laughed and left Elizabeth's office, closing the door behind her.

Elizabeth swiveled her back to the door and surreptitiously wiped a tear away from her face. She got no satisfaction from the report that Darcy was unhappy. She had almost hoped to hear that he was in a great mood—at least then one of them would be happy.

After taking a deep breath, Elizabeth pushed down the lump in her throat and opened her file again. But it was useless for her to try to concentrate; the specter of Darcy floated through her mind. Tomorrow she had to face Darcy the Judge, and he was not nearly as kind as Darcy the Lover. She could expect him to notice her poor preparation and, if he was back to his old self, to call her out on it.

Making every effort not to run into Darcy, Elizabeth bolted to her car just before five. The relief she felt by making it safely through her first day was short-lived as the anxiety of facing him the next day set in. Hoping to ease some of her tension—or perhaps to beat it into exhaustion—she went to the gym and took a long, long run on the treadmill, iPod blasting in her ears.

Earlier that morning when Darcy pulled into the courthouse parking lot and immediately spotted Elizabeth's car, his stomach first jumped with excitement, then dropped in disappointment. Things were going to be very, very different now that they were back. He snuck in through the rear entrance to avoid the possibility of a surprise meeting; he wasn't sure how well he would handle seeing her. His docket revealed that he would not have to find out today, as she was not scheduled to appear before him, but the rest of the week looked to be difficult. His relief at avoiding a painful confrontation was matched only by his irritation that he would not get the chance to see Elizabeth.

And as usual, his irritation got the better of him. As the morning progressed, his demeanor became sterner, his criticisms harsher, and his patience thinner. Even his secretary was not spared. Hoping to avoid any social interaction, he barked his lunch order to her and retreated to his office. He wouldn't have been surprised if she had spit in his sandwich, but luckily his lack of appetite spared him from finding out.

He sat morosely at his desk, pressing bread crumbs into his blotter and recalling the feel of Elizabeth's skin against his cheek, when his cell phone rang. The caller ID showed "Charley." In no mood to field Bingley's meandering conversation, Darcy ignored the call. He then saw that he had also missed a call from Georgiana. He did not respond to her text inviting herself to dinner.

Lunch did nothing to soothe his temper, and he powered through his afternoon docket even more angrily than the morning's. Instead of encouraging the attorneys to work out their differences, as he usually did, he made veiled threats of sanctions and made rulings that bound the parties into uncomfortable positions. He was in no humor to persuade people to do the right thing. It gave him a masochistic pleasure to see once-cocky counsels squirm under his glare. His normally lenient stance on first-time offenders and unsophisticated plaintiffs was not in play today: he dismissed the claim of a seventy-year-old widow against her hooligan neighbor and ordered an unemployed father to immediately pay back child support or face jail before sending a prostitute and her john to jail for thirty days. Still, at the end of the day, he felt no better.

When he got home, Georgiana was already there cooking dinner. For the first time in his life, he regretted that she had a key, and wished that she had not come to see him.

"Hi. You didn't return my call," she noted indignantly as he entered.

He slammed the door without responding. She rolled her eyes before ducking back into the kitchen.

"How was Mrs. R?" she called.

"Fine," he replied curtly.

He hoped if he made rudimentary conversation, he could satisfy Georgiana's mothering instincts and then usher her out as soon as possible. Tossing his cell phone and keys on the counter next to hers, Darcy sat tiredly at the table and bit his tongue while she carried on a one-sided conversation.

"Will, what's wrong?" she asked after a half hour of total silence from him. He blinked and looked up from his untouched dinner, as if seeing her for the first time.

"Nothing, sorry. Busy day tomorrow. I'm behind." It took a monumental effort to bite even those words out.

She observed him for a moment, and then picked up her cell phone from the counter. "I have a new puppy. He's really cute," she announced as she pulled up the photo album function of her phone. Wrinkling her brow, she realized she had his phone, not hers.

"Who is this?" She handed him the phone.

Darcy took the phone from her hand, and his heart exploded in a spasm of pain as he saw Elizabeth's face. They were lying in bed together—he was asleep, and she was grinning at the camera. He snapped the phone shut.

"It's no one," he said.

"Uh, then why is she in your bed?"

"It's no one."

It was a miracle that he managed to sound so calm. He clenched the phone tightly in his hand, resisting the temptation to look at the picture again, to scroll through and see if she had taken any other photos.

"I'm sorry, I've invaded your privacy," Georgiana said quietly.

He did not respond, did not even look at her as he squeezed the phone in his hand with white knuckles. Pain and rage coiled tightly in his chest, his breaths slow and deliberate, his face eerily blank of expression. As if sensing an ominous calm before a dangerous storm, Georgiana hastily gathered her things.

"I'll leave you alone. Call me tomorrow," she said as she hurried out the door. A few steps down the hall, she jumped when she heard the phone smash against the door.

Darcy picked up the pieces of the shattered cell phone. Instantly he regretted his temper tantrum. He wanted to see the photo again, to try to remember when it might have been taken. He wanted to read her expression. Was she wrinkling her nose like she did so often when she smiled? Was she smiling dreamily or mischievously? Was this the first morning, or later? He cursed himself, picked up his house phone, and dialed.

"Darcy?" came Bingley's voice. "I've been trying to call you for—"

Darcy cut him off. "Can you get her cell number for me?"

"I'll try."

Darcy hung up without another word. He had always been in tight control of his emotions, and losing his temper did not sit well with him. This facet of his personality was unacceptable, and he needed to regain control. Now.

The next day, anticipation sat like a lead weight in her gut as Elizabeth steeled herself for her first glimpse of Darcy. When he strode into the courtroom, the other attorney said cheerfully,

"Welcome back, Your Honor. Do anything fun on your vacation?"

In their other world—the world where she was Lizzy and he was Will—he would have made a joke about doing *her*. But they were back in the real world, and Darcy only replied with a low "Thank you, Mr. Johnson." His eyes flicked to her, then to his desk. "Good morning, Ms. Bennet."

Elizabeth murmured a greeting, knowing he must hear the waver in her voice. Could he hear her heart pounding too? While her opponent made his case for taking a deposition, Elizabeth twisted her fingers nervously behind her back. She presented her counter arguments, avoiding her usual lengthy exchanges. When both had made their cases, Darcy quietly ruled against Elizabeth before calling a recess and quickly exiting the courtroom.

Elizabeth exhaled the breath she had been unconsciously holding and closed her eyes. Had he seemed disappointed in her performance? She blindly stuffed her file into her briefcase and rushed back to her office. Once safely at her desk, she pressed the heels of her palms to her eyes, willing herself to calm down. Adrenaline had flooded her body the moment she saw Darcy. Now her fight-or-flight response had abated and she felt empty, deflated. She had never known that love could be so draining. Her five-minute encounter felt more like a five-mile sprint. With no hope of doing any more work that morning, Elizabeth went to the gym and took a yoga class, seeking peace from her turmoil.

After seeing Elizabeth, Darcy had to retreat to his chambers to regain his calm. Seeing her look so exhausted, and obviously not up to her job, distressed him. Was this what they could expect for the rest of their lives? Painful, awkward meetings that made him want to leap over the bench and comfort her? He ran a trembling hand through his hair and paced his office. He would give his right arm to see her in private. Should he call her? Could he risk it?

Unable to resist, he spent his lunch break at the local electronics store, transferring his destroyed phone's memory card to a new phone. Within twenty minutes he was sitting in his car staring at the photo that had provoked such a reaction in him. Elizabeth was smiling impishly at the camera. Even through the haze of pain, he felt himself smiling back at her, and his finger touched the image lightly, inadvertently closing the picture to a black screen. With her face no longer before him, his smile faded.

It was almost too much to hope that Jane would give Elizabeth's number to Bingley, especially if she knew that it was Darcy who wanted it. When the text message containing her number finally arrived, Darcy spent a long, long time weighing the advantages and drawbacks of calling her. In the end, he never came to a decision, and went for a long, long run instead.

Elizabeth's foul mood did not improve the next day, but she did allow Charlotte to persuade her to have lunch in the cafeteria. Distracted by the potential of seeing Darcy, Elizabeth barely listened to Charlotte's animated conversation. To her credit, Charlotte tried to buoy her spirits. Unfortunately, she chose to do so by concocting an outrageous story about Elizabeth's passionate but ill-fated love affair with a mysterious man while on vacation. The farce hit too close to home and Elizabeth had a hard time laughing it off. Matters were made worse and her fears were realized when she saw Darcy enter the cafeteria. Her feeble smile faded and she ducked her head to avoid his gaze.

"You are so seriously distracted. Thinking about all the hot love you got during vacation?" Charlotte snorted when Elizabeth failed to laugh at her story.

Elizabeth, trying to play along, smiled weakly and said, "What makes you so sure I had so much great sex during my vacation?"

"When you stop putting the cream in the coffee, it gets bitter."

Elizabeth's laugh was hollow as she watched Darcy beneath lowered lashes. He stared at her for a long moment, then left.

A few moments later Elizabeth's cell phone rang, showing an unidentified number. Charlotte grinned as she looked at the phone.

"Loverboy is calling!" Unable to continue, Elizabeth stood without answering her phone.

"I'm going back to work," she said and left, leaving Charlotte in surprised silence.

When she reached her office, Elizabeth checked her message.

"Elizabeth, it's Will. Please call me."

The unexpected sound of his voice—she had no idea how he got her number—threw her for a loop. But returning his call was out of the question. She wasn't ready to talk to him yet, but even if she was, it only delayed the inevitable. It had to end. Both of their careers were at stake.

The next day's status conference in front of Darcy did not go well. Ashamed of her previous day's performance, and determined to go on as if nothing lay between them, Elizabeth had ensured that she was well prepared. In the old days, she would have made her argument and, if Darcy disagreed, they would butt heads. But in the old days, it had never taken on a personal edge; his criticisms of her case had never felt like criticisms of *her*. Now, knowing how tender he could be, she felt the lash of his tongue more sharply. He seemed more vigilant, as if he did not trust her to play fair, as if he thought she would take advantage of his feelings for her. He was cold, businesslike, and ready with sharp, probing questions to ensure that no one—especially *she*—tried to pull the wool over his eyes. It was a tough afternoon, and Elizabeth returned to the office feeling as if she had been through the wringer.

As she sat at her desk staring into space, her cell phone rang, showing an unidentified number. She knew it must be Darcy, and that she should not answer. It took an enormous effort to resist answering, and her relief was palpable when the ringing stopped. By the end of the day she had three messages from him asking her to call. The temptation was so seductive that she found herself reaching for the phone. Instead, she went to the gym and took two consecutive spin classes.

Exhausted both emotionally and physically, Elizabeth collapsed on her bed after a hot shower. She looked at her cell phone for a long moment before her curiosity conquered her caution, and she checked her messages. She was both relieved and disappointed that there were no further messages from Darcy. There was, however, a picture message from Jane showing a margarita. With a wry smile, Elizabeth opened her stored pictures to send back her usual response—a "Just Say No" sign. Instead, she found herself looking at a picture of Darcy kissing her cheek in Trafalgar Square. The forgotten image seared her heart and rising tears stung her throat. Unable to resist any longer, she paged through the rest of the album. There she stood under the granite lions, and now they both looked contentedly into the camera. When she saw the picture of him in his riding breeches, boots propped on the ottoman and riding crop in his hand, she shook with silent tears. Not until after her phone battery died was she able to cry herself to sleep.

Friday saw Darcy in his worst mood yet. He reduced one attorney to tears and ejected another from the courtroom for not knowing the rules of evidence—all before lunch. In the hallway outside, attorneys whispered warnings and passed wary glances at each other. By the time Elizabeth arrived for her afternoon trial, an ominous silence had fallen over the courtroom.

Past experience had taught Elizabeth that she had better be well-prepared for a trial with Darcy, and her current emotional state allowed her to immerse herself in obscure case law. She was the most thoroughly prepared she had ever been.

All her legal research did not, however, prepare her for Darcy's anger. His face was a dark cloud threatening a storm as he called the case to order. She took a deep breath and squared her shoulders, and before long they were sparring like never before. He overruled her objections and she put them on the record for appeal. Their voices rose over each other, even to the concern of the other parties. They wrangled over evidence, with Darcy ruling in favor of Elizabeth's opponent. When she persevered in her arguments, Darcy glared at her.

"Ms. Bennet, you are walking a very fine line today," he said in a dangerous tone.

"What planet's laws are you following?" she finally exclaimed in exasperation, throwing her hands up in the air. A hush fell over the already quiet courtroom. Darcy's face reddened, and he stood up.

"I am calling a five-minute recess." He tossed his gavel on the bench. "Ms. Bennet, I'll see you in my chambers. Now." His tone brooked no argument. The opposing counsel stood to follow them.

"*Alone*."

Elizabeth's face flushed, and she slammed her file on her table before following Darcy to his chambers. Both walked in silence, their body language exuding fury as they passed his secretary. He opened the door to his office and closed it firmly after she had stepped in.

"Elizabeth, what the hell are you doing out there?"

"I'm preserving my case for appeal from your misguided rulings."

"Your objections are baseless, and you're not laying the foundation for your evidence."

"You're ruling against me just to prove you're not playing favorites."

The conversation would have been perfectly normal if he hadn't swept her into his arms and started kissing her hungrily as soon as the door was closed. Completely forgetting her determination to resist him, she returned his kisses eagerly.

"Why won't you return my calls?" he asked her between kisses.

"It's over, remember? It was all a dream," she answered huskily.

"No, that was the reality, this is the nightmare. I don't want to do this anymore." He stepped back from her, breathing heavily. His hair was mussed from her grabbing fingers.

"I don't, either. You promised it would end when we got back," she said in a low voice. "This is unethical."

"Elizabeth, I can't do this. I need to see you. We'll work something out."

"I can't see any way out," she stated. She put a hand to his face and wiped away a smudge of lipstick then smoothed down his hair. He pulled her suit jacket back in place.

"I'll think of something," he said and opened the door, cutting off any response she may have had. They returned to the courtroom.

"Mr. Johnson, I am removing myself from this case," Darcy announced as he returned to his bench.

"What? You can't do that!" Elizabeth cried.

Mr. Johnson also began to protest. Darcy held up his hand to both of them.

"During my conversation with Ms. Bennet, we discussed the merits of her argument. It was unintentional, but it was an *ex parte* communication, and I would feel more comfortable removing myself from this case."

"That's baloney!" Elizabeth exclaimed hotly. Darcy's face reddened again, and he glared at her. She recovered herself and lowered her voice. "It was not a conversation on the merits; it was a *technical* point."

"Ms. Bennet, would you like to return to my chambers and rehash our conversation or would you like me to sanction you now?" he said through gritted teeth, the dangerous tone creeping back into his voice. Her temper flared again. She pulled her checkbook out of her purse.

"Should I make the check to F. Darcy? Middle initial U?" she retorted angrily. He threw the gavel on his bench.

"Chambers. NOW!" he ground out, pointing at the hallway. She followed him, aware they were leaving a courtroom of gaping disbelief in their wake.

He closed the door and pulled her into his arms again, kissing her.

"I *cannot* be on this case," he said as he nuzzled her ear.

"Not after that, you can't," she admitted, chagrined. She rolled her head back to expose the tender flesh of her neck to him.

"Please see me tonight," he said huskily against her jawline.

"We shouldn't."

He was kissing her throat now. "I need to see you. Please." Her fingers had again curled in his wavy hair, and she hungrily sought his kisses.

"Will, this can't work."

"It *can*, we just have to make it work," he reassured her. He put his lips to hers again and gave her a passionate, probing kiss that seemed to suck the willpower out of her. His hands were beneath her suit jacket, splayed across her back. Then he slid one hand down to cup her bottom.

"Lizzy, please, I need you," he whispered in her ear. His voice shook with the depth of his feelings.

Elizabeth nodded in defeat, resting her head on his chest. He stroked a hand over her hair.

"Come to my place at eight o'clock," he said. "Nobody we know lives in my building. It will be safe." He gave her a gentle squeeze and released her to write his address on a business card.

"This is wrong," she said, troubled, as she took the card. He tipped her chin up with his forefinger, forcing her to meet his gaze.

"No, this is right. *We* are right. We have to work around the rule." She nodded again and straightened her jacket. He tucked a tendril of hair behind her ear and kissed her again.

They both returned to the courtroom, their faces flushed with desire that was construed as anger by everyone who saw them.

"Please take this case to Judge Clayton," Darcy ordered. Elizabeth said nothing. She regretted her retort to him. It had shown blatant disrespect for him in the courtroom, and by not sanctioning her for that behavior, he looked weak.

"Your Honor, I'm very sorry for my comment earlier. Please let me apologize. I am very sorry," she said clearly and genuinely contritely so that everyone would hear.

"Thank you, Ms. Bennet. Apology accepted." He saw that she was saving face for him, and he appreciated it.

Elizabeth drove home berating herself for her lack of willpower. Her resolution to end it with Darcy was no match for her desire to be with him, and for a moment, she had let herself believe that they could work it out. But once she was away from his seductive embrace, common sense returned. A clandestine affair didn't appeal to her; there was no joy or honor in sneaking around. Unless one of them took a drastic career detour—such as him stepping down from the bench, or her moving her practice to another jurisdiction—a romantic relationship was simply not possible. As she changed out of her business suit into a peasant skirt, tank top, and sandals, she decided that it was best to make a clean, firm break, and she promised herself that she would do exactly that… right after she met him tonight.

Feeling heavy with guilt, Elizabeth drove into downtown San Francisco and managed to find a parking spot a block away from Darcy's building. She was politely intercepted by the doorman, who called Darcy to ensure that she was expected. Then with an approving nod, the doorman waved her toward the elevator. "Twenty-first floor, Ms. Bennet."

Her nervousness climbed as the elevator glided silently to the top floor. By the time she reached the twenty-first floor, her heart was hammering and her mouth was dry. She took a deep breath and stepped into the hallway, barely taking notice that Darcy's penthouse occupied the entire floor. Her hand hesitated as she reached for the doorbell, and for a wild moment she nearly turned tail and ran away. Then she closed her eyes and pushed the button.

A second later the door flung open and before her stood Darcy, his face anxious. They stared at each other in frozen silence until, shaking himself, he stepped aside.

"Come in."

Elizabeth stepped into the foyer, noting the rich hardwood floor and warm honey lighting. It was a sophisticated yet comfortable foyer, giving her the same feeling of welcome she had felt at Pemberley. She rubbed her hands over her arms, trying to soothe her goose bumps.

"I was afraid you would change your mind," he admitted as he led her into the living room.

"I almost did." Her feet sunk into plush carpet, tickling her toes over the soles of her sandals. The room was furnished in dark woods accented by leather chairs, a comfortable sofa, and carelessly tossed throw pillows. The décor was masculine without exuding machismo, much like the man himself.

"Nice place," she said, avoiding his hungry gaze by staring pointedly at a painting.

"Don't," he said from behind her. She felt his fingers brush over her shoulder.

"Don't what?"

"Don't pretend there's nothing between us." He turned her to face him. "Lizzy, I've missed you so much," he whispered, pulling her gently to him. One hand splayed across her low back while the other tangled in her hair. He dipped his head and pressed his lips to hers. His arms tightened around her, and she responded to his kiss by twining her arms around his neck. The kiss deepened, drawing their bodies closer together. His hand tucked under her top, feeling her smooth skin against his palm.

She was helpless to stop him—she didn't *want* to stop him—when he hotly kissed her neck. By the time his lips dropped to her bare shoulder, soft moans came from her throat.

"All I think about is you. I can't eat. I can't sleep. I can't work." His voice sounded tired and strained, and Elizabeth realized that he was as miserable as she was. He knew their dilemma, and was as trapped by his feelings as he was by the rules that bound them. Darcy broke the kiss and took a deep breath before resting his chin atop her head. "It wasn't just sex, Lizzy. You know that. It was something more." Then, cupping her face in his palms, he searched her eyes. "Tell me you felt it too," he pleaded.

Unable to avoid that green gaze, she nodded and closed her eyes. "Yes," she whispered. Elizabeth turned her face into his palm and kissed it. Darcy caught her lips in another kiss, searing away her pangs of conscience by inflaming her emotions.

A moment later, he had lifted her in his arms and carried her to his bedroom. Sweeping aside the pillows, Darcy laid her gently on the bed before leaning over her. Clothes were peeled aside, revealing bare skin to exploring fingertips that lingered on every dip and hollow, tasting every rise and curve of flesh. Elizabeth inhaled his clean, mossy scent, losing herself in absorbing each sensation. Every sound that came from his lips tasting her skin, every electric zing as his fingers brushed over her eager and sensitive body, every beat of his heart against hers, held her rapt. When he finally buried himself in her, her sigh was as much one of relief as pleasure—at last she was whole.

They made love as twilight fell, and lay wrapped in each other's arms as darkness settled around them. Darcy's ragged breathing calmed, and his finger traced tender, lazy circles on her arm. Elizabeth pressed her nose into his neck and savored what she knew were the last moments of this affair.

"My term ends next April." His hushed voice broke the silence. "We could wait until then to be together."

She let out a quiet, humorless laugh. "Aren't we closing the barn door after the horse is already out?"

"I'm trying to do the right thing."

"I know. I'm sorry. I don't know if I can wait for that long."

"We could…"

"No. I won't sneak around."

"No. Of course not, I'm sorry. I don't know what I'm saying."

They fell into another silence.

"You could look into another area of law, one where we wouldn't have a conflict," he suggested.

"And give up everything that I've worked for?" She sat up and looked indignantly at him. "Why am I the one who has to sacrifice everything? Why don't *you* quit?"

"I can't quit, we're already short two judges!" He looked at the ceiling and rubbed his eyes. "I have a responsibility. I *can't* quit."

"I have responsibilities, too. I have clients who expect me to fight for them. I can't just dump them because I want to sleep with the judge."

Darcy nodded and Elizabeth settled back into his side, nestling her head against his shoulder.

"What do we do, then?" he finally asked.

"What we both know we have to do."

"I can't end this."

"Then I will." She sat up and pushed her hair from her face before swinging her feet over the edge of the bed. She shoved her arms through her shirt and jerked it over her chest. "It's not in either of our characters to lie and deceive everyone. You know as well as I do that it has to end." She stood and shimmied into her skirt before scuffing into her sandals. Darcy sat up and glared at her as she walked toward the door.

"And I'm supposed to just accept that? To see you every day and pretend that nothing ever happened? How is that any less a lie?"

Elizabeth paused and said over her shoulder, "It was always a lie, Will. We both knew what we were doing was wrong, but we were too selfish to stop. Now we're too selfish to make it work. It's just the price we have to pay."

Then she left.

Chapter 16

FANNY EYED THE CUCUMBER, Roquefort, and walnut tea sandwich with suspicion before popping it into her mouth. She chewed once, and an expression of bliss came over her face. She had always loved afternoon tea at the Ritz Carlton, even if it did cost an arm and a leg. As a little girl, her mother brought her here on special occasions or when she needed cheering up. It was a tradition she continued with her own girls, though Elizabeth had always felt the tradition too *frou-frou* for her sensibilities. Lou, on the other hand, was all about the elegant setting and over-the-top harpist.

"I think she's going to throw her back out," he said, nodding toward the swaying musician.

"That is a woman of great talent," Fanny replied. "Just look at her hairdo."

"What?" Lou laughed.

"Well, it's pinned and coiffed so elegantly that either it's a wig or she's got a stylist, and if she can afford either one she must make a pretty penny." Fanny nodded, having satisfactorily taken

Lou down her meandering path of logic. Lou only laughed and shook his head. Fanny popped another mini-sandwich into her mouth and chewed.

"What's wrong with Lizzy?" she asked around a slice of cheese.

"Where do I begin?"

"No, Louis! I'm serious. She hasn't been the same since she came back from England. Has she told you anything?"

"What makes you think something is wrong?"

"Oh, for heaven's sake, Lou! Can't you see that she's lost weight? I know my Lizzy, she never met a cookie she didn't like, and Pilates only gets you so far. She has only come to dinner once this week and even then she never made fun of me, not once! Now you tell me there's nothing wrong with her."

Lou paused over his tea, debating whether he could share any information with Fanny. The look of genuine worry that creased Fanny's face softened him.

"She met a man there, and it didn't work out," he said heavily.

Fanny clapped her hands together and gave out a childish laugh.

"Oh, how wonderful!"

"Fanny, darling, didn't you hear me? It didn't work out."

"Oh, well that doesn't matter, all that matters is that she isn't gay!"

"Hey! What's wrong with being gay?"

"Nothing, dear, you look wonderful in pink, but I want *grandchildren*."

"Fanny," Lou said gently, "Lizzy is devastated. Really. I think you should let up a bit on the marriage and family routine."

"So who is this idiot who dumped my daughter?"

"That, I'm afraid, I am not at liberty to reveal."

Fanny propped her chin on her fist and gave Lou a wistful look. "She never would tell me all the things she told you. I think she's even closer to you than she is to Jane."

"Well, Lizzy and I have been through a lot together. My parents weren't too happy when I came out, you know. She was always there for me."

"Yes, I know. I'm glad she's got you to confide in. I always considered you one of my girls, you know."

"I know."

"You'll look out for her, won't you?"

"I will."

"Good. Now, I seem to have misplaced my wallet..."

Making good on his promise to her mother, Lou insisted that Elizabeth come to his place that night for a little slumber party. With that prick Darcy messing with her mind, Elizabeth could use a night of female bonding. He had his supply of ice cream, donuts, and Diet Coke. They were going to have an old-fashioned sleepover, if he had to bind and gag her to do it.

It wasn't even dinner time yet, but Lou was already in pajama bottoms and a T-shirt with a wine glass in his hand when Elizabeth walked in. He took in her ragged appearance and without hesitation pulled her into his arms for a long, warm hug. He kissed the top of her head and silently cursed Darcy.

"You okay, sweet pea?" he asked, pressing his forehead to hers. She nodded and gave him a short, half-hearted laugh. He stood back and took her coat and overnight bag. "Let's get the bad part over with. Tell me what an asshole he is," Lou said as he settled onto the couch.

Elizabeth helped herself to a glass of wine and shook her head. "Honestly, I really don't want to talk about it. Let's talk about something else."

She ducked her head into his refrigerator and wrinkled her nose. Gay or not, he was still a bachelor, and he had an ample supply of mold and other unidentifiable substances in his fridge. "We'd better order pizza," she said, closing the door.

"I'm already on it," Lou replied. "I've also invited someone else over."

"Who?" Elizabeth asked, indignant that he would invite a third wheel to their pajama party.

"Charlotte Lucas."

"Charlotte? When did you suddenly get all cozy with her?"

"Can you keep a secret?" he asked.

She rolled her eyes at him. "Uh, I slept with my judge. I *think* I can keep a secret."

"I keep running across her at gay bars. She's a lezzie, Lizzy," he said with a smirk.

Elizabeth raised her eyebrows again. Charlotte Lucas, gay? *Of course*. How could she have missed it?

"You're not trying to set us up, are you? Because I'm in a really bad emotional place right now," she joked.

Lou grimaced and shook his head. "No, you're not her type."

As if on cue, Charlotte arrived with her own overnight bag, and all talk of Darcy blissfully came to an end. They drank a couple of bottles of wine and ate pizza and ice cream. It did not take long for them all to get drunk.

By nine o'clock, they had formed their own band called the Sexy Bitches and were jumping up and down on Lou's bed, singing Madonna songs into hairbrushes.

By ten o'clock, Charlotte had braided Elizabeth's hair and half of Lou's into cornrows.

By eleven o'clock, Lou had crooned Olivia Newton-John's "I Honestly Love You" to a picture of Colin Firth.

Hours later, Lou was sandwiched between them on the bed. Charlotte had drifted off to sleep, and Elizabeth was just hovering on the edge herself, when Lou whispered to her.

"Feeling better?"

Elizabeth smiled drowsily and nodded. She would survive. Once again, Lou had come to the rescue.

"Will, where have you been?" came Caroline's voice over his phone on Sunday. He silently swore and cursed himself for answering it.

"You know perfectly well I was on vacation with your brother," he replied coolly.

She laughed. "So prickly! I always did like that about you. We need to go over this purchase of Georgie's. I want to make sure all the provisions are right," she said.

He sighed. Caroline was arranging Georgiana's purchase of a house with funds from her trust fund which, as trustee, Darcy was required to approve.

"Of course, I'd forgotten. Can you meet me for lunch tomorrow?" he asked tiredly.

"Not today?"

Darcy looked down at himself: wrinkled boxer shorts, stained T-shirt, unshaven cheek. There was a possibility he might smell bad too.

"No, tomorrow is better," he replied.

On Monday, Darcy watched Elizabeth with depressed scrutiny. She sat in the back of his courtroom chatting quietly with her opposing counsel. It was Jim Roberts, the attorney who had suggested that Darcy ask Elizabeth out on a date so long ago at the Assembly Room. It felt like a lifetime ago.

Jim was sitting behind her, leaning forward and talking low in her ear in a gesture that Darcy plainly recognized as a come-on. When Elizabeth put her hand over her mouth and stifled a laugh, Darcy felt a surge of jealousy and had to ask the party before him to repeat his point. *How can she be acting as if everything is normal?*

He found himself straining to hear what Elizabeth was saying. She and Jim were whispering and giggling. How could she be *flirting?*

"Mr. Roberts, perhaps you and Ms. Bennet would like to take your conversation outside my courtroom?" Darcy said sternly.

Jim flushed and leaned back silently in his chair. Elizabeth glared at Darcy, her nostrils flaring, pursing her lips. Then she dropped her eyes to her lap. He felt smugly satisfied that he had ruined Jim's little come-on.

When Darcy finished the case immediately before him, Elizabeth and Jim came forward to present a settlement document for his approval. He approved it without comment and handed it back to Jim.

"Thank you, Your Honor," Elizabeth said deferentially.

Darcy could hear the sarcasm in her voice, but he did not respond, and she followed Jim out of the courtroom. Darcy was beginning to feel like he needed a drink.

He met Caroline an hour later at a local coffee shop. She was waiting for him at a stool by the window. When she saw him, she stood and hugged him.

"Will, it's so good to see you again," she said as she kissed his cheek, lingering just too long for mere friendship. Darcy put his hands on her arms and gently put some space between them.

"Thank you. You look well," he said. He didn't really know that she looked particularly well but remembered that she liked hearing that she did.

She smiled. "Thank you, it's Prada."

He nodded with approval that he did not really feel.

"Charles certainly was refreshed by his vacation. You don't look so well, though. Have you lost weight?" she said.

He shrugged and looked down at his tea.

"You should come out for the weekend. The salt air will do you good," she suggested, resuming her seat at the window bar.

"I don't have consumption, Caroline," he replied, rolling his eyes.

She rested her chin in her palm as she looked at him. "Why don't you take me out to dinner and tell me your troubles?"

He looked sideways at her and smiled. They hadn't been together for almost a year, yet she remained steadfast in her pursuit of him. He had to admire her persistence. It wasn't that she wasn't beautiful or enjoyable company; it was that she was just not to his liking. He had simple, natural tastes. He liked fruit versus cheesecake, running on a path versus a treadmill, vanilla perfume versus Obsession. Caroline was not simple and natural—she was exotic, complex, always impressing him with a mix of textures and smells. Her appearance was never lacking, never a thread or hair out of place. She had a beautifully sculpted body as a result of dedicated personal training and, he thought, perhaps some silicone.

And yet, her perfect appearance was off-putting. He liked flaws and imperfections, like the wrinkle between Elizabeth's brows that appeared when she was frustrated, or her little belly roll that showed she enjoyed ice cream a little too often. Imperfections were honest; perfection was not. He could not now comprehend how he could have found Caroline attractive, or how he could have been satisfied with the "comfort" she brought him. Everything was so clear to him now.

"Thank you, but no," he answered, smiling at her.

She sighed and gave him a coquettish look.

Darcy's eyes were drawn to the window where, to his horror, he saw Elizabeth and Charlotte Lucas walking past. Both looked at him, Elizabeth with something like shock and Charlotte with something like humor. His heart sank. Of course Elizabeth would walk by when he was sitting next to a blatantly flirting Caroline. *Of course*. He put a shaky hand on the back of his neck and resisted the urge to run after her and tell her that it wasn't what it looked like.

Caroline perceived his changed mood and sighed. His expression told her it was back to business as usual. With resignation, she pulled out her portfolio and reviewed the documents. They finished their coffee, he in silence, she in observation. He was different, changed somehow.

That afternoon, Darcy tried to catch Elizabeth's eye, but she refused to be caught. She gave a perfunctory performance in court and left quickly.

Elizabeth had been not just shocked but also hurt by seeing Darcy with the vaguely familiar lovely brunette in the coffee shop. Had they merely been talking, she would not have minded, but the woman was so blatantly trying to get into his pants, and he looked like he was enjoying the attention!

She tried to ignore it, but it left Elizabeth in a seriously foul and depressed mood. After all, he was a very, very handsome man, and he wasn't likely to rush into a quick one-night stand, was he? And she did break it off with him… but just because she couldn't have him didn't mean he could just throw himself at the next pretty woman, did it? And Charlotte… Charlotte would not let her forget it. She laughed and said she hoped old Darcy was finally getting some poontang to make everyone else's life easier. She wouldn't *stop* saying it, either!

For the rest of the week, Darcy looked longingly at Elizabeth. When she succeeded in getting Charlotte to take her cases, he left her messages on her cell phone. When she refused to return his calls, he sent her flowers with no card. By Thursday, he was at wit's end at her resolution to ignore him. He was going to have to call in the big guns. He decided to consult an old friend—who just happened to be Elizabeth's boss.

"Will, to what do I owe this pleasure?" Mr. Gardiner asked pleasantly when he took Darcy's call.

"Well, Milton, I thought it had been a long time since we'd had a drink after work and I wanted to invite you out this evening," Darcy said easily.

"I don't mind if I do!" Mr. Gardiner replied cheerfully, and they agreed to meet at six.

Milton Gardiner, a stout, genial man in his early sixties, had been a sort of mentor to Darcy when he first arrived in the States. Although they'd not worked together for nearly a decade, the two remained friends. Darcy was counting on that friendship now.

They met at the Top of the Mark, a landmark restaurant in San Francisco that boasted spectacular views of the city and bay. Once they had ordered drinks, they settled into a quiet, comfortable corner and spent a few minutes catching up.

"I expected you to be retired and sunning yourself in San Diego by now," Darcy commented.

"Ha! I wish! I'm afraid my plan to move quietly to San Diego has been foiled. Instead, I'm opening an office there."

"Really! What happened?"

"My practice is being purchased by DeBourgh & Associates, and they want to open an office in San Diego. As part of the deal, I agreed to open the San Diego office, hire their staff, and get the office running. DeBourgh will hire her own attorneys. It's more than I wanted to do, but it will be worth the payout. I'll be able to retire very comfortably when everything is completed."

They talked a little more about the merits of San Diego, and then Darcy cleared his throat.

"Actually, Milton, the reason I asked you to join me was that I wanted to ask you for some advice. May I pick your brain, off the record, of course?" Darcy asked as he swirled his drink, gazing at the dimly reflected cubes of ice.

"Of course. May I assume that this is a theoretical situation?" Mr. Gardiner asked, assuring Darcy in so many words that their discussion would remain between them.

"Yes." Darcy took a swig of his drink, building his courage. "Let's suppose a judge became interested in a lawyer who appears regularly before… her. What is your opinion on the ethical situation of a judge dating a lawyer?" he asked without looking at Mr. Gardiner.

Mr. Gardiner thought for a moment. "It's not completely unheard of, but it is sticky. I think the judge would have to remove… herself… from all of that attorney's cases, possibly from the cases of that attorney's firm, unless the attorney willingly exempted… himself… from appearing before that judge."

Darcy nodded. "I thought as much. And when do you think removal is appropriate? Meaning at what stage of the relationship?" Darcy continued. Mr. Gardiner looked at him through lowered lids.

"Well, that's difficult to say, but I would think as soon as the judge understands that there is a mutual, serious interest. Let's say they go on a couple of dates, but there's no spark. I don't think the judge would be obligated to remove himself. But let's say they date steadily for a couple of months, then I think the judge has an obligation to notify all concerned parties of the relationship and the possibility of a conflict. Then the parties can decide whether they want to waive the conflict. Most likely in that situation, the attorney... himself... should not appear but someone from his firm may."

Darcy nodded. "And if it progresses beyond dating? What if they become intimate, serious?"

Mr. Gardiner chuckled. "I don't think there's any doubt—the attorney may not make any material appearances before the judge. The firm will need to advise everyone of the possible conflict, and the parties can determine whether to strike the judge from the case. In no circumstances should that attorney be trying cases before the judge. Even if the judge could maintain impartiality, the appearance of conflict would be overwhelming and would jeopardize every case. Now, Darcy, do you want to tell me what's going on? Knowing that Judge Clayton is married, I highly doubt she is dating one of the attorneys appearing before her." Mr. Gardiner, eager for some juicy gossip about Darcy's love life, leaned forward.

Darcy sighed and put down his glass. "If I remove myself, I would need to disclose the relationship. I would rather that she voluntarily withdrew from my cases to avoid the need to offer an explanation. I've not tried any of her cases since we became involved, but I don't want the appearance of bias to put any of her past cases in jeopardy. If we reassign her cases now, we can skate by without much problem, I think." Darcy raised his eyes to Mr. Gardiner, who waited expectantly. "Will you reassign Elizabeth's cases before me to other attorneys in your office?" Darcy asked quietly.

Mr. Gardiner's expression remained expectant, until realization sunk in. "Elizabeth?" he said quietly. Darcy nodded. "That can't be. She hates you."

"We did get off on the wrong foot, but we've worked it out."

"When… when did this happen?" Mr. Gardiner choked out.

"We met at the seminar in London. It happened so fast." Darcy seemed lost in thought for the moment. "There was nothing going on before then, I swear it. But things progressed so quickly that it would be natural for anyone to think we have been involved far longer."

Mr. Gardiner blew out a breath. "Darcy, I am disappointed in you," he said quietly. "I thought you had more self-control."

The criticism stung Darcy. "Milton, you know that I am not an impulsive man. I am very serious about Elizabeth. I have considered the implications of our relationship carefully, and this relationship is important enough to ask you this favor."

Mr. Gardiner nodded slowly. "Does she feel the same?"

"I believe she does. But you know Elizabeth. She is so damned headstrong that as soon as you give her a piece of advice, she does the opposite just to prove you wrong. And usually, she does." He smiled briefly. "The problem is that if she suddenly begins striking me as a judge, it will look suspicious.

I think she feels that her clients won't approve. I felt that if perhaps you were able to rearrange her trials and assign mine to other attorneys, then it would be your decision and not hers."

"Then you haven't discussed this with her?"

Darcy shook his head. Telling Milton that Elizabeth had refused his calls would probably not work in Darcy's favor.

"This may have implications beyond my current attorneys," Mr. Gardiner said slowly. "The DeBourgh buyout may be affected if the entire firm is prohibited from appearing before you."

Darcy swore. "Then it must be done immediately," he said. "I won't have your retirement affected by this."

"Elizabeth won't take kindly to my rearranging her cases without an explanation."

"She will be furious if she finds out that I spoke with you."

"Nevertheless, I won't do it without her consent," Mr. Gardiner replied.

"And if she refuses?"

"Then you'll have to remove yourself voluntarily from her cases."

Darcy groaned, and ran a hand through his hair. "God, I'm sorry, Milton. I've made a total mess of it."

"Does anyone else know?"

"Her sister and my best friend, but no one else that I know of. They understand the situation, and I am confident that they will reveal nothing. Besides, they aren't in the legal community."

"In any event, make certain they understand the importance of keeping this under their hats. Hopefully, Elizabeth will see sense and agree not to appear before you."

***

The next afternoon, Mr. Gardiner asked Elizabeth to come to his office. He closed the door behind them, gestured her to take a seat on the leather sofa in his office, and sat next to her.

"Elizabeth, I understand that you are having some trouble with Judge Darcy," he began delicately.

"We do have our arguments," she murmured, looking into her lap.

"It has been suggested that perhaps it is better that you not appear before him."

"Who has suggested that?"

Mr. Gardiner sighed. "He has."

Elizabeth felt a flush creep up her neck to her cheeks. "Did he say why?"

"He did. Elizabeth, you are both playing a dangerous game."

"We aren't. I ended it, he just won't accept it," she replied, humiliated beyond belief that she was having this conversation with her boss.

"Look, Elizabeth, I'm telling you this as a friend and, I hope, a surrogate father. Don't play this game. You can't win. It's emotionally difficult for both of you and can be professionally devastating to all of us. As your boss, I'm telling you that you cannot appear before him; whether that's voluntary or involuntary is your choice."

"I know," she said miserably. "I wanted to just go on as if nothing had happened, but he won't let me."

"Perhaps because it's not so easy for him."

"It's not easy for me, either, but at least I'm trying to do right by everyone!" she exclaimed.

"Lizzy, there *is* no way to do that. The bell can't be unrung. Now you have to do the right thing and stay out of

Will's courtroom. Then you're free to see him or not, whichever you please."

"It's not that simple!" she cried, scrubbing a tear from her cheek. "What if, after all this trouble, it turns out it was nothing but a fling? What do I do then? You know it's always harder for a woman. His reputation won't be hurt, but *mine* will. Everyone will say 'Oh, there's that attorney who slept with the judge to win her cases.' Who can survive that?"

"What do you want to happen?"

"I don't know!"

"I can't protect you when I'm gone, you know. DeBourgh will fire you in a heartbeat if she gets a whiff of this, so you'd better make a decision fast. Until you decide, I think the best thing for you is a little distance. I'm sending you to San Diego instead of me."

"What?!"

"Lizzy, I can't risk the livelihood of this entire firm for your bad decision, well-intentioned though it might be. Either you go and figure out what you want, or I'm afraid you'll have to leave the firm. I'm sorry." He placed a comforting hand on hers. "As long as I am here, there will be a place for you when you come back."

She nodded curtly. "When would I have to leave?"

"I had planned to go next week. I can have your cases covered in the meantime, while you get your affairs in order." She stood to leave. "Elizabeth, don't be angry with him. Will did what he thought was best, for both of you," Mr. Gardiner said.

She laughed mirthlessly. "Really? He won't accept that it's over, ratted me out to my boss, and is forcing me to relocate to San Diego. How thoughtful of him! How shall I ever repay such kindness?"

She stormed from Mr. Gardiner's office and back to her own, where she paced angrily. It was nearly five o'clock. Darcy would likely still be at work. She strode to the elevator and punched the button, then stomped toward his secretary.

"Is Judge Darcy still in?" Elizabeth asked through gritted teeth.

His secretary, surprised, asked, "Is he expecting you?" Her hand crept toward the phone.

"He *ought* to be," Elizabeth fumed and headed toward his door, swung it open, and slammed it behind her. Darcy looked up from his desk, startled. Over his phone intercom, his secretary was saying, "Ms. Bennet is on her way to see you."

"Thank you." Darcy punched off the intercom. She stood before him, hands on hips, cheeks flaming, looking as if she were ready to go into battle.

"What's wrong?" he asked cautiously, walking slowly toward her.

"What's wrong? Well, since you asked so nicely, I'm relocating to San Diego. Happy?" she replied tightly.

"What?!" He took a few steps closer to her.

"Yes, Mr. Gardiner felt it would be prudent to get a few miles between us. Thank you so much for revealing my most intimate affairs to my boss!"

"You can't go! You quit, right?"

"Don't be absurd! Of course I didn't quit. I just said I'm relocating to San Diego. Are you deaf?"

Darcy's anger was rising. "I asked him to take you off my cases!"

"Congratulations, you succeeded!"

"You don't have to go."

"Yes, I do." Suddenly, Elizabeth's energy waned. She wanted to cry. She pressed her fingers on her forehead.

Darcy closed the space between them. "Is this what you want, Elizabeth? Do you really want it to end?"

She leaned against the door and looked toward the ceiling. "You said what happens in England, stays in England."

"That was before I fell in love with you."

"You are screwing up my career."

"Doesn't it mean anything to you that I love you?" He put his arms on either side of her, effectively trapping her against the door. She could smell that mossy scent again and it threatened to lull her back into his arms. She fought it.

"You love me? Since when? Since you got me transferred?" she asked tiredly.

"I told you that I loved you in England," he answered softly, the hurt evident in his voice.

She turned her head away from him and laughed. "Yes, once when you were drunk and once during sex. How am I supposed to take that seriously?"

"I told you I would never lie to you!"

"I didn't think you were lying. I just didn't think you meant it. Would it kill you to say it over dinner?"

"I'm saying it now. I love you." She didn't answer. "Lizzy, do you love me?" he asked quietly. She looked away. "Elizabeth, do you *love* me?" he demanded, becoming angry.

She looked down but did not answer.

"*Do you love me?*" he shouted at her.

"*Yes!*" she shouted back.

"*Then tell me, dammit!*" He pounded his hands on the door on either side of her for emphasis.

"*What difference does it make?*" she cried, pushing him in the chest, freeing herself from the enclosure of his arms. She turned her back to him and took a deep breath and pressed her fingers to her eyes, willing herself not to cry. "What difference does it make?" she whispered.

Darcy put his arms around her from behind. "It makes a difference to *me*," he said, hugging her. "All I want is to know you love me. Tell Milton that you won't go to San Diego. Quit and we'll find you a different job, one where we can be together without any conflict."

Elizabeth pulled away from him and turned to face him, arms crossed over her chest. She was furious with him for interfering and for forcing her to make a choice. "You don't get it, do you? I don't want to find another job, and I don't want to quit. You can't rule my life the way you rule your courtroom! You can't just make a decision and that's the end. What about what *I* want?"

He stood speechless. She shook her head and dropped her arms to her side.

"Look, this has gotten completely out of hand. I think we need to take a break," she said.

"Take a break?" he repeated stupidly.

"I'll be gone for several months, setting up the office in San Diego. I think the drama of this affair has blown everything out of proportion. Maybe with a little distance, we can put this back into perspective."

He laughed humorlessly. "And in the meantime, I sit here twiddling my thumbs, waiting for you to figure out what you want?" he retorted. She didn't answer, and he stared angrily at her.

"I'm not asking you to wait for me," she said finally.

He did not respond. After an uncomfortable silence, she left. She marched past the unabashedly eavesdropping secretary and strode angrily to her car, managing to drive home before she let her rage, frustration, and heartbreak flood forth.

Darcy, on the other hand, was taking his ire out elsewhere. He marched angrily to the elevator and punched the button. He threw open the door to Gardiner & Associates and stormed directly to Milton's office.

"What did you do?" he said furiously, slamming the office door behind him. Mr. Gardiner turned in surprise.

After a moment, Mr. Gardiner said, "I saved all of our careers and gave her some breathing space."

"You stabbed me in the back! I came to you for help!" Darcy fumed.

"Stabbed you in the back? That's rich! You sneak around, knowing you are in serious ethical violation, and then expect me to dig you out? You nearly wreck my retirement. You force me to send one of my best attorneys away. I'm sorry, I'm not quite seeing the knife in *your* back!"

Darcy paced angrily, hundreds of retorts on his tongue, none of which rang true. Milton was right. He had botched this badly. He needed to calm down, to recalibrate his mind so that he could think straight.

He sat wearily on Mr. Gardiner's couch. Mr. Gardiner silently offered him a glass of scotch. Darcy waved it away.

"I want you to understand that I am in love with her," Darcy said quietly, his head in his hands.

"Then you need to give her this time. I have a feeling Elizabeth will come back to you. But she's angry right now, and the more you push, the harder she will resist. You should know that by now. She is independent, some would say stubborn. But she is good at heart, and she will figure it all out in her own time."

"And if she doesn't?"

"Well, then you will have to go after her and remind her why she fell in love with you in the first place."

Chapter 17

DESPITE HER ANGER AT Darcy for the role he played in her transfer, Elizabeth came to welcome the relocation to San Diego. In her heart she knew that Darcy meant well, but she was undecided in her own mind what she wanted. She knew she loved him, but the ethical conflict loomed. His high-handedness in telling Mr. Gardiner encroached too far upon Elizabeth's free will.

Perhaps more importantly, however, Elizabeth was afraid that if she did commit to Darcy—and essentially gave up her career—that she would grow to resent him, and that would ultimately destroy whatever relationship they had. At a minimum, the transfer would give her breathing space to clear her head and decide what she wanted. For now, she just wanted to be alone.

It took only two weeks of burying herself in viewing leasing properties by day and working on appeals by night for Elizabeth's exhaustion to overcome her anger. Long evenings alone without Jane or Lou gave her time to reflect on whether she'd made the right choice. Thoughts of Darcy no longer made her beat her pillow in frustration. Instead, she began to wonder how he was, what he was doing, and how well he was getting over her. Each evening she returned to her suite, showered tiredly, ate listlessly, and fell into bed, beat but unable to sleep. Every night she picked up her phone to call Darcy, and every night her courage flagged. She'd left things badly with him and wasn't sure she could bear the rejection if he decided that the affair wasn't worth saving. Too proud to summon Lou for company, she spent the Fourth of July alone in her bed, watching fireworks on television, and hugging a pillow to her chest.

Lou Hurst paced aimlessly outside the courthouse, waiting for Charlotte, with whom he'd become closer since Elizabeth's departure three weeks ago. With his Blackberry in hand, he sat at a vacant bench and checked his email, hoping for some word from Elizabeth. A moment later, a shadow fell over him. He looked up and was surprised to find Darcy standing beside him. Lou's guard instantly went up.

"Hello, Will," he said coldly.

"Where is she?" Darcy asked quietly.

"Where you sent her, San Diego."

"Do you know where she's staying?"

"Yes." Lou did not elaborate. Over Darcy's shoulder, Lou saw Charlotte walking toward them.

"Will you tell me?"

"No." Lou stood, tucked his Blackberry into his jacket pocket, and looked squarely at Darcy. "She doesn't need any more of your mind games."

Darcy barked out a bitter laugh. "My mind games? I've been nothing but straight with her from the start. She's the one playing games. 'I love you, but I don't want to see you.' 'It feels right but it's wrong.' 'I think I'll move to San Diego,'" Darcy mimicked.

At that moment, Charlotte joined them.

"Hello, Judge. Hi, Lou. You two know each other?"

Lou said nothing. He knew Elizabeth's relationship with Darcy was a secret, and if he was to help her recover from this sham romance, the less said the better.

But Darcy nodded. "Through Ms. Bennet," he said, not taking his eyes away from Lou.

Lou looked at him in annoyance. Darcy turned his attention to Charlotte.

"Speaking of Ms. Bennet, where has your little friend been these last few weeks?" he asked, smiling genially at her.

"Didn't you know? Lizzy was transferred to San Diego for a few months," she said.

"Ah, San Diego. Lovely town. I hope Milton has put her up at the L'Auberge Del Mar. It's the best hotel there," Darcy said.

Charlotte laughed. "Lord, no! She's at the Westin."

Darcy smiled in satisfaction and looked slyly at Lou, who became visibly angry.

"Come on, Charlotte, we don't want to take up any more of the judge's time," Lou urged, taking her by the elbow.

"Oh, I'm in no hurry," Darcy said pleasantly.

"Well, we *are*," Lou retorted with bare civility. He tugged Charlotte by the arm, but she seemed reluctant to leave Darcy behind.

"Would you like to join us for dinner?" she asked Darcy before Lou could protest.

"Yes, it happens that I'm free tonight," Darcy said without hesitation.

Charlotte blinked in surprise. Clearly, she had not expected him to accept. "Oh. Uh, okay, well, come on."

She glanced apologetically at Lou, who glared back at her. The three walked in silence toward the Assembly Room, where they quickly found an empty table before Charlotte excused herself to the restroom.

"Very funny," Lou growled at Darcy.

Darcy leaned across the table toward Lou. "You are her best friend. Don't you want her to be happy?"

"I suppose you think she'll be happy with *you?*"

"Why don't you ask *her?*" Darcy bit out.

"From what she's told me, you're only making her miserable."

"What exactly has she told you?"

Lou opened his mouth to spit out a list of offences and stopped short. For all her confidences in Lou, Elizabeth had never once said anything *bad* about Darcy. Oh, she was annoyed by him, and the relationship was breaking her heart, but she'd never blamed Darcy for any of it. His confidence wavered. He clamped his mouth shut and watched the emotions flicker across Darcy's face. He saw resentment and then uncertainty and then, ultimately, sadness.

Darcy looked down at his hands. "I won't ruin your dinner," he said quietly. He took a deep breath. "Tell Elizabeth..." He paused. "Tell her that I miss her." With that, Darcy rose and walked quickly from the bar.

Lou sat in surprised silence. In his loyalty to Elizabeth, he'd assumed that Darcy was the cad, a playboy villain who swept her off her feet then dumped her when things got sticky. But this brief interaction made him think twice. Darcy hadn't acted like a skirt-chaser. He'd acted like someone who was *hurt*.

Charlotte returned from the restroom. "Where did the judge go?" she asked.

"He remembered he had to be somewhere, said he was sorry," Lou replied absently. He was already typing a message to Elizabeth on his Blackberry:

<We need to talk.>

Darcy drove home depressed. He understood Elizabeth's anger and need for space. He had made a huge blunder by going to Mr. Gardiner, and only Mr. Gardiner's quick thinking and discretion kept them all from disaster. His natural inclination to solve the problem quickly had backfired badly for him.

He was further frustrated by the loyalty of Elizabeth's friends. Jane and Bingley had both been uncharacteristically tight-lipped about Elizabeth, Mr. Gardiner had flatly refused to discuss her, and Lou was outright hostile. Even though he had tricked Charlotte into revealing Elizabeth's location, what good was it if she didn't want to see him?

Sitting at his kitchen table, Darcy rubbed his eyes and sighed. How had he gotten into this mess?

"Hey."

Darcy opened his eyes at the sound of Georgiana's soft voice. The condominium, which Darcy had purchased from a down-on-his-luck musician, had a soundproof music room where he kept a piano for Georgiana. She'd evidently been practicing when he came home.

"Hey," he answered with a half-smile.

"You seem down," she remarked, sitting down beside him.

"I'm all right," he answered, his overprotective instincts preventing him from burdening her with his troubles.

"Why don't you get your guitar and play with me?" she suggested. When he first shook his head, she took his hand and pulled him from the chair. Finally, with a reluctant sigh, Darcy sat on a padded bench in the music room and tuned his guitar. The simple act of making music, of improvising and creating sound from strings and wood, lightened his spirits. After two hours and a couple of beers, Darcy had cheered considerably.

"I have a group of friends, and we play in a coffee shop every Friday night," Georgiana said casually. "We need a guitarist."

Darcy let the invitation hang in the air for a moment, then said, "I'll sit in until you find one." The time he would have to devote to practicing would give him something—anything—else to do than mope about Elizabeth.

Chapter 18

THE ANNOUNCEMENT OF JANE'S engagement to Bingley at the end of July gave Elizabeth the perfect excuse to return to Meryton. She wanted to talk to Jane, to confide her heartbreak to her, and to learn anything she could of Darcy. She wavered back and forth and, on impulse, purchased a ticket Friday afternoon to return in time for dinner that night. By the time she had packed, it was too late to call Jane.

As the taxi dropped her at the house she shared with her sister, Elizabeth was suddenly struck by how homesick she was. As soon as she was in the door, she wrapped her arms around a surprised Jane in a tight hug.

"Hi, Janey," she muffled against her shoulder. Jane laughed, returning the hug with equal emotion.

A moment later, a sniffling Elizabeth pulled away. "Surprise!" she laughed, wiping her eye with the back of her hand. "Are you going somewhere?" she asked, disappointed, noticing for the first time the forest green silk dress that swept gracefully over Jane's shoulders.

"Not exactly," Jane answered hesitantly. "I'm having a few friends over for a dinner party. An engagement party."

"An engagement party? You didn't tell me you were planning anything," Elizabeth replied, stung by the exclusion.

"Will's coming," Jane replied, biting her lip. "I didn't want you to have to see him." She rubbed Elizabeth's arms. "If you want to come, you're welcome. If you want to hide, I won't tell him that you're here."

"I'm certainly not going to hide from him," Elizabeth said with determination. "I can be in the same room with him for a few hours." She didn't feel nearly as confident as she sounded. She was not sure she was ready to see Darcy yet; her stomach was already tumbling like an acrobat at the thought.

"Are you sure?" Elizabeth nodded. "Then you'd better go change. Remember, the best revenge is looking fabulous." As Elizabeth began to climb the stairs toward her room, Jane called after her, "That black satin number should do the trick."

Elizabeth chuckled and shook her head, but didn't question Jane's taste, and after freshening up, she shimmied into the sleek, sleeveless dress with the plunging neckline in front and a deep V in the back. She draped a long, gold chain with small diamond studs over her neck and began to search for shoes. Her eyes landed on the red python-skin stilettos she'd bought in London, but the ache the memory brought to her chest made her pass them over for a pair of gold strappy heels. There was no knowing how the evening would go, but she didn't want to seem as if she was purposefully reminding him of their affair.

She brushed her hair and did what she could to tame her curls into something presentable. Her eyes looked almost too dark in her pale face, and she hurriedly applied bronzer to put some color back in her cheeks. One last swipe of lipstick and she was ready. With a deep breath, Elizabeth gathered her courage and made her way downstairs, her stomach coiling into a tighter knot with each step.

Instantly she saw Darcy across the living room, even though his back was to her. She recognized his broad shoulders and the way his blazer hung on them, his hair curling slightly over the collar. He had that same stance of casual elegance that she remembered from Pemberley. Every shred of emotion that she had managed to bury over the last few weeks wormed its way to the surface in icy prickles. The only thought in her mind was that she still loved him and wanted nothing more than to go to him.

She was, therefore, shocked and dejected to see a tall, slender brunette in a lovely saffron dress snake her hand into the crook of his elbow.

"Elizabeth!" At the sound of her name, Elizabeth turned just in time to avoid Darcy's piercing look. "Elizabeth, so good to see you again!" Richard Fitzwilliam said as she walked toward her with an eager grin. He gave her a warm hug and kissed her on the cheek.

"I'm afraid I'm the unlucky thirteenth guest," she said to him, willing herself not to look in Darcy's direction.

"No worries, my date ditched me. You can be 'Sharon' tonight," Richard grinned, tucking her hand in his elbow. "Unless you have a date?" he asked with mock suspicion. She shook her head and allowed him to lead her to the dinner table. As they sat down, Elizabeth was eternally grateful to see that Jane had hastily placed her as far from Darcy as possible.

Richard, who Elizabeth recalled to be an incorrigible flirt, was living up to her recollection. He casually draped his arm over her chair as they talked, making good eye contact and leaning in close to hear what she said. Every once in a while, his hand brushed over her shoulder as he made some point. Once, a million years ago, Elizabeth would have appreciated the attention. Now it made her cringe inwardly as she wondered what Darcy must be thinking.

So caught up in her self-conscious worries was Elizabeth that she did not realize until it was too late that Richard was telling the whole table about her karaoke performance.

"And then she spanked herself!" he exclaimed, causing the whole table to laugh appreciatively. The whole table except for Darcy, whose glare Elizabeth could feel boring into her head even as she stared unblinking at the person across from her, smile frozen in place. *Could this really get any worse?* she wondered. Of course it could.

The elegant brunette, who Elizabeth recognized as the woman from the coffee shop but who she had managed to avoid meeting, was leaning in close to Darcy's ear and whispering something with a secret smile on her lips. Moments later, she stood to toast the newly engaged couple.

"To Charles and Jane. I don't know how two people could be more alike in their temperaments, generosity, and kindness. They are the type of people one wants to detest," she said, to laughter. "But, of course, you cannot help but love them. I wish you many years of happiness, and I think I speak for everyone here when I say we would all be fortunate to have one tenth of the love you have for each other." She raised her glass. "Love long."

"Thank you, Caroline," Bingley said, raising his glass to her.

Caroline. Caroline Bingley. Charley's sister, and Darcy's on-again, off-again lover. Elizabeth felt her heart sink to new depths of depression as she glanced over at them. Caroline had placed one hand over Darcy's while she sipped from her wine glass. Darcy stared at his untouched dinner plate, his jaw clenched.

All the irrational hopes of a romantic reunion that had sprung to Elizabeth's heart died a miserable death when she saw Caroline lean over and kiss Darcy's cheek. Tears glazed her eyes and before Richard could notice them, she excused herself for some air. She left the house and walked to the sidewalk, rubbing her hands over her arms and blinking away her tears as she did. Moments later, Darcy was behind her.

"Was your performance for *him?*" His voice was angry and bitter.

"Who?" she asked tiredly.

"My cousin."

"Your cousin?"

"Yes. Richard Fitzwilliam, my cousin. Or didn't you know?"

"How was I supposed to know he was your cousin?" she asked, annoyed by his accusatory tone.

"Yes, Fitzwilliam is such a common name. There are thousands of us running around dating you."

"Sorry, next time I'll check your family tree before I go out on a date," she snapped over her shoulder. "I see you haven't lost any time taking up with old friends."

"There's nothing going on with Caroline," he answered quickly.

"Somebody ought to tell *her* that."

"Why do you care? You told me not to wait for you."

"I did. Did you expect me to wait for you?" She could barely keep her temper in check as jealousy and anger flared in her chest.

Darcy grabbed Elizabeth's arm and spun her around to face him just as Caroline called his name from the porch. Elizabeth looked pointedly at his hand, squeezing her arm so tightly, before raising her eyes to his. His hand dropped to his side, fist clenching and unclenching.

"She's very lovely. You'd better get back to her, or you'll be sleeping alone tonight."

Elizabeth skirted around him and walked toward the house, arranging her features into an expression of calm pleasantness. She murmured a soft "Excuse me," as she squeezed past Caroline into the house, Darcy fast on her heels.

"Who is she?" Caroline asked, still within Elizabeth's earshot.

"No one."

Darcy's response inflamed Elizabeth's fury further. *No one?* Not even "an ex girlfriend" or "Jane's sister"? She would teach him that she was *no one!*

She joined Richard at the table, slipped her hand easily into his, and spent the rest of the evening flirting with him for all she was worth. By the end of the night, he was infatuated with her. And Darcy was furious.

When the party began to break up and the guests began to leave, Richard persisted by Elizabeth's side, determined to have a moment alone with her. Darcy had the same inclination and resolutely stayed. Jane and Bingley looked worriedly at each other, seeing Darcy's anger, Caroline's suspicion, Elizabeth's spite, and Richard's amusement.

"Don't you have an early meeting tomorrow?" Darcy said to Richard, annoyed.

"Darcy, have you *met* my charming date? Who could possibly want to leave her just to make an early meeting?" Richard laughed, squeezing Elizabeth's hand. Elizabeth tilted her head at Darcy and smiled.

"I don't believe I've had the pleasure of meeting your date, Judge Darcy," she said sweetly.

"Caroline, this is Elizabeth Bennet. She is Jane's sister," he said formally. "Caroline is Charley's sister, Elizabeth. She'll be helping Jane over the next few months with the wedding preparations." He smiled lazily at Elizabeth and snaked his arm around Caroline's waist. "Elizabeth is an attorney who, until recently, regularly appeared before me. She has transferred to a San Diego office."

With that little speech, Darcy effectively told Elizabeth that he would be seeing a lot of Caroline and not much of her, told Richard that Elizabeth was not readily accessible, and eased Caroline's claws out of him by letting her know that Elizabeth was safely hundreds of miles away.

Caroline extended her hand to Elizabeth. "It's always a pleasure to meet any of Darcy's co-workers," she said warmly.

Richard watched the interaction between the three and seemed to quickly understand the dynamics. He put his arm possessively around Elizabeth's waist and drew her close.

"San Diego is not so far away—just a couple of hours by plane. I'll be down to visit you very soon," he said warmly. Then he drew her close and kissed her soundly on the lips.

Stunned, Elizabeth kissed him back rather chastely and then said breathlessly, "I can't wait."

Richard grinned widely. Darcy fumed and stood rooted to his spot.

"Won't you see me to the door, love?" Richard said to Elizabeth, pulling her gently by the arm toward the door—and out of Darcy's earshot.

"Richard..." Elizabeth began.

Richard looked up at her from buttoning his jacket. "Caroline is not to be underestimated. You will need to fight her tooth and nail for him." Elizabeth looked at him in surprise. He grinned. "I knew it was too good to be true—you weren't that crazy about me before. I'll manage, especially if it means bringing Will down a notch." Elizabeth laughed, and he slipped his arms around her waist. "He's such a snob sometimes, it irks me. I remind him of what an incorrigible scamp I am at every opportunity." With that, he swept Elizabeth into a dip over his knee and kissed her. She whooped with laughter and returned his kiss.

Richard slipped out with a mischievous glance at Elizabeth. She bit her lip as she closed the door behind him, then turned and studiously kept her eyes on the floor.

"I think I'll hit the hay," she announced.

"Yes, we should be going, Will. Good night, Ms. Bennet. Good night, Jane, Charley," Caroline said, smiling. She hugged Jane and Bingley and then took Darcy's hand.

"Let's go home, sweetie," she said warmly. He pressed his lips together but said nothing. He allowed himself to be led out the door. An hour later, as Elizabeth lay curled on her bed in her pajamas, fending off tears with a will of iron, her cell phone rang. She hastily wiped her nose and cleared her throat.

"Hello?"

"It's me. I left my coat here. Will you come down and let me in? I don't want to disturb Jane and Bingley." Darcy's smooth voice from the other end set her stomach in a knot again. It was becoming annoying how he could twist her emotions so easily. And annoyance was her friend, because it kept misery at bay.

"You're not fooling anyone, but I'll come down," she sighed.

He was waiting at the door when she opened it and thrust his coat toward him. Her hair was pulled up into a knot at the top of her head, and she was barefoot in a pair of low-slung loose cotton pants and a tank-top with no bra.

"Can't I come in?" he asked, not taking the coat.

"Won't Caroline be lonely?"

He rolled his eyes and stepped forward, pushing the door open. She stepped aside to allow him to come in and closed the door behind her. When he still did not take the coat, she clutched it to her chest.

Darcy turned to look at her. She was as he loved her most—natural, tousled. Even in his anger with her, his pulse quickened, and he wanted to kiss her.

"Why didn't you tell me you would be coming to town?" he asked.

"It was spontaneous," she answered.

"How long will you be here?"

"I leave tomorrow evening."

He closed the distance between them again. "Elizabeth, this is ridiculous. Why won't you call me? There's nothing to stop us from being together now," he said. He took the coat from her hands and tossed it aside. "No conflict, no scandal, nothing." He put his arms around her waist. "Nothing." He brushed his lips across hers. She did not return his kiss.

"Nothing except your new girlfriend," she replied. He pulled his head back.

"Caroline is not my girlfriend."

"Fine. Friend with benefits, then," she replied, pulling away from his arms.

"You know very well that I am not like that," he said angrily. "There is nothing between Caroline and me. Which is more than I can say for you and Richard! Are you sleeping with him?"

She looked at him in outrage. "You have a lot of nerve!" she exclaimed.

"You fell into my bed quickly enough, why not take up with my cousin?" he spat out bitterly. Even as the words came out he mentally berated himself. He was not winning her back.

"I think you'd better leave," she said hotly, picking up his coat and throwing it at him. He caught it and stood still, checking his anger.

"I want to marry you," he blurted. *What on god's earth was he doing?* Words that never crossed the reasoning part of his brain were coming out of his mouth!

"Really? As much as I'd like a husband who thinks I'm a whore, I'm going to have to decline. Get out."

She flung open the door for him. He held his coat. She hitched her thumb toward the driveway. Thinking that he had done enough damage for one night, he left.

His hands shook as he drove home. He was filled with rage, remorse, and heartache. What the hell was his problem? Why couldn't he control himself when he was around Elizabeth? His whole intent in returning had been to ask her to see him, to let him fly down every weekend to be with her. Not to propose and certainly not to insult her.

He unlocked the door of his penthouse and tossed his keys on the counter. Sitting at the table in the dark, he looked out over the city and replayed every moment he had ever had with her in his head. He let out a shaky sigh and put his head in his hands. After long moments of struggling with self-control, he expelled a sob and let tears come. He did not hear Georgie enter the room but felt her arms around his shoulders. He turned into her chest and let her comfort him. After a few moments, he wiped a hand over his face.

"Will, no woman is worth this torment," she said softly.

"I keep making it worse," he laughed humorlessly, shaking his head. "Every time I see her, I go with good intentions, and then something happens, and I push her further away."

Haltingly and with gentle prodding from Georgie, he related their entire history to her, from first meeting to last. He left out the juicy bits, but she got the idea. She sighed sympathetically and held his hand.

"I'm an idiot. I have brought this on myself."

She nodded. "Will, you've never had to pursue a woman—ever. You're insecure, and it's making you do crazy things. I know exactly what you're going through. I only have two bits of advice: First off, don't let it destroy you, don't let it change who you *are*. Second, try to fix it, but don't call her, don't see her. You don't have enough self control when you're around her. Write Elizabeth a letter, pour it all out, and see what happens. Women are terribly romantic about letters, you know."

Chapter 19

ELIZABETH'S TRIP BACK TO San Diego was an endurance test to see how long she could go before she had to brush tears from her cheek. She never went more than a minute. Seeing Darcy had been shock enough, and for a brief moment, she had let herself fantasize that she could let everything go and just rest her head against his chest and be comforted. But Caroline's presence had shattered Elizabeth's fantasy with all the subtlety of a sledgehammer.

Even if Darcy did deny that he and Caroline were romantically involved, the fact remained that he had returned to her, had sought *some* sort of refuge from her. Jane had warned Elizabeth in England to be careful, and in her usual fashion, Elizabeth had ignored her. Well, she was paying the painful price now. The entire plane ride—and the taxi ride as well—was filled with images of Darcy taking comfort in Caroline's arms… and her bed. It wasn't the first time Elizabeth cried herself to sleep over Darcy.

When Elizabeth picked up her mail a few days later, she was

startled to find an envelope addressed to her in Darcy's strong, neat hand. As she turned the envelope over and over, she imagined a hundred different scenarios, none of which ended well. The coward in her wanted to return the letter unread, but every other molecule in her body wanted to know what he had to say—even if it was that he never wanted to see her again.

Taking a deep breath, Elizabeth carefully opened the envelope.

Dear Lizzy,

Before I say anything, let me first apologize for my absolutely atrocious behavior to you at Jane's party. I was an immature asshole, and you deserved none of it. Whether or not you have been involved with Richard in the past is none of my business, and you were perfectly right to throw me out.

I realize that the dilemma in which we find ourselves is harder for you than it is for me. You're the one who has to sacrifice if we are to be together. You think that I don't care about the ethical problems, but that's not true. I just care more about us. I wanted so badly to make things work that I got tunnel vision. I am admittedly used to having my own way. I jeopardized you, Mr. Gardiner, and myself with my reckless behavior, and I am truly sorry.

But your solution—to act as if nothing has happened—was no better. No matter what happens in the future, we cannot change the fact that we did become involved. It can't be undone, and I would never want to.

You can be in no doubt of what I want. I want to wake up with your breath on my neck and your hair in my face. I want to feel your heartbeat under mine. I want the sun to feel warm again and to have the emptiness in my chest filled. I want us back.

Now what remains is for you to tell me what you want. If you want to be with me—if you love me—I need you to tell me. If you need more time, I'll wait. But if I'm just hanging on to a dream, I need to know so that I can move on. Whatever it is that you want, I'll do. Just know that no matter what you decide, I love you.

Will

Elizabeth bit her lip uncertainly. In a perfect world, she would call him and tell him that she loved him and wanted to be with him. But this wasn't a perfect world. Her departure to San Diego provided only a temporary fix to their dilemma. What would happen when she returned to San Francisco? He was still only one of two judges, and there was still an ethical conflict. Her unenviable choice was to either give up Darcy, or to give up the career that she'd built. Her uncertainty about the potential longevity of their relationship made the second option feel far too risky.

The whole situation gave her a headache of monumental proportions. Rubbing her temples, Elizabeth set the letter aside and picked up the phone. An hour later, she was flat on her stomach as a gentle-handed woman smoothed clay over her back and eased the tension from her muscles. Under the expert hands of the masseuse, Elizabeth's mind slowed until she could look at her dilemma calmly and rationally. This was an important decision that would affect the rest of her life. A knee-jerk reaction was the worst thing she could do. She promised herself that she would not be hasty, but knew he deserved an answer by the end of the week.

***

Darcy was hiding. There was no other word for it. After three weeks of being shuttled from barbecues to dinners to the movies by Bingley, Darcy wanted nothing more than to be alone in his misery. He had not heard from Elizabeth in the ten days since the disastrous engagement party, and it was too soon to expect a response to his letter, sent mere days before. All he wanted was to sit in the dark and get completely drunk.

The insistent ringing of his doorbell for the past minute was spoiling that plan. Darcy sighed and opened the door. Outside stood Caroline, her finger still on the buzzer as she smiled brightly at him.

"What?" he asked tiredly.

"You're so pissy when you're moping. I'm here to cheer you up." Without waiting for an invitation, which he would likely not have issued in any event, Caroline pushed past him and strode to his kitchen. "I brought sushi," she called.

Darcy watched her with a mixture of annoyance and amusement. He had to give her credit for her persistence, but he was in no mood to laugh; he was enjoying his self-pity.

"Why don't you tell me what's wrong," she suggested as she sat next to him on the couch. He took the chopsticks she offered and used them to listlessly push a kappa roll across the plate.

"I'm fine."

"Yes, you're the picture of sunny optimism. How much weight have you lost in the last month?"

"I don't have much of an appetite these days," Darcy admitted, setting the sushi plate on the coffee table and rubbing a hand over his face. He accepted the glass of wine Caroline offered him.

"I'm a great listener," she cajoled.

"I don't want to talk about it." Darcy quaffed the wine quickly and welcomed the refill. On his empty stomach, the alcohol went straight to his head, and he began to feel drowsy. He put his head against the sofa back and closed his eyes, only to open them again when Caroline pressed her lips to his.

"Caro—" he began to protest.

"Shhh."

Darcy closed his eyes again and let her kiss him, relishing for the moment the simple pleasure of being desired. But as she straddled his lap, he shook his head. "No, Caroline."

"This says yes," she countered, stroking a hand over his traitorously aroused groin. "You're in dire need of a sexual interlude, and I'm going to give it to you." She made her point by wrapping her arms around his neck and kissing him again.

It occurred to Darcy that perhaps he could have a night of pleasure instead of torment. He closed his eyes again and tried to imagine that it was Elizabeth whose fingers were unfastening his collar buttons, that it was Elizabeth who was responding to his now probing lips. He caught her face in his hands, but it was too narrow. The hair under his fingertips was too sleek, and her breast felt too large in his palm. He inhaled deeply, but instead of sunshine and pears, he smelled incense and cloves. Her mouth didn't taste right, and she was not supple and soft against his chest. She was too long, too slender, and too… too not Elizabeth.

Ashamed, Darcy opened his eyes and turned his face away from Caroline's. "No," he said harshly as he firmly slid her from his lap to the couch. He put his head in his hands and clenched his eyes shut, disgusted with himself. "I just can't."

"What's *wrong?*" she asked, her voice hurt and confused.

"It's all wrong. Everything is wrong." Trying to imagine Caroline as Elizabeth was a futile exercise. He could find Elizabeth in a darkened room full of a hundred women: he knew every inch of her, every sound of her, every smell of her.

"Is there someone else?" Caroline asked quietly. Darcy nodded once. "Who is she?"

"Jane's sister. I'm sorry."

Caroline stood from the couch, hugging herself. She paced a moment before asking him, "Do you love her?"

Darcy looked at Caroline with watery eyes and laughed. "For God's sake, Caroline, are you *blind?* Look at me! I'm a wreck!" He swallowed hard and closed his eyes again, clenching and unclenching his jaw as he tried to maintain his composure. "I'm sorry," he repeated.

"No, it's okay," she replied. "You've never led me to believe we were anything more than friends. It was a nice arrangement, but I never expected more. You don't need to be sorry." She sat next to him on the couch. "I hate to see you this way. Is there anything I can do?"

Darcy looked at her and saw her in a whole new light. Yes, she could be shallow and self-centered, and sometimes damned annoying, but she'd always been a good friend to him. Above all, they had always been good friends.

He shook his head and over the rest of the bottle of wine, recounted the whole pathetic situation to her. "Sounds like you're fucked," she laughed.

"It could work, but she'd have to give up litigating in our jurisdiction, and she's already made a good name for herself. It's not fair to her."

"You know, I've always felt that one's career is secondary. I don't mean that women should sacrifice everything for men, but that you make the most of what you've got. Great jobs come and go, but great men… well, you should hold on to those."

Darcy laughed, then stopped, alarmed by the cat-like gleam in Caroline's eyes. She poked the tip of her tongue out the corner of her mouth and smiled slyly.

"What are you up to?" he asked warily.

"Maybe you should remind her of what she's missing."

"What are you talking about?"

"All's fair in love and war, Darcy."

Elizabeth dropped the letter in the slot at the post office Saturday morning and tried to let go of the tension in her gut. She had been a little late on the promise to answer Darcy's letter by the end of the week, but it had been a grueling experience, and she was fighting the urge to jam her arm into the slot to retrieve the letter and burn it.

"Well, there's no going back now," she muttered to herself as she climbed into her car. "Jane will give me a pep talk." The relief she felt knowing that in a short time she would be picking up her sister at the airport and spending a relaxing weekend with her was palpable. As different as the two sisters were, each was the other's closest confidante, and Elizabeth needed Jane more than ever to distract her from constant fretting over Darcy.

"Lizzy, I've missed you," Jane said as they hugged tightly at the airport. A while later they were in swimsuits, lounging by the pool and sipping margaritas while Jane caught Elizabeth up on the local gossip.

"Poor Daddy," Elizabeth snorted as she rifled through a stack of photos handed to her by Jane. "Does Mom ever close her mouth? And look, Lydia with a different guy in every picture. What a surprise! Ooh, what's this? Jane, are you making porn?" Elizabeth laughed as she came across a picture of Bingley, wearing nothing but a sheet and a satisfied grin.

Jane snatched the picture from Elizabeth, blushing and giggling. "He always looks that way," she insisted, playing innocent.

Suddenly, Elizabeth fell silent. In her hand was a picture of Darcy and Caroline, laughing with wine glasses in hand. Jane, catching Elizabeth's crestfallen expression, gently took the picture from her.

"How is he?" Elizabeth asked, her voice unsteady.

"He seems... quiet," Jane answered cautiously.

"Is he seeing Caroline again?"

"I'm really not sure. They're together a lot, but then again, they're both in the wedding party."

"What does Charley say?" Elizabeth persisted.

"You know Charley, he's clueless. You want me to ask him?"

Elizabeth pressed her palm to her eyes and shook her head, willing herself not to cry as she thought of the letter she'd posted that morning.

"I wouldn't say they're serious," Jane offered and took Elizabeth's hand. "But I *would* say he's unhappy, and he misses you."

Chapter 20

"WHY DO YOU HAVE that grin on your face?" Caroline asked as she slid into the booth across from Darcy for their dinner date. He glanced up from the letter he was reading, already creased from too many handlings since the day before, then folded it and tucked it into his jacket pocket.

"Just had some good news, that's all," he shrugged, and picked up his fork.

The letter had been short and to the point, so it was easy for Darcy to memorize it: *Will, I just need time to figure out what to do. I still love you. It's not fair of me to ask you to wait, so I won't. I hope to see you when I visit Jane on the weekend of August 20th. Love, Lizzy*. Even though she was hedging her bets, Darcy was buoyed by Elizabeth's letter. *I still love you*. At least it wasn't a blanket rejection.

"I need your help on a charity thing I'm doing," Caroline said as she drizzled vinaigrette over her salad.

"Of course I'll help out," Darcy replied absently. "Just tell me what I need to do."

"It's a benefit for the Pediatric Aids Foundation," Caroline began. "Charles is involved and has participated in the charity function before, but this year he can't. So we were hoping you could step in."

"Sure. What is it, a fund drive or something?"

"Something like that."

"Oh, I'm good at meet-and-greets," he said, perking up. "I wonder where my tuxedo is," he trailed off, mentally cataloguing his closet.

"It's a charity auction," she clarified.

"You need me to buy something?" He took a bite of his steak, closing his eyes and savoring the flavor. Since reading Elizabeth's letter for the first time yesterday, his appetite had returned—he couldn't get enough of a good steak. And pears. He loved pears.

"No, actually, I need your help with the auction itself."

"What's being auctioned?"

"You are."

"I am what?" he asked, taking another bite of steak.

"You are being auctioned."

He stopped chewing and took a drink of wine. "Sorry, I thought you said I was being auctioned." He smiled. She nodded. The smile disappeared from his face, replaced by a frown. "What do you mean?"

"It's a bachelor auction." When Darcy put down his fork and leaned back in his seat, looking displeased, Caroline hastily continued, "It's been very successful for the past four years, and every year Charles auctions himself. But this year he doesn't want to because he's engaged. I need you to fill his slot."

"A bachelor auction? You mean, I go up on stage and women bid on me, and I go out on a date with the highest bidder?" She nodded. "Absolutely not." He crossed his arms over his chest.

"Why not? It's for a great cause. Charles always has a blast. It's a lot of fun. Besides, I really need you to do this. The auction is two weeks away, and I don't have a replacement yet." Caroline looked pleadingly at him.

"Do you have any idea how humiliating that sounds?"

"Will, honestly, you really take yourself too seriously. A lot of great guys do this. We have doctors, lawyers, politicians, sports figures, local celebrities. It's all in good fun, it's for a good cause, and it's not at all humiliating. It's not some strip club. You don't have to dance or anything, you just stand up there and women bid on you."

"What if I don't get any bids?" he sulked. "*That* would be humiliating."

Caroline laughed. "You, not get any bids? Have you looked in the mirror lately? Charles usually pulls in about $10,000, and he's just cute. You're gorgeous—I'm counting on you for at least $15,000."

"Can't I just contribute $15,000?"

"Of course you could, but you'd still have to do this for me. I need a warm body to fill the slot. Charles isn't willing to do it. I'm begging you as a personal friend and as an upstanding member of society. Please, let me sell you at auction."

The corner of Darcy's mouth curled up in a reluctant smile. Caroline really could be persuasive when she tried. He picked up his fork and resumed eating his steak.

"I'll do it if you promise to outbid anyone who you think I couldn't stand to go on a date with. I'll pay for it. You know me well enough. No hunchbacks, no sailors, no transvestites."

"Look, you could use the action, tranny or not. When's the last time you got lucky?"

"What day is this?"

"August 8th."

"Too bloody long ago, then."

"What's the status of the Elizabeth situation?"

"I'm now officially on hold." He said it proudly, as if he'd just been awarded a gold star.

Caroline shook her head. "Someone needs to slap some sense into that girl," she muttered. Then she jabbed her fork at Darcy. "I'm telling you, you need to let her know that you're not just going to wait around forever."

"But I would."

"Yes, but you can't let *her* know that!" she exclaimed, rolling her eyes at him. "Honestly, Will, you sound so desperate. You have to play hard to get! It's the oldest trick in the book. I know I never want anything so bad as when I know I can't have it."

"I can't believe that I'm taking relationship advice from you," he said, shaking his head.

"Darcy, believe it or not, you are the only one who I could never conquer." He looked down at his wine but said nothing. "Why?" she asked him curiously.

"Why what?"

"Why couldn't I conquer you?"

He laughed. "I don't know. I think you're just too exotic for me. I mean, you fly to Sumatra to buy coffee beans. You dye your own clothes after making your own dye. You have a *tattoo*, Caroline. I can't keep up with that."

"What *do* you like?" she said leaning forward, intrigued.

He paused, took a sip of wine, and sighed. "I like *her*."

"Care to elaborate?"

He shrugged. "I can't explain it, it just is. I like Elizabeth. Everything about her. The way she smells, her hair, her jokes, the way she moves, the way she laughs. All her imperfections, to me, combine into one perfect whole. I feel like I'm missing something when she's not here, like I've forgotten my wallet. Something just isn't *right* without her."

Caroline grinned and put her chin in her palm. "Who knew you were such a romantic?"

He laughed. "Romantic? Really? I feel like an idiot. She makes me do things I would never dream of doing before I met her."

"Like what?" Caroline asked, smirking.

"No," he smiled. "I won't tell you."

"Did it involve leather chaps?" she asked slyly. He laughed and shook his head. "Pity," she murmured.

He lifted his eyes up from his wine glass. "It did, however, involve a riding crop."

The weekend of August 20th came far too quickly for Elizabeth's liking. When she'd sent Darcy her letter last week, she was feeling optimistic. If she knew for certain how serious he was, whether their relationship would actually go anywhere, then she'd consider making a career change. But that was before Caroline entered the picture. Admittedly, Elizabeth kept insisting that Darcy not wait for her, but she hadn't actually expected him to go back to Caroline. She was willing to take him at his word when he'd denied being involved with Caroline at Jane's engagement party, but that was three weeks ago. As they both knew too well, *anything* could happen in that amount of time.

"You okay?" Jane asked Elizabeth, rubbing her hand as they drove from the airport to the house.

"I told Will that I wanted to see him this weekend, and now I'm having doubts," Elizabeth admitted.

"Have you made any arrangements?" Elizabeth shook her head. "Then why don't we try something safe, where you don't have to be alone with him. He's been playing guitar with his sister at a coffee shop in town; we can go and see him there tonight." Elizabeth nodded, her stomach still churning.

After dinner, Elizabeth was sitting in the back of a crowded coffee bar trying to blend into the wallpaper. She was sure Darcy would not be expecting her, so she felt a slight advantage having the element of surprise. But when she saw his head bowed over a guitar, a curl of hair falling over his forehead as he tuned the strings, her toes literally curled in her sandals with anxiety. She slouched lower in her seat and chewed her thumbnail.

For an hour Darcy and Georgiana, accompanied by a vocalist, played Celtic music. At first, it brought back painful memories of Pemberley to Elizabeth. But the first pang eased into a dull ache, and by the third song even that had evaporated completely as the music affected her as it had the first time she heard him play. She could no longer ignore her feelings: she was in love with him, and no amount of career satisfaction would fill the gaping hole that would eat at her heart forever if she didn't at least try to make it work. With a renewed sense of hope, she stood at the end of the set and pushed her way through the crowd toward Darcy. Her path was intercepted by Caroline, who reached Darcy first, but when she retreated for coffee, Elizabeth advanced.

She stood behind him, just out of his line of vision, and said, "That was really beautiful."

At the sound of her voice, Darcy spun around, his eyes instantly landing on her. For a moment his mouth worked silently, too shocked to speak.

"Elizabeth," he managed to get out. She nodded and smiled, a nervous giggle bubbling up from her chest.

"Is this a bad time?" she asked.

"No! No, of course not! I wasn't expecting you to arrive until tomorrow," he stammered. "I'm just surprised to see you here." His cheeks had gone a ruddy red.

"How are you?" she asked, struggling against the urge to fling her arms around his neck and kiss the very life from him.

At last, a smile crept to his face. "Better, now," he said. His reaction forced the nervous giggle from her chest, and she covered her mouth like a schoolgirl, blushing. "You look well."

"Thank you." There was an awkward pause and then both started to talk at the same time.

"Are you busy—" he began, while she said, "I thought maybe—"

Both stopped with a little laugh, and then he said, "You first."

"I thought maybe we could have dinner tomorrow night, if you're not busy."

"Absolutely, I was going to suggest the same thing," he agreed. They both fell silent for another moment, each searching the other's face for some hint of what to do.

"Lizzy," he said softly, stepping closer to her and placing one hand on her upper arm. "I'm so glad—"

"Ms. Bennet! What a surprise to see you here!"

Elizabeth tore her attention from Darcy to find Caroline before her with her long legs, skinny hips and big boobs, handing Darcy a cup of coffee. "Here you go, dear." She took a sip of her coffee and looked back at Elizabeth, smiling politely. "Are you in town visiting Jane?" she asked, tilting her head to one side. Elizabeth looked up—way up—at Caroline, whose high-heeled boots put her a good seven inches taller than Elizabeth. Elizabeth, sensing that this could be a high-stakes game, returned Caroline's question with a single nod.

"Darcy's a great player, isn't he?" Caroline continued, touching Darcy's arm. Elizabeth could hear the undertone in Caroline's voice, and she wasn't praising his guitar skills.

"Is he?" she replied, casting a glance at Darcy.

"Oh, yes. I've known him for years, and he just gets better and better." Caroline's smile was not completely hidden by the sip of coffee she took, and Elizabeth was certain it was by design.

"He seems to have more guitars than he can handle," Elizabeth replied.

"Oh, he can handle them," Caroline assured her. "In fact, he seems to go through them pretty quickly. I guess he's still looking for the perfect fit."

"And until then, he returns to the old standby?"

"Yes. New instruments can be so temperamental."

"I guess there's some benefit to playing an instrument that's been broken in by the rest of the band," Elizabeth said sweetly.

The sly smile slipped from Caroline's lips a notch.

"Elizabeth, you remember my sister, Georgiana? You met in Tahoe," Darcy interceded hastily. Even he could sense that they were on the verge of a royal catfight.

Elizabeth's claws receded, and she turned her attention to Georgiana.

"Oh, yes, I remember, you thought Will was my dad," Georgiana laughed. "Poor old man."

"Elizabeth, we were just going to go have dinner across town, would you like to join us?" Darcy asked, his eyes hopeful that she would accept.

"Oh, yes, please do come along. I'd love to get to know you better. Since we'll be sisters," Caroline added. Elizabeth recalled then that Caroline was Bingley's sister, soon to be Jane's sister-in-law. Her stomach dropped.

"No, thanks, I've lost my appetite."

"We'd better go, our reservations are in twenty minutes," Georgiana reminded Darcy. He nodded, and threw one puzzled, longing look at Elizabeth before being pulled away by Caroline and Georgiana. Elizabeth slowly counted to ten as she watched them leave.

Lou Hurst looked at the photo ID on his cell phone: an extended middle finger with black nail polish on it. He flipped it open.

"How did it go?" he asked anxiously.

"I've got competition," Elizabeth replied.

"Lady Boobs-a-Lot?" he asked, referring to Caroline.

"Yep. She's catty too."

"I know you. You can match her bitch-slap for bitch-slap."

"I need help, Lou! I don't know how to handle this!" she said, sounding as if she were on the verge of crying.

"Do you think he's sleeping with her? Or is she just messing with you?"

"How the hell do I know? I'm so clueless right now. Why does it have to be so damned complicated?"

Lou laughed. And laughed.

"What's so fucking funny, Queenie?" she said angrily. He laughed again.

"Lizzy, I've never seen your panties so twisted! You're positively chafing!"

"Fuck you, Lou."

"Now, don't be mad at me. *I* didn't sweep you off your feet and then dump you in the garbage."

She sighed in frustration. "What should I do?"

"How do I know?" he said gently. "He's human. Who knows what his motivations are? Do what your heart tells you to do and hope for the best."

Chapter 21

DO WHAT YOUR HEART tells you to do, and hope for the best had been Lou's advice. Elizabeth found it ironic that her heart was telling her to murder Caroline Bingley and dispose of the body in the San Francisco Bay.

"No, those flotation devices on her chest will keep her from sinking," she muttered to herself as she steered her car toward Darcy's place. "Better to give her the dirt nap." Homicidal fantasies had filled her mind for the past twenty-four hours.

Elizabeth already regretted her decision not to join them for dinner the previous night. Not only had she given Caroline even more unsupervised time with Darcy, but she'd also lost an opportunity to size up the competition. Only two hours after they'd separated, Elizabeth had called Darcy to firm up their plans for tonight—and to make sure that Caroline hadn't gone home with him.

Jealousy was not an entirely new emotion for Elizabeth, but the intensity of the envy she felt when she saw Darcy with Caroline was startling. Her rational mind told her that Darcy was not the kind of man to sleep with one woman while pursuing another, but the green-eyed monster in her heart told her that Caroline wasn't likely to take no for an answer. Why, oh why, had she been so stupid to tell Darcy not to wait for her?

As the elevator glided up to Darcy's floor, Elizabeth composed herself. She had to be pleasant, not petulant, sunny, not sour. Depending on his greeting, perhaps she would even kiss him hello. She smoothed a hand over her skirt, pulled a piece of lint from her sleeve, squared her shoulders, and walked purposefully to his door.

Her carefully choreographed entrance was derailed by the fact that Darcy was on the phone when he opened the door for her. He smiled at her apologetically as he listened to the person on the other end.

"Yes, I understand. I will," he said into the phone. "I—Yes, I will. I *understand*... Yes." He gave Elizabeth an exasperated look and rolled his eyes as he dropped his keys into his pocket. Then he firmly interrupted the voice at the other end mid-sentence. "*Caroline*, I have to go. We'll talk tomorrow." He hung up the phone and tossed it on a chair.

Elizabeth bit her tongue at the sound of Caroline's name. The woman was like poison ivy: let one tentacle take root in the foundation, and soon she'd be pulling the whole building down. Elizabeth was determined that Caroline was not going to destroy her relationship with Darcy. She was perfectly capable of doing *that* herself.

"You look beautiful," Darcy said, stepping closer to her. Elizabeth rubbed her hands over her arms, putting a barrier between them. She couldn't kiss him with Caroline's name still on his lips. Apparently sensing her hesitation, Darcy stepped back and cleared his throat.

"Shall we go?" he suggested cheerfully. Elizabeth nodded.

They found a quiet corner in a cozy restaurant overlooking the city lights, and Elizabeth tried to forget about Caroline. Darcy asked her questions about the progress of the San Diego office, and she asked him to update her on local news. They had a long discussion about an appeal that Elizabeth was writing, exchanging ideas back and forth, so that by the time they were served coffee, Elizabeth was feeling like herself again.

"When will you be in town again?" he asked, tentatively stroking one finger over her hand.

"I could come in next weekend," she suggested, "if you're not busy."

He grimaced. "I'm actually busy next Saturday, all day."

"Oh? What are you doing?"

"Caroline talked me into this charity auction thing," he said, stirring his coffee.

"You seem to be spending a lot of time with Caroline," Elizabeth commented, pulling her hand away from him. He blinked at her in surprise.

"We're friends."

"You were more than friends before," she reminded him gently.

"That was before. This is now."

"Do you think she really believes that you're just friends?"

"Yes, I do."

Elizabeth snorted and shook her head. "Will, for someone who is usually so perceptive, sometimes you can be amazingly dense."

"And for someone who is usually so open-minded, sometimes you can be incredibly judgmental."

"I know what I saw last night."

"What did you see last night?"

"I saw a woman guarding her territory. She might as well have peed on you."

"Oh, please, Elizabeth. Don't be ridiculous," Darcy laughed.

"I'm telling you, she's got her eye on you."

"Are you saying that you don't trust me to know when Caroline is trying to seduce me? As if I might just wake up one morning and find that I'd shagged her all week long? Sorry, love, that only happens with you." His annoyance was evident, and Elizabeth felt herself approaching dangerous territory. She began a tactical retreat.

"I'm sorry, Will. I'm not saying that I don't trust you. I'm saying I don't trust *her*."

"Are you asking me to stop being friends with Caroline? Fine. I'll stop being friends with Caroline if you'll drop Lou."

"It's not the same, Lou is *gay!*"

"It is the same. If you don't trust me, where does that leave us?"

"I don't know, where *does* it leave us?"

Darcy let out a bitter laugh. "You're asking me? It's all I can do to get you to talk to me, let alone dictate where our relationship is going."

"Okay, look. I don't want to fight about this. How about we see where we are before we start exiling friends from each other."

"Fine."

"Fine."

Both were mute during dessert, and a heavy silence hung over them as they drove back to Darcy's place. Once he had parked, Darcy put his hand over Elizabeth's.

"Elizabeth, I'm sorry. I don't want to fight with you."

Elizabeth sighed and squeezed his hand. "I'm sorry too. But I don't like Caroline. She gives me the heebie-jeebies."

"Do you really want me to stop being her friend?"

"No, I just want you to establish some boundaries. She doesn't have any. Anyway, it doesn't matter since we don't know where we are. I can't tell you to give up your friends any more than you can tell me to give up my career. It's just something we need to feel out."

"I don't suppose there's any chance you'll be coming up for a nightcap?" he asked. She shook her head.

"No, it's too soon for me. It will just make things harder."

"I understand." He fell silent for a moment, then said, "Come on, I'll walk you to your car."

When they reached her MINI Cooper, Darcy took Elizabeth's hand and pressed her fingers to his lips. "I think we've made a little progress," he said.

"Yes, I haven't thrown anything at you," she laughed.

"Drive safely, okay?"

Elizabeth nodded and climbed into her car, watching Darcy wave as she drove away.

"What is it with women?" Darcy asked with disgust as he stabbed a piece of coffee cake with his fork. "You all have trust issues." The meeting with Caroline to finalize his biography for the auction pamphlet had veered off course with Darcy's foul mood.

"Another lover's spat?" Caroline asked sympathetically.

"We had this odd discussion. I told her that we're just friends, but Elizabeth thinks you're a threat."

"It's about time!" Caroline said, exasperated.

"What?" Darcy paused, fork midway to his mouth.

"I've been giving her all the signals, it's about time she started playing hardball."

"What are you talking about?"

"Will, I told you. She needs to know that you're not just sitting around pining over her, day and night. If she thinks she has some competition, she'll make a move. I've been giving her and Jane plenty to chew on."

"Do you mean to say that she was right? You were staking your claim on me?"

"Well, yes, but I don't mean it. I'm just forcing her hand."

"Bloody hell!" Darcy dropped his fork with a clatter and raked his hands through his hair. "You *bloody* women!"

"Is it working?"

"That's not the point!"

"What did she say?"

"You will stop this ridiculous charade immediately!" Darcy stood, fuming. He tossed a few bills on the table to pay for their coffee and shook his head. "I thought you were my friend, Caroline." He strode toward the exit, and Caroline hastily followed him outside.

"Will, I *am* your friend! Wait! Where are you going?" she called after him.

"Home. And don't call me!" he spat over his shoulder.

Caroline watched him as he stalked down the street, his shoulders hunched against a brisk wind, unsure for the first time in her life whether she had done the right thing.

Chapter 22

DARCY PACED NERVOUSLY BACKSTAGE as a hockey player was auctioned off to a horde of screaming women. The Empire Room of the Sir Francis Drake Hotel was teeming with San Francisco's most powerful women, all dressed in glittering gowns and all eager to contribute to a worthy cause while showcasing their wealth. Considering the net worth of the elite audience, Darcy had expected the crowd to be more… dignified. Instead, it was as if a bachelorette party had broken out, complete with diamond-bedecked middle-aged women vying to stuff dollar bills into any waistband that strutted by. He just hoped to get the evening over with as soon as possible without too much humiliation and with his virtue intact.

As much as he wanted to, Darcy could not renege on his promise to Caroline. He was still furious with her, but the Pediatric Aids Foundation still needed him for the auction. In an effort to avoid her, he had declined to use the offered hospitality suite—to which Caroline, as an auction organizer, had free access—and reserved his own room. It was a mere bonus that he wouldn't have to share the shower with twenty other bachelors.

"Are you still mad at me?" Caroline's posture was uncharacteristically hesitant as she poked her head around the corner.

"Yes," he replied, not even looking in her direction.

"I'm really sorry. I was only trying to help."

He didn't answer; instead he intently studied a poster on the wall.

"I'll come clean to her, if that's what you want."

"I don't want anything from you, Caroline. I don't even want to have this discussion." He heard her sigh, and a moment later, the clack of her heels faded as she walked down the hallway. Darcy ran a hand through his hair.

"Judge Darcy, you're up!" the director called as the emcee on stage began Darcy's introduction.

"Our next bachelor is Fitzwilliam Darcy, a circuit judge here in Meryton. Judge Darcy was born and raised in England and came to California several years ago to open an office for his international law firm. He was later appointed to superior court circuit judge by the governor. He is one of the youngest judges ever to be appointed in the county."

Darcy's stomach churned as he heard, "Will, please come on out so we can get a good look at you." He stepped out onto the stage wearing his judicial robe—another one of Caroline's brilliant ideas. The crowd booed.

"Will is thirty-eight years old, stands six foot four, weighs in at a svelte 210 pounds, and has beautiful green eyes. Oh! He looks even better close up than he does in our catalogue!" the emcee tittered. Darcy swallowed, then plastered a grin on his face.

"Will's hobbies are playing guitar, riding horses, fencing, and riding motorcycles. You may also be interested to know that he was a racecar driver while he was in college. He lives in the fast lane, ladies!" There was more cheering.

"Judge Darcy, if you could just show us your legal briefs?" the emcee shouted into the microphone. Cursing Caroline to the seven foulest levels of hell, Darcy took off his robe, revealing his tailor-made Dolce and Gabbana suit. As the crowd's boos changed to cheers, he squinted into the dimly lit room, further blinded by the spotlight as he strode to the middle of the stage.

"Can we start the bidding at $1,000?" the emcee called. Darcy's mouth went dry. The bidding quickly escalated to $10,000, and soon there was a fierce competition among five women determined to have a date with Darcy.

Hoping to end the torture soon, Darcy encouraged the bidding. He leaned over to the emcee's microphone and said, "Come on, ladies, it's for a good cause. Have pity on me, and take me out on a date!"

He mentally cringed when the emcee grinned and said, "Well, girls, you could hear that lovely accent aaaaaaaaaallllllllllll night long! Get out your checkbooks!"

"Twenty thousand!"

Darcy's head snapped at the sound of a distinctly familiar voice. He shaded his eyes against the spotlight and searched the audience, hoping that his ears were deceiving him. They were not.

There stood Elizabeth, bidding paddle in hand, a grin on her face as she waved it in the air.

"Twenty-five," came another bid.

"Thirty!" Elizabeth called.

Frantically Darcy searched the crowd for Caroline. When he found her, he nodded in her direction. She immediately raised her paddle and called, "Thirty-five!"

"Thirty-seven," came another bid.

"Thirty-eight," bid Elizabeth. Darcy looked again at Caroline.

"Forty!"

"Forty-five," Elizabeth immediately countered. He saw her shoot an angry look at Caroline. He swung back to Caroline and nodded.

"Fifty!"

"Fifty-five," was Elizabeth's response. This time, when Darcy signaled Caroline to bid, Elizabeth caught the movement. He saw her brows crease in confusion as Caroline made the next bid for sixty thousand dollars.

"Going once." Darcy stood ready to signal Caroline again if Elizabeth made another bid.

"Going twice." Elizabeth slowly lowered her paddle.

"Sold for sixty thousand dollars to our own Caroline Bingley. I think that's a record, Judge Darcy! You better make it worth Caroline's while! And Caroline, that better not be coming out of our fund!"

Darcy ignored the emcee's obnoxious innuendos and watched Elizabeth as she gave him one long, furious glare and tossed her paddle on the table. Without another glance, she began to push her way out of the room.

A moment later, Darcy was hustled off the stage by the director. Blood rushing in his ears, he searched frantically for Elizabeth, looking down the hallway then dashing to the lobby. He caught sight of her hair bobbing angrily amongst the crowd of guests.

"Elizabeth!" he called after her. She stopped, squaring her shoulders before she turned toward him. Her face was a mask of fury, her cheeks flushed and her eyes snapping as he approached her. "Elizabeth, wait," he said quietly as people began to look at them. "Let me explain. Can we go to my room and talk?" Without waiting for her response, Darcy led her to the elevator, nodding politely as they squeezed into the lift with other hotel patrons. Upon reaching his floor, he led Elizabeth to his room and let her in.

After hanging the "Do Not Disturb" sign on the handle, he closed the door turned around. The sound of her palm striking his face registered just a brief second before the pain did. Astonished, he lifted one hand to his flaming cheek and stared at her. She packed quite a wallop.

"Is *that* your choice?" she shouted at him. He was still too stunned to respond. "You *motherfucker!* I can't believe you!" He could see her shaking uncontrollably. At last his mind began to work again.

"Elizabeth—" he began, and reached out to touch her arm. She flung off his hand with a wild gesture.

"Just friends? What a crock!"

"Elizabeth!"

"Do you and Caroline laugh at me over breakfast every morning? Is this your little love nest?"

"*Stop!* Listen to me!" he grabbed her by the arms again and shook her once. "I am not, and *never was*, seeing her."

"You are so full of *shit!*"

"I am not *lying* to you!"

"You were signaling Caroline. You *told* her to outbid me!"

"Of *course* I did! That has to be your life savings! I couldn't have you spend that kind of money over this stupid, *stupid game!*"

He dropped his hands from her arms and clutched his head in frustration. Both were breathing hard.

"I hate you," she said hotly.

He threw his hands up in the air in exasperation. "What's new, Elizabeth? I can't do anything right with you! I try to see you, and you refuse. I tell you I love you, and you move to San Diego. I keep you from throwing away your life savings, and you tell me you hate me. You give me every reason to think you don't want me, and then you freak out when you see me with someone else. What do you want me to do? I don't know what to do anymore! Just tell me what to do, and I'll do it!" he shouted at her.

They glared at each other, both panting with anger. Darcy began to pace. When he had regained control of his temper, he turned to face her again.

"Elizabeth," he started again. "I am not seeing her. Caroline is nothing more than a friend. I swear it on my mother's grave." There was no more solemn vow he could make.

It broke his heart when he saw Elizabeth's face begin to crumple. She sank onto the sofa and buried her face in her hands, sobbing. Kneeling before her, Darcy put his hands on her knees, rubbing them gently.

"Lizzy, this has to stop. Either we go forward together, or we end it for good. Neither of us can bear any more heartbreak."

She nodded, still crying, and wiped her cheek with the back of her hand. Unable to watch her cry, he sat on the sofa next to her and pulled her close, kissing the top of her head.

"What will it be?" he asked quietly, caressing her arm.

"I wanted to surprise you. I wanted to make this grand gesture that told you how I felt, and instead, you had Caroline outbid me. I can't compete against her."

"Lizzy, there *is* no competition. You're the only one I want. Why can't you see that?"

"Because she's always there." They sat in silence for a long moment before she said, "I don't know how much more of this I can take."

"Me either. You've got to make a choice, Lizzy. For both our sakes."

She nodded, wiping her eyes again. "I know. I've just made my choice."

When she did not look up at him, Darcy felt his throat begin to close. *What a tragically ironic end to the love of my life,* he thought. He felt her arms tighten around his waist, as if to give him a final good-bye, and he buried his face in her hair, inhaling the scent of pears for one last time.

"Lizzy," he said, his voice pleading, "don't."

"Don't make me go back to San Diego," she whispered.

His heart stopped for a beat and then sprang to life again when the meaning of her words penetrated his mind.

Chapter 23

DON'T MAKE ME GO back to San Diego, she had said. Elizabeth simply could not participate any longer in the ridiculous charade of pretending she did not need Darcy to breathe life into her soul. She was completely miserable without him and only felt whole when they were together. If she could stay at her firm and avoid having him as her judge, she would; if she could not, then she would work something else out. The choice that had tortured her for weeks now seemed so startlingly clear, that she could not remember why she had ever hesitated. She loved him, and that was all that mattered.

She tipped her face up to his and gave him a tremulous smile. "I know I can be a brat, but if you'll have me, I want to stay here. With you."

Darcy stroked his thumb over her cheek. "Do you mean it?" he whispered. She nodded and kissed the palm of his hand, closing her eyes as two more tears trickled out. He wiped them away and touched his nose to hers. Tentatively, Elizabeth pressed a soft kiss to his lips. For one heart-stopping second, he did not respond. Then, he wrapped his arms around her and crushed her to his chest, returning her kiss with all the pent-up ardor of the past two months.

Their mouths opened and shifted, tongues tasted and withdrew, lips nibbled and caressed. She curled her fingers into his hair and inhaled his intoxicating clean, mossy scent. His skin tasted woodsy, and his chin rasped against hers, bringing to life memories that had comforted her through long, lonely nights. The touch of his lips on hers awakened a hunger in her that had lain dormant out of sheer determination.

Gently, she loosened his tie and pulled it from around his neck, then pushed his jacket from his shoulders. Eager to feel his skin against hers, she tugged his shirt from the waistband of his trousers. Her fingers unfastened each button of his shirt until his chest was bare beneath her palms. His chest hair scratched under her hands and his breath caught as she grazed his nipple with the pad of her thumb. A soft moan came from Darcy's throat.

She dropped her lips to nibble Darcy's jawline as he deftly unbuttoned her blouse, his hands hot as they splayed against the skin of her back. The slip of silk slid down her arms and she shivered as his lips brushed over her shoulder. In one swift move, Darcy stood and pulled Elizabeth to her feet. Kissing, they stumbled toward the bedroom, leaving a trail of shirts, pants, shoes, skirt, hose, bra, and underwear. Her feet swung from the floor as Darcy scooped her into his arms and crossed the remaining distance to the bed.

Elizabeth closed her eyes and sighed as Darcy's lips blazed a trail from her throat to her breast. His knee pressed between her legs, sending a shock of desire through her. She arched her torso against his and stroked her hand over the dip of his spine. Her fingers tested the dimples of his low back, and then skimmed over his firm rear. An unguarded gasp escaped her lips when his tongue rasped over her nipple, pleasure spreading in a hot flush up her chest to her face.

"I've missed you," he whispered against her belly. "I've missed how you taste, how you smell." He spread her legs and ran the flat of his tongue along her wet core, curling the tip to dip in just beyond her folds, before moving up the length of her body to draw a kiss from her lips. She tasted herself on his lips and tongue.

Darcy's long, lean torso covered hers, the muscles of his back firm under her searching fingers. She ran the arch of her foot along his calf, sliding her thigh along his hip, his erection pressed insistently against her stomach.

"I love you, Will," she whispered. He caught her gaze and brushed a lock of hair from her face, caressing her cheek. He stroked is thumb across her lower lip.

"Again."

"I love you."

His hands clutched her curves, holding her close as he thrust into her. Her hips rose to meet his, and each movement brought a soft groan from him, a quiet exhalation of pleasure whispered in her ear. They fell into a sensual rhythm, passion ebbing and flowing as their lips hungrily sought to quench the drought. Fingers twined and legs twisted, muscles clenched and unclenched. Nothing could be heard but their shallow breaths.

Desire coiled in a tight ache until Elizabeth could bear no more. She gasped against Darcy's throat, and he caught her lips in a hot kiss. One of his hands clutched her hip and the other tangled in her hair as he strained to bring her to release. When her body suddenly flushed hot, she let out a stifled cry and tensed, arching against him as pleasure blossomed from between her legs. Instantly, Darcy's taut body stilled as he groaned against her lips, unable to stop the intense ripple of ecstasy that shot through him as he climaxed.

Both shuddered and gasped, tightening their embrace as they shared the intimacy of making love and the pleasure of pleasing. They were bound together by this act, this expression of their innermost longings laid bare only for each other. Vulnerability and sanctuary mingled with desire and satisfaction, the purest demonstration of love and trust.

Darcy's hand released its grip on her bottom and soothed a tender caress over Elizabeth's thigh. The hand clutching her hair now stroked her cheek as he looked down on her.

"Say it again," he asked quietly.

"I love you."

He closed his eyes, as if she put his mind at ease, and swallowed. Then he opened his eyes again.

"I love you, Elizabeth Bennet, and I'll never stop."

Darcy stared gloomily at his desk Monday morning. The weekend had been wonderful; Elizabeth had stayed with him, and they'd spent hours working out their issues and planning for the future. It was now settled that they were "together" and they would deal with the consequences of their relationship—whatever they might be—as a couple. The easiest resolution would be to make sure Elizabeth was taken off any cases over which Darcy was already the judge. They made a plan to approach Mr. Gardiner together and see what he was willing to do to accommodate them.

The sex had been spectacular. It reminded him of those giddy days at Pemberley, when they had been happy and uninhibited, when none of the troubles of the real world had touched them. Having Elizabeth back was like having a splash of color on a gray canvas; it breathed new life into him. Without her, his home felt sterile and empty, and the bed taunted him with its spaciousness. Darcy rather liked being pushed to the edge of the mattress by her greedy legs. The comfort of a thin duvet was cold, indeed.

Yet the fact remained that she had to complete her obligation in San Diego. Now he sat sullenly looking at his calendar and wishing the weekend—and her next visit—was already upon him.

The monotony of his depression was broken when the mail clerk delivered a package to him late in the afternoon. He glanced at the label, marked "Personal and Confidential," then saw that it was postmarked in San Diego. He opened it in the privacy of his chambers, and what he saw made his jaw drop.

Inside was a black and white photograph of Elizabeth wearing black pants and a white shirt, opened to reveal a bustier that he recognized as the one she had worn at the jazz club in London. He shook the box, and out fell the black silk bustier. On the back of the picture he saw Elizabeth's slanted handwriting.

This photograph reminds me of a certain night in London. To be honest, the events of the night are somewhat hazy in my memory. I remember your agitation in the shops and your annoyance at me for wearing a suit. I also remember how hot the club was and your smile when we danced. I remember crashing glass and the hardness of the table. I remember your laugh, and how you couldn't stop. It's been so long since I felt your laugh rumbling in your chest. I miss it terribly. Promise me that you'll laugh when I see you again.

Darcy pulled out the lacy bustier and looked closely at it. He had not remembered it in any detail. He saw now its fine lace and boning, the hooks on the back, the delicate black lining. It was soft and smooth under his fingers. How could she have worn this tiny thing and he not remember, in vivid detail, every inch of it?

He looked at the photo again. Elizabeth was standing with her hands in her pockets, leaning one shoulder against the wall. Her hair fell in large, dark curls around her shoulders. She looked relaxed, pensive. She looked beautiful.

When he called her that night, Darcy couldn't keep the smile from his voice. "That was a delightful surprise," he said when she answered her phone.

She laughed. "I hope it passed courthouse security without too much inspection."

"I imagine our mail sorter is very appreciative."

"Do you remember me wearing it? You were awfully drunk that night."

"Yes. I believe that's when I first told you that I loved you."

"I believe you had some fascination with my shoes."

"I'm looking forward to seeing them again," he murmured.

Elizabeth laughed huskily. "You'll have to wait until this weekend."

They rang off a few moments later, and Darcy crawled into bed, the bustier in his hand.

On Tuesday afternoon he was surprised to receive another package marked "Personal and Confidential." Darcy closed his chambers door and opened it with anticipation. Out fell another photograph and folded leather pants. The photograph showed Elizabeth sitting in a chair, barefoot in the leather pants and unbuttoned white shirt—the bustier was missing from the picture. He turned the photo over.

I have always loved these pants. They are impractical, tight, and impossible to care for. I only wear them once a year. The last time I wore them, I was with you. Do you remember? I did a little dance. You laughed at me. Later you told me you wanted to bronze them.

He looked at the picture again. With a little lurch in his chest, he realized that Elizabeth was doing a long-distance striptease. He put his head in his hands with a weak laugh and prayed for the weekend.

"Is this going to go on all week?" he asked that night over the phone.

"It will end when I run out of clothes."

"Lizzy, you are driving me crazy. Why didn't we shag more last weekend?"

"Because I didn't want another case of love rash."

When no package had arrived by two o'clock on Wednesday, Darcy became agitated. He paced in his office and wondered if she had forgotten or if perhaps it had been lost. When it arrived an hour later, he practically tore it open. Out fell a white shirt and another photograph.

In the picture, Elizabeth knelt on the floor, knees apart, wearing only the white shirt with the sleeves rolled up. Her bare thighs showed beneath the edge of the shirt. He looked at the photo for a long, long time before he turned it over.

This is your shirt. I remember the exact day you wore it. I wore it the next morning, because I loved how it smelled. Did you know that you smell like fresh air and moss? I love the smell of you. It says strength and warmth and springtime. I never told you how much I love your smell. I found this shirt in my suitcase, and I have slept in it every single night since. For a long time, I couldn't wash it; the scent of you still clung to it. Alas, at some point it had to be washed, but not before it smelled like both of us. Now it only smells like me. It is a lonely smell, and I have decided to give it up.

He read the note twice, and then turned the picture back over. He put his face in the shirt. She was right, it smelled like her. He called her immediately.

"I miss you," Darcy said huskily when she answered.

"It's awful, isn't it?" she teased.

"I love the way you smell. It's feminine and sexy and makes my mouth water."

"Keep that in mind for this weekend."

Darcy spent all day Thursday waiting for his package. He asked his secretary three times, but no package. He even went to the mail room to see if it had been misplaced, but to no avail. He frowned, returned to his chambers, and picked up the phone.

"Did you run out of clothes already?"

She laughed. "I thought this one should be opened at home."

Elizabeth was right. The photograph showed her kneeling on the floor with her bare back to him, wearing nothing but a black thong. Her hair was swept over her shoulder, baring her entire back and neck for his admiring gaze while she looked at him over her shoulder beneath lowered lashes. The corner of her mouth was curled in a slight smile.

The silky black thong slipped over his fingers as it fell from the envelope. He raised it to his nose. It smelled of citrus and pears: tangy and sweet. Darcy closed his eyes and inhaled deeply. The scents evoked a flood of memories of nights spent at

Pemberley. It tugged both at his heart and his groin. He opened his eyes and turned the photo over.

The last time we were together at Pemberley, you put kisses all over my back. You left your marks on me. It took two weeks for them to go away. But now I think I am ready for another set.

"Elizabeth, you are the worst tease I have ever known," he said quietly when she answered her phone.

"I think you should go to work late tomorrow if you can," she said mischievously.

He laughed quietly. "I'll see what I can do. How late will I be?"

"It should arrive before nine."

"And you? When will you arrive?"

"My flight leaves at 3:15."

On Friday morning, Darcy called his secretary to advise her that he would be in late and to please alert all the attorneys with morning appearances. Then he waited anxiously for the FedEx man.

He received a slender envelope at 8:45. He looked at the envelope for a long time, heart thudding. He carefully pulled the cord on the envelope and opened it. He pulled out the photograph.

Elizabeth was lying on her back on the floor with her face turned to the side, facing the camera. Her elbows were bent over her head, tendrils of hair hanging from her fingertips. Her back was slightly arched, pushing her breasts up and emphasizing the transition from slender waist to curved rear. Her legs were bent at ninety degrees, crossed ankles resting on a chair. Her expression was a mixture of innocence, humor, and seduction. She wore nothing at all, not even a necklace.

With shaking hands he turned the photo over.

I surrender was all she had written on the back. He shivered.

They had surrendered to each other at Pemberley, and it had led to the two most blissful weeks of his life. Could he hope that they could recapture that? His response to these pictures promised that at least on his part, their reunion would be intense.

What could he do but respond in kind? He changed his clothes and set up the camera. He took several photos, edited the best on his computer, and emailed it to her.

"You'd better be ready when you get here," he said when she answered her phone.

She laughed. "Is that a threat or a promise?"

"I think you should check your email."

"Really? Is this safe for work, or should I wait until I get back to my hotel?"

"Lizzy, I'm not a porn star like you," he said, smiling. "I have to get going. Call me when you leave for the airport."

Elizabeth grinned as she checked her email. Attached was a black and white photo of Darcy standing in his hallway, one arm braced against each wall. His damp hair curled slightly and his head tilted to the side. A soft smile curved the corners of his mouth. He was wearing his riding pants and boots and nothing else.

The caption read, *Please come home to me*.

That evening, Darcy picked Elizabeth up at the San Francisco airport. Since security protocols prevented meeting her at the gate, Darcy met her at the curb—and what a meeting it was. There was no modesty in their greeting as she flung her arms around his neck and kissed him with all the pent-up passion of a week's longing. He returned the kiss with equal enthusiasm, grasping her face with eagerness and laughing giddily for those brief moments when their lips parted. Finally, under the disapproving glare of the security agent, Elizabeth tossed her bag into the Audi's backseat and climbed into the car.

From the moment she folded her legs under the dash, Darcy sought the skin beneath the hem of her skirt. His palm brushed her thigh, and she crossed her legs, trapping his hand in a warm cocoon of pear-scented flesh.

"God, it's good to have you back," Darcy breathed, barely able to keep his eyes on the road.

"I'll feel better when I'm *on* my back," she teased, giving his hand a squeeze with her legs.

"Not again," he laughed, recalling another car ride in London, and the near-disaster her teases had provoked then.

"Not again? You mean you want me on top this time? Alright."

"I love that you're so horny."

"Oh yeah? Tell me about it."

"Need I elaborate?" Darcy inched his hand farther up her thigh and gave a seductive caress.

"No. But it would be sexy if you did."

"Well, your blouse is very pretty," he began chastely.

"Oh, no, that won't do at all!" she laughed.

"Hmmm. All right then. You have lovely, warm, chocolaty eyes."

"Better," she grinned and pushed his hand a little further up her skirt. "But not quite good enough."

"I love the way you smell," he tried. Elizabeth leaned over the gearshift and nuzzled her nose against Darcy's ear. "Keep going," she said huskily.

"I can't resist you," he confided.

"Then stop trying." She kissed the side of his neck, letting her tongue taste his salty skin. He let out a soft moan and tried his best to kiss her and drive at the same time. His racing skills were the only thing that saved them from an embarrassing crash—how would he explain to the police why his penis was in her hands?

After what seemed like an eternity, Darcy pulled into the underground garage of his building and parked. Elizabeth immediately climbed onto his lap and renewed her assault on his lips.

"Let's go up," he murmured, unable to imagine how they could possibly make love with the steering column in her back. She nodded and climbed off his lap. Darcy hastily zipped up his trousers and then climbed out. As they walked toward the elevator, Elizabeth skipped in front of him and put her arms around his waist.

"Just one more," she pleaded. With a soft laugh, Darcy kissed her while guiding her—backwards—toward the elevator and pressed the call button. Once inside, still entwined in her arms, he pressed the button for his floor and the lift jolted to life.

"Jesus, how I love your kisses," he rasped against her lips. "Your mouth tastes like warm caramel."

"I love how you feel against me," she replied, pressing her body tight against his.

As Darcy's head descended for another kiss, Elizabeth's hand grappled on the button panel until she found the stop button. She pulled it, bringing the elevator to a halt.

"What are you doing!" Darcy exclaimed, laughing as he pulled away from her. "You're setting off the alarm."

"I don't hear anything," she replied, continuing her efforts to seduce him by attacking the buttons of his shirt.

"It's silent. This building is full of rich bastards who don't want to be disturbed by some poor fool stuck in the elevator. But security knows that we've stopped." He made his point by disengaging the stop button and setting the elevator back on its trek to the twenty-first floor.

"Oh, come on, sweetie. Live a little," she pouted.

"I don't normally do my 'living' in public elevators." Then he grinned as she reached for the stop button. They swatted hands for a moment before she pretended defeat.

"You're such a do-gooder," she groused. "I bet you answer the phone every time it rings, even when you're in the shower."

"If I think it's you, then yes," he answered, gathering her into his arms again for a conciliatory kiss. She began to unbutton his shirt, and as he tried to avoid her advances, she hastily pulled the stop again.

"Stop it!" he laughed, releasing the button again. "There's probably a hidden security camera! We can't do anything in here!"

"Really? Not even this?" she asked as she brushed her hand over his crotch. "I've thought *long* and *hard* about this."

"What if someone gets on the elevator?" he pleaded, although he did not remove her hand this time.

"That's why I keep pulling the stop button, you ninny." Her hand stroked over the bulge of his burgeoning erection and she drew his head down for another kiss. Her massage—even through his trousers—was exquisite, and Darcy found himself not wanting to wait any longer, either. He pulled the stop button, initiating the silent alarm once again.

"You're going to get me arrested," he sighed as he shrugged out of his jacket. Then, resigning himself to the knowledge that the security team was likely about to enjoy a live pornographic performance, gave in to her demands. It was no use to resist. She was already unbuttoning her blouse.

"Tell me what you like," she breathed, her nipples peaking under the delicate lace of her bra.

"I love the way your titties fit in my hands," he whispered and cupped her breasts, edging the lace away and stroking his thumbs over her nipples. Her soft moan was answered when he dipped his head to taste the flesh released by his fingers.

"I love that your pussy is hot and tastes like pears," he rasped, using his free hand to pull up her skirt and stroke a finger along her sex. Then he withdrew his finger and put it in his mouth, tasting her tangy flavor. Elizabeth pulled it from his mouth and put it in her own, sucking on his finger.

"I love it when you touch me," he continued against her throat. In response, Elizabeth unzipped his trousers and plunged her hands inside, stroking and cupping him with maddening talent.

"I love it when you taste me," he ventured. His confession was answered by Elizabeth dropping to her knees and taking him into her mouth. He tipped his head back and closed his eyes while her tongue danced over his skin, bringing goose bumps to his arms and a flush to his cheeks.

"Christ, I want to fuck you," he groaned. She lifted herself onto the railing and spread her legs. He pushed her skirt up, thumbs tracing her folds. "Do you want me to fuck you?"

"Yes," she whispered.

After fumbling with a condom, he pushed into her, and she leaned her head back against the wall, arms wrapping tightly around his neck.

"Good?" he asked.

"Yes," she gasped.

"Harder?"

"Yes."

"Deeper?"

"Oh, yes."

He pushed into her, and she squirmed against him.

"Fuck me," she said against his neck.

She wrapped her legs tightly around him, drawing him in as far as she could. He used the railing as leverage to push himself into her, feral grunts coming from his throat while she stifled her own wild, hoarse moans. Her nails dug into his back as she reached orgasm with a throaty growl. He reached his own with an animalistic snarl and the satisfaction of a conqueror, her lower lip caught between his teeth.

They remained clutched together, languid in released tension, for a long moment. Their heartbeats slowed, and Darcy lazily opened his eyes. He was just about to kiss her when the phone in the elevator call box rang. Instinctively, Darcy picked it up. Elizabeth looked up at him, one eyebrow cocked in disbelief.

"This is building security. We're reading a malfunction on elevator car number four. The stop button has been engaged. Do you need assistance?"

"Uh, no," Darcy answered, dazed. "We're fine." At least the security team had the grace to let them finish the act before offering rescue.

"Please disengage the stop button, sir."

"Uh… in a minute."

"Sir, please identify yourself."

"Oh bloody hell!" Darcy exclaimed, and hung the phone up in a panic. He hurriedly tucked his shirt into his pants and zipped them up.

"I told you, you always answer the phone!" Elizabeth accused as she buttoned her blouse.

"They'll be sending the police along any moment now," he said nervously. Softening, Elizabeth put her arms around his waist and began to kiss his jawline.

"We're stopped between floors. It'll take them at least thirty minutes to get in here. If we go now, they'll never know it was us."

"Oh, God, I'm going to be arrested."

"I'm sure you can pull some strings to get us off the hook."

"You're such a bad influence on me," he laughed, shaking his head and putting his arms around her. After another kiss, he released the elevator and it shuddered back to life. Then he retrieved his jacket from the floor and shrugged into it.

"I wonder if I can get fired for indecent exposure," he mused as the elevator climbed past the eleventh floor.

Elizabeth crossed her arms over her chest and leaned against the railing. "Sweetie, take a look around. There's no camera. Nobody can prove that we were, um, bumping uglies."

"I may have to just buy the building and confiscate and destroy all the surveillance videos, just to be sure," he said.

"What am I going to do with you?" she laughed, shaking her head.

"Come away from the railing, darling," he said, pulling her to his side as the elevator doors opened. "God only knows what goes on in these elevators."

Chapter 24

"DON'T BE NERVOUS," DARCY said reassuringly as Elizabeth paced in his chambers. They had borne four weeks of a long-distance affair, but her assignment was over. Now was the time to face the music.

"How do I look?" she asked, smoothing down the pleat of her skirt.

"You look very professional."

Darcy's speakerphone buzzed. "Yes," he answered.

"Judge Boyd will see you now."

Elizabeth glanced at Darcy, wide-eyed. He gave her a kiss on the forehead.

"It will be fine," he said, squeezing her arms encouragingly, while ignoring the anxiety in his own stomach. "Let's go."

Darcy opened the door for Elizabeth and together they walked down the hall to the presiding judge's chambers.

"Come in, have a seat," Wendell Boyd invited as he opened his chambers door. Already seated was Milton Gardiner. "What can I do for you?" he asked once Elizabeth and Darcy were settled in two leather chairs.

"I have a bit of a situation," Darcy began, clearing his throat. "I need to recuse myself from Ms. Bennet's cases."

"I see." Wendell leaned back in his chair. "May I ask why?" he said after a moment.

"We've developed a personal relationship that would make it improper for me to decide any of her cases," Darcy replied matter-of-factly.

"How far back does this go? Do we need to worry about retrying anything?"

Darcy shook his head. "There was about a two-week period where some interaction was unavoidable. I removed myself from the only trial. All of the other hearings were status or settlement conferences where any decision I made was preliminary and could be revisited by the trial judge."

Wendell shifted his gaze to Mr. Gardiner. "And your concern is whether Will needs to remove himself from all of your firm's cases, correct?"

"Yes. If so, it could have dire consequences on the sale of my firm."

Wendell looked up at the ceiling for a moment, thinking. "Of course, you'll have to disclose your conflict and if there's any objection, the case can be reassigned, but I don't think you need to take the action of removing yourself from the entire firm."

"I know this may make things difficult for Judge Clayton, so I just want to say that I am willing to do whatever is necessary to make the transition smooth," Elizabeth offered.

"Actually, your timing couldn't be more perfect," Wendell said, leaning forward. "I got this memo this morning." He pushed a sheet of paper across the desk to Darcy, who picked it up and read it.

"They've lifted the hiring freeze?" Darcy asked in disbelief.

Wendell nodded. "Looks like they found some money in someone's couch cushions. Enough for two new positions, three if Will retires."

"How soon will you be hiring?" Mr. Gardiner asked.

"My hope is to have two new judges within three months." He turned his blue eyes to Darcy. "Let me reiterate. I hope to hire *two* new judges, not three. I still hope you will reconsider your retirement plans."

Darcy nodded, too surprised to say anything. Wendell turned his attention to Elizabeth.

"In the meantime, I think that if the parties got conflict waivers it would still be possible for you to appear. Now, I don't know if you want to actually go through all that trouble, and frankly on a criminal case it's unlikely the prosecution would agree to a waiver. But you know your cases best and whether it would be a bigger headache to transfer to Frances than to get a waiver. I'll leave that up to you."

"Well, that settles it!" Milton said, rubbing his hands together. "Elizabeth, we'll meet next week to go over your cases. Now I'm going to be late for dinner, and my wife really hates that, so I'd better get going." They all rose and shook hands before parting ways.

"That was astonishingly painless," Elizabeth said as they pulled onto the freeway.

"Yes, I'm waiting for the other shoe to drop," Darcy laughed.

"Oh, I'll bear the brunt of that. You know Judge Clayton is going to screw up all of my cases."

"Look at it as an opportunity to make your name with the Court of Appeals."

"Yes. You know..." she began thoughtfully. "I quite like doing appeals. You're not in the trenches, so to speak. It's more academic. It's actually less stressful that what I do now."

"Are you thinking of shifting gears to specialize in appeals?"

"I have been, yes. It would keep me out of your courtroom, and I'd still be able to work with my clients whenever they wanted to do an appeal."

"That sounds very—pardon the pun—appealing."

"I don't think I can pardon that pun, it was awful. But seriously, what do you think?"

Darcy considered for a moment, then gave her his honest opinion. "I think you'd be very good at it, and I think it's something that you should do if it really makes you happy."

"You won't think I'm doing it just because we're a couple, will you?"

"I think whatever you do, you'll do it because it's right for you, regardless of how it affects me. If it happens to resolve our problem, then that's great. But if it doesn't, then we'll find another way around it. What's important to me, above all, is that you be happy."

Elizabeth stroked his hand with hers, then kissed it. "That's why I love you."

"And then we did it in the elevator." Elizabeth held a red lacy teddy up to her chest. It was the day after her meeting with Judge Boyd—and the elevator sexcapade—and Lou was taking her lingerie shopping as a welcome back gift.

"In the elevator?" Lou exclaimed, shocked. He shook his head at the teddy, and she hung it back on the rack.

"In the elevator."

"Lizzy, you little tramp! I'm very proud of you," he laughed. "Remind me to start carrying wet wipes everywhere."

He picked up a pair of garters and showed them to her. When she wrinkled her nose, he put them back. She picked up a yellow, gauzy baby doll nighty and glanced at him for approval. He nodded and said, "Try that on," as he followed her to the dressing room.

"What do you think?" she asked as she opened the door for him.

Lou smiled. "Very pretty. I think he'll like it."

She came out and they rifled through panties. He picked up a pair comprised of a small mesh triangle and three strings. He frowned.

"Really, what is the point?" he said. He held them to his waist. "No support, doesn't conceal anything. Why not just go without?"

"I believe those are more of a hair net," Elizabeth commented.

"So, are you moving in with Judge Horndog?" Lou asked as they continued on to the sale rack.

"I don't think I'm ready for that just yet. I mean, you have to have your mail forwarded, and I still share the house with Jane. Besides, he'd probably make me do all the laundry, and you know I hate laundry. I'd rather just buy new underwear."

"Glad you have your priorities straight. What's the deal with Jane now? You mentioned last week that she and what's-his-face were having problems."

"Yeah, it's all a huge mess. She's mad at him because his sister was all over Will, and he keeps defending her."

"You know, you and Jane have the weirdest taste in men. I mean, Charley is such a space cadet, and Will always looks like he's sucked on a lemon. Captain Conundrum has a sidekick, General Malaise."

"Hey, come on," Elizabeth laughed. "Will smiles at me all the time."

"I'll believe it when I see it. If he were my boyfriend, he'd have a smile plastered on his face twenty-four-seven."

"Oh, really. And just how do you think that would happen?"

"Blow jobs, my dear Lizzy. I know all the secrets."

Elizabeth looked at him with hungry curiosity. "Tell me, or I'll never tell you when your ass looks fat again."

They spent forty minutes in a Starbucks with Lou drawing diagrams for Elizabeth's edification. Once in the car, he actually unzipped his pants and showed her more.

"Lou, I don't know what I'd do without you," Elizabeth finally said, her sides aching from laughing all day.

"Friends mean a lot, Lizzy." Lou glanced at Elizabeth, his humor replaced with a sincere expression. "A man can't be without them."

"I know," she sighed. "Are you trying to tell me to give Will the okay to be friends with Caroline?"

"I'm saying that his friendship with her is no different than our friendship. Except that if I wasn't gay, you'd be sleeping with me because you couldn't resist. But the point is, you trust him, and you believe him when he says there was nothing going on between them. And if you come to terms with that, maybe Jane will too. It's affecting more people that just you, honey."

Elizabeth rolled her eyes. "Honestly, Lou, why do you always have to be the voice of my conscience? Can't you just be the devil on my shoulder?"

Lou stopped the car in front of her house. "Doing good deeds is how I get my wings. And you know I need some wings to wear with my leather chaps in the Gay Pride Parade." Elizabeth climbed out of the car and ducked her head back in the window.

"Okay, I get it. If you love something, set it free, *blah, blah, blah*. I hate it when you're right."

She blew him a kiss and started toward her house when Lou called out the window, "And remember! *Wax on, wax off!*"

Chapter 25

"WHAT DO YOU MEAN, the wedding is off?" Fanny cried, her shrill voice ringing against the kitchen's ceiling. "It can't be off! Call Charley right now and tell him it's back on."

"Mom! Please! Can't you see Jane's upset?" Elizabeth replied, her arm wrapping protectively around Jane's shoulder as she sat weeping at the kitchen table.

"Of course I see she's upset, Lizzy, I'm not an idiot! But she'll feel much better once she calls Charley and tells him the wedding is *back on*." Fanny jabbed her finger on the tablecloth for emphasis.

"It's too late, I can't call him," Jane wailed, a sob hiccupping between her words.

"Oh, this is all my fault," Elizabeth moaned. "I'm so sorry, Janey."

"Your fault? How is it your fault?" Fanny leapt onto Elizabeth's words, eager for a scapegoat to blame for months of intense planning gone down the drain.

"It's a long story, Mom," Elizabeth sighed.

"No, it's not. Charley's sister tried to steal Elizabeth's boyfriend, and Charley refuses to admit that she was wrong to do it. That's the long and short of it." Jane wiped her eyes and cleared her throat. "Now I'll just have to find a job at another hospital and resign myself to the fact that I'm going to be an old maid."

"Is *that* all?" Fanny laughed. "Look, Jane, this is not a reason to cancel the wedding. Lord knows I hated your father's sister when we got married."

"You hated my sister?" Tom asked indignantly, catching Fanny's last sentence as he entered the kitchen for a beer.

"Of course not, Tom. Go back to your hockey-ball game, or whatever it is you're watching. I've got more important things to worry about here." She gave her husband a dismissive wave of the hand over her shoulder and turned back to Jane. "Now, as I was saying, I *hated* your father's sister when we got married." Tom let out an irritated grunt and left the kitchen, beer in hand.

"Which one?" Jane sniffled.

"Madeline."

"Aunt Maddie? How could you hate her? She's wonderful!" Elizabeth cried, shocked to learn that her favorite aunt was on her mother's shit list.

"Exactly. She's perfect in every way, a real Mary Poppins. She never smoked hash, never drank a beer, finished college without taking any time off, and became the perfect housewife. I still hate her, sometimes. But the point is I didn't marry *her*. I married your dad, who I loved dearly and still do to this day."

"You told me you liked my sister!" Tom called from the living room.

"Oh Tom, shut *up!* Jane, do you love Charley?"

"Yes, of course I do."

"Is this the only thing that's keeping you apart? That he defended his sister who tried to sleep with Lizzy's boyfriend?

Wait… Lizzy has a boyfriend?" Fanny's train of thought was derailed by the notion that Elizabeth, at last, had found someone. "When did this happen?!"

"Mom, we're talking about Jane, not me. For God's sake, woman, focus!" Elizabeth pleaded. She turned her attention back to Jane.

"Jane, Will and I have gotten over Caroline. We've moved on. You and Charley need to too."

"You're dating *Will?* Charley's best man?" Fanny screeched. "The tall one, with the to-die-for accent and bedroom eyes?"

"Eww, Mom, please! You're grossing me out!" Elizabeth exclaimed, observing her mother's fawning expression. If anything could turn Elizabeth off Darcy, it was imagining him with her *mother*.

"But he won't say she was *wrong*," Jane pouted, drawing Elizabeth's attention back.

"Well, honey, she wasn't. I mean, if I understand it correctly, she was just trying to help him out by making me jealous. And it worked, and now we're back together, so she wasn't technically wrong."

"*Back* together?" Both Jane and Elizabeth ignored Fanny's outburst.

"Lizzy, how can you be so casual about it? Doesn't it make you furious to know that she was scheming behind your back? That she played everyone for idiots?"

"Of course it does, but I try to keep the big picture in mind. Will was never interested in her, he didn't know what she was doing, it made me open my eyes, and now we're together. I can't see her coming between us again, and I really don't think you should let her come between you and Charley. So he defends his sister. Don't you think that's kind of honorable of him? I mean, he loves her unconditionally, just like he loves you."

Jane mulled on this for a moment.

"When did this happen with Will?" Fanny asked in a stage whisper.

"Mom! Please! I'll tell you about it *later*," Elizabeth hissed.

"I guess I didn't really think of it like that," Jane said slowly. "I've been so intent on making him apologize for what she'd done. But that's not really fair, is it? I mean, I wouldn't apologize to Will for those pants you're wearing tonight. The blame for those falls squarely on your shoulders."

"What's wrong with my pants?" Elizabeth replied defensively, glancing down at her khakis, before she caught Jane's half-smile. "So, do you think you should call him and make up?"

"I think I should do it in person."

"I'll drive you there." Elizabeth grinned as they stood.

"Wait just one minute, Miss Lizzy! Don't you step out of this house until you tell me all about Will!"

"Mom, I made a solemn vow to Will, and I'm going to keep it. What happens in England stays in England." Elizabeth and Jane left the house, arm-in-arm, leaving a fuming Fanny in their wake.

Mrs. Bennet had planned her dream wedding for Jane, and luckily for her it was not for naught. Now that Bingley and Jane were back on track, they had managed to trim the guest list to only 200, and even that had been a battle. Using Bingley's money, Fanny Bennet had outdone herself. But when the day finally came on the last Saturday of November, with the ceremony held in San Francisco's Grace Cathedral, no one could deny that it was a splendid affair.

Elizabeth stood before the mirror with Jane in their dressing room. Jane, a vision of angelic beauty with her ball gown of cascading duchess satin and cathedral train, adjusted her triple-tiered tulle veil for the ninth time. Her mother adjusted it back to its original position.

"Stop fussing, Jane," Fanny said softly. "You look lovely, like Grace Kelly." She stood back and smiled at Jane. As she and Elizabeth gazed with misty satisfaction at Jane, a soft knock came from the door.

"Come in," Elizabeth called.

Darcy poked his head in. "Mrs. Bennet, your husband has lost something; he's asked you to come help him," he said coming into the room. Fanny nodded once, sniffled, then squared her shoulders before marching out the door to take care of anyone who dared to threaten the planned perfection of her day.

Because Elizabeth had stayed with Jane the night before, she had not seen Darcy yet. He looked, quite honestly, devastatingly handsome in his tuxedo. Elizabeth wasn't one to be impressed by such finery, but she had to admit, Darcy would look good in just about anything—or nothing. She arched one brow as vivid images began to enter her mind.

"What?" Darcy asked, looking down critically at his tuxedo. "Is there lint on my lapel?"

"No, nothing." Elizabeth grinned.

"Lizzy! Come here at once!" Fanny's voice held a faint hint of panic. Elizabeth saw Jane's eyes flash toward the door, her own face showing signs of panic. With a placating gesture, Elizabeth headed toward the door.

"How are you feeling?" Darcy asked as he stood behind Jane at the mirror.

She laughed, but it sounded a little too shrill. "Like I'm about to face a firing squad. I can't believe how many people are going to be there. What if I forget my vows? What if I trip going down the aisle? What if my mother remembers how she normally behaves?"

Darcy laughed softly and put his hands on her arms, somehow avoiding stepping on the voluminous gown around her.

"Jane, think about it. What's the worst thing that could happen today?"

"Well, they could drop the cake or somebody could faint or my dress could get torn..." she began, reciting the laundry list of disasters that had accumulated in her mind over the last twenty-four hours.

Darcy smiled and squeezed her arms gently. "No, Jane. The worst thing that could happen is that you miss the joy of your own wedding with silly worries. This is the only day in your life when you will marry Charley. What do you want your memories to be? That one of the tables was missing a centerpiece? Or that this was one of the happiest days of your life?"

Jane met his eyes in the mirror and let out a slow exhale. Then she smiled and her tense shoulders relaxed. "You're a great guy, Will," she said, squeezing his hand on her shoulder. "No wonder Charley likes you so much."

Elizabeth returned to the dressing room to see her boyfriend and her soon-to-be-married sister in a somewhat tender embrace.

"Hey now!" she laughed as she closed the door behind her. Darcy looked up at her and smiled.

"Disaster averted?" he asked as he pulled away from Jane.

Elizabeth nodded. "Missing boutonniere," she explained. "Not found but replaced. The wedding can go on." She had pulled a flower from her own bouquet to make her father a new one.

Darcy looked at her for the first time today. "You look very nice," he said smiling.

"I hope so or this very expensive dress will have been all for nothing," she teased. She wore a floor-length satin and organza bridesmaid gown in a rich cranberry color that set off her creamy skin. Small, jeweled butterflies held her hair in a chignon.

Darcy walked to her and gave her a soft, lingering kiss just near her ear. "I lied, you look ravishing," he said quietly.

"You're looking your usual dashing self." She grinned at him. He shrugged, as if to say *I can't help it*.

"I missed you last night," he said for her ears only. "It's hard to sleep without you."

"Am I so boring that you use me as a sleep aid?"

"On the contrary, your vigorous workouts are excellent for wearing me out," he rejoined quietly and brushed his lips across hers. "Try not to make a habit of not being there." His hand lingered delicately on her shoulder, thumb stroking her neck lightly. His other hand sneaked around her waist and pulled her closer to him.

"Will, control yourself. It's Jane's wedding day."

"And what of it? I'm not marrying her. I have other prospects in mind," he said and kissed her. She was just putting her arms around his neck when Mrs. Bennet bustled back in.

"Oh, you two, I suppose another one will be just around the corner. But one wedding at a time, one at a time. Let's go, we're ready to start," she said as she walked toward Jane.

Darcy pulled back from Elizabeth but not before he gave her a meaningful look. Exactly what the meaning was, she wasn't sure. Maybe it was, *Yes, another wedding is around the corner*, or perhaps, *Your mother certainly is presumptuous*, or possibly even, *I wish we were having sex right now*.

The wedding ceremony was unfortunately very formal and very long. There were several bouts of kneeling and rising and recitations of prayers in both English and Latin. Elizabeth's preference was for something less formal and more heartfelt, but then, this really was her *mother's* wedding, not Jane's. Elizabeth's eyes crept up to find Darcy's already on her. Her heart skipped a beat, and she briefly imagined that she was marrying him as she listened to the vows, and she wondered if he were doing the same thing.

Finally, the ceremony ended, and the recessional played. Elizabeth took Darcy's arm, and they walked down the aisle out of the church into the brisk, but luckily, sunny day. There was another hour of photos and confusion before they were able to get into the hired Rolls Royce and drive to the reception at the luxury hotel where most guests were staying. Elizabeth and Bingley helped Jane get her dress, flowers, and veil all into the car while Darcy discussed directions with the chauffeur. Finally, they arrived at the hotel and were announced to the waiting crowd.

Elizabeth and Darcy each gave teasing, heartwarming toasts, danced the obligatory first dance, and helped with the cake cutting. When at last their obligations were complete, they found a moment together.

"Want to dance?" Elizabeth asked, her arms snaking around his waist.

"No, remember the jazz club in London? I don't dance well."

"How else am I supposed to press my lonely body against yours?" she teased.

"Well, your hair seems to be coming a little loose. Maybe we need to go upstairs to our room and freshen up?"

She nodded and with a mischievous glance, led him by the hand from the reception to the elevator. Both blushed, remembering their amorous adventure in another elevator, but the crowded lift prevented any replay of that incident. Once inside their room, however, all bets were off.

"I can't believe how much I miss you when you're gone," he said as he kissed her neck and pulled off his tuxedo jacket. "Twenty-four hours without you and I'm some kind of randy wreck." She laughed as their hands scrabbled to undress each other, until at last her dress fell to a cranberry puddle at her feet. Darcy's expression, however, did not convey lust.

"What kind of sex-defying contraption is that?" he asked indignantly, looking with consternation at her supportive undergarment.

She laughed. "Here, you have to unhook this first," she said softly, pulling his hands to her undergarment. "And then this unzips here," Elizabeth continued, guiding his hands.

He found it strangely sexy that she was showing him how to undo a garment that could have been his grandmother's.

"And this is the last snap," she said, guiding his hand between her legs.

"That should have come undone first," he said with a mischievous grin. She shook her head.

"Then I wouldn't be completely naked, would I?" she said as she pushed the garment down.

"No indeed," Darcy breathed. His vest and shirt were quickly discarded, and he held her close to him.

"Can I take your hair down?" he asked. She shook her head.

"No, we do have to go back downstairs. Let's try not to mess it up," she said. She kissed him and ran her fingers over his chest while he pressed her back with his hands. He made a little moaning noise as her fingers brushed across his nipples. Elizabeth smiled under his kiss, then dipped her head to attend to his nipples. She put her open mouth on one, letting her hot breath warm it. She kissed it softly, then she put the flat of her tongue on it, stroking it across the puckered skin. He closed his eyes and let his hand rest on her shoulder, the other continuing to stroke her back, working its way to her butt.

She took his nipple in her mouth and sucked. He grunted and squeezed her rear. She trailed kisses down his chest, across the flat expanse of his belly. Elizabeth pushed him to a seated position on the bed and knelt before him. She spread his legs and kissed his thighs before taking him into her mouth.

He looked down and watched her head move, jeweled butterflies glinting in the lamplight. Her dark hair bobbed against his pale thighs, a sight he could never tire of seeing.

"Yes," he whispered. He closed his eyes again, letting the sensations she evoked wash over him. His fingers worked carefully into her hair, the need to guide her head overtaking any concern for her hairdo. His thigh muscles flexed, tense with desire battling self-control. Then she did something with her tongue, something that completely undid him, something that provoked such an erotic response that he had no control; he spent himself with his hands tangled in her hair, a pin jabbing his palm, pain shooting through him at the same time as the exquisite pleasure of coming in her mouth.

"Oh... my... *God!*" he exclaimed.

There was a knock at the door.

"Lizzy, what are you doing in there? Everyone is asking for you!" came her mother's voice. Elizabeth opened her eyes and looked at Darcy, his member still in her mouth. Darcy cleared his throat.

"Lizzy is in the bathroom, Fanny. We'll be down in a few minutes." Elizabeth gave him an approving swirl of her tongue, forcing a quiet grunt from his throat.

"Don't take too long coming!" Fanny called before leaving.

"No chance of that," Darcy laughed quietly. "Where on earth did you learn that little trick?"

"I'll give you one gay guess."

"Lou? Lou showed you how to give a seismic blow job?"

"Yes, and believe me, it's no simple task."

Darcy pulled her from her knees to sit on his lap, where his hand fell to the joint between her legs and began to massage.

"That may call for some payback."

"I'm all for calling in my debts." She grinned as he swung her to lie on the bed. She was just enjoying his breath tickling her inner thigh when there was another knock on the door.

"Go away!" they both shouted in frustration, before shooting each other grins.

"Elizabeth, you have ten minutes before we get a lock-out key and drag you downstairs!" came Lou's voice.

"If you'd stop disturbing me I'd only need five!" she shouted back. They heard his laugh fade as he walked away.

"Only five minutes, that's a lot of pressure," Darcy murmured before dipping his head between her legs.

"I have every confidence you can accomplish the task."

He did accomplish the task, passing with flying colors as indicated by the sharp pull Elizabeth gave his hair while expelling her now-familiar gasp of pleasure. They took a few moments to calm down, a brief moment to simply lie with each other, legs twisted in a lazy embrace, before pulling themselves from the bed to freshen up.

Once downstairs, Fanny corralled Elizabeth to some unknown duty and Darcy found himself at the bar next to Lou. They said nothing at first, merely acknowledging each other's presence by nodding at their reflections in the mirror behind the bar.

"It seems I have misjudged you, Mr. Hurst. I owe you an apology," Darcy said to him, staring straight ahead. Lou said nothing. "And a car," Darcy continued. He saw the corners of Lou's mouth curl up in a reluctant smile. "And possibly a retirement plan of some sort," Darcy concluded.

Lou laughed. "She wouldn't take *all* of my advice," Lou replied and took a sip of his drink.

"There was nothing lacking in her performance, I assure you," Darcy replied and took a sip of his own drink. Their eyes met in the mirror.

Lou replied, "Yes but it would be vastly improved by the removal of her front teeth."

Darcy burst out laughing.

Chapter 26

TIME SEEMED TO SLIP through Elizabeth's fingers no matter how hard she tried to savor every moment. Already she'd been back at Gardiner & Associates for three months, spending most nights at Darcy's place. She was one change of address card away from officially living with him, and he did all the laundry.

Time went so fast that Christmas, with all its commercial and familial pressures, snuck up on Elizabeth and practically mugged her. It did, after all, leave her penniless and with a splitting headache.

"Lizzy, I can't tell you how much I appreciate you hosting Christmas dinner this year. What with Jane's wedding, my nerves are nearly torn to shreds!" came Mrs. Bennet's shrill voice over the phone.

"It's no problem, Mom. Put Dad on, would you?"

"Yes, dear?" came her father's voice.

"Dad, I'm begging you, please don't let Mom start on about me not being married again this year. I can't take the humiliation."

"But Lizzy, it's a Christmas tradition, like Uncle Teddy's eggnog-and-prune fudge," Mr. Bennet protested with a laugh.

"Daddy!" Elizabeth pleaded.

Mr. Bennet laughed and assured Elizabeth that he would do his best. Elizabeth wondered if she should tell Darcy not to come at all. Twice she dialed his number but hung up.

"Why do you keep calling me and hanging up?" Darcy asked her a few moments later when she answered her phone.

"Will, I don't know if I want you to come to Christmas dinner. I don't think I can stand the embarrassment that my family will put me through."

"Elizabeth, don't be silly. They can't be that bad. You and Jane turned out okay."

"An aberration, I assure you. You will be pounced on by Lydia, who will try to recruit you for her escort service. Kitty will name-drop all the famous people she's served dessert to. Mary will bore you to death with the religiosity of post-Soviet literature. And my mother... oh, my mother! I shudder to think," she said.

"Have I ever told you that I have an uncle who insists that the healthiest form of exercise is to jog around his grounds in nothing but socks and trainers?"

"Eeesh!"

"Look, don't be concerned that I'm going to be offended or insulted or embarrassed. I can take it. If there's some other reason you don't want me to come, then say it." He had used that gentle, persistent tone that said he was not to be swayed.

"You've been warned," she sighed dramatically, but was secretly pleased that he wanted to spend the holiday with her.

Lou arrived first, shaking the rain off his umbrella on the front porch. Elizabeth smiled widely as he gave her a hug and a kiss on the cheek.

"Smells great!" he said as he hung his coat in the closet. "Who's going to be here?"

"Mom and Dad, Lydia, Kitty, Mary, Jane and Charley, Will, and Caroline."

"Caroline! Lady Boobs-a-Lot? Why on earth is she coming?" Lou exclaimed as he headed toward the kitchen, following the smells of turkey and stuffing.

"Jane wanted me to invite her, and I figured if she's going to be my sister-in-law, we should try to get along. Besides, maybe my family will frighten her off."

"Very forward-thinking of you."

She slapped his hand as he dipped his finger into a pan of gravy, but he still managed to get a taste.

"Get that, would you?" she called to Lou when the doorbell rang.

Lou let Jane, Bingley, and Caroline in and took their coats. Bingley and Jane gave Elizabeth warm hugs and kissed her cheek. Caroline hung back and then presented a surprised Elizabeth with a bottle of wine.

"Thank you for inviting me," she said almost shyly.

"You're welcome," Elizabeth stammered. Caroline watched Jane and Bingley over her shoulder as they headed toward the living room before turning to Elizabeth.

"Look, I know we got off on the worst possible footing and I don't expect us to be best friends. But I want to thank you for helping patch things up with Charley and Jane. He didn't deserve to be caught up in my mess."

"No, I didn't like seeing Jane so unhappy either. And I know your friendship was important to Will. Just, you know, stay out of his pants."

Caroline laughed. "Not a problem. I'm in his cousin's pants."

"Richard?" Elizabeth exclaimed, and Caroline nodded. Elizabeth shook her head at the seemingly incestuous relations of their group of friends. "If he rings your bell," she laughed, glad to have the threat of Caroline nullified by the intervention of a man more suited to her.

Mary, Kitty, and Lydia were the next to arrive. They bustled in and hung their coats, laughing and hugging everyone. The house was ringing with giggles as the sisters caught up with each other over glasses of wine.

The doorbell rang again, and Elizabeth opened it to greet her parents.

"Lizzy, darling, you look lovely," Mrs. Bennet said dreamily. Elizabeth looked at her father in horror as the cloud of cannabis washed over her. He shrugged sheepishly and grinned. Mrs. Bennet made her way sedately to her family, hugging daughters and exclaiming at how lovely each one of them looked and asking for some crackers.

"You got her *high?*" Elizabeth gasped in a hushed tone.

"It was the only way, dear. But don't worry, I'm the designated driver."

Her mortification only increased when she saw Darcy step onto the porch.

"Oh, hello, Will," Mr. Bennet said pleasantly, shaking his hand.

"How are you, Tom?"

"Oh, you know, hiding from all the wedding planning," he laughed, winking at Elizabeth.

Elizabeth drew Darcy into the kitchen as Mr. Bennet made his way toward the living room. From there she heard Lydia laugh, "Lord, Mom, have you been smoking *pot?*" Elizabeth closed her eyes and wished herself under the floorboards.

"It's good for glaucoma," her mother replied loftily.

"If you *have* glaucoma," Lou laughed.

"An ounce of prevention, you know," was her mother's response.

"More like a dime bag. Jesus, Fanny, how much did you smoke?"

Elizabeth opened her eyes and saw Darcy grinning at her. He kissed her quickly and whispered, "Thank you for inviting me after all. And thank you for inviting Caroline. It was very big of you." He winked at her and gave her rear end a surreptitious squeeze. Elizabeth giggled and kissed Darcy's chin before taking her glass of wine into the living room.

The turkey nearly fell on the floor and the mashed potatoes were lumpy, but otherwise Elizabeth counted the evening a success. Her family teased Darcy as if he was one of their own children, and Elizabeth was proud to note that Darcy gave as good as he got. She supposed that it was a good thing that he'd gotten to know her family through Jane and Charley while she was in San Diego; it left the whole awkward "this is my date" phase out of the relationship.

They drank far too much wine, which made the gag-gift exchange hilarious. But one by one, people began to get tired, and the party began to break up. Darcy took his place next to Elizabeth at the door, saying good night to everyone as they left. After giving Elizabeth a hug good night, Mrs. Bennet turned to Darcy and, to his surprise, gave him a hug as well. Elizabeth rolled her eyes as Mrs. Bennet rested her cheek on Darcy's chest, a slightly-intoxicated grin on her face.

"You are a very nice man, Will," she sang. "You should marry my daughter." She emphasized her meaning with three resounding smacks on his chest. Darcy winced and laughed.

"Mom, you were doing so well," Elizabeth sighed. Her mother smiled at her.

"Your father thinks he's so clever, but I know what's going on! Tom! Bring the bag of weed home with you. We'll finish it off tonight."

Elizabeth pressed her fingers to her forehead. "Jesus Christ," she laughed.

"All right, come on, Fanny. Let's roll you into the car," Mr. Bennet laughed.

"Speaking of rolling…" Mrs. Bennet began, but Elizabeth cut off the rest of the sentence by closing the door.

Turning to Darcy, Elizabeth said, "Please don't have my parents arrested."

He laughed and put his arms around her. "I didn't see anything. I'm sure your mother was wearing some organic perfume, like patchouli. Who am I to argue that she wasn't carrying around fresh oregano?"

"Nice try," she laughed and hugged him.

"Ah, well, then perhaps you will just have to bribe me," he said suggestively. She ran her fingers over his bottom.

"Are you soliciting me?"

"I believe I am. Is it working?"

"I believe it is." He kissed her and worked his hands down her back to her own bottom.

He pulled back from her and said, "Why do you always have your hair up?"

She put her arms around his neck. "Because you like to take it down," she replied simply. He smiled and pulled the band from her hair, letting it fall over her shoulders.

She kissed him, drawing his lips to hers.

"Lizzy," he said against her lips. "Your mother was right."

"I sincerely hope you're talking about the ounce of prevention," she replied and kissed him again.

"No. Elizabeth—"

"Will, if you propose to me right now because my mother told you to, so help me God, not only will I refuse, but I'll never, *ever* forgive you."

"Okay," he laughed, then sought another kiss from her. "I can take a hint. You only want me for my body. It's so demeaning. Can we go to bed now?"

Once in her bedroom, Elizabeth undressed and fell into bed on her back, exhausted. Darcy climbed in next to her, and lay on his side, head propped up on his hand.

"That wasn't bad at all, was it? I'm afraid to say, you seem to fit in with my family. That goes in the 'con' column, in case you're keeping score," she said sleepily.

"I did have one last Christmas gift," he said, opening his hand before her. Hanging from his fingers was a pair of brilliant asscher-cut drop diamond earrings. She looked up to him, shocked. He smiled. "Don't thank me, it's a gift to myself. I wanted to see them on you."

He watched as she put the earrings on and turned to face him. He nodded approvingly. "Even better than I imagined," he said.

She smiled and pushed him onto his back, straddling him. "I don't know what I've done to deserve you," she said, kissing him.

"Undoubtedly it was something very naughty. Perhaps it involved an encounter at an all-girls school? And I'm sure short skirts and knee socks were involved," he said, smiling against her lips. She laughed and put her arms around his neck, grasping the iron post headboard behind him.

"You are a kinky man, Mr. Darcy."

He looked at her in perfect tenderness and stroked a curl of her hair. "No, Ms. Bennet, in fact my tastes are very simple. My favorite color is Elizabeth. My favorite song is Elizabeth. My favorite flavor of ice cream is Elizabeth. My favorite flower is Elizabeth. My favorite fruit is the pear, because it smells like Elizabeth." This simple declaration was made with a sincerity that stilled her heart. She could say nothing else.

Instead, she kissed him and caressed him, held him until he was breathless. Darcy let out a sigh of pleasure as she joined their bodies. She pulled herself along him, arching her body in the moonlight. He ran his fingers over her peaks and valleys, tracing each contour as if to commit it to memory. Elizabeth whispered his name against his neck while he trailed his finger over her spine. He gently rolled her to her back.

His hands felt the curve of her waist, the swell of her hips, the line of her thigh as it moved along his side. He stretched over her body, no end and no beginning to each; they were the same.

Darcy sensed, rather than heard, their heartbeats become synchronized. He could feel her heartbeat inside his own chest. When Elizabeth drew breath, *his* lungs filled. He did not know how he would take another breath on his own without her. He was experiencing her with a clarity he had never before known. If he strained, he could hear her thoughts like whispers inside his head: *this is what it means to love*.

Their trembling sighs mingled into one breath. She knew that his skin tingled when her fingertips brushed over it. She felt the coursing of his blood in her own veins. She would never be Elizabeth again, and he would never be Will again. Their souls would be forever colored by the essence of other.

They expelled soft cries at the same time, breathing into each others' mouths, names whispered in ardor.

She trembled within his shaking arms, both too overcome to speak. His fingers still curled in her hair, his breath slower but still hot against her ear. Their bond had been powerful, their connection beyond the physical. Each felt shaken as the sublime connection eased its grip, and released them back into their own consciousnesses. Darcy wanted to weep, mourning the loss of that perfect union of awareness. He heard her shuddering exhalation and kissed away the salty wetness on her cheek.

They settled into a comfortable embrace, arms and legs entwined. As they drifted off to sleep, Darcy murmured, "Happy Christmas, Elizabeth." Indeed, it was.

Chapter 27

MILTON GARDINER'S RETIREMENT PARTY was held on a luxury yacht in the San Francisco Bay in the first week of February. At least two hundred guests were in attendance, and at least half of those were attorneys with whom both Darcy and Elizabeth were acquainted. Although their relationship was now common knowledge, both tried to keep a professional distance, especially in light of Darcy's decision not to retire. After all, he no longer wanted to go back to England; everything he wanted was right here.

To avoid the appearance of arriving together, Darcy dropped Elizabeth off then circled the block for fifteen minutes. When he finally boarded the yacht, his eye was immediately drawn to her. Even after seeing her every single day in every state of dress and undress, he always felt a thrill when he saw her. Tonight her skin was warmed by the peach silk dress she wore. It draped over her breast, softening her curves, and skimmed over her hips to end just above the knee. Her hair was swept back in a soft bun, wavy tendrils slipping free only to be tucked behind her ears.

The earrings he had given her for Christmas sparkled subtly against her skin.

When her smoky eyes met his along with that teasing half-smile that made his knees turn to jelly, he swallowed and nodded in acknowledgment. Then, determined to appear professional, he turned to greet a friend. They mixed and mingled in separate circles until the yacht pulled out just as the sun set. As the craft passed under the Golden Gate Bridge, Darcy managed to find a moment alone with Elizabeth.

"Did I tell you how lovely you look tonight?" he asked quietly.

She shook her head and smiled. "No, but it's duly noted, Your Honor."

He grinned and took a step away from her as another attorney approached and again they went their separate ways.

Dinner was served, and they ate at separate tables. The alcohol flowed freely and everyone began to get a little drunk. As the toasts to Milton began, Darcy walked to the back of the room and stood behind the crowd. Once Judge Boyd had taken the stage for a speech, Elizabeth joined Darcy, who sneaked his hand to her low back.

As the speech droned on, Darcy's hand slipped lower onto her rear. He slid a hand slowly over her cheek, fingers tracing the curve where cheek met leg. He ran a finger back up, lightly trailing her rear cleavage. She tried to repress her smile but failed. He looked resolutely ahead, giving no sign of his hand's explorations. He ran his hand again over her cheek, cupping it and caressing it. Then he gave her bottom a light smack and pulled his hand away from her.

The interminable speech continued, and Darcy wandered out onto the deck for some bracing, libido-dousing air. He turned and looked into the ballroom and again admired Elizabeth's figure. Then he realized with a start that she was—*they* were—plainly visible to anyone on deck. He looked to his left and saw a group of about eight attorneys, male and female, looking at him. Some raised their glasses to him, others gave him a thumb's up—all were grinning and laughing. He recognized all of them, knew their names. Every. Last. One. *Jesus fucking Christ,* he thought, and quickly looked away from them. And was surprised to realize that he didn't care. He laughed to himself.

A moment later, Elizabeth joined him. "He certainly does admire Milton!" she grinned as she stepped up to the railing beside him. He smiled. She looked out over the water and saw the shimmering city lights in the distance. When she shivered in the breeze, Darcy removed his jacket and draped it over her shoulders. She turned to thank him.

He kissed her.

"Will!" she said, pulling back. "There are people everywhere," she reminded him.

"I don't care." Darcy took a pin out of her hair and flung it into the water. Another followed shortly after. She looked at him in shock and amusement.

"I don't care, Elizabeth, I love you." He put his fingers into her hair and let it cascade over her shoulders. He kissed her again. "I love you." She laughed at him and returned his kiss.

He did his best to ignore the catcalls coming from their ready-made audience.

"Go get her, Judge!"

"Dar-*cy*, Dar-*cy*, Dar-*cy!*"

"The *Looooove Boooat*."

He pulled one hand from her hair and extended his middle finger at them, much to their delight. They hooted and laughed but did not leave. He sighed. He had carried his mother's ring in his pocket for three weeks now, looking for the perfect opportunity to propose. None had arisen; something had always gone amiss. An unfortunate phone call, a distraction, an interruption, an argument. Clearly, the universe was not bending to his will on this.

Right. This is it. Now or never, you coward. Get down on bended knee. Recite a love poem. Tell her how lovely she is in the moonlight, never mind the cursed fog cover. Ask her to be yours and spend eternity with you. Make it good! Don't screw it up!

"Marry me," he demanded. *No no no!!!* That wasn't romantic *at all!*

"Yes, Judge Darcy," she answered seriously, but a smile twitched at the corner of her lips. His heart stopped for just a moment, then roared back to life.

She gave him a long kiss and said with an amused smirk, "Is that the best you could do?"

"Yes—No. Er, Elizabeth, I love you more than life itself, you would make me the happiest man alive if you consent—"

"Stop! I liked the first one better!"

He slanted a smile at her. "How about, 'Marry me, wily wench, and we'll sail the seven seas together?'"

"No, that's not quite it, either," she laughed.

He sobered slightly, but his eyes twinkled. He pressed his forehead to hers.

"You must *at least* allow me to tell you how ardently I admire and love you, and I beg you to end my suffering and please be my wife."

She swallowed. "Yes, I like that one. That's the one we'll tell the grandkids," she murmured against his lips. He smiled and kissed her deeply again.

He pulled the ring from his pocket and held it up. Together they looked at a three-carat emerald cut diamond with two half-carat kite diamonds on each side, set in a platinum filigree and pave band.

"Oh, Will, it's stunning," she whispered, though she could not see its brilliance in the dark.

"I realize it may not be to your taste, and we can get a different one later. But if you like it, I'd like you to have it. It was my mother's," he said quietly, looking first at the ring, and then, almost shyly, to her.

"Your mother's? Shouldn't Georgiana have it?"

He shook his head. "No, it's for you. I… it's incredibly sentimental to me, and I want you to have it."

"Then nothing would make me happier." She smiled warmly at him. He put it on her finger and kissed her. Their private audience was cheering loudly and whistling. In fact, the ballroom had erupted into polite applause, as Judge Boyd had taken that moment to end his speech. Neither heard a thing.

Although Elizabeth was convinced that her mother would notice the shift in the earth's gravity as soon as she became engaged, Darcy assured her that they did, indeed, need to tell her parents by some method other than an anonymous note tacked to their car. Fanny Bennet's rapturous reaction lived up to all of Elizabeth's expectations, and yet, somehow, she didn't mind. Having just hosted the society event of the decade with Jane's wedding, Mrs. Bennet was quite prepared to have a toned-down event. But, alas, it was not to be, for Darcy had other ideas. For while he, too, wanted a small wedding, he wanted to be married at Pemberley, which involved flying half of their guests to England and providing lodgings for a week's stay. Thankfully, Elizabeth convinced him that hiring a wedding planner would be by far the wisest decision, and they both found their lives made much more bearable by the arrangement.

The weeks flew by, and suddenly, almost without explanation, Elizabeth found herself back in her old bedroom at Pemberley, her wedding dress hanging from a hook on the door. She was to be married the very next day, and all her family and friends were gathered in England for the event. Now, her last night as a single woman, Elizabeth and Lou lay on her bed holding hands and quietly contemplating the next day.

"Are you going to live here?" he asked.

"No, but we've talked about spending our summers here once we have kids. Maybe later in life we'll move here, but not in the foreseeable future."

Lou gave her a sly grin. "So you're getting married tomorrow. Has your mama told you what to expect on your wedding night?" he asked.

Elizabeth laughed and shook her head. "Young ladies are not supposed to know such things. Could you tell me, Auntie Lou?"

"Well, it is your duty as a wife, but it will be a terrible experience. He will take out his lollydoodle and insult you with it. You must just close your eyes and lie still, it will be over soon." Lou demonstrated by flopping onto his back beside her, stiff as a board, eyes closed, fists clenched and jaw set in grim determination. "Just remember, if you are lucky, you will bear him ten sons within the first two years. Then you won't ever have to do it again." He opened one eye and looked at her.

"Don't project your own experience onto me," she teased, then grew pensive. "I wish you could have been my bridesmaid," she said.

"Don't be ridiculous, you know I look dreadful in green," he replied, propping his head up with her pillows.

She slipped an arm around his waist. They lay together in silence for a few moments.

"Promise me this will never change," she said quietly.

"I rather think Darcy would object to my sleeping over," he laughed quietly, wrapping a lock of her hair around his forefinger.

"You know what I mean," she said, pinching him gently.

Lou was silent for a moment. Then he said, "I can't promise that it won't ever change, Lizzy. People grow and take different paths in life. We have always been best friends, but now Darcy is your best friend, and that's the way it *should* be. But I can promise you that I'll always be there for you, and I'll always love you. And that's the way it should be too."

She laid her head on Lou's chest and listened to his steady heartbeat. He had been her rock for fifteen years. Had he not been gay—and had she not met Darcy—they would likely have married. Her parents loved Lou, and he fought with her sisters as often as she did. He was a brother to her, the brother her parents had never given her.

But this chapter was ending; another would begin tomorrow. She could not imagine any ending to the story that did not include growing old with Darcy.

"Of all this you're going to be mistress," Lou said pensively. "You'll have a lot of money, great cars, fabulous clothes…"

"You don't really think any of that matters to me, do you?"

"No, but I couldn't have parted with you for anyone less worthy," he said quietly.

Elizabeth Bennet Darcy's wedding day flashed by like a well-loved videotape; it ran too quickly in some parts, too slowly in others, but at the conclusion was the happy ending.

She was not at all nervous. She went for a run, showered, ate a hearty breakfast, and got her hair done. Her mother again exuded the unnerving calm she had shown at Jane's wedding, keeping her voice appropriately modulated and carrying on intelligent conversations. By the time she was in the chapel's changing room being zipped into her Monique Lhuillier Chantilly lace halter sheath, Elizabeth had reached a near zen-like state: this was her destiny, and she was content to be swept along by the stream of karma.

She shrugged into the dress coat that was to be worn within the chapel and fitted the floor-length veil on her head. A bouquet of wildflowers hung casually in her hand.

"Oh, Elizabeth, you look so lovely," Jane breathed. Elizabeth smiled in the mirror at Jane. "How can you be so relaxed?"

"What could possibly go wrong? All that matters is that we're married at the end of it all."

"We're ready, let's get you into the waiting area," Fanny huffed as she entered the room. She stopped short when she saw Elizabeth and smiled. "Oh, Lizzy," was all she said and dabbed a corner of her eye with a handkerchief. Elizabeth hugged Fanny tightly, finally comprehending why her mother's fondest wish was to have her daughters happily married. Elizabeth wanted nothing more herself.

"Well, well," Fanny sniffled. "Let's get you going. We don't want to leave Will waiting." She dabbed her eyes again, and flashed Elizabeth a brilliant smile. "Let's go, I know your father wants to see you." They gathered Elizabeth's skirts, veil, and flowers and stepped into the waiting area outside the chapel. Her father, dressed in a black tuxedo and looking better than she had seen him in years, beamed proudly when his eyes fell on her. She smiled and tucked her hands into his.

"My little Lizzy," he said quietly, giving her fingers a gentle squeeze. He blinked back tears and hugged her gingerly so as not to crush her dress. For the first time all day, Elizabeth felt a little lump in her throat.

"Don't you dare cry. Your mother will kill me if you ruin your makeup," Mr. Bennet said, wagging his finger at her. Elizabeth laughed, nodded, and swallowed. Then she turned to face the chapel doors and her fate.

Darcy stood patiently at the front of the church. Elizabeth was late, but he didn't care. She would get there. He felt as if his entire life had led to this one single event: he had never been so sure of anything before. He would be making it up as he went along for everything after, but this—this was *meant* to be.

The string quartet's music changed, signaling the beginning of the ceremony. Darcy turned to face the doors at the end of the aisle, his heart pounding with anticipation. When the doors opened, all he could see were two silhouettes framed by bright white light. Then, as they stepped forward, Darcy saw Elizabeth. Perhaps it was the veil, or her smile, or the overwhelming sense of rightness that washed over him, but she had never looked so lovely to him as she did at that moment. Their eyes locked and held until her father gingerly placed her hand in Darcy's.

"Take good care of her," Thomas whispered, his voice hoarse with emotion.

"I will," Darcy promised, unable to take his eyes from Elizabeth. He thought it more likely that she would take care of him, but he would to his last breath always try to make her happy.

"You're late," he whispered.

"Get used to it."

The impish grin that he so loved flirted with the corners of her mouth, and he felt his own smile curling in response. Remembering the solemnity of the task at hand, they turned their attention to the reverend.

Neither would afterwards remember much of the ceremony. They had not written their own vows, instead preferring the simple traditional words of the Anglican Church:

"With this Ring I thee wed, with my Body I thee worship, and with all my worldly Goods I thee endow; In the name of the Father, and of the Son, and of the Holy Ghost. Amen."

Then, as quickly as it had begun, it was over and they were man and wife. Applause washed over them as Darcy took her in his arms and sealed his vows with a heartfelt kiss. With her hand in his, they then strode back down the aisle, flower petals strewn over them as they made their way to the exit. As the doors opened and the bright June sunlight filtered in, Darcy paused.

"Happy anniversary," he grinned as he turned to her.

"Already?" she laughed.

"Yes. Exactly one year ago today, we fell in love. Right here, at Pemberley."

Elizabeth wrapped her arms around his waist and tipped her face up to his. "Well, then, I think I'd like an anniversary kiss." Darcy smiled as he cupped her face and dipped his lips to hers.

A discreet cough behind them alerted them to the wedding coordinator's presence, and they ended their kiss to be led back to the main house for the reception. Once they had been tucked away into the study, they embraced again.

"At last," Darcy sighed into her neck. He closed his eyes and drew in a deep breath, pears and wildflowers intoxicating him. "I love you, Mrs. Darcy," he whispered.

"And I love you, Will. How does one go about asking her new husband for another kiss?"

"No need to ask," he chuckled, and pressed his lips to hers again.

Elizabeth would only recall bits and pieces of the reception: silly toasts made by Jane and Bingley, being blinded by flashbulbs, and meeting new relatives whose names she could never hope to remember. Mostly she would remember the sensation of Darcy's thumb stroking over her wedding band, reassuring both of them that this was no dream, that they had finally married. They danced the required dances, ate the required cake, and kissed the required kisses. While they both shared the joy of seeing their families so happy, they both wanted nothing more than to be alone, to feel for the first time the intimate solitude of marriage.

And so, promptly at nine o'clock, they made their exit.

"Er, I should warn you," Darcy began as they waved good-bye at the ballroom door.

"Yes?"

"There's this family tradition..."

The family tradition became evident as the Darcy family did not remain respectfully seated at their tables and wish the newlyweds good night. No, they promptly rose and began blowing noisemakers and waving bits of cloth—napkins, handkerchiefs, anything they could find.

"A tradition?" Elizabeth asked skeptically as they turned to ascend the stairs, unable to ignore the small parade of people who were lining up behind them.

"Um, yes. Goes waaaaay back. Something about proving that we've consummated our marriage."

Elizabeth turned to Darcy, her face a mask of horror.

"Will! I'm not going to—" she began.

"No, no, of course not," he laughed. "It's a silly little tradition. We just have to give them something."

They reached the top landing and walked toward the rear bedroom—Darcy's bedroom, with which Elizabeth was already intimately acquainted. He opened the door and they stepped inside, closing the door behind them. The crowd gathered outside their door, noisemakers and cheers clearly audible through the heavy oak door.

"How long will they stay out there?" she asked.

"Until we give them something," he replied.

"Give them something?"

"Yes, just a little token. To prove that, uh, well…"

Elizabeth began to laugh, his meaning becoming clear. As he shrugged out of his jacket, she loosened his tie. With a wink and a saucy grin, she opened the door and tossed the tie out to the waiting guests. The tie was met with a raft of cheers, but they did not go away when she closed the door.

"Nobody cares if I get naked," he laughed, pulling her close to him. "We'll have to give them something to prove that *you're* getting naked." He knelt before her and rolled one of her stockings down to her ankle then shook it out. With a flourish, he opened the door and tossed the stocking out to the anxious crowd. Another burst of cheers followed, and as he closed the door, the party triumphantly carried their trophies back to the ballroom.

"Your family really is a bunch of perverts."

They laughed, and then they fell silent, as if neither knew what to say. Darcy looked at Elizabeth and felt his chest tighten. He remembered the first time he made love with her, in this very room. He felt that eagerness again, the anticipation of the beginning of something *wonderful*. With a little laugh, he caught her up in his arms and kissed her. It broke the awkwardness of the moment, and both felt the rush of being newly married and madly in love.

She turned in his arms, inviting him to unzip her dress. Reluctant to rush, he instead kissed her neck, letting his lips linger at the hollow beneath her ear. Slowly, he brushed his fingertips across her shoulders and under the straps of her gown. Sweeping her hair aside, he kissed the warm skin of her bare shoulder, forging a sensual trail into the curve of her neck where his breath ruffled the curls at the nape of her neck. With a smile, he recalled the seductive power of those curls, they way they had so entranced him to the point of distraction. Now—and forever—he could pay them the attention they so deserved.

With fingers that trembled ever so slightly, he unzipped her dress, catching their images reflected in the mirror. The light played on her skin, warming her peach tones and deepening the hollows of her collarbones. One strap fell from her shoulder, and he coaxed the other strap to her elbow before the dress fell in a ruffled puddle at her feet.

She stood before him, reflected in the mirror, in lacy white panties and just one stocking. Her smooth skin slid beneath his palms as he stroked his hands over her chest, cupping each perfectly molded breast in his hands, nipples peeking between his fingers. With a shiver, she turned in his arms and brushed her nose against his throat. He lowered his head to meet her lips. His hands splayed across the bare skin of her back, his tanned skin contrasting against her pale skin. He traced the curve of her bottom, his fingertips pressing into that soft flesh.

"Lizzy," he whispered hoarsely, trembling with love, anticipation, and satisfaction all at once. Elizabeth tucked her fingers into the waistband of Darcy's pants, unfastened them, and pushed them down before sneaking her hands around his waist to explore his firm rear. Then, between kisses and breathy laughs, they undressed each other.

But for her one stocking, they stood naked before each other for the first time as husband and wife. She picked up her bouquet and began to pull flowers from it and place them in her hair. He took over and released her hair from its loose binding. When he was satisfied, he took the remainder of the bouquet and pulled off petals, sprinkling them on the bed sheets.

Elizabeth began to remove her stocking, when Darcy stopped her.

"No, leave it. It's sexy," he said, smiling. Then, lying back on the bed, he folded her in his arms. Their hands began a hungry exploration, tracing over familiar territory with a new eagerness. Fingers twined and legs twisted. He nipped her thighs, kissed her nipples, and tasted her folds. She stroked the long lines of his muscles, arched against his body, pressing her soft curves against his lean angles. Finally, he pulled her atop his lap, their chests pressed together, and with a moan of pleasure, thrust himself into her.

"My god, Lizzy, you're so beautiful," he whispered reverently against her throat. She let out a husky laugh and pushed him backwards onto the bed, straddling him while her hair fell in a curtain around their faces. Darcy tipped his head back and closed his eyes, a smile on his lips as she rode him, unable to keep soft moans from escaping his chest every time she changed pace or rhythm.

When at last he opened his eyes, his breath was stolen by the sheer beauty of his wife. Her hair hung in soft curls, sprinkled with wildflowers. Her face held a mix of humor, tenderness, and seduction as she caught his expression. Naked as she was, her cheeks dusted with light freckles, her eyes bright and clear, she looked like a nature element, a wood nymph set on stealing his heart. He relinquished it with ease.

He rolled her to her back, eager for the sensual rise of her hips against his. As he kissed her eyelids, her cheeks, her nose, and her lips, his hand caressed her side, until it came to rest on the lace top of her stocking. Her ankles pressed into his calves, and his fingers gripped her thigh.

"Elizabeth." Her name bubbled from his lips unbidden, pushed out by the volume of joy in his chest. There was no room left for air. She smiled under his vocal caress and tightened her arms around him.

"Yes, Will, I'm your Lizzy. Make me yours," she whispered.

He thrust himself into her with undiluted passion, his breath coming in gasps. Completely heedless of who might hear, he let himself go. The bed creaked and groaned under their movements.

When she dug her fingers into his low back and arched her torso into his, he heard her sharp intake of breath just before she cascaded over the edge of orgasm. Then she was pulsing around him, writhing beneath him, her cries muffled into his neck as she invited him to join in her pleasure.

He clung on for a few short seconds before he began to shudder with a crashing paroxysm of desire.

"Lizzy!" His cry then dissolved into an incoherent groan of unadulterated bliss. He had never before been so compelled to express his pleasure vocally, to let her *hear* how much pleasure she brought him. Upon reflection later, he supposed it had to do with the sheer, shout-at-the-top-of-your-lungs, lunatic joy he was feeling. But at the moment, he really was beyond coherent thought.

Chapter 28

IT WAS NINE O'CLOCK the next morning before either of them even stirred, and another hour before they rose. Mrs. Reynolds had ventured to attempt to rouse them but retreated upon hearing the unmistakable and unguarded sounds of love-making when she approached their door.

Elizabeth lay back against the pillows, smiling in cat-like satisfaction. Darcy leaned against the post at the foot of the bed, a similar expression softening his features as he faced her. She gently placed her foot against his chest, and he stroked her ankle absently.

"You will wear me out, woman," he said softly.

She chuckled quietly and pulled one of the scattered flowers from under her hip. She perched the withered, broken thing jauntily behind her ear.

"You're a very chatty lover, you know. You go two days without saying anything, and as soon as we start, you're making speeches. It's quite amazing," she teased him.

"Perhaps I have an oral fixation."

She laughed, and he stroked a hand over her calf. She agreed that indeed he had an oral fixation, but as it was a very pleasurable obsession, she forgave it.

"We really should get up. We have guests," she said without making any move to get out of bed.

"Yes. You first," he replied with a languid smile. They looked at each other for a few more moments and then both laughed. "We're hopeless."

"We do have to catch a flight this afternoon. Are you ever going to tell me where we're going?"

"It's a surprise. I'll tell you that it's a four-hour flight. I'm sure you'll figure it out when we get to the airport. Have you packed a bathing suit?" He smiled.

When she could wheedle no more from him, they reluctantly rose and dressed to meet their guests for the wedding brunch. While Darcy was normally fastidious about his grooming, his languid mood this morning overcame him. He did not shave. He pulled on a T-shirt and jeans and was content to appear barefoot. Elizabeth ran a careless brush through her hair, aiming only to get most of the flower petals out. She slipped into a pair of jeans and put on Darcy's suit shirt from the previous day, tucking it halfway into her jeans and rolling up the sleeves. They shared a final lingering embrace before they exited their room.

They entered the dining room, Darcy's hand resting possessively on Elizabeth's shoulder, thumb stroking the back of her neck. Most of their guests laughed, either privately or outright, at the completely besotted expression on Darcy's face. They were forgiven their rudeness in oversleeping, and they circulated through the room together, hugging and greeting their guests.

Try as he would to maintain his dignity, Darcy was unable to stop touching his wife. He held Elizabeth's hand or let his hand rest on her waist as they walked about the room. When they sat at their table, he put his hand on her leg. He brushed her hand when passing the butter dish. Finally, he stopped trying to suppress his desire. He put his hand on the back of her neck and pulled her to him for a lingering kiss. She smiled under his lips and there was a little murmur of "awww"s in the room.

Elizabeth stepped onto the deck of the yacht with a sense of wonderment. She had been surprised indeed to learn that the first five days of their honeymoon were to be spent sailing in the Greek islands aboard the *Star Gazer*, a fifty-foot yacht owned by Thanos Latsis, a close friend of Darcy's. They were greeted warmly by Thanos and his wife, who introduced them to the crew. Both Darcy and Elizabeth experienced a little shiver when she was introduced as "Mrs. Darcy." Thanos winked and grinned, then with warm hugs and a gift of champagne, he left them. They waved as the ship pulled out from dock into the sinking sun.

Darcy stood by the railing with his arm around Elizabeth, watching the mainland grow smaller as they sailed away. She nestled her head into his shoulder, and he stroked her arm. The sun cast a golden glow on them, warming them despite the wind.

"Do you remember my telling you about an uncle who runs around his estate in nothing but trainers?" Darcy said into her ear. She smiled and nodded. "That's Thanos. He's not technically an uncle, but he was very close to my father. I was sorry that he couldn't make it to our wedding." He paused for a moment.

"My father would have loved you," he said quietly. "And I think you would have liked him."

"Tell me about him," she said, snuggling into his arm.

"He loved a pretty woman with a lively mind." Darcy grinned before planting a kiss atop her head and hugging her tightly to him. Elizabeth sensed the regret he felt that his parents did not survive to see his wedding day.

For a brief moment, her throat stung, and she hugged him more tightly. Then she said, "I'm very sorry that you lost both your parents. I can't imagine what it must be like. And I know it's no substitute but my parents like you very much, and they've taken Charley in as their own. I'm sure they will do the same with you."

Darcy laughed softly and kissed her forehead. "Yes, I'm looking forward to getting to know your parents better. It will be good to feel like a part of a family again."

Their return to the real world after their honeymoon saw them looking happy, healthy, and tan. While Elizabeth had the option of merely avoiding any cases before Darcy, the idea of specializing in appeals had become increasingly attractive. She enjoyed research, she loved to write, and she liked the satisfaction of making law. The transition from trial lawyer to appellate lawyer would be gradual, but she was content with her decision and confident in her abilities.

But her decision to focus on appeals did not take them into completely separate circles, and their first day back to work saw them back in the same courtroom with Elizabeth having a minor matter taken off calendar to allow for transfer to another attorney.

"This will be transferred to Ms. Lucas, correct, Ms. Bennet?" Darcy asked as he reviewed the order taking the case off calendar.

"Yes, Your Honor."

"Excellent. Any chance it will settle prior to trial?"

"Anything is possible."

Darcy glanced up at Elizabeth, spying the smirk toying about her lips.

"Are you being impertinent with me, Ms. Bennet?" he asked, suppressing his own grin.

"Not at all, Your Honor. I'm being just as respectful as I ever was."

"Indeed," he replied sardonically before signing the order. "Ms. Bennet, I'll have you perform service."

"I'll bet you will," she said with a wink. He coughed to cover his laugh before handing her the order. Without blinking, she handed it to her opposing counsel, who hid his own snicker as he turned away.

"You know," Elizabeth said quietly, so that the other attorneys in the room would not hear, "I don't think I like you calling me Ms. Bennet. I think I'd like to be called Ms. Darcy. It sounds so much more important to be married to the judge."

"Now, Ms. Bennet, we wouldn't want anyone to say I was playing favorites."

"My husband might be offended if I didn't take his name, you know. He's an old-fashioned sort of man."

"Really?"

"Yes, he's a bit of a curmudgeon. Gets very cranky when I don't *perform service*."

"You, Ms. Bennet, are an incurable flirt."

"Somebody should warn my husband."

"Somehow I think he already knows."

"Do you think it upsets him that I tease him without mercy?"

"Upsets him?" Darcy replied with a smile and rested his cheek on his fist. "No, Ms. Bennet. I daresay your husband is a very lucky man."

Epilogue

DARCY LIFTED HIS HEAD from the pillow and propped it on his palm. He sighed contentedly and looked down at the warm body sleeping next to him. He watched her sleep for a few moments then, unable to resist, he brushed a dark brown curl from her forehead. Sleepy eyelids fluttered open and soft brown eyes focused on him.

"Good morning, sweet pea," he said gently. A smile spread across her face.

"What are you smiling at?" he laughed softly.

"I don't think she's smiling, I think she has gas," said the *other* person in his bed.

"Don't be ridiculous, Lizzy, she's smiling at her daddy, who she thinks is the most handsome man in the whole world. Aren't you, Emma?" he said, not looking up. Emma gurgled and waved a hand at him.

Finally Darcy looked up at Elizabeth, who watched them with a tender smile on her face.

"Aren't you getting up soon?" he asked her.

"Soon," she replied but did not move. She held his gaze for a few moments longer.

"Ahhh… I think she's hungry," he said as he uncurled the tiny fingers now clenching his chest hair, pursed little lips straining toward his nipple. "I'm sorry, little one, but that tap is dry," he laughed.

Elizabeth unbuttoned her nightshirt and curled Emma into her arms. The baby found her nipple and fed hungrily.

Darcy lay back in bed. The last six weeks had been pure, unadulterated bliss. He had not thought it possible to be happier than he had been on his wedding day, but the year since that day had relaxed into comfortable happiness, relieving him from that roller-coaster giddiness he had felt then with Elizabeth.

But that was before Emma. He had not thought it possible to cram any more love into his heart but somehow he had. The first moment he held her six weeks ago—red and squalling, angry at being born—the world had stopped. Nothing had existed but him and this hopelessly fragile, helpless, writhing ball of curly hair and strong lungs. How he had managed not to dissolve into joyful, hysterical tears he will never know.

They didn't normally bring her to bed with them but sometimes Darcy couldn't help himself. If she fussed, he wanted to hold her. Even if she didn't fuss, he wanted to hold her. A few hours ago, he had heard Emma stir in her crib, and he instantly woke and brought her to bed.

The revolting contents of her diaper did not deter him. He was sure he could win a contest on changing her onesie in record time. His favorite sound was the cooing little voice that she seemed to save just for when he held her.

He smiled as he looked up at the ceiling. There was no doubt he was going to be a very indulgent father. He could imagine playing Barbies with her, teaching her to ride a bicycle, and how to swim. He was sure she would want dance lessons, so he would be taking her to class and carrying her little gym bag for her. Maybe she would want to play soccer too, so he'd have to work that into her schedule. Then there would be piano lessons, of course. How he would work horseback riding in as well, he wasn't sure. He spent the next ten minutes planning out her entire extracurricular career through middle school.

He looked over at Elizabeth as she gazed down at Emma. They seemed like some modern day Madonna and child—her loose hair fell in ringlets around her shoulders, her nightshirt open to reveal her very ample bosom, the child suckling quietly in her arms. Just then, Elizabeth raised her eyes to him. They held their gaze for a moment over the head of their baby, communicating a private moment of pure and unadorned love.

When the baby was finished, Elizabeth rose and put Emma in her crib. She returned to the bed, snuggling under the coverlet with a contented sigh, pushing her rear into his hips. She was asleep a moment later.

Both were exhausted after nights of feeding every two hours, but Darcy insisted that he get up with Elizabeth every time. Sometimes, when Elizabeth was plainly exhausted, he let her sleep and fed Emma with pumped milk. Those were magical moments for him, even though they didn't feel so magical the next morning.

Darcy was a changed man. The days of having no pictures in his wallet were over; it now bulged with wedding pictures, baby pictures, pictures of Elizabeth and Jane—anything that made him smile was jammed into his increasingly undersized wallet. He was constantly finding new pictures on his cell phone, taken by Elizabeth and left to surprise him. His domestication rather took him by surprise, yet he wore it comfortably, for he had never really wanted anything more than a family of his own.

Both Darcy and Elizabeth felt extremely fortunate these days. Elizabeth's choice to focus on appeals gave her much more flexibility to work from home and kept them away from any professional conflicts. It was no mystery that Darcy's professional discontent evaporated with the achievement of his personal happiness; he was reinvigorated and tackled each case with an enthusiasm he hadn't had in years. When he decided to run for re-election, he won handily.

As he watched Elizabeth, her breaths soft as she slept, he remembered all they had gone through to get where they were today. The heartache of their breakup had pitched him into a darkness he never wanted to know again, and he counted himself lucky that they had been able to work out their conflict. For of all the trials Darcy had ever had, winning Elizabeth had been the hardest—and the one most worth the winning.

The End

Acknowledgments

The author would like to thank Casey Childers, Mary Miner, Lee Parsons, and Deborah Styne for their tireless support, suggestions, talent, and editorial contributions. Without their assistance, this book would never have made it beyond my hard drive. Thanks also go to my agent, Kevan Lyon, and my editor, Deb Werksman—thank you both for your efforts to make this book the best it could be.

About the Author

Sara Angelini is an attorney living in the San Francisco Bay area. After graduating from West Virginia University with a Master's Degree in Animal Sciences, she gave up her dream of becoming a veterinarian when she realized that she only liked her own pets. She moved to California with her husband to pursue law school. She often fills her legal pads with dialogue or plot ideas while ostensibly listening to deposition testimony. *The Trials of the Honorable F. Darcy*, inspired by Colin Firth's smoldering haughtiness and an insatiable curiosity about what made Mr. Darcy tick, is her first novel. She lives with her husband and daughter.

Pemberley By the Sea

Abigail Reynolds

"Romance fans will be carried along by the smoldering heat between Cassie and Calder." —*Kristine Huntley, Booklist*

Pride and Prejudice with sun, sand, seafood, and surf

Marine biologist Cassie Boulton has no patience when a modern-day Mr. Darcy appears in her lab on Cape Cod. When their budding romance is brutally thwarted by their families, Calder tries to set things right by rewriting the two of them in the roles of Mr. Darcy and Elizabeth Bennet from *Pride and Prejudice*…but will Cassie be willing to supply the happy ending…?

"The couple's wit and chemistry make them worth rooting for." —*Publisher's Weekly*

"The type of novel you will want to keep at the top of your 'to be re-read' book stack." —*Austen Prose*

"Jane Austen fan or not you cannot help but love Abigail Reynolds' *Pemberley by the Sea.*" —*Love Romance Passion*

978-1-4022-1356-4
$14.95 US/ $15.99 CAN/ £7.99 UK

An Offer You Can't Refuse

Jill Mansell

"The perfect read for hopeless romantics who like happily-ever-after endings."—*Booklist*

Nothing could tear Lola and Dougie apart... except his mother...

When Dougie's mother offers young Lola a £10,000 bribe to break up with him, she takes it to save her family. Now, ten years later, a twist of fate has brought Dougie and Lola together again, and her feelings for him are as strong as ever.

But how can she win him back without telling him why she broke his heart in the first place?

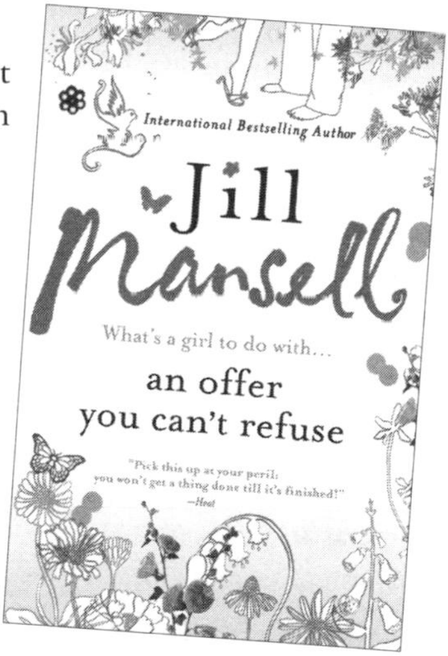

"Mansell knows her craft and delivers a finely tuned romantic comedy."
—*Kirkus Reviews*

"A fast pace and fun writing make the story fly by." —*Publisher's Weekly*

"Endearingly optimistic and full of attitude." —*Saturday Telegraph*

978-1-4022-1833-0 • $14.00 US

Miranda's Big Mistake

Jill Mansell

"Mansell's novel proves the maxims that love is blind and there's someone for everyone, topped with a satisfying revenge plot that every jilted woman will relish." —*Booklist*

Even the worst mistake of your life can lead to true love in the end...

Miranda's track record with men is horrible. Her most recent catastrophe is Greg.

With the help of her friends, Miranda plans the sweetest and most public revenge a heartbroken girl can get. But will Miranda learn from her mistake, or move on to the next "perfect" man and ignore the love of her life waiting in the wings...?

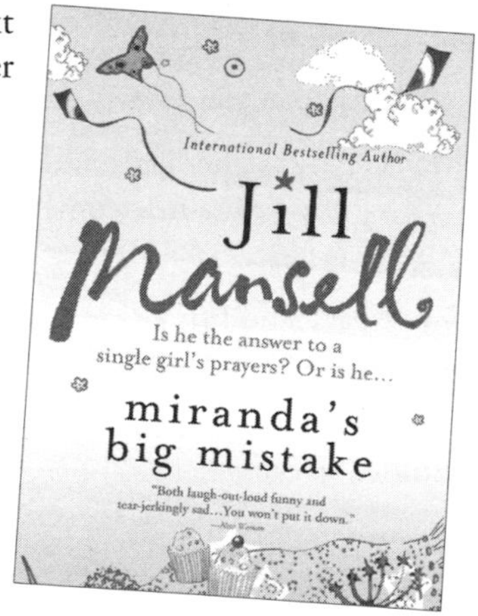

"An exciting read about love, friendship, and sweet revenge —fabulously fun"
—*Home and Life*

"A fantastic fun read!"
—*Wendy's Minding Spot*

"An absolute romp of a read!"
—*A Bookworm's World*

978-1-4022-1832-3 • $14.00 US

Fire Me

Libby Malin

"Humorous and full of heart, *Fire Me* is a sharply written novel about life, love and the good ole 9-5."
—*Melissa Senate,* author of *See Jane Date*

How to lose your job and find true love…

Fed up with impossible deadlines and meaningless busywork, Anne Wyatt goes to work one day determined to resign. But that's the day her boss announces someone is going to get laid off—and with a generous severance package. Now Anne has one day to ruin her career...

Anne's hysterical tactics are unwittingly undermined by Ken, the handsome graphic designer in the next cubicle, who has his own ideas for liberation from the corporate grind...

"*Fire Me*…had this reader chuckling out loud." —*Lancaster Sunday News*

"For hijinxs and crazy shenanigans that'll leave you chuckling to the bewilderment of those around you, I highly suggest this book." —*Love Romance Passion*

"A light-hearted romp of a book..."
—*A Bookworm's World*

978-1-4022-1757-9
$12.99 US/ $13.99 CAN/ £6.99 UK

Dating da Vinci

Malena Lott

"Delightfully affirming romance!" —*Booklist*

She knows she shouldn't take him home...

His name just happens to be Leonardo da Vinci. When the gorgeous young Italian walks into Ramona Elise's English class, he's a twenty-five-year-old immigrant, struggling to forge a new life in America—but he's lonely, has nowhere to live, and barely speaks English...

Picking up the pieces of her life after the death of her beloved husband, linguist and teacher Ramona Elise can't help but be charmed by her gorgeous new student. And when he calls her "Mona Lisa" she just about loses her heart...

"Malena Lott's charming, heartfelt novel about how grieving widow Ramona Elise gets her groove back will have you cheering 'bravissimo.'"
—*Jenny Gardiner,* Award-winning author of *Sleeping With Ward Cleaver*

"A remarkable tour de force. This story will make you laugh, cry, and fall in love all over again."—*Single Titles*

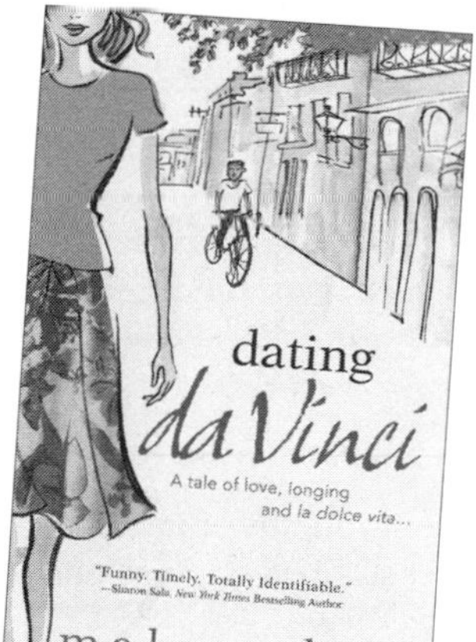

978-1-4022-1393-9
$12.95 US/ $13.99 CAN/ £6.99 UK

Mr. Darcy Takes a Wife

LINDA BERDOLL

"Wild, bawdy, and utterly enjoyable...Austenites who enjoy the many continuations of her novels will find much to love about this wild ride of a sequel." —*Booklist*

Hold on to your bonnets!

Every woman wants to be Elizabeth Bennet Darcy—beautiful, gracious, universally admired, strong, daring, and outspoken—a thoroughly modern woman in crinolines. And every women will fall madly in love with Mr. Darcy—tall, dark and handsome, a nobleman and a heartthrob whose virility is matched only by his utter devotion to his wife...

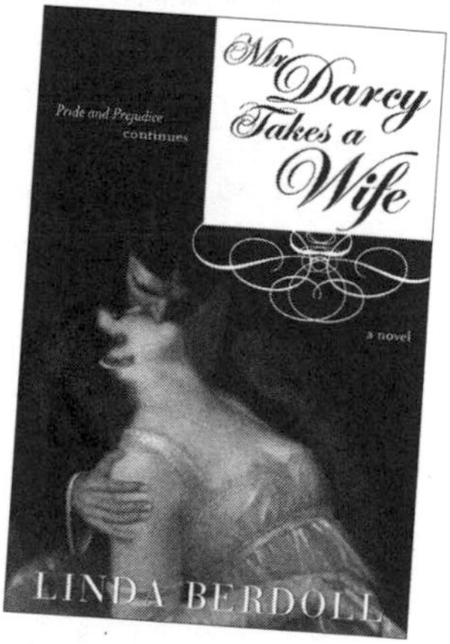

"Masterfully aligns Jane Austen's characters, taking us further into their lives and intrigue. Linda Berdoll, I am in awe...The regular Jane Austen community is in an uproar over this scandalous enlightenment."
—*Pop Syndicate*

What Readers Say:

"I thoroughly enjoyed this book, once my eyes stopped popping and I readjusted my lower jaw."

"Lizzy and Darcy like never before!!"

"Shocking and lusty... I loved every minute of it."

978-1-4022-0273-5
$16.95 US/ $19.99 CAN/ £9.99 UK